The coming Race

THE
WESLEYAN
EARLY CLASSICS OF
SCIENCE FICTION
SERIES
General Editor
Arthur B. Evans

EDWARD BULWER-*L*YTTON The

Edited with an introduction by DAVID SEED

Wesleyan University Press *Middletown, Connecticut*

coming Race

Published by

Wesleyan University Press,

Middletown, CT 06459

www.wesleyan.edu/wespress

The Wesleyan edition

of *The Coming Race* © 2005 by Wesleyan University Press

Introduction and critical materials © 2005 by David Seed

All rights reserved

Printed in the United States of America

ISBN 0-8195-6749-3 (Cloth)

Cataloging-in-Publication Data is available from the Library of Congress

CONTENTS

NOTE ON THE TEXT

The whereabouts of the manuscript of
The Coming Race are not known. The text
used for this edition is taken from that of
the Knebworth Edition of Bulwer-Lytton's
works published by George Routledge,
1873–77, with obvious errors corrected.

ACKNOWLEDGMENTS

My grateful thanks to the following who helped with this project at different stages: the Consumer Services division of Unilever Bestfoods, Robert Crossley, Arthur Evans, and Marie Mulvey Roberts. I am particularly grateful to Andrew Brown of Cambridge University Press, who generously shared information with me at the beginning of this project and whose bibliographical work on Bulwer-Lytton remains a model of scholarship.

The Coming Race (1871) is an example of what one reviewer called "satiric utopias," which are "marked by great confidence in the material inventiveness of man, and great distrust of his capacity for real spiritual progress of any kind."[1] As its title suggests, the novel explores the evolutionary theme of imminent supersession by a more advanced form of humanity whose lifestyle reveals the perceived inadequacy of the narrator's social norms. The novel thus belongs in a cluster of late Victorian speculations about the possible directions human evolution might take: whether finance might supplant religion as happens in Samuel Butler's *Erewhon* (1872) or the city be replaced by a neo-feudal rural society as in Richard Jefferies's *After London* (1885). Butler sets up his narrative through a description of exploration—hence the novel's subtitle, *Over the Range*. Similarly, *The Coming Race* opens with an account of how its American narrator explores the recesses of a mine and then falls into an underground world. This sequence of exploration followed by the discovery of a lost race was to recur in H. Rider Haggard's novel *King Solomon's Mines* (1885), which combined the lost race theme, topographical exoticism, and imperial anxieties over who ruled Africa.

The Victorian period marked not only a phenomenal surge in the sheer number of novels published; this productivity was tied to a constant ongoing debate about the nature of fiction, what sort of themes it should engage with and how these themes should be represented. Although Edward Bulwer-Lytton (1803–73) was a contemporary of the great Victorian realists, he wrote within the different generic conventions of the historical romance, the Newgate novel (based on lurid crimes recorded in the *Newgate Calendar*), and occult narrative, among others. Not only did he avoid the limitations of a single genre, but he was also encouraged by his longstanding love of German literature to use fiction as a means of metaphysical speculation. Within the debate over the nature of fiction that took place around the middle of the century, Bulwer-Lytton was an ardent supporter of what he termed "idealism" in opposition to documentary realism. Under the influence of German metaphysicians like Hegel, he saw art as the embodiment of ideas.[2] In a note that he added to his novel *Zanoni* in 1853 he discusses this dimension to his fiction in terms of "typical meanings" hinted at by the surface narrative. These latent meanings would only be accessible to the most perceptive reader since the "essence of type is mystery. We behold the figure, we cannot lift the veil."[3] Using less mystical terms, Bulwer-Lytton mounted a similar argument in his essay "Certain Principles of Art in Works of the Imagination," where a recognition of general types can offset unfamiliarity. "In the hands of great masters of fiction," he declares, "we become unconsciously reconciled, not only to unfamiliar, but to improbable, nay, to impossible, situations, by recognizing some marvellous truthfulness to human nature in the thoughts, feelings, and actions of the character represented."[4] This is Bulwer-Lytton's charter for the extraordinary. Speculative works like *Zanoni* and *A Strange Story* were written to challenge what he calls in the latter work the "absorbing tyranny of every-day life." In "Certain Principles" he singles out for special praise Hawthorne's *Transformation* (i.e., *The Marble Faun*), *Gulliver's Travels* (the "greatest work of pure imagination and original invention" of its age), and Johnson's *Rasselas*.

None of these works could be described as science fiction, although they have connections with the genre that was emerging during the nineteenth century. Here one of the seminal works is generally acknowledged to be *Frankenstein,* a novel that Bulwer-Lytton admired and to which he alludes within *The Coming Race.* It is possible that he responded particularly to Frankenstein's own account of his search for ultimate knowledge, a search culminating in his famous experiment. This narrative sequence was followed later in the century in *The Strange Case of Dr. Jekyll and Mr. Hyde.* Although Bulwer-Lytton does not describe an actual experiment, he did adopt the narrative persona of "some Scholar or dabbler in Science," and he expressed fears to his editor that some parts were "very dry." Years before Wells popularized the term "Scientific Romance," Bulwer-Lytton devised a narrative that he described as "perhaps a romance but such a romance as a Scientific amateur . . . might compose."[5] Like his contemporaries, Bulwer-Lytton used his fiction as a means of intellectual speculation. Similarly, Samuel Butler debated Darwinian issues in his novel *Erewhon* (1872) and its sequel, *Erewhon Revisited* (1901), as well as in his nonfiction.

UTOPIAN THEMES

Bulwer-Lytton visited Robert Owen's experimental industrial community at New Lanark, Scotland in the 1820s, but by the time he mentioned him in *The Coming Race,* Bulwer-Lytton's early enthusiasm had given way to a judgment on Owen as an unsuccessful social experimenter. The rational society of Bulwer-Lytton's underground race, the Vril-ya, may be an embodiment of the millenarian world Owen outlined in his own writings. *A New View of Society* (1813) explores the collective formation of character in a world where reason has removed social antagonism. Similarly, in his *Book of the New Moral World,* which he composed between 1836 and 1844, Owen described the current state of society as a "pandemonium," whereas in the coming new age truth itself would become a religion and society would be organized on a basis of reason and equality. The Vril-ya have similarly evolved out of a "wrangling" period of conflict into a uniformity of rational belief virtually unquestioned.

Bulwer-Lytton's future society attempts to conflate aristocracy with utopian egalitarianism and his narrator draws justificatory analogies with the Guardians in Plato's *Republic* and with the princely order of Sir Philip Sidney's *Arcadia*. In *England and the English* (1833) he expressed his satisfaction at the way the British aristocracy had been involved in the country's general life, and after the European political upheavals of 1849 he wrote a friend that an aristocracy was an essential insurance against chaos.[6] In *The Coming Race* the Vril-ya thus embody the idealized qualities of an aristocracy—refinement, serenity, and a life of leisure—which they rationalize as offering the only alternative to chaos and barbarism. But, despite the narrator's instant admiration for the members of this regime as a "noble order," political strife has not completely disappeared; it has only been pushed to the remote margins of the underground world. The stability of the Vril-ya is reflected in the millenarian aspects of Bulwer-Lytton's society, where selected elements of social life have ceased to change: there is no longer any war; government is no longer needed nor a police force since crime has died out; and all the population has become vegetarian. Even literature itself, in an anticipation of *Brave New World,* has become an antiquarian interest since the social conflicts described in older writings simply no longer exist. One reason why these conflicts do not exist lies in the erasure of the whole working class and the leveling upward of society. The godlike serenity of the Vril-ya was only one factor among many that prompted a reviewer to argue that the novel's main line of argument proved "that a pure democracy is a thing as little to be realised as it is to be desired."[7] The equality of the Vril-ya had been achieved at the cost of human emotion and any drive toward distinction, a price too high for that reviewer to stomach.

The limited number of critics addressing *The Coming Race* have tended to take the novel as an anti-utopia ridiculing the inhuman order of the Vril-ya. Darko Suvin has argued that here the "novel of individualistic psychology and the tradition of parabolic abstraction meet for the first time." He locates a disparity between a utopianism applied to children only and the differentiation of adults by wealth. Bulwer-Lytton had unswervingly opposed the utopian claims made by the leaders of the French Revolution, clinging to a faith in an enlightened socially engaged aristocracy; but for Suvin, "even a perfect, aristocratic collectivism could abolish [social] strife, together with class and national hatred, only by issuing in soul-crushing mediocrity."[8] The force *vril* suggests a homogeneous unified social organization that would be questioned by the sort of contradiction Suvin finds, a contradiction revealed in the description of Vril-ya society as an "aristocratic republic."

AUTOMATA AND THE LOSS OF INDIVIDUALISM

Within the social structure Suvin identifies, the humanoid automata that perform menial tasks implicitly represent docile social drones. Although automata had been manufactured since the eighteenth century, it was in the following century that they began to be described in fiction as labor-saving devices. In the section of his anthology of nineteenth-century science fiction (*Future Perfect*, 1966) devoted to such inventions, H. Bruce Franklin describes a mechanized utopia of 1844 where displaced humans have become the slaves of their machines. He reads Herman Melville's tale "The Bell-Tower" (1855) as a parable of automation taking over the role of a human workforce. Here a figure designed to strike the clock bell at regular intervals actually kills its own inventor.[9] Bulwer-Lytton's automata are genderless humanoid "figures" performing the functions of domestic servants. There is no suggestion in *The Coming Race* of the opposition between humans and machines that was emerging in nineteenth-century science fiction and that was to become a major theme in the genre. The unity of Vril-ya society is local and depends on an excluded margin of "barbarians," and accordingly one issue preoccupying the narrator is the question whether he will be admitted to this privileged group. Since he is denied access to vril, his expulsion remains only a matter of time. And, although he naively dreams of participating in an emerging super race, he is actually condemned to death to protect the purity of the Vril-ya. In other words, the narrator falls victim to his own racial obsolescence. The very fact that the Vril-ya possess automata suggests a sophisticated technology that could be directed to domestic or military purposes. I. F. Clarke has pointed out that one of the reasons for German victory in the Franco-

Prussian War was superior military technology, and it may be that the automata figure not only "in place of an underclass" but also as replicants, which could be used for military purposes.[10]

For James L. Campbell Sr. *The Coming Race* belongs with Bulwer-Lytton's last novels, *The Parisians* and *Kenelm Chillingly* (both 1873). He argues that in each work Bulwer-Lytton "expostulates against the popularity of social and political theories he thought undermined individual character and national life."[11] Campbell helpfully alerts the reader to the ways in which Bulwer-Lytton's dystopian ironies cut two ways: against the religious controversies and hypocrisy of Victorian England and against the contradictions and emerging imperialism of the United States. Like Gulliver, Bulwer-Lytton's narrator is therefore a butt of the novel's ironies as much as a means of revealing them to the reader; and this fact was recognized by the *Athenaeum* reviewer who saw how the narrator's certainties are upset by his experiences, particularly his central beliefs: "Steeped to the lips in his national liberalism, he regards freedom as the complete emancipation of individual action, not the reconciliation of the subjective to the higher will."[12] Bulwer-Lytton's multiple allusions to contemporary science throughout the novel all focus on forces linking the material with the spiritual, the organic with the inorganic. Cumulatively they establish connectedness as a condition of being that tacitly ridicules the narrator's atomistic attitudes as perversely working against the order of nature.

The Coming Race AS A GOTHIC NOVEL

In his history of science fiction, *Trillion Year Spree* (1986), Brian Aldiss argues that the genre developed in tandem with the Gothic such that individual works often display characteristics of both genres: *Frankenstein* is a record of both an experiment and a destructive "haunting" by the product of that experiment; *Dr. Jekyll and Mr. Hyde* similarly describes an experiment and the collapse of ego unity that results. *The Coming Race* also has a double nature.

It describes a human species of the imminent future whose emergence depends on the equally imminent demise of current Western humanity. Bulwer-Lytton draws on the "last man" theme that had been used by Thomas Campbell and Mary Shelley. The narrator's journey underground to a "world without a sun" (a phrase borrowed from Campbell) takes him into a literal and metaphorical eclipse reflecting his perceived evolutionary obsolescence. This descent novel underscores Bulwer-Lytton's preoccupation with endings, which can be seen in such titles as *The Last Days of Pompeii* and *The Last of the Barons*. These novels frequently end with a battle or a scene of destruction (Pompeii by volcanic eruption, the Roman Capitol by fire in *Rienzi*) marking a transition from one phase or regime to another. *Kenelm Chillingly*, for instance, concludes with a tableau where Kenelm's father symbolically leads him across Westminster Bridge toward the unknown fate that await the "Man of the Young Generation." Fiona Stafford has argued that Bulwer-Lytton had been fascinated by the theme of racial extinction from the 1820s onward, a fascination revealed in the fact that "almost all the principal characters in Bulwer's historical romances are last-of-the-race figures."[13] These are not final endings, of course. Even the gloomiest examples include hints of a new historical phase about to start.

The novel's evocation of a world underground draws partly on the experiences of Aeneas being taken to the Land of the Shades by the Sibyl in book 6 of Virgil's *Aeneid* and also on the descriptions of Pandaemonium in *Paradise Lost*. The underworld of *The Coming Race* is a place of "mephitic gases," which are associated with volcanic regions and abandoned mines. Like the opening location of *Paradise Lost*, it is a place of dismal chaos. And, pursuing the analogy with this poem, the Vril-ya can be read as quasi-Miltonic angels about to emerge from underground. Like Aeneas, the narrator finds an underground road leading his way to an enormous city. This city's massive architecture, as we shall see, draws on John Martin's images; the spacious hall and naphtha lighting echo Milton's Pandaemonium. When the narrator looks out across the landscape, the "roseate flame" created by distant rivers recalls a similar light when Faust conjures up the Spirit of the Earth through necromancy. In short, all these details suggest that the narrator has descended into a form of hell where he can no longer organize his impressions in any rational or consistent way. In every sense, he is lost. His eventual return to the surface has the symbolic psychological relief of a resurrection toward normality.

JOHN MARTIN AND THE SUBLIME

The scientific and evolutionary aspects of *The Coming Race* point toward the future; its Gothic aspects point toward endings and the past. When describing the College of Sages in the underground capital, Bulwer-Lytton relates the building's "massiveness and solidity" to the pictures of John Martin, which he admired throughout his life. In *England and the English* Bulwer-Lytton singled Martin out for special praise as the "greatest, the most lofty, the most permanent, the most original genius of his age," adding that "vastness was his sphere."[14] Bulwer-Lytton's focus on the large idea of his works brought a grateful response from the artist, who wrote to Bulwer-Lytton in 1849 to express his appreciation of the latter's discrimination: "The judgement of the less refined critics," he complained, was "limited to the material detail, whilst the higher spiritual aim is entirely overlooked."[15] William Feaver has argued that Martin's "imaginative documentary interests" were further developed by such writers as Haggard, Doyle, Verne, and Wells, presenting Martin as a important link between the Gothic and late Victorian science fiction.[16]

Martin's prints and paintings of legendary cities like Nineveh, Babylon, and Pandemonium depict those cities through enormous buildings supported by heavy pillars in perspective lines that stretch away out of sight. A repeated tension emerges between the apparent stability and permanence of these structures and the forces that bring about their destruction emerging from distant or raised vortices in the pictures. The spaciousness of Bulwer-Lytton's city, together with its lamps, open squares, and orderly lines of shops all echo the theme of city planning that is visible in several of Martin's works. But these must also have sharpened Bulwer-Lytton's sense of the sublime, especially in the vast underground settings like that of Martin's *Pandemonium* where the massive architectural structures and dwarfed human figures recede into the surrounding darkness. Bulwer-Lytton applies a Burkean notion of the sublime as a scale of perception so vast that it inspires fear in his narrator. The latter's first glimpse of the underground world is a vertical one, down into the depths of a chasm within which he can vaguely perceive a massive building, apparently constructed in the Egyptian style. This vertiginous image sets a tone for the narrator's experience of the spaces of this new world in that it inspires awe mixed with fear. Just as Gulliver has his spectacles, so he carries his pocket telescope, a signal of his difficulties in dealing with scale and distance. However impressive the sights, the narrator repeatedly registers difficulty in seeing beyond a certain distance. Like the underground world Bulwer-Lytton describes in his 1830s serial "Asmodeus at Large" (see the appendix), the sheer expanse of the place defies the limits of the observer's vision. For one reviewer of the novel this produced a disconcerting visual effect. Although *The Coming Race* refers to the gas lamps of this underground city, he complained that "we are haunted throughout the book by the difficulty of conceiving any *distant prospect* but one which would be mainly composed of the lights themselves."[17] Bulwer-Lytton draws attention to the challenges presented to the narrator through the example of paintings in Aph-Lin's city building, which seem to resemble those of Cranach but lack a center. In other words, the paintings reflect a realism of detail without the perspective that would make those details cohere around a point of view. The result is disturbing: "The effect was vague, scattered, confused, bewildering—they were like heterogeneous fragments of a dream of art" (chap. 4). Thematically these paintings relate to the narrator's difficulties in seeing whole scenes in the novel.

The Coming Race thus has an important Gothic dimension that sheds a somber light on its predictive dimension. The narrator experiences a series of disorientations after his fall into the underworld. The relation between sea, land, and air becomes confused. He sees creatures that have no known relation to any living fauna. And when he meets a human being, the latter has a face like that of a sphinx, at once penetrating and totally inscrutable. Egyptian allusions in Bulwer-Lytton regularly denote mystery and imply the possession of a sacred knowledge inaccessible to the observer. The drama of the novel peaks at moments when the narrator is experiencing crises of fear: awe before the dreadful features of the Vril-ya; terror at the monster emerging from the subterranean lake; and despair when his means of ascending back to his home world seems to be blocked. The narrator oscillates between respect for the evident sophistication of the underground culture and a conviction that it is demonic. If these beings are truly going to take over the earth, this terror implies that something even worse than extinction is in store for the narrator's society.

DARWINIAN THEMES

The Victorian age was perceived as a period of rapid social and scientific change, so universally that Walter Houghton has suggested that "transition" was one of the key terms of the age.[18] In *England and the English,* published shortly after the upheavals of the first Reform Bill, Bulwer-Lytton states: "Every age may be called an age of transition—the passing on, as it were, from one state to another never ceases; but in our age the transition is *visible.*" He goes on to characterize the times as full of uncertainty, "an age of disquiet and doubt—of the removal of time-worn landmarks, and the breaking up of the hereditary elements of society" under the impact of Benthamite questioning, and concludes: "The age then is one of *destruction!*"[19] The evolutionary theories that saturate *The Coming Race* help systematize this perception of transition through their promulgation of absolute laws, which present biological and other modes of change as an irresistible destiny.

From all explanations of change, the contentious issue of evolution made itself felt in the works of many novelists in the Victorian age. One of the most dramatic aspects of Darwin's theories was his notion of species rivalry: the struggle for existence. In the famous fourth chapter of *The Origin of Species* (1859), "Natural Selection; or the Survival of the Fittest," he pointed out that the struggle was at its most severe between members of the same species and then considered the example of the inhabitants of countries: "As all the inhabitants of each country are struggling together with nicely balanced forces, extremely slight modifications in the structure or habits of one species would often give it an advantage over others."[20] It is ambiguous whether Darwin is describing the relation of humans to their environment, to other humans, or to other species.

The Coming Race is based on similar premise of racial displacement. Bulwer-Lytton was absolutely explicit about applying Darwin when explaining the novel to his editor John Forster:

> The only important point is to keep in view the Darwinian proposition that a coming race is destined to supplant our races, that such a race would be very gradually formed, and be indeed a new species developing itself out of our old one, that this process would be invisible to our eyes, and therefore in some region unknown to us. And that in the course of the development, the coming race will have acquired some peculiarities so distinct from our ways, that it could not be fused with us, and certain destructive powers which our science could not enable us to attain to, or cope with.[21]

In March 1870 he returned to this central conception of evolutionary displacement as follows: "The coming race, though akin to us, has nevertheless acquired by hereditary transmission, etc., certain distinctions which make it a different species, and contains powers which we could not attain to through a slow growth of time; so that this race would not amalgamate with, but destroy us. And yet this race, being in many respects better and milder than we are, ought not to be represented terrible, except through the impossibility of our tolerating them, or they tolerating us, and they possess some powers of destruction denied to ourselves."[22]

There is some evidence that Bulwer-Lytton incorporated allusions to *The Descent of Man*, published in the same year as *The Coming Race*, into his novel. For example, in chapter 16 we are told how the Vril-ya gradually lost their body hair through the application of the "law of sexual selection." Darwin makes exactly the same point in chapter 20 of *The Descent of Man*, where body hair is included as a secondary sexual characteristic. For Darwin, human body hair represents the traces of the "uniform hairy coat of the lower animals" (*The Descent of Man*, chap. 1). In his account, hairlessness was introduced by the female of the species; thus there is a suggestion that the loss of hair reflects both evolutionary progress and a certain feminization of the species. Similarly, as we shall see in the next section in detail, Bulwer-Lytton demonstrates the evolutionary superiority of the Vril-ya through their skill at language, which was perceived by Darwin and other scientists as a crucial factor in illustrating the difference between humans and other species. The nearest alternative to language that Darwin admits is birdsong, and it is striking that the Vril-ya possess caged birds trained so efficiently that their song resembles opera. Not only do they acquire the narrator's language in record time; they also possess a language that shows an advanced composite of Aryan roots and morphology.

In fact, there is an ambiguity about the status of the Vril-ya, who do not directly exemplify Darwin's model for human progress. First of all, their skulls are described as "brachycephalic." Within the anthropology of the period, brain size was correlated with intelligence; therefore, the more civilized races had larger brains. If their brains grew, this would alter the size of the skull, elongating it into "dolichocephalic" (literally, "long-headed") proportions. But the opposite has happened with the Vril-ya. Then there is their idealization of the frog. This preoccupation is described in chapter 16 at the point where we are told of their hairlessness. Here Bulwer-Lytton imitates Darwin's procedure of regularly comparing human characteristics with those of other species. For the latter, the frog was definitely a member of a lower order of creatures. For T. H. Huxley, however, the frog was a creature symbolically important in his formulation of a theory that humans and other animals were conscious automata. In 1870 Huxley gave a talk to the Metaphysical Society on the question "Has the Frog a Soul?" where he considered the two main traditions of explaining behavior: through automatism and through animism. While Huxley was heading toward the first of these, Bulwer-Lytton remained throughout his life resolutely hostile to materialist explanations of consciousness and behavior. The Vril-ya's idealization of the frog could therefore be read as an absurd inversion of Darwinian evolution, where advanced humans actually celebrate the traces in them of an earlier, more primitive creature; and it could also be seen, possibly with a glance at Huxley who used the frog to demonstrate physical reflexes, as a satire on a society that was converting itself into human automata.

The notion of species rivalry with its attendant possibility of supplantation or extinction had been well established by the time Bulwer-Lytton came to work on his novel and informed later nineteenth-century speculative novels like Jefferies's *After London* that, as Gillian Beer states, showed the "throttling power of a few dominant species."[23] *The Coming Race* is a future-directed narrative where the evident strength and physical well-being of the Vril-ya as well as their intellectual accomplishments suggest the imminence of their emerging as humanity's heirs. There is also the factor of technology, which gives them further credentials: their applications of vril and their automata. We shall see cases of a robotized population in later hollow earth novels.

PHILOLOGY

The study of philology demonstrated through its investigations of linguistic origins that language itself was subject to evolutionary change. The fact that Bulwer-Lytton dedicated *The Coming Race* to the leading proponent of philology, Max Müller, reflects Bulwer-Lytton's sensitivity to linkages between race, language, and evolution that had emerged by the 1860s in Britain. Etymology as a metaphor of general evolutionary descent and change had been adopted by Darwin from Charles Lyell.[24] In the hands of Max Müller a conception of language emerged as being as independent of human choice as geology or biological evolution. Like those sciences, language too underwent gradual mutations as it changed from phase to phase; and, again like those sciences, it too was subject to absolute laws. Thus, on the one hand, Max Müller promoted a message of transience ("generations after generations have passed away, with their languages"); on the other, he yoked language to science in terms that would have appealed to a Victorian audience's hunger for systems.[25]

Etymology had already figured in Bulwer-Lytton's early novels *Eugene Aram* (1832) and *Zanoni* (1842), where linguistic origins supply the credentials of his eponymous hero, but philology takes on a central significance in *The Coming Race*.[26] Here Bulwer-Lytton quotes from Max Müller's 1868 Rede Lecture "On the Stratification of Language" in which an extended analogy is drawn between the study of geology and the study of linguistic history. For Max Müller writing is a necessary evil—necessary because it gives philologists their raw material—in arresting the natural evolution of speech. Just as geologists extrapolate the evolution of the earth's surface from strata, so philologists can infer the history of word change from the different phases of language. "Unless some languages had been arrested in their growth during their earlier stages, and had remained on the surface in this primitive state," philology could not exist. Muller waxes positively lyrical over the new light that philology can shed on human evolution: "In the successive strata of language thus exposed to our view, we have in fact, as in Geology, the very thread of Ariadne, which, if we will but trust to it will lead us out of the dark labyrinth of language in which we live, by the same road by which we and those who came before us, first entered into it."[27] Max Müller's metaphors of learning suggest a movement from darkness to light, from confinement to open space; but Bulwer-Lytton's narrator is trapped for most of the novel within a labyrinth of unknown size that is inadequately lit for the most part.

When *The Coming Race* was being set up for publication, Bulwer-Lytton explained to his editor: "The language of the Vrilya is much modelled on Max Müller's . . . theories of the formation of language. Many of the words are Sanscrit [*sic*]—others Welch [*sic*]—one or two as you observe Greek, & the rest fanciful but still framed according to philosophical theory."[28] The narrator of *The Coming Race* is clearly an amateur philologist himself and plans to publish a study of the Vril-ya language, which will demonstrate its "union of simplicity and compass." The detailed account of this language given in chapter 12 clearly mimics a philological study and follows Max Müller's phases of evolution (taken from Humboldt, as he admits) from juxtaposition through combination to inflection. Vril-ya is thus presented as a more efficient form of Western linguistic evolution, whose mainstream sign is the Aryan verb radical *ya*. Bulwer-Lytton accepts unquestioningly Max Müller's designation of monosyllabic Chinese as the most "primitive" surviving language, a "photograph" of "man in his leading-strings" (formerly used to teach children to walk), and gives a pastiche philological account of Vril-ya structure and grammar.[29] This account covertly demonstrates the superiority of the Vril-ya's culture to the narrator's own in a number of important respects. First, by transposing Max Müller's example of the Aryan root *nak* and modifying European examples (*nax* for Latin *nox* or Greek *nyx*, i.e., "night"), Bulwer-Lytton implies that the Vril-ya language alone contains within itself the range of varieties to be found in the Indo-European languages. Indeed, it symbolizes the active potential of the whole tradition that its suffix *ya* is the Aryan root meaning "to go." Second, having established its scale, Bulwer-Lytton suggests that the culture has a spiritual dimension in terms like *veed* (immortal spirit) or *veedya* (immortality), which echo the Sanskrit *veda* or sacred knowledge (Max Müller himself was a Sanskrit scholar and constantly drew on that language for his examples of word change).

Throughout chapter 12 of *The Coming Race,* Bulwer-Lytton carefully naturalizes Vril-ya by juxtaposing familiar terms and paradigms with unfamiliar usages. The nouns follow a traditional pattern of declension, which resembles that of Latin. Affixes echo English ("too"/"to") or German ("zu") though their meaning has been shifted. Most importantly, Bulwer-Lytton plays on the gender associations of terms to imply that traditional masculinity has become displaced by a new and active form of femininity. The Vril-ya term for "man," "an," echoes the classical Greek "aner" but reduces the term to an indefinite article. Similarly the term for "woman," "gy," is also taken from the classical Greek "gyne," but masculinizes it into the American homophone "guy." Bulwer-Lytton also inverts the symbolism of the final letter of the English alphabet. As in his earlier narratives *Zicci* and *Zanoni* Bulwer-Lytton invests the letter *z* with a special hermetic symbolism suggestive of the magical skills demonstrated by the protagonists of Gothic fiction. In *The Coming Race* z-compounds signify pleasure and even love; in other words, they signify far more positive possibilities than mere endings. Thus Bulwer-Lytton's female protagonist Zee is separated by a whole alphabet from her male counterpart Aph-Lin and personifies a characteristically modern, that is, American, form of "zed." Although C. A. Simmons is correct alphabetically to state that Zee "suggests ending," the specific national associations of her name equally suggest modernity and rapid change.[30] There is a pointed irony in the fact that the most dynamic member of the Vril-ya, the root of whose name is an obvious contraction of "virile," should be a woman. As we shall see, the novel expresses deep anxiety about gender roles and social behavior.

Bulwer-Lytton establishes a central link in the novel between technology, America, and the New Woman. The narrator proudly basks in his American nationality, in which "Europe enviously seeks its model and tremblingly foresees its doom" (chap. 7), but he unconsciously betrays his country's imperial ambitions, vulnerability to financial corruption, and tendency to social inversion. Like Gulliver in Brobdingnag, his pride gradually collapses before the apparently superior social organization of his hosts and the irresistible technology of vril. Again like Gulliver, he is infantilized into a "small barbarian," an un-evolved "froglet" to be used as the plaything of the young woman Zee. As the novel progresses, the narrator's role shifts from that of utopian visitor, who takes in the sights and explanations of the underground world, to that of would-be reformer. Casting himself ludicrously as both a utopian and an "absolute sovereign," he speculates about how he might redesign the world of the surface. However, his dream of power thinly masks a deep-seated fear of the Vril-ya.

In *Kenelm Chillingly* Bulwer-Lytton had dramatized his unease over contemporary social trends. His narrator is mistaken for an American because of his "length of limb," "gravity of countenance," and evident education. Kenelm is equally disturbed by a visible change in the manners of young ladies whose use of cosmetics and new habits of speech reflect a "slang of mind, a slang of sentiment, a slang in which very little seems left of the woman, and nothing of the lady" (bk. 4, chap. 6). *The Coming Race* draws on the debate about the position of women, which was fed by John Stuart Mill's polemical essay *The Subjection of Women* (1869). Mill directed his main argument against the rationalization of system-atic repression as "natural" and ironically questioned the special value attached to meekness and submissiveness as an "essential part of sexual attractiveness."[31] For Mill and for Mary Wollstonecraft before him, gender was constructed to a significant extent—and perhaps entirely—by social custom, and the most efficient way to counteract this social slavery was through education. Against this explanation, physiologists like Darwin argued that the sexual behavior of each gender was tied to physical stature and "nature." Thus, for Darwin, "the male is the more active member in the courtship of the sexes," whereas the female is "less eager than the male."[32]

In *The Coming Race* Bulwer-Lytton's use of the device of inversion in discussions of gender politics has the effect of estranging the narrator from the apparently human figures he meets. The first females startle him by being taller than the men and not at all timid. Zee is a member of the College of Sages and thus well fitted to play the role of tutor to the narrator. Although Bulwer-Lytton presents the latter as an American, he displaces aspects of American social style (Zee's name, the absence of hereditary titles, etc.) onto a society that represents the narrator's future. The Vril-ya seem to display a heightened rationality based on their apparent control of their own evolutionary situation through Malthusian checks on population size and the law of sexual selection. Aph-Lin puts the case for nurture ("we are all formed by custom"), and his voice proves to be indistinguishable from that of his daughter Zee since both couch their explanations in the rational expository style used by Mill. The sexual overtures of Zee coincide with the narrator's discovery that his life is at serious risk. Aph-Lin warns his guest: "If you yield, you will become a cinder" (chap. 22). Not only does the narrator find that he has been infantilized and then reduced in the species hierarchy to a carnivorous animal; but in this warning he is reminded how tenuous his hold on life is. Recoiling from the absence of maidenly decorum common to "most civilized countries, except England and America," he falls back on a prim insistence that Zee's behavior is "improper" and defensively rationalizes her femininity as a kind of motherly care. The narrator's feelings for Zee become increasingly colored by fear and the apprehension that marriage to her will be a form of death. The contrast over which gender has the prerogative to propose marriage is described by a young Gy as a "strange reversal of the laws of nature" (chap. 25) and this turns into a more pointed danger for the narrator once he becomes the object of a princess's erotic attention. In short, through Zee and her kind, according to one scholar, Bulwer-Lytton satirizes "both the Victorian women's rights movement and the fast, mannish young women described in E. Lynn Linton's 'Girl of the Period' articles in the *Saturday Review*."[33] The allusion here is to the novelist Eliza Lynn Linton, who gained notoriety in 1868 by publishing the first of a series of attacks on contemporary trends in female behavior. For Linton, the "girl of the period" (which became a catchphrase of the time) was an independent being who rejected the restrictions of domesticity and parental authority. Linton's contribution to the women's rights movement of the 1860s, which was being fed by American campaigners, was oddly contradictory. Linton herself actually embodied a professional independence in her choice of career, and, although she seemed to be regretting the demise of female charm, she directed a telling irony against men's expectations, declaring: "Men do not care for brains in excess in woman."[34] The association between *vril* and women throughout the novel constantly hints at the latter's "supposedly stronger sexual energy," as Darko Suvin notes.[35] Zee's evident capacity for independent thought and action, her display of sexual initiative and her physical strength, are all described implicitly by Bulwer-Lytton as a displacement of sexuality from one gender to the other, symbolized by her possession of the "virile" vril staff. This symbolism is further reinforced by the phallic physiological detail that the Vril-ya possess unusually large thumbs. Gender anxieties in the novel are expressed as threats to the narrator's life. The crowning irony comes in the conclusion when the threatening female actually proves to be the means of the narrator's liberation from the underworld.

One reviewer of *The Coming Race* noted the topicality of its depiction of the relations between the sexes, yet was evidently uneasy at the fact that Bulwer-Lytton's female characters were stronger but more obedient, commenting: "We presume all this is burlesque."[36] Another reviewer noted the alarming speed with which American women were "invading" all those areas of social activity that were previously the domain of men, including sports.[37]

Where Bulwer-Lytton hints at the supersession of men, Mary E. Bradley Lane's *Mizora: A Prophecy* (1881) describes a single-gender utopia where men have become totally extinct. Not even the word for "man" persists in their language, and paintings of male figures are shut away in the archives of this republic. Lane's narrative uses the same frame convention of the hollow earth to set up the visit by a young Russian woman through an arctic opening (Symmes's Hole) to an underworld. Generations ago, scientists discovered the means of reproducing life without any male participation. Mizora is an ideally ordered "land of brain workers," full, like Bulwer-Lytton's utopia, of spacious villas and broad streets.[38] Also like Bulwer-Lytton's underground race, the Mizoreans have discovered a method of travel by flight and have organized their society so as to minimize conflict and labor. Both worlds are presented as satirical comments on the nineteenth century, in Lane's case on Reconstruction America. The major difference, however, between the two writers lies in Lane's apotheosis of applied engineering in depicting a world run on totally scientific principles; this leaves the workings of the brain an inexplicable mystery. *Mizora* contrasts strikingly with Bulwer-Lytton's attempts to imagine a worldview combining material and mental dimensions. There is a further difference between the two narrators. In *Mizora*, Vera Zarovitch expresses unqualified admiration for the utopian society she experiences with all the zeal of a convert, whereas Bulwer-Lytton's unnamed American moves from fear to admiration and, in the end, to recoil from the Vril-ya.

TEUTONISM

The Coming Race was published immediately after the Franco-Prussian War, which had suggested to Max Müller the importance of unity between the "Teutonic" nations, namely, Britain, Germany, and the United States. C. A. Simmons has documented how Bulwer-Lytton's novel, together with works like George Tomkyns Chesney's *The Battle of Dorking,* published in 1871 and read by Bulwer-Lytton while his own novel was being prepared for press, grew out of a historical period when "language and national Destiny are linked with the Anglo-Saxon origins of the English."[39] Bulwer-Lytton had earlier in *Harold; or, The Last of the Saxon Kings* (1848) idealized the Anglo-Saxons as a "magnificent race of men" who demonstrated a "passion for freedom, individual and civil" (chap. 2). The historian Léon Poliakoff has shown how the combination of Sir Walter Scott's influence and the wave of Teutonism that swept through Britain in the 1840s, promoted by Thomas Carlyle and others, had its impact on Bulwer-Lytton and his contemporaries.[40] Add to these influences evolutionary theory and philology, and we can more closely understand one of the last moments of realization by the narrator of *The Coming Race* when he senses that the Vril-ya, "descended from the same ancestors as the great Aryan family" (chap. 26), will supersede his own race and the others of the West. In short, Bulwer-Lytton's narrator succumbs completely to what H. G. Wells was later to describe as Max Müller's "unaccountable assumption that language indicated kindred" and endorses the latter's speculations about race.[41]

Max Müller's philological studies had the effect of confirming the Aryan nations' political and economic supremacy as an inevitable result of evolution. Accordingly, we might expect Bulwer-Lytton's novel to endorse a similarly upbeat interpretation of its own historical moment, but there are signs in *The Coming Race* of Bulwer-Lytton's balancing evolutionary optimism against the gloomier implications of the "last man" theme. By displacing evolutionary superiority on to the Vril-ya, Bulwer-Lytton makes the position of the narrator problematic since he comes to recognize his own inferiority before this other race. Gillian Beer has shown how in evolutionary writing hierarchy was achieved by projecting the "model of the single life cycle" onto a range of different phenomena.[42] Like Gulliver in the land of the Houyhnhnms, the narrator accepts the right of his hosts to reclassify him, which they do by designating him a "Tish" (an exclamation of insignificance) or "froglet," that is, an unformed creature. As he becomes caught in the role of freak, the features of Victorian masculinity—his full facial whiskers—turn into a stigma, a visual sign of his difference from the humans around him.

THE FORCES OF NATURE

The Victorian period saw not only astonishing advances in science but also a sustained attempt to apply scientific principles of investigation and analysis to what would now be called the paranormal. During Bulwer-Lytton's lifetime, scientists were investigating such phenomena as atmospheric magnetism, mesmerism, electro-biology, and the Odic force. All of these topics and more find mention in *The Coming Race*. It was a later sign of this interest when the Society for Psychical Research was founded in 1882, a society that numbered distinguished writers and scientists among its membership. Virtually every major novelist produced narratives dealing with the supernatural including Dickens, who helped establish a fashion for Christmas ghost stories. Bulwer-Lytton's story "The Haunted and the Haunters" (1859) was a successful example of this genre. Here a skeptical narrator is drawn against his will to admit a ghostly presence in a London house. His attitude toward this strange phenomenon approaches Bulwer-Lytton's own in that it leaves the door open to other dimensions of experience: "Now, my theory is that the Supernatural is the Impossible, and that what is called the supernatural is only something in the laws of nature of which we have been hereto ignorant." Part of that something, he continues, may be a "material fluid—call it Electric, call it Odic, call it what you will."[43] There are many signs of Bulwer-Lytton's serious pursuit of this kind of inquiry into the nature of reality. In 1861 he met the French occultist Eliphas Levi, and the two formed a group to study clairvoyance, magic, and related phenomena. In his essay "On Art in Fiction" (1838) Bulwer-

Lytton laid out some of the elements that he particularly valued in the novel. He expressed an impatience with excessive detail and had strong reservations about Scott's virtual exclusion of the "metaphysical operations of stormy and conflicting feelings."[44] This was a point he returned to in his 1845 preface to *Night and Day*, where he describes himself as "searching for new regions" in his writings.

Bulwer-Lytton's metaphysical curiosity, a quality shared by many Victorian writers and helpfully surveyed in Robert Lee Wolff's *Strange Stories* (1971), helps to explain the recurrence in his fiction of questers, seekers after knowledge like Adam Warner in *The Last of the Barons,* who is presented as a scientist but described as a "wizard" and a "philosopher." In "The Tale of Kosem Kesamin, the Magician," which Bulwer-Lytton claimed to have devised in his childhood, the young narrator receives the following instruction from the magician about his "first fathers": "Their knowledge pierced into the heart of things. They consulted the stars—but it was to measure the dooms of earth; and could we recall from the dust their perished scrolls, you would behold the mirror of the living times."[45] Here we see the privileging of ancient wisdom, the transcendent visionary nature of that wisdom, and its potential applicability to the present, themes that recur in Bulwer-Lytton. The Egyptian sage Arbaces in *The Last Days of Pompeii,* for instance, seeks to "put aside the veil of futurity" and see the disaster that is threatening the city. Several critics have pointed to Bulwer-Lytton's fascination with the occult, and in *Zanoni* he dramatized the encounter between ancient wisdom and the youthful desire for knowledge through the dialogues where Clarence Glyndon, a young English artist, learns from the mysterious and apparently ageless seer Zanoni. This "explicitly Rosicrucian text," which impressed the novelist Harriet Martineau so much that she devised a key to its symbolism, is punctuated by rhapsodies to the "Venerable Brotherhood" that has preserved a wisdom potentially capable of explaining life itself: "The laws of Attraction, of Electricity, and of the yet more mysterious agency of that Great Principle of

Life . . . were but the code in which the Theurgy of old sought the guides that led it to a legislation and science of its own" (*Zanoni*, bk. 3, chap. 5).[46] Set against the spiritual and political upheaval of the French Revolution, this novel establishes an opposition between spiritual and material values repeated in Bulwer-Lytton's novels of the 1860s, but even more significantly it describes a principle of connection that looks forward to vril. Zanoni's tutor, the scientist Mejnour, claims "to find a link between all intellectual beings in the existence of a certain all-pervading and invisible fluid resembling electricity, yet distinct from the known operations of that mysterious agency—a fluid that connected thought to thought with the rapidity and precision of the modern telegraph" (bk. 4, chap. 5). Until the end of the nineteenth century when J. J. Thomson discovered the electron, literary representations of electricity straddled the material and the immaterial in this way. Bulwer-Lytton's spiritualization of electricity anticipates Marie Corelli's later application, in novels like *A Romance of Two Worlds* (1886) and *The Life Everlasting* (1911), of electricity as a force uniting all life, a kind of "Electric Spirit," as she calls it, whose credibility she felt was strengthened by the discovery of radium.

EXPLORING THE SPIRITUAL: *A Strange Story*

A Strange Story (1861), which was to influence Bram Stoker's *Dracula*, continues this theme through an extended debate over the nature of reality and was planned by Bulwer-Lytton to "embrace all the modern learning of mysticism."[47] Its narrator, Allen Fenwick, is a doctor who announces at the beginning of the novel "my creed was that of a stern materialist" (chap. 1) but who is then gradually forced by extraordinary events to believe in the paranormal. Fenwick's encounters with different male characters—the women function as observers, sources of romantic entanglement, or experimental subjects—always involve a temporary discussion of the metaphysical controversies of the period: the nature of mind, the evidence for the existence of the soul, mental projection, and so on. His main "tutor" is an elderly pathologist named Faber who encourages him to find evidence of the inexplicable, even the supernatural, in writers like Bacon, Descartes, and Faraday. As a complacently modern scientist, Fenwick faces his real antagonist in the mysterious Margrave, who has learned the secret of the elixir of life from a Middle Eastern sage. Through his magic wand, a clear anticipation of the vril staff in *The Coming Race*, Margrave can throw his victims into a trance that forces them to lose their will and follow his directions. Once the wand comes into Fenwick's possession, he is triggered by its resemblance to an electrified rod into speculating on the exact nature of the force it contains, deciding that it may be an elemental vital fluid everywhere in Nature. Here again the novel anticipates the vril force, but through rather different evolutionary ironies. In *The Coming Race* the narrator is so bemused by the Vril-ya technology that its functioning seems positively magical, whereas Fenwick personifies a presumption of scientific progress that the extraordinary undermines. *A Strange Story* is packed with the signs of evolutionary theory; amateur naturalists have their collections of stuffed apes, which can transform houses into museums. But the neatness of these exhibits, reflecting the categories of Victorian science, is symbolically disrupted at the points where ancient magic enters the narrative.

Bulwer-Lytton dramatizes the fact that the wisdom of the past is not dead and relates the episodes of trance and automatism to the mid-Victorian debates that were going on about the limitations and ambiguities of sensory perception.[48] In particular the novel problematizes the division between mind and matter by using the argument from analogy, a common extrapolative strategy in science fiction. Just as Descartes found a "flame" in man, so scientists have discovered that most matter contains electricity. Whatever the ironies directed against the narrator in *The Coming Race*, his intellectual eclecticism and desire for a field theory of meaning were entirely congenial to Bulwer-Lytton, who repeatedly attempted to stimulate scientific inquiry into so-called spiritualism. He disliked this term because it obscured his conviction that "natural agencies are apparent in all the phenomena."[49] Indeed, throughout his career Bulwer-Lytton demonstrated an interest in mesmerism, Rosicrucianism, séances, in short an interest in any field that challenged a simple materialistic explanation of the world. In 1853 he wrote to Lord Walpole that his inquiries were unsettling rational presumptions: "I have been pursuing science into strange mysteries since we parted, and gone far into a spiritual world, which suffices to destroy all existing metaphysics and to startle the strongest reason."[50] Electricity came to carry a symbolic weight for Bulwer-Lytton in that it linked the animate and inanimate in Nature. The narrator of *The Coming Race* is virtually the last in a whole series of seekers described by Bulwer-Lytton, and one recent reprint of the novel carries glosses encouraging the reader to use it as a guide to spiritual enlightenment.[51]

Bulwer-Lytton's use of his fiction as a forum for metaphysical speculation reflects his independence of any individual religious denomination or creed. As his biographer Leslie Mitchell has shown, Bulwer-Lytton was constantly drawn to the spiritual, but independently of any institutional religion. For him, religion was demonstrated through two processes: humanity's capacity to receive images of God and his conviction that prayer should be "equated with the release of all imaginative sensibilities."[52] Thus the very idea of a divine prime mover or creator was crucial to Bulwer-Lytton's conception of the world. Chapter 14 of *The Coming Race*, which discusses the Vril-ya's religion, reflects the importance of this issue for Bulwer-Lytton. The deity is carefully indicated through expressions independent of religious sects ("the All-Good") and is revered for primal acts of creation where life is set in motion from form to form. Bulwer-Lytton alludes to Ralph Waldo Emerson's notion of compensation (discussed in his *Essays*, first series), whereby every instance of disease, for example, is balanced by positive vitality, and concludes the chapter with a quotation from the American naturalist Louis Agassiz's *Essay on Classifi-*

cation where the latter argues that the design of Nature implies that it has been created by a "reflective mind." If that is so, then every living creature possesses an "immaterial principle." In the novel that principle is symbolized by vril.

VRIL: THE LIFE FORCE

The mysterious force vril occupies a central role in *The Coming Race*. On 20 March 1870 Bulwer-Lytton explained the concept to John Forster as follows:

> I did not mean Vril for mesmerism, but for electricity, developed into uses as yet only dimly guessed, and including whatever there may be genuine in mesmerism, which I hold to be a mere branch current of the one great fluid pervading all nature. . . . Now, as some bodies are charged with electricity like the torpedo or electric eel, and can never communicate that power to other bodies, so I suppose the existence of a race charged with that electricity and having acquired the art to concentre and direct it—in a word, to be conductors of its lightnings. If you can suggest any other idea of carrying out that idea of a destroying race, I should be glad. Probably even the notion of Vril might be more cleared from mysticism or mesmerism by being simply defined to be electricity and conducted by those staves or rods, omitting all about mesmeric passes, etc. Perhaps too, it would be safe to omit all reference to the power of communicating with the dead.[53]

Vril is introduced into the novel as a benign therapeutic force before being identified as a weapon. Clearly it served as a synthesizing concept for Bulwer-Lytton, linking different areas of experience. This notion emerged in his writings as early as the 1840s: in *Zanoni* (1842) the Eastern sage Mejnour "professed to find a link between all intellectual beings in the existence of a certain all-pervading and invisible fluid resembling electricity, yet distinct from the known operations of that mysterious agency" (*Zanoni,* bk. 4, chap. 5). Just as vril is repeatedly related to the will in *The Coming Race*, so the physician narrator of *A Strange Story* (1862), Allen Fenwick, conducts experiments on inducing an electric current by the exercise of will. The critic A. C. Christensen has even seen vril as an anticipation of nuclear power.[54]

The exact nature of the vril force is difficult to pin down. For one critic it reveals the sinister underside to the uniformity of Vril-ya society, representing the "terrifying ruthlessness which allows them to eliminate anyone who disturbs the even tenor of the society."[55] Recent writers on *The Coming Race* have rightly stressed how vril draws together technological, biological, and psychic factors, as Susan Stone-Blackburn has pointed out.[56] This mysterious force resembles electricity, but it can never be quite defined.[57] Its working is shown first in the novel by the simple act of touch. Only when it functions as a weapon used to kill a monster does the vril rod seem to emit a "flash of lightning," but even here it can hardly be read as a prototype of a death ray. Bulwer-Lytton's careful vagueness of description leaves the nature of the force open to different interpretations, even linking it to the will of the operator. Bruce Clarke has recently argued that vril is loosely based on the Victorian concept of ether and "models energy by transferring it from natural to human agency." Bulwer-Lytton thus constructs an "analogue of the power technologies now driving the transportation and communication systems assisting the transfers of wealth that run the British Empire." Clarke reads the novel as an imperialist parable whose politics is confirmed by the fact that the ability to control vril is transmitted racially from generation to generation. He argues: "The Vril-ya have achieved super-humanity by mastering a form of subtle humanity and then co-evolving with it, integrating their biological and technological being."[58]

Around the turn of the century a Vril-ya Club was formed in London, and publications that applied Bulwer-Lytton's term began appearing.[59] In 1911 an anonymous tract titled *Vril; or, Vital Magnetism* appropriated Bulwer-Lytton's term for the purpose of expounding a doctrine that conflated philology (*vri* was an ancient root signifying life), mind power, and the new physics of particles and molecules. It was claimed that Bulwer-Lytton took vril from "ancient occult writings" and that the term had at least three levels of meaning: a cosmic principle, the "power of action and movement," and the "energy which performs the functions of life in the living organism."[60] The pamphlet stuck close to the spirit of *The Coming Race* in hypothesizing a force that straddled mind and matter, uniting the principles of the nervous system, the energy content of food, and even breathing methods into a kind of cosmic holism.

There is a pointed historical irony in the fact that Bulwer-Lytton's novel influenced the naming of a commercial product that was created following the Franco-Prussian War. After the siege and surrender of Paris, the French army sought ways to supply their forces with more nourishing food in the belief that this played a part in the fall of Paris. A Scot, John Lawson Johnston, was awarded the contract of producing tinned beef from the early 1870s onward. Initially called Johnston's Fluid Beef, the product grew in popularity and was renamed ("over a cigar") Bovril by combining the prefix *bo-* (i.e., "ox" or "beef" in Latin) with *vril*. Bovril was first sold in Britain at the 1886 Colonial and Continental Exhibition in London and subsequently was promoted as a national asset and a form of "liquid life" during the Boer War, when Rudyard Kipling lent his name to a chorus of praise for the product. An advertisement in the *Daily Mail* in 1900 asserted: "Doctors, nurses, officers, soldiers and newspaper correspondents unite in bearing testimony to the great popularity of Bovril at the Front as an Invigorating and Nourishing Food, preparing the soldier for battle and aiding him in recovery when weakened by wounds and disease."[61]

Bulwer-Lytton might have been doubly bemused to learn that his semimystical term "vril" had been appropriated by commerce and then turned toward the cause of British imperialism, were it not for the fact that in *The Coming Race* the vril staff becomes the embodiment of an ultimate, irresistible power exploited by the regime to subjugate the minorities who exist on its margins. The appropriation of that concept by George Griffith for his second novel, *Olga Romanoff* (1894), is both explicit and limiting. Whereas Bulwer-Lytton carefully left vague the applications of vril, Griffith concentrates exclusively on aerial military technology in his twenty-first-century narrative. The Aerians (a combination of "air-eans" [i.e., creatures of air] and "Aryans") who rule this world simply put into practice what Bulwer-Lytton had speculated about as theory. One character explains: "We have realised, to all intents and purposes, the dream that Lytton dreamt when he wrote that book. . . . All that the Vril-Ya did in his dream we have accomplished in reality, and more than that."[62] This so-called realization involves a simplification of Bulwer-Lytton's multidimensional concept into the single issue of world domination through the exercise of military supremacy in the air.

FROM THEOSOPHY TO NAZISM

Given Bulwer-Lytton's long-standing interest in the occult, it is hardly surprising that *The Coming Race* had an influence on figures like Madame Blavatsky. S. B. Liljegren has demonstrated the ways in which Blavatsky drew on Bulwer-Lytton's novels—particularly *The Last Days of Pompeii*, *Zanoni*, and *The Coming Race*—for her own *Isis Unveiled* (1877). Blavatsky's huge synthesis of science, religion, and philosophy, *The Secret Doctrine* (1888), also drew on Bulwer-Lytton in seeing vril as a new designation for a "terrible sidereal Force" known to the ancients; and by the turn of the century Bulwer-Lytton's title phrase had become assimilated into Theosophical discussions of the imminent coming race to be revealed with the new cosmic cycle.[63] Bulwer-Lytton's work was named by Aleister Crowley as an influence on his poem *The Mother's Tragedy* (1898), and Crowley placed Bulwer-Lytton's *Zanoni* and *A Strange Story* at the head of his list of recommended literature in his *Magick in Theory and Practice* (1929). Race theory and spiritual change combined in the Theosophist writings of

Annie Besant, who was herself an admirer of Bulwer-Lytton. She believed that an occult hierarchy was directing world history according to a Great Plan and, like Bulwer-Lytton, saw the present age as a "transition period" in which the first signs of the new race were beginning to emerge. This "coming race"—she repeats the phrase constantly—was to grow out of the Aryans and would be characterized by higher psychic faculties and a faith in Reason. "We are living in an environment," she declared, "that is destructive of the higher evolution, and at our peril we leave it as it is when the Coming Race must inevitably be born."[64] Like Bulwer-Lytton, she did not elaborate on how this evolutionary change would take place; she only insisted on its inevitability.

Theosophy spread from Britain to Germany toward the end of the nineteenth century, taking with it Blavatsky's version of Bulwer-Lytton's ideas. The revival of occultism in Germany produced new editions of Bulwer-Lytton's works, and ultimately *The Coming Race* was appropriated by a number of secret organizations in Germany in their formulation of an ideology of Ariosophy, a fusion of Aryan race doctrine, Nordic mythology, and Theosophy.[65] From the 1910s onward the Thule Society, the Golden Lodge, and the Vril Society to varying degrees incorporated Bulwer-Lytton's novel into the lore of Atlantis and emerging theories of racial superiority. The German rocket scientist Willy Ley admitted to being a member of one of these communities, whose "disciples believed they had secret knowledge that would enable them to change their race and become the equals of the men hidden in the bowels of the Earth." Bulwer-Lytton's subterranean world was evidently taken to be a model of imminent developments within the world and his narrative to be a parable of power: "Whoever becomes master of the vril will be master of himself, of others round him and of the world."[66] Ley asserted that the German Ariosophists' beliefs were founded directly on Bulwer-Lytton's novel: "The subterranean humanity was nonsense, *Vril* was not. Possibly it had enabled the British, who kept it as a State secret, to amass their colonial empire."[67]

Founded in 1918 (and joined by the young Adolf Hitler the following year), the Thule Society was ostensibly a literary club but in reality a secret political organization numbering among its members specialists in the occult who were familiar with Bulwer-Lytton's novel. It has been alleged that one such figure, Karl Haushofer, had many meetings with Hitler while he was writing *Mein Kampf*; and that Haushofer went on to found in Berlin the Luminous Lodge or Vril Society, dedicated to the awakening of the Aryan race. Accordingly, there are reports that during the 1930s the Nazis explored caves and Antarctica to find the Vril-ya and conducted experiments into the construction of a saucer-shaped Vril Machine that would work on an antigravity principle. Partly by the very nature of this material, hard historical facts on the relation of German occultism to the Nazi ideology have been difficult to locate. In the most professional examination of this topic, Nicholas Goodrick-Clarke has questioned the importance of the Thule Society and the reliability of Ley's statements, suggesting that the Vril Society never existed. However, Goodrick-Clarke does document the ways in which Bulwer-Lytton's writings, and particularly *The Coming Race*, played a part in the Nazi belief in a super race that would take control of the world through harnessing cosmic forces and ancient wisdom.[68]

EVOLUTION IN THE WORKS OF BULWER-LYTTON'S CONTEMPORARIES AND BEYOND

One year after *The Coming Race* was published, Samuel Butler's *Erewhon* appeared, and some reviewers attributed its success to the influence of Bulwer-Lytton's novel. Butler was so stung by this judgment that in his preface to the second edition of *Erewhon* he took pains to stress that he had finished his own satire in 1871 and made a point of not looking at *The Coming Race* (which subsequently startled him by its similarities) until he had finished his last corrections. One of Butler's biographers has noted that Butler changed the name of one of his characters from Zelora to Zulora when he discovered Zee in *The Coming Race*.[69] Such details aside, both works concern themselves with the superseding of humanity, in Bulwer-Lytton's by a higher race, in Butler's by technology. The inset "Book of the Machines" explains the Erewhonian destruction of machines as growing out of this fear of becoming redundant. Based on the premises that machines are tools and tools externalized limbs (a notion popularized in the 1960s by Marshall McLuhan), the Erewhonian author speculates that even human consciousness has been shaped by machines. Far from being the mere implements of human use, these devices pose a potential threat summed up as the "art of the machine—they serve that they may rule" (*Erewhon*, chap. 24).

This same theme was picked up by George Eliot, who applauded John Blackwood for publishing *The Coming Race*, in a dialogue-essay "Shadows of the Coming Race," collected in *Impressions of Theophrastus Such* (1879). Here the case for machines being seen as extensions of man is put by the speaker Trost (in German, "comfort" or "reassurance") and the contrasting case for supersession put by the narrator. Trost insists that humans will retain their central function as the "brains" of these machines, while his companion proposes an altogether different Darwinian case that "the process of natural selection must drive men altogether out of the field." As fewer physical demands are made on humans, they will degenerate physically and "will naturally, as the less energetic combinations of movement, subside like the flame of a candle in the sunlight." Drawing an analogy with geological evolution, the narrator hypothesizes a coming race of "beings who will be blind and deaf as the inmost rock, yet will execute changes as delicate and complicated as those of human language and all the intricate web of what we call its effects."[70] Within this dialogue it is the narrator who has the last say and who puts the most cogent case, expressing essentially the same anxiety as that presented in *The Coming Race*, an anxiety that much later Isaac Asimov was to call the "fear of supplantation."[71] Asimov ties this fear historically to ambivalence toward technology arising from the Industrial Revolution, which is precisely the tension within George Eliot's dialogue. Bulwer-Lytton, however, imagined supplantation in racial and national as well as technological terms.

Because both writers shared many common evolutionary concerns, it is not surprising to find elements of Bulwer-Lytton's novel incorporated into H. G. Wells's *The Time Machine* (1895). There are a number of specific echoes in Wells's descriptive details (references to the Sphinx, the buildings, the underground machines). Wells takes his Time Traveller to a similar future world of leisure, but one where the Traveller's individuality comes under no threat. Where Bulwer-Lytton's American immediately registers fear before the subterranean beings, Wells's Traveller feels "like a schoolmaster amidst children" (chap. 4). Although her name partly echoes that of Bulwer-Lytton's Zee, the infantile Weena lacks Zee's strength or stature; her name more likely was suggested by Arowhena in *Erewhon*. Quite literarily, she is a "wee" version of Bulwer-Lytton's mild-mannered but threatening future woman. Stephen Derry has argued that *The Time Machine* draws on Bulwer-Lytton's novel through "parody with an agenda of patriarchal reclamation."[72] However, his suggestion of parody ignores the broader issue of the degeneration of humanity that was popularized around the turn of the century by Max Nordau and T. H. Huxley (whose lectures the young Wells attended) as a general fate hanging over civilization rather than awaiting any specific racial groups.

Aspects of *The Coming Race* were also selectively woven into Bernard Shaw's *Back to Methuselah* (1921). Shaw had read the novel in his youth and, as B. G. Knepper points out, praised it in an 1887 lecture on fiction. Knepper argues that Shaw was particularly interested in the notion of vril, which he interpreted as "primarily a product of will"; it adapted variously as a mind ray, vortex, or means of communication in Shaw's later writings.[73] "The Tragedy of an Elderly Gentleman," the third in the *Back to Methuselah* sequence, is the work that bears the most signs of Bulwer-Lytton's influence. The elderly gentleman of the title is displaced into a future where his race has become obsolete. Among other things, he has difficulties with the terms of human classification that derive directly from an analogy used by Bulwer-Lytton. He complains that "everybody here keeps talking to me about primaries and secondaries and tertiaries as if people were geological strata."[74] The characters he encounters have z-names, one woman being called Zoo. They use a tuning-fork device similar to the vril rod to communicate by a form of radio. And one of the main regimes of this future age is the Turanian Empire, whose name is taken, via Bulwer-Lytton, out of Victorian philology. As in *The Coming Race,* much of the dialogue satirizes the gentleman's presumptions of decorum and social order, using evolutionary theory to demonstrate the inevitability of change. Like Bulwer-Lytton's narrator, the elderly gentleman is the last of his kind, already a walking anachronism.

UNDERGROUND WORLDS AND THE HOLLOW EARTH

Apart from its allusions to Hades and Hell, the setting of *The Coming Race* draws on an emerging tradition of depicting alternative societies through worlds underground, which continues to be used in science fiction (see the last section of the bibliography). One of the earliest examples of this tradition, Ludvig Holberg's *Journey of Neils Klim to the World Underground* (1741), probably suggested to Bulwer-Lytton some aspects of his own narrative. Like the narrator of *The Coming Race,* Klim descends into the underworld down a rope that breaks. He too is attacked by a monster, comes upon an impressive, spacious city, and engages in extended dialogues with the underground rulers about the constitution of society. He too is astonished by the subservience of men in a province where the "order of things is indeed inverted."[75] Klim too is an impressionable conservative who is disturbed by the spectacle of men working in the kitchen or women taking the sexual initiative in relationships.

The notion of a hollow earth is used by Holberg as a facilitating device for his plot, but the hollow earth had been promoted as a geological reality from 1818 through the 1820s by Captain John Cleves Symmes of Ohio. Symmes campaigned for exploration of the polar regions, where, he claimed, there were vast openings into the earth's interior, each one becoming known as "Symmes's Hole." *Symzonia,* a utopian novel published in 1820 under the pen name of Adam Seaborn (possibly Symmes himself), it describes the experiences of sailors who discover this inner world, the inhabitants of which criticize humans of the surface for being violent and slaves to their passions.[76] Thus was set a pattern of voyage narratives that culminated in travelers encountering a subterranean race whose culture is much advanced. The vogue for hollow earth narratives peaked around the turn of the century. Charles Willing Beale's *The Secret of the Earth* (1899), for instance, describes how two Americans construct an airship and fly to the North Pole, where they explicitly confirm Symmes's theory and extend his polar explorations. Once they sail inside the earth, they encounter a race so advanced that it seems to have dispensed with labor altogether, but then—and this becomes another standard feature of hollow earth fiction—wonderment shifts into horror at the barren desert that constitutes most of the underground terrain, compelling the airmen to make their escape.

A much closer coincidence of themes and concerns with *The Coming Race* can be found in Jules Verne's *Journey to the Center of the Earth* (1864; English translation, 1871). Here the narrator's uncle, Professor Lidenbrock, combines an interest in mineralogy and philology that conveniently enables him to decipher a message in Runic script left for the explorers by their precursor. The descent underground, as in Bulwer-Lytton's novel, feeds the narrator's sense of moving into an evolutionary past, even of stepping out of contemporary reality into a world of myth where fossil creatures come alive. The two monsters that do battle in front of the travelers resemble the reptiles that Bulwer-Lytton's narrator encounters. In both novels the creatures are animated versions of antediluvian mammals, characterized not only by size but also by their huge eyes and jaws, the physical signs of malign intent and predation.

Verne's evocation of an underground world so huge that it seems to have its own "sky" anticipates Bulwer-Lytton's descriptions and explicitly refers to hollow earth theory, but Verne does not use the subterranean setting to imagine any kind of alternative society. There is some evidence, however, that *The Coming Race* influenced *Les Indes noires* (*The Black Indies*, 1877). In 1876 Louis-Jules Hetzel sent Verne a manuscript translation of Bulwer-Lytton's book, *Les Races futures*, recommending it as a novel "full of ideas."[77] *Les Indes noires* develops the narrative frame of *The Coming Race*—departure from and return to a mine—into a central subject. Set in central Scotland, the novel describes the discovery of a natural labyrinth of underground galleries, which are converted into a coal mine. The largest cavern, compared by Verne to the Mammoth Cave in Kentucky, becomes the temporary site of Coal Town until the lake on the surface bursts its floor and floods the cave. Verne follows Bulwer-Lytton in evoking the sublime vastness of underground space but does not use the setting as an alternative social location.

In *The Coming Race* Bulwer-Lytton conflates the notion of the hollow earth with traditional representations of the underworld. As early as the 1830s he had been using the underground as a fantasy location from which to comment ironically on contemporary England (see the appendix), and in his 1871 novel he complicates his descriptions of the world of the Vril-ya by incorporating details associated with Hell. Both the enormous building the narrator encounters and the use of naphtha lighting recall Milton's description of Pandaemonium in *Paradise Lost* and as a result make it impossible to read the underground world as an unqualified utopia. By having his narrator descend into a projected future, Bulwer-Lytton inverts the trope of progress as an ascent. By intermittently suggesting that the underground is a kind of Hell with its warring elements, "mephitic gases," and similar features, he gives expression to the narrator's shifting responses, which slide from initial admiration to final rejection.

The notion of a hollow earth as the habitat of a lost race was used by C. J. Cutcliffe Hyne in his *Beneath Your Very Boots* (1889), which describes the discovery by an English traveler of an underground "nation" (the Nradas) descended from the ancient Britons.[78] Although these people are shown to be technologically advanced, Hyne has no interest in developing a consistent utopia. By contrast, Joseph O'Neill's *Land under England* (1935) uses the same lost underground race convention to satirize the brainwashing methods of totalitarian regimes. Whereas Hyne has his narrator travel in search of adventures, O'Neill dramatizes the potential threat to democracy posed by a people descended from the Romans who have institutionalized group behavior through a form of hypnosis.[79]

Hollow earth conventions were used around the turn of the century to dramatize developments in the United States that were tied loosely to the exploration of the polar regions. William Reed's *The Phantom of the Poles* (1906) is unusual in limiting itself to scientific questions, positing a hollow earth to "solve" the various uncertainties of explorers like Nansen. William R. Bradshaw's *The Goddess of Atvatabar* (1891) is more typical in describing an increasingly fantastic sequence of adventures introduced by a sea voyage that casts away the crew underground. In his introduction, Julian Hawthorne (Nathaniel's nephew) cites *The Coming Race* as a precursor text dealing with spiritual ideals, but *The Goddess of Atvatabar* has a high-minded rhapsodic style quite different from Bulwer-Lytton's tone. Bradshaw's narrator, Lexington White, views this new world as paradisiacal and technologically advanced (they have electronically powered flying machines), imbued with a culture where the ideal and the practical have harmonized: "Invention had raised humanity from the depths of slavery, ignorance, and weakness to a height of empire undreamed of in earlier ages."[80] The term "empire" might make us pause in this account of progress, and indeed when a goddess in Atvatabar steps down from her divine role because of a burgeoning romance with White, war breaks out between two factions. The last sections of the novel describe a struggle for naval supremacy resulting in a victory for the side commanded by White, and the novel ends with him installed as co-ruler of this domain. Behind the adventure narrative lies a description of American military superiority explicitly linked to the politics of the outside world.

The hollow earth in some narratives becomes the site for spiritual education. John Uri Lloyd's *Etidorpha* (i.e., Aphrodite) (1895), textually one of the most complex instances of the genre, presents a story-within-a-story set in motion by the encounter of the primary narrator, Lewellyn Drury, with a strange old man. The latter leaves Drury a manuscript describing how he joins an occult society in his search for ultimate knowledge. He is taken into an underworld through a cavern in Kentucky after he has symbolically shed his old identity, and there he is instructed by a sightless sage into the secrets of the natural world. Like Bulwer-Lytton's fiction, *Etidorpha* challenges materialist presumptions about reality, which is shown to depend on energy identified with spirit as opposed to matter. The old man learns that the earth floats in a kind of fluid or ether, similar to the elemental force described in *A Strange Story*.

Bulwer-Lytton's notion of the life-force vril is repeated in William Alexander Taylor's *Intermere* (1901), in which an advanced subterranean civilization is run on new applications of electricity, the "life-giving, life-preserving and life-promoting principle, the superior and fountain of all law affecting the material Universe and intervening space."[81] This elevated rhetoric gives us a sign that Taylor's utopia is a spiritual one, where the excesses of nineteenth-century industry are screened by a dispersal of small manufacturing plants around the country. Intermere embodies an idealized version of America; there, luxury has disappeared, and society is organized on a homestead principle. The narrator's experience of this new world is thus a kind of education in the failures of America to realize its own potential, an extended tuition in the "grand possibilities of human life" (19), which are being smothered by his actual society.

Taylor's cautious exploration of social themes contrasts with H. Rider Haggard's better-known *When the Earth Shook* (1919), which combines the lost race motif and an exotic South Seas setting with fears of cultural subversion. A group of gentleman adventurers gain access to an "Under-world" whose ancient inhabitants have discovered a means analogous to radium of prolonging life indefinitely. Both their great city and the "death-rods" used by the ruler's guards echo Bulwer-Lytton, as does the attempted marriage between the hero, Arbuthnot, and the king's daughter. However, the historical moment of the novel's publication soon after World War I gives the question of power more urgency than it has in *The Coming Race*. The capacity of the Vril-ya to fly reflects their greater mobility than surface humanity. Haggard applies this more directly in the technology of planes that can bomb cities, and he sets his narrative against a background of apocalyptic destruction that this technology makes possible.

Evolution was easily incorporated into hollow earth fiction also. John Wyndham's *The Secret People* (1935) combines Verne's subject of converting the Sahara into an inland sea with the lost race theme.[82] Here, the conversion has actually taken place, and a couple whose plane crashes into the New Sea are sucked underground by a whirlpool. In the earth's depths they discover a race of pygmies that apparently has been isolated for thousands of years from the rest of the human race.

THE IMPORTANCE OF *The Coming Race*

The publication of Bulwer-Lytton's novel initiated a science fiction revival in the decades that followed. For Darko Suvin this revival was triggered variously by the 1867 Reform Bill, the Franco-Prussian War, the Paris Commune of 1871, and a general perception of the instability of social values.[83] In the short term, *The Coming Race* made an impact on writers like Wells and Shaw; since then, it has stayed in print largely because of its continuing appeal in mystical and theosophical circles. Although the novel was first published anonymously, its authorship was an open secret, and, as the bibliography to the present edition shows, *The Coming Race* has been reprinted far more times than any of Bulwer-Lytton's other works, under at least four different titles. It is also a text in which different cultural currents intersect. *The Coming Race* related directly to both sides of the Franco-Prussian War: on the German side to the promotion of Aryan cultural superiority, and initially to the French in their adoption of the beef extract Bovril. The latter was subsequently promoted by the British government in support of its imperial program during the Boer War and later to promote national well-being in the First and Second World Wars. The book's metaphysical dimension, particularly its description of vril as a vital principle, was incorporated into Theosophy and the occult; and *The Coming Race* continues to attract interest from New Age presses. Finally, it was woven into the continuing debates over the relation between race and nation and over the evolution of military technology.

The coming Race

Inscribed to

MAX MÜLLER

in tribute of respect

and admiration

CHAPTER I   I am a native of ——, in the United States of America. My ancestors migrated from England in the reign of Charles II., and my grandfather was not undistinguished in the War of Independence. My family, therefore, enjoyed a somewhat high social position in right of birth; and being also opulent, they were considered disqualified for the public service. My father once ran for Congress, but was signally defeated by his tailor. After that event he interfered little in politics, and lived much in his library. I was the eldest of three sons, and sent at the age of sixteen to the old country, partly to complete my literary education, partly to commence my commercial training in a mercantile firm at Liverpool. My father died shortly after I was twenty-one; and being left well off, and having a taste for travel and adventure, I resigned, for a time, all pursuit of the almighty dollar, and became a desultory wanderer over the face of the earth.[1]

In the year 18—, happening to be in ——, I was invited by a professional engineer, with whom I had made acquaintance, to visit the recesses of the —— mine, upon which he was employed.

The reader will understand, ere he close this narrative, my reason for concealing all clue to the district of which I write, and will perhaps thank me for refraining from any description that may tend to its discovery.

Let me say, then, as briefly as possible, that I accompanied the engineer into the interior of the mine, and became so strangely fascinated by its gloomy wonders, and so interested in my friend's explorations, that I prolonged my stay in the neighbourhood, and descended daily, for some weeks, into the vaults and galleries hollowed by nature and art beneath the surface of the earth. The engineer was persuaded that far richer deposits of mineral wealth than had yet been detected, would be found in a new shaft that had been commenced under his operations. In piercing this shaft we came one day upon a chasm jagged and seemingly charred at the sides, as if burst asunder at some distant period by volcanic fires. Down this chasm my friend caused himself to be lowered in a 'cage,'[2] having first tested the atmosphere by the safety-lamp. He remained nearly an hour in the abyss. When he returned he was very pale, and with an anxious, thoughtful expression of face, very different from its ordinary character, which was open, cheerful, and fearless.

He said briefly that the descent appeared to him unsafe, and leading to no result; and, suspending further operations in the shaft, we returned to the more familiar parts of the mine.

All the rest of that day the engineer seemed preoccupied by some absorbing thought. He was unusually taciturn, and there was a scared, bewildered look in his eyes, as that of a man who has seen a ghost. At night, as we two were sitting alone in the lodging we shared together near the mouth of the mine, I said to my friend,—

"Tell me frankly what you saw in that chasm: I am sure it was something strange and terrible. Whatever it be, it has left your mind in a state of doubt. In such a case two heads are better than one. Confide in me."

The engineer long endeavoured to evade my inquiries, but as, while he spoke, he helped himself unconsciously out of the brandy-flask to a degree to which he was wholly unaccustomed, for he was a very temperate man, his reserve gradually melted away. He who would keep himself to himself should imitate the dumb animals, and drink water. At last he said, "I will tell you all. When the cage stopped, I found myself on a ridge of rock; and below me, the chasm, taking a slanting direction, shot down to a considerable depth, the darkness of which my lamp could not have penetrated. But through it, to my infinite surprise, streamed upward a steady brilliant light. Could it be any volcanic fire; in that case, surely I should have felt the heat. Still, if on this there was doubt, it was of the utmost importance to our common safety to clear it up. I examined the sides of the descent, and found that I could venture to trust myself to the irregular projections or ledges, at least for some way. I left the cage and clambered down. As I drew near and nearer to the light, the chasm became wider, and at last I saw, to my unspeakable amaze, a broad level road at the bottom of the abyss, illumined as far as the eye could reach by what seemed artificial gas-lamps[3] placed at regular intervals, as in the thoroughfare of a great city; and I heard confusedly at a distance a hum as of human voices. I know, of course, that no rival miners are at work in this district. Whose could be those voices? What human hands could have levelled that road and marshalled those lamps?

"The superstitious belief, common to miners, that gnomes or fiends dwell within the bowels of the earth, began to seize me.[4] I shuddered at the thought of descending further and braving the inhabitants of this nether valley. Nor indeed could I have done so without ropes, as from the spot I had reached to the bottom of the chasm the sides of the rock sank down abrupt, smooth, and sheer. I retraced my steps with some difficulty. Now I have told you all."

"You will descend again?"

"I ought, yet I feel as if I durst not."

"A trusty companion halves the journey and doubles the courage. I will go with you. We will provide ourselves with ropes of suitable length and strength—and—pardon me—you must not drink more to-night. Our hands and feet must be steady and firm to-morrow."

CHAPTER 2

With the morning my friend's nerves were re-braced, and he was not less excited by curiosity than myself. Perhaps more; for he evidently believed in his own story, and I felt considerable doubt of it: not that he would have wilfully told an untruth, but that I thought he must have been under one of those hallucinations which seize on our fancy or our nerves in solitary, unaccustomed places, and in which we give shape to the formless and sound to the dumb.

We selected six veteran miners to watch our descent; and as the cage held only one at a time, the engineer descended first; and when he had gained the ledge at which he had before halted, the cage re-arose for me. I soon gained his side. We had provided ourselves with a strong coil of rope.

The light struck on my sight as it had done the day before on my friend's. The hollow through which it came sloped diagonally: it seemed to me a diffused atmospheric light, not like that from fire, but soft and silvery, as from a northern star. Quitting the cage, we descended, one after the other, easily enough, owing to the juts in the side, till we reached the place at which my friend had previously halted, and which was a projection just spacious enough to allow us to stand abreast. From this spot the chasm widened rapidly like the lower end of a vast funnel, and I saw distinctly the valley, the road, the lamps which my companion had described. He had exaggerated nothing. I heard the sounds he had heard—a mingled indescribable hum as of voices and a dull tramp as of feet. Straining my eye farther down, I clearly beheld at a distance the outline of some large building. It could not be mere natural rock, it was too symmetrical, with huge heavy Egyptian-like columns, and the whole lighted as from within. I had about me a small pocket-telescope, and by the aid of this I could distinguish, near the building I mention, two forms which seemed human, though I could not be sure. At least they were living, for they moved, and both vanished within the building. We now proceeded to attach the end of the rope we had brought with us to the ledge on which we stood, by the aid of clamps and grappling-hooks, with which, as well as with necessary tools, we were provided.

We were almost silent in our work. We toiled like men afraid to speak to each other. One end of the rope being thus apparently made firm to the ledge, the other, to which we fastened a fragment of the rock, rested on the ground below, a distance of some fifty feet. I was a younger and a more active man than my companion, and having served on board ship in my boyhood, this mode of transit was more familiar to me than to him. In a whisper I claimed the precedence, so that when I gained the ground I might serve to hold the rope more steady for his descent. I got safely to the ground beneath, and the engineer now began to lower himself. But he had scarcely accomplished ten feet of the descent, when the fastenings, which we had fancied so secure, gave way, or rather the rock itself proved treacherous and crumbled beneath the strain; and the unhappy man was precipitated to the bottom, falling just at my feet, and bringing down with his fall splinters of the rock, one of which, fortunately but a small one, struck and for the time stunned me. When I recovered my senses I saw my companion an inanimate mass beside me, life utterly extinct. While I was bending over his corpse in grief and horror, I heard close at hand a strange sound between a snort and a hiss; and turning instinctively to the quarter from which it came, I saw emerging from a dark fissure in the rock a vast and terrible head, with open jaws and dull, ghastly, hungry eyes—the head of a monstrous reptile resembling that of the crocodile or alligator, but infinitely larger than the largest creature of that kind I had ever beheld in my travels. I started to my feet and fled down the valley at my utmost speed. I stopped at last, ashamed of my panic and my flight, and returned to the spot on which I had left the body of my friend. It was gone; doubtless the monster had already drawn it into its den and devoured it. The rope and the grappling-hooks still lay where they had fallen, but they afforded me no chance of return: it was impossible to re-attach them to the rock above, and the sides of the rock were too sheer and smooth for human steps to clamber. I was alone in this strange world, amidst the bowels of the Earth.

CHAPTER 3

Slowly and cautiously I went my solitary way down the lamplit road and towards the large building I have described. The road itself seemed like a great Alpine pass, skirting rocky mountains of which the one through whose chasms I had descended formed a link. Deep below to the left lay a vast valley, which presented to my astonished eye the unmistakable evidences of art and culture. There were fields covered with a strange vegetation, similar to none I have seen above the earth; the colour of it not green, but rather of a dull leaden hue or of a golden red.

There were lakes and rivulets which seemed to have been curved into artificial banks; some of pure water, others that shone like pools of naphtha. At my right hand, ravines and defiles opened amidst the rocks, with passes between, evidently constructed by art, and bordered by trees resembling, for the most part, gigantic ferns, with exquisite varieties of feathery foliage, and stems like those of the palm-tree. Others were more like the cane-plant, but taller, bearing large clusters of flowers. Others, again, had the form of enormous fungi, with short thick stems supporting a wide dome-like roof, from which either rose or drooped long slender branches. The whole scene behind, before, and beside me, far as the eye could reach, was brilliant with innumerable lamps. The world without a sun[1] was bright and warm as an Italian landscape at noon, but the air less oppressive, the heat softer. Nor was the scene before me void of signs of habitation. I could distinguish at a distance, whether on the banks of lake or rivulet, or half-way upon eminences, embedded amidst the vegetation, buildings that must surely be the homes of men. I could even discover, though far off, forms that appeared to me human moving amidst the landscape. As I paused to gaze, I saw to the right, gliding quickly through the air, what appeared a small boat, impelled by sails shaped like wings. It soon passed out of sight, descending amidst the shades of a forest. Right above me there was no sky, but only a cavernous roof. This roof grew higher and higher at the distance of the landscapes beyond, till it became imperceptible, as an atmosphere of haze formed itself beneath.

Continuing my walk, I started,—from a bush that resembled a great tangle of seaweeds, interspersed with fern-like shrubs and plants of large leafage shaped like that of the aloe or prickly pear,— a curious animal about the size and shape of a deer. But as, after bounding away a few paces, it turned round and gazed at me inquisitively, I perceived that it was not like any species of deer now extant above the earth, but it brought instantly to my recollection a plaster cast I had seen in some museum of a variety of the elk stag, said to have existed before the Deluge. The creature seemed tame enough, and, after inspecting me a moment or two, began to graze on the singular herbage around undismayed and careless.

CHAPTER 4

I now came in full sight of the building. Yes, it bad been made by hands, and hollowed partly out of a great rock. I should have supposed it at the first glance to have been of the earliest form of Egyptian architecture. It was fronted by huge columns, tapering upward from massive plinths, and with capitals that, as I came nearer, I perceived to be more ornamental and more fantastically graceful than Egyptian architecture allows. As the Corinthian capital mimics the leaf of the acanthus, so the capitals of these columns imitated the foliage of the vegetation neighbouring them, some aloe-like, some fern-like. And now there came out of this building a form—human;—was it human? It stood on the broad way and looked around, beheld me and approached. It came within a few yards of me, and at the sight and presence of it an indescribable awe and tremor seized me, rooting my feet to the ground. It reminded me of symbolical images of Genius or Demon that are seen on Etruscan vases or limned on the walls of Eastern sepulchres—images that borrow the outlines of man, and are yet of another race. It was tall, not gigantic, but tall as the tallest men below the height of giants.

Its chief covering seemed to me to be composed of large wings folded over its breast and reaching to its knees; the rest of its attire was composed of an under tunic and leggings of some thin fibrous material.[1] It wore on its head a kind of tiara that shone with jewels, and carried in its right hand a slender staff of bright metal like polished steel. But the face! it was that which inspired my awe and my terror. It was the face of man, but yet of a type of man distinct from our known extant races. The nearest approach to it in outline and expression is the face of the sculptured sphinx[2]—so regular in its calm, intellectual, mysterious beauty. Its colour was peculiar, more like that of the red man than any other variety of our species, and yet different from it—a richer and a softer hue, with large black eyes, deep and brilliant, and brows arched as a semicircle. The face was beardless; but a nameless something in the aspect, tranquil though the expression, and beauteous though the features, roused that instinct of danger which the sight of a tiger or serpent arouses. I felt that this manlike image was endowed with forces inimical to man. As it drew near, a cold shudder came over me. I fell on my knees and covered my face with my hands.[3]

CHAPTER 5   A voice accosted me—a very quiet and very musical key of voice—in a language of which I could not understand a word, but it served to dispel my fear. I uncovered my face and looked up. The stranger (I could scarcely bring myself to call him man) surveyed me with an eye that seemed to read to the very depths of my heart. He then placed his left hand on my forehead, and with the staff in his right gently touched my shoulder. The effect of this double contact was magical. In place of my former terror there passed into me a sense of contentment, of joy, of confidence in myself and in the being before me. I rose and spoke in my own language. He listened to me with apparent attention, but with a slight surprise in his looks; and shook his head, as if to signify that I was not understood. He then took me by the hand and led me in silence to the building. The entrance was open—indeed there was no door to it. We entered an immense hall, lighted by the same kind of lustre as in the scene without, but diffusing a fragrant odour. The floor was in large tesselated blocks[1] of precious metals, and partly covered with a sort of matlike carpeting. A strain of low music, above and around, undulated as if from invisible instruments, seeming to belong naturally to the place, just as the sound of murmuring waters belongs to a rocky landscape, or the warble of birds to vernal groves.

A figure, in a simpler garb than that of my guide, but of similar fashion, was standing motionless near the threshold. My guide touched it twice with his staff, and it put itself into a rapid and gliding movement, skimming noiselessly over the floor. Gazing on it, I then saw that it was no living form, but a mechanical automaton.[2] It might be two minutes after it vanished through a doorless opening, half screened by curtains at the other end of the hall, when through the same opening advanced a boy of about twelve years old, with features closely resembling those of my guide, so that they seemed to me evidently son and father. On seeing me the child uttered a cry, and lifted a staff like that borne by my guide, as if in menace. At a word from the elder he dropped it. The two then conversed for some moments, examining me while they spoke. The child touched my garments, and stroked my face with evident curiosity, uttering a sound like a laugh, but with an hilarity more subdued than the mirth of our laughter. Presently the roof of the hall opened, and a platform descended, seemingly constructed on the same principle as the "lifts"[3] used in hotels and warehouses for mounting from one story to another. The stranger placed himself and the child on the platform, and motioned to me to do the same, which I did. We ascended quickly and safely, and alighted in the midst of a corridor with doorways on either side.

Through one of these doorways I was conducted into a chamber fitted up with an Oriental splendour; the walls were tesselated with spars, and metals, and uncut jewels; cushions and divans abounded; apertures as for windows, but unglazed, were made in the chamber, opening to the floor; and as I passed along I observed that these openings led into spacious balconies, and commanded views of the illumined landscape without. In cages suspended from the ceiling there were birds of strange form and bright plumage, which at our entrance set up a chorus of song, modulated into tune as is that of our piping bullfinches. A delicious fragrance, from censers of gold elaborately sculptured, filled the air. Several automata, like the one I had seen, stood dumb and motionless by the walls. The stranger placed me beside him on a divan, and again spoke to me, and again I spoke, but without the least advance towards understanding each other.

But now I began to feel the effects of the blow I received from the splinters of the falling rock more acutely than I had done at first.

There came over me a sense of sickly faintness, accompanied with acute, lancinating[4] pains in the head and neck. I sank back on the seat, and strove in vain to stifle a groan. On this the child, who had hitherto seemed to eye me with distrust or dislike, knelt by my side to support me; taking one of my hands in both his own, he approached his lips to my forehead, breathing on it softly. In a few moments my pain ceased, a drowsy, happy calm crept over me; I fell asleep.

How long I remained in this state I know not, but when I woke I felt perfectly restored. My eyes opened upon a group of silent forms, seated around me in the gravity and quietude of Orientals —all more or less like the first stranger; the same mantling wings, the same fashion of garment, the same sphinx-like faces, with the deep dark eyes and red man's colour; above all, the same type of race—race akin to man's, but infinitely stronger of form and grander of aspect, and inspiring the same unutterable feeling of dread. Yet each countenance was mild and tranquil, and even kindly in its expression. And strangely enough, it seemed to me that in this very calm and benignity consisted the secret of the dread which the countenances inspired. They seemed as void of the lines and shadows which care and sorrow, and passion and sin, leave upon the faces of men, as are the faces of sculptured gods, or as, in the eyes of Christian mourners, seem the peaceful brows of the dead.

I felt a warm hand on my shoulder; it was the child's. In his eyes there was a sort of lofty pity and tenderness, such as that with which we may gaze on some suffering bird or butterfly. I shrank from that touch—I shrank from that eye. I was vaguely impressed with a belief that, had he so pleased, that child could have killed me as easily as a man can kill a bird or a butterfly. The child seemed pained at my repugnance, quitted me and placed himself beside one of the windows. The others continued to converse with each other in a low tone, and by their glances towards me I could perceive that I was the object of their conversation. One in especial seemed to be urging some proposal affecting me on the being whom I had first met, and this last by his gesture seemed about to assent to it, when the child suddenly quitted his post by the window, placed himself between me and the other forms, as if in protection, and spoke quickly and eagerly. By some intuition or instinct I felt that the child I had before so dreaded was pleading in my behalf. Ere he had ceased another stranger entered the room. He appeared older than the rest, though not old; his countenance, less smoothly serene than theirs, though equally regular in its features, seemed to me to have more the touch of a humanity akin to my own. He listened quietly to the words addressed to him, first by my guide, next by two others of the group, and lastly by the child; then turned towards myself, and addressed me, not by words, but by signs and gestures. These I fancied that I perfectly understood, and I was not mistaken. I comprehended that he inquired whence I came. I extended my arm and pointed towards the road which had led me from the chasm in the rock; then an idea seized me. I drew forth my pocket-book and sketched on one of its blank leaves a rough design of the ledge of the rock, the rope, myself clinging to it; then of the cavernous rock below, the head of the reptile, the lifeless form of my friend. I gave this primitive kind of hieroglyph to my interrogator, who, after inspecting it gravely, handed it to his next neighbour, and it thus passed round the group. The being I had at first encountered then said a few words, and the child, who approached and looked at my drawing, nodded as if he comprehended its purport, and, returning to the window, expanded the wings attached to his form, shook them once or twice, and then launched himself into space without. I started up in amaze and hastened to the window. The child was already in the air, buoyed on his wings, which he did not flap to and fro as a bird does, but which were elevated over his head, and seemed to bear him steadily aloft without effort of his own. His flight seemed as swift as any eagle's; and I observed that it was towards the rock whence I had descended, of which the outline loomed visible in the brilliant atmosphere. In a very few minutes he returned, skimming through the opening from which he had gone, and dropping on the floor the rope and grappling-hooks I had left at the descent from the chasm. Some words in a low tone passed between the beings present: one of the group touched an automaton, which started forward and glided from the room; then the last comer, who had addressed me by gestures, rose, took me by the hand, and led me into the corridor. There the platform by which I had mounted awaited us; we placed ourselves on it and were lowered into the hall below. My new companion, still holding me by the hand, conducted me from the building into a street (so to speak) that stretched beyond it, with buildings on either side, separated from each other by gardens bright with rich-coloured vegetation and strange flowers. Interspersed amidst these gardens, which were divided from each other by low walls, or walking slowly along the road, were many forms similar to those I had already seen. Some of the passers-by, on observing me, approached my guide, evidently by their tones, looks, and gestures addressing to him inquiries about myself. In a few moments a crowd collected round us, examining me with great interest, as if I were some rare wild animal. Yet even in gratifying their curiosity they preserved a grave and courteous demeanour; and after a few words from my guide, who seemed to me to deprecate obstruction in our road, they fell back with a stately inclination of head, and resumed their own way with tranquil indifference. Midway in this thoroughfare we stopped at a building that differed from those we had hitherto passed, inasmuch as it formed three sides of a vast court, at the angles of which were lofty pyramidal towers; in the open space between the sides was a circular fountain of colossal dimensions, and throwing up a dazzling spray of what seemed to me fire. We entered the building through an open doorway and came into an enormous hall, in which were several groups of children, all apparently employed in work as at some great factory. There was a huge engine in the wall which was in full play, with wheels and cylinders, and resembling our own steam-engines, except that it was richly ornamented with precious stones and metals, and appeared to emit a pale phosphorescent atmosphere of shifting light. Many of the children were at some mysterious work on this machinery, others were seated before tables. I was not allowed to linger long enough to examine into the nature of their employment. Not one young voice was heard—not one young face turned to gaze on us. They were all still and indifferent as may be ghosts, through the midst of which pass unnoticed the forms of the living.

Quitting this hall, my guide led me through a gallery richly painted in compartments, with a barbaric mixture of gold in the colours, like pictures by Louis Cranach.[5] The subjects described on these walls appeared to my glance as intended to illustrate events in the history of the race amidst which I was admitted. In all there were figures, most of them like the manlike creatures I had seen, but not all in the same fashion of garb, nor all with wings. There were also the effigies of various animals and birds wholly strange to me, with backgrounds depicting landscapes or buildings. So far as my imperfect knowledge of the pictorial art would allow me to form an opinion, these paintings seemed very accurate in design and very rich in colouring, showing a perfect knowledge of perspective, but their details not arranged according to the rules of composition acknowledged by our artists—wanting, as it were, a centre; so that the effect was vague, scattered, confused, bewildering—they were like heterogeneous fragments of a dream of art.

We now came into a room of moderate size, in which was assembled what I afterwards knew to be the family of my guide, seated at a table spread as for repast. The forms thus grouped were those of my guide's wife, his daughter, and two sons. I recognised at once the difference between the two sexes, though the two females were of taller stature and ampler proportions than the males; and their countenances, if still more symmetrical in outline and contour, were devoid of the softness and timidity of expression which give charm to the face of woman as seen on the earth above. The wife wore no wings, the daughter wore wings longer than those of the males.

My guide uttered a few words, on which all the persons seated rose, and with that peculiar mildness of look and manner which I have before noticed, and which is, in truth, the common attribute of this formidable race, they saluted me according to their fashion, which consists in laying the right hand very gently on the head and uttering a soft sibilant monosyllable—S.Si, equivalent to "Welcome."

The mistress of the house then seated me beside her, and heaped a golden platter before me from one of the dishes.

While I ate (and though the viands were new to me, I marvelled more at the delicacy than the strangeness of their flavour), my companions conversed quietly, and, so far as I could detect, with polite avoidance of any direct reference to myself, or any obtrusive scrutiny of my appearance. Yet I was the first creature of that variety of the human race to which I belong that they had ever beheld, and was consequently regarded by them as a most curious and abnormal phenomenon. But all rudeness is unknown to this people, and the youngest child is taught to despise any vehement emotional demonstration. When the meal was ended, my guide again took me by the hand, and, re-entering the gallery, touched a metallic plate inscribed with strange figures, and which I rightly conjectured to be of the nature of our telegraphs. A platform descended, but this time we mounted to a much greater height than in the former building, and found ourselves in a room of moderate dimensions, and which in its general character had much that might be familiar to the associations of a visitor from the upper world. There were shelves on the wall containing what appeared to be books, and indeed were so; mostly very small like our diamond duodecimos, shaped in the fashion of our volumes, and bound in fine sheets of metal. There were several curious-looking pieces of mechanism scattered about, apparently models, such as might be seen in the study of any professional mechanician. Four automata (mechanical contrivances which, with these people, answer the ordinary purposes of domestic service) stood phantom-like at each angle in the wall. In a recess was a low couch, or bed with pillows. A window, with curtains of some fibrous material drawn aside, opened upon a large balcony. My host stepped out into the balcony; I followed him. We were on the uppermost story of one of the angular pyramids; the view beyond was of a wild and solemn beauty impossible to describe,—the vast ranges of precipitous rock which formed the distant background, the intermediate valleys of mystic many-coloured herbage, the flash of waters, many of them like streams of roseate flame, the serene lustre diffused over all by myriads of lamps, combined to form a whole of which no words of mine can convey adequate description; so splendid was it, yet so sombre; so lovely, yet so awful.

But my attention was soon diverted from these nether landscapes. Suddenly there arose, as from the streets below, a burst of joyous music; then a winged form soared into the space; another, as in chase of the first, another and another; others after others, till the crowd grew thick and the number countless. But how describe the fantastic grace of these forms in their undulating movements! They appeared engaged in some sport or amusement; now forming into opposite squadrons; now scattering; now each group threading the other, soaring, descending, interweaving, severing; all in measured time to the music below, as if in the dance of the fabled Peri.[6]

I turned my gaze on my host in a feverish wonder. I ventured to place my hand on the large wings that lay folded on his breast, and in doing so a slight shock as of electricity passed through me. I recoiled in fear; my host smiled, and, as if courteously to gratify my curiosity, slowly expanded his pinions. I observed that his garment beneath then became dilated as a bladder that fills with air. The arms seemed to slide into the wings, and in another moment he had launched himself into the luminous atmosphere, and hovered there, still, and with outspread wings, as an eagle that basks in the sun. Then, rapidly as an eagle swoops, he rushed downwards into the midst of one of the groups, skimming through the midst, and as suddenly again soaring aloft. Thereon, three forms, in one of which I thought to recognise my host's daughter, detached themselves from the rest, and followed him as a bird sportively follows a bird. My eyes, dazzled with the lights and bewildered by the throngs, ceased to distinguish the gyrations and evolutions of these winged playmates, till presently my host re-emerged from the crowd and alighted at my side.

The strangeness of all I had seen began now to operate fast on my senses; my mind itself began to wander. Though not inclined to be superstitious, nor hitherto believing that man could be brought into bodily communication with demons, I felt the terror and the wild excitement with which, in the Gothic ages, a traveller might have persuaded himself that he witnessed a sabbat[7] of fiends and witches. I have a vague recollection of having attempted with vehement gesticulation, and forms of exorcism, and loud incoherent words, to repel my courteous and indulgent host; of his mild endeavours to calm and soothe me; of his intelligent conjecture that my fright and bewilderment were occasioned by the difference of form and movement between us which the wings that had excited my marvelling curiosity had, in exercise, made still more strongly perceptible; of the gentle smile with which he had sought to dispel my alarm by dropping the wings to the ground and endeavouring to show me that they were but a mechanical contrivance. That sudden transformation did but increase my horror, and as extreme fright often shows itself by extreme daring, I sprang at his throat like a wild beast. In an instant I was felled to the ground as by an electric shock, and the last confused images floating before my sight ere I became wholly insensible, were the form of my host kneeling beside me with one hand on my forehead, and the beautiful calm face of his daughter, with large, deep, inscrutable eyes intently fixed upon my own.

CHAPTER 6

I remained in this unconscious state, as I afterwards learned, for many days, even for some weeks, according to our computation of time. When I recovered I was in a strange room, my host and all his family were gathered round me, and to my utter amaze my host's daughter accosted me in my own language with but a slightly foreign accent.

"How do you feel?" she asked.

It was some moments before I could overcome my surprise enough to falter out, "You know my language? How? Who and what are you?"

My host smiled and motioned to one of his sons, who then took from a table a number of thin metallic sheets on which were traced drawings of various figures—a house, a tree, a bird, a man, &c.

In these designs I recognised my own style of drawing. Under each figure was written the name of it in my language, and in my writing; and in another handwriting a word strange to me beneath it.

Said the host, "Thus we began; and my daughter Zee, who belongs to the College of Sages, has been your instructress and ours too."

Zee then placed before me other metallic sheets, on which, in my writing, words first, and then sentences, were inscribed. Under each word and each sentence strange characters in another hand. Rallying my senses, I comprehended that thus a rude dictionary had been effected. Had it been done while I was dreaming? "That is enough now," said Zee, in a tone of command. "Repose and take food."

CHAPTER 7

A room to myself was assigned to me in this vast edifice. It was prettily and fantastically arranged, but without any of the splendour of metal work or gems which was displayed in the more public apartments. The walls were hung with a variegated matting made from the stalks and fibres of plants, and the floor carpeted with the same.

The bed was without curtains, its supports of iron resting on balls of crystal; the coverings, of a thin white substance resembling cotton. There were sundry shelves containing books. A curtained recess communicated with an aviary filled with singing-birds, of which I did not recognise one resembling those I have seen on earth, except a beautiful species of dove, though this was distinguished from our doves by a tall crest of bluish plumes. All these birds had been trained to sing in artful tunes, and greatly exceeded the skill of our piping bull-finches, which can rarely achieve more than two tunes, and cannot, I believe, sing those in concert. One might have supposed one's self at an opera in listening to the voices in my aviary. There were duets and trios, and quartettes and choruses, all arranged as in one piece of music. Did I want to silence the birds? I had but to draw a curtain over the aviary, and their song hushed as they found themselves left in the dark. Another opening formed a window, not glazed, but on touching a spring, a shutter ascended from the floor, formed of some substance less transparent than glass, but still sufficiently pellucid to allow a softened view of the scene without. To this window was attached a balcony, or rather hanging-garden, wherein grew many graceful plants and brilliant flowers. The apartment and its appurtenances had thus a character, if strange in detail, still familiar, as a whole, to modern notions of luxury, and would have excited admiration if found attached to the apartments of an English duchess or a fashionable French author. Before I arrived this was Zee's chamber; she had hospitably assigned it to me.

Some hours after the waking up which is described in my last chapter, I was lying alone on my couch trying to fix my thoughts on conjecture as to the nature and genus of the people amongst whom I was thrown, when my host and his daughter Zee entered the room. My host, still speaking my native language, inquired, with much politeness, whether it would be agreeable to me to converse, or if I preferred solitude. I replied, that I should feel much honoured and obliged by the opportunity offered me to express my gratitude for the hospitality and civilities I had received in a country to which I was a stranger, and to learn enough of its customs and manners not to offend through ignorance.

As I spoke, I had of course risen from my couch; but Zee, much to my confusion, curtly ordered me to lie down again, and there was something in her voice and eye, gentle as both were, that compelled my obedience. She then seated herself unconcernedly at the foot of my bed, while her father took his place on a divan a few feet distant.

"But what part of the world do you come from," asked my host, "that we should appear so strange to you, and you to us? I have seen individual specimens of nearly all the races differing from our own, except the primeval savages who dwell in the most desolate and remote recesses of uncultivated nature, unacquainted with other light than that they obtain from volcanic fires, and contented to grope their way in the dark, as do many creeping, crawling, and even flying things.[1] But certainly you cannot be a member of those barbarous tribes, nor, on the other hand, do you seem to belong to any civilised people."

I was somewhat nettled at this last observation, and replied that I had the honour to belong to one of the most civilised nations of the earth; and that, so far as light was concerned, while I admired the ingenuity and disregard of expense with which my host and his fellow-citizens had contrived to illumine the regions unpenetrated by the rays of the sun, yet I could not conceive how any who had once beheld the orbs of heaven could compare to their lustre the artificial lights invented by the necessities of man. But my host said he had seen specimens of most of the races differing from his own, save the wretched barbarians he had mentioned. Now, was it possible that he had never been on the surface of the earth, or could he only be referring to communities buried within its entrails?

My host was for some moments silent; his countenance showed a degree of surprise which the people of that race very rarely manifest under any circumstances, howsoever extraordinary. But Zee was more intelligent, and exclaimed, "So you see, my father, that there is truth in the old tradition; there always is truth in every tradition commonly believed in all times and by all tribes."

"Zee," said my host, mildly, "you belong to the College of Sages, and ought to be wiser than I am; but, as chief of the Light-preserving Council, it is my duty to take nothing for granted till it is proved to the evidence of my own senses." Then, turning to me, he asked me several questions about the surface of the earth and the heavenly bodies; upon which, though I answered him to the best of my knowledge, my answers seemed not to satisfy nor convince him. He shook his head quietly, and, changing the subject rather abruptly, asked how I had come down from what he was pleased to call one world to the other. I answered, that under the surface of the earth there were mines containing minerals, or metals, essential to our wants and our progress in all arts and industries; and I then briefly explained the manner in which, while exploring one of these mines, I and my ill-fated friend had obtained a glimpse of the regions into which we had descended, and how the descent had cost him his life; appealing to the rope and grappling-hooks that the child had brought to the house in which I had been at first received, as a witness of the truthfulness of my story.

My host then proceeded to question me as to the habits and modes of life among the races on the upper earth, more especially among those considered to be the most advanced in that civilisation which he was pleased to define as "the art of diffusing throughout a community the tranquil happiness which belongs to a virtuous and well-ordered household." Naturally desiring to represent in the most favourable colours the world from which I came, I touched but slightly, though indulgently, on the antiquated and decaying institutions of Europe, in order to expatiate on the present grandeur and prospective pre-eminence of that glorious American Republic, in which Europe enviously seeks its model and tremblingly foresees its doom. Selecting for an example of the social life of the United States that city in which progress advances at the fastest rate, I indulged in an animated description of the moral habits of New York. Mortified to see, by the faces of my listeners, that I did not make the favourable impression I had anticipated, I elevated my theme; dwelling on the excellence of democratic institutions, their promotion of tranquil happiness by the government of party, and the mode in which they diffused such happiness throughout the community by preferring, for the exercise of power and the acquisition of honours, the lowliest citizens in point of property, education, and character. Fortunately recollecting the peroration of a speech, on the purifying influences of American democracy and their destined spread over the world, made by a certain eloquent senator (for whose vote in the Senate a Railway Company, to which my two brothers belonged, had just paid 20,000 dollars), I wound up by repeating its glowing predictions of the magnificent future that smiled upon mankind—when the flag of freedom should float over an entire continent, and two hundred millions of intelligent citizens, accustomed from infancy to the daily use of revolvers, should supply to a cowering universe the doctrine of the Patriot Monroe.[2]

When I had concluded, my host gently shook his head, and fell into a musing study, making a sign to me and his daughter to remain silent while he reflected. And after a time he said, in a very earnest and solemn tone, "If you think, as you say, that you, though a stranger, have received kindness at the hands of me and mine, I adjure you to reveal nothing to any other of our people respecting the world from which you came, unless, on consideration, I give you permission to do so. Do you consent to this request?"

"Of course I pledge my word to it," said I, somewhat amazed; and I extended my right hand to grasp his. But he placed my hand gently on his forehead and his own right hand on my breast, which is the custom among this race in all matters of promise or verbal obligations. Then turning to his daughter, he said, "And you, Zee, will not repeat to any one what the stranger has said, or may say, to me or to you, of a world other than our own." Zee rose and kissed her father on the temples, saying, with a smile, "A Gy's tongue is wanton, but love can fetter it fast. And if, my father, you fear lest a chance word from me or yourself could expose our community to danger, by a desire to explore a world beyond us, will not a wave of the *vril*,[3] properly impelled, wash even the memory of what we have heard the stranger say out of the tablets of the brain?"

"What is vril?" I asked.

Therewith Zee began to enter into an explanation of which I understood very little, for there is no word in any language I know which is an exact synonym for vril. I should call it electricity, except that it comprehends in its manifold branches other forces of nature, to which, in our scientific nomenclature, differing names are assigned, such as magnetism, galvanism,[4] &c. These people consider that in vril they have arrived at the unity in natural energic agencies, which has been conjectured by many philosophers above ground, and which Faraday thus intimates under the more cautious term of correlation:—

"I have long held an opinion," says that illustrious experimentalist, "almost amounting to a conviction, in common, I believe, with many other lovers of natural knowledge, that the various forms under which the forces of matter are made manifest have one common origin; or, in other words, are so directly related and mutually dependent, that they are convertible, as it were, into one another, and possess equivalents of power in their action."[5]

These subterranean philosophers assert that, by one operation of vril, which Faraday would perhaps call 'atmospheric magnetism,'[6] they can influence the variations of temperature—in plain words, the weather; that by other operations, akin to those ascribed to mesmerism,[7] electro-biology,[8] odic force,[9] &c., but applied scientifically through vril conductors, they can exercise influence over minds, and bodies animal and vegetable, to an extent not surpassed in the romances of our mystics. To all such agencies they give the common name of vril. Zee asked me if, in my world, it was not known that all the faculties of the mind could be quickened to a degree unknown in the waking state, by trance or vision, in which the thoughts of one brain could be transmitted to another, and knowledge be thus rapidly interchanged. I replied, that there were among us stories told of such trance or vision, and that I had heard much and seen something of the mode in which they were artificially effected, as in mesmeric clairvoyance;[10] but that these practices had fallen much into disuse or contempt, partly because of the gross impostures to which they had been made subservient, and partly because, even where the effects upon certain abnormal constitutions were genuinely produced, the effects, when fairly examined and analysed, were very unsatisfactory—not to be relied upon for any systematic truthfulness or any practical purpose, and rendered very mischievous to credulous persons by the superstitions they tended to produce. Zee received my answers with much benignant attention, and said that similar instances of abuse and credulity had been familiar to their own scientific experience in the infancy of their knowledge, and while the properties of vril were misapprehended, but that she reserved further discussion on this subject till I was more fitted to enter into it. She contented herself with adding, that it was through the agency of vril, while I had been placed in the state of trance, that I had been made acquainted with the rudiments of their language; and that she and her father, who, alone of the family, took the pains to watch the experiment, had acquired a greater proportionate knowledge of my language than I of their own; partly because my language was much simpler than theirs, comprising far less of complex ideas; and partly because their organisation was, by hereditary culture, much more ductile and more readily capable of acquiring knowledge than mine. At this I secretly demurred; and having had, in the course of a practical life, to sharpen my wits, whether at home or in travel, I could not allow that my cerebral organisation could possibly be duller than that of people who had lived all their lives by lamplight. However, while I was thus thinking, Zee quietly pointed her forefinger at my forehead and sent me to sleep.

CHAPTER 8

When I once more awoke I saw by my bedside the child who had brought the rope and grappling-hooks to the house in which I had been first received, and which, as I afterwards learned, was the residence of the chief magistrate of the tribe. The child, whose name was Taë (pronounced Tar-ee), was the magistrate's eldest son. I found that during my last sleep or trance I had made still greater advance in the language of the country, and could converse with comparative ease and fluency.

This child was singularly handsome, even for the beautiful race to which he belonged, with a countenance very manly in aspect for his years, and with a more vivacious and energetic expression than I had hitherto seen in the serene and passionless faces of the men. He brought me the tablet on which I had drawn the mode of my descent, and had also sketched the head of the horrible reptile that had scared me from my friend's corpse. Pointing to that part of the drawing, Taë put to me a few questions respecting the size and form of the monster, and the cave or chasm from which it had emerged. His interest in my answers seemed so grave as to divert him for a while from any curiosity as to myself or my antecedents. But to my great embarrassment, seeing how I was pledged to my host, he was just beginning to ask me where I came from, when Zee fortunately entered, and, overhearing him, said, "Taë, give to our guest any information he may desire, but ask none from him in return. To question him who he is, whence he comes, or wherefore he is here, would be a breach of the law which my father has laid down for this house."

"So be it," said Taë, pressing his hand to his heart; and from that moment, till the one in which I saw him last, this child, with whom I became very intimate, never once put to me any of the questions thus interdicted.

CHAPTER 9

It was not for some time, and until, by repeated trances, if they are so to be called, my mind became better prepared to interchange ideas with my entertainers, and more fully to comprehend differences of manners and customs, at first too strange to my experience to be seized by my reason, that I was enabled to gather the following details respecting the origin and history of this subterranean population, as portion of one great family race called the Ana.

According to the earliest traditions, the remote progenitors of the race had once tenanted a world above the surface of that in which their descendants dwelt. Myths of that world were still preserved in their archives, and in those myths were legends of a vaulted dome in which the lamps were lighted by no human hand.[1] But such legends were considered by most commentators as allegorical fables. According to these traditions the earth itself, at the date to which the traditions ascend, was not indeed in its infancy, but in the throes and travail of transition from one form of development to another, and subject to many violent revolutions of nature. By one of such revolutions, that portion of the upper world inhabited by the ancestors of this race had been subjected to inundations, not rapid, but gradual and uncontrollable, in which all, save a scanty remnant, were submerged and perished. Whether this be a record of our historical and sacred Deluge, or of some earlier one contended for by geologists, I do not pretend to conjecture; though, according to the chronology of this people as compared with that of Newton, it must have been many thousands of years before the time of Noah.[2] On the other hand, the account of these writers does not harmonise with the opinions most in vogue among geological authorities, inasmuch as it places the existence of a human race upon earth at dates long anterior to that assigned to the terrestrial formation adapted to the introduction of mammalia. A band of the ill-fated race, thus invaded by the flood, had, during the march of the waters, taken refuge in caverns amidst the loftier rocks, and, wandering through these hollows, they lost sight of the upper world for ever. Indeed, the whole face of the earth had been changed by this great revulsion; land had been turned into sea—sea into land. In the bowels of the inner earth even now, I was informed as a positive fact, might be discovered the remains of human habitation—habitation not in huts and caverns, but in vast cities whose ruins attest the civilisation of races which flourished before the age of Noah, and are not to be classified with those genera to which philosophy ascribes the use of flint and the ignorance of iron.

The fugitives had carried with them the knowledge of the arts they had practised above ground—arts of culture and civilisation. Their earliest want must have been that of supplying below the earth the light they had lost above it; and at no time, even in the traditional period, do the races, of which the one I now sojourned with formed a tribe, seem to have been unacquainted with the art of extracting light from gases, or manganese, or petroleum. They had been accustomed in their former state to contend with the rude forces of nature; and indeed the lengthened battle they had fought with their conqueror Ocean, which had taken centuries in its spread, had quickened their skill in curbing waters into dikes and channels. To this skill they owed their preservation in their new abode. "For many generations," said my host, with a sort of contempt and horror, "these primitive forefathers are said to have degraded their rank and shortened their lives by eating the flesh of animals, many varieties of which had, like themselves, escaped the Deluge, and sought shelter in the hollows of the earth; other animals, supposed to be unknown to the upper world, those hollows themselves produced."

When what we should term the historical age emerged from the twilight of tradition, the Ana were already established in different communities, and had attained to a degree of civilisation very analogous to that which the more advanced nations above the earth now enjoy. They were familiar with most of our mechanical inventions, including the application of steam as well as gas. The communities were in fierce competition with each other. They had their rich and their poor; they had orators and conquerors; they made war either for a domain or an idea. Though the various states acknowledged various forms of government, free institutions were beginning to preponderate; popular assemblies increased in power; republics soon became general; the democracy to which the most enlightened European politicians look forward as the extreme goal of political advancement, and which still prevailed among other subterranean races, whom they despised as barbarians, the loftier family of Ana, to which belonged the tribe I was visiting, looked back to as one of the crude and ignorant experiments which belong to the infancy of political science. It was the age of envy and hate, of fierce passions, of constant social changes more or less violent, of strife between classes, of war between state and state. This phase of society lasted, however, for some ages, and was finally brought to a close, at least among the nobler and more intellectual populations, by the gradual discovery of the latent powers stored in the all-permeating fluid which they denominate Vril.

According to the account I received from Zee, who, as an erudite professor in the College of Sages,[3] had studied such matters more diligently than any other member of my host's family, this fluid is capable of being raised and disciplined into the mightiest agency over all forms of matter, animate or inanimate. It can destroy like the flash of lightning; yet, differently applied, it can replenish or invigorate life, heal, and preserve, and on it they chiefly rely for the cure of disease, or rather for enabling the physical organisation to re-establish the due equilibrium of its natural powers, and thereby to cure itself. By this agency they rend way through the most solid substances, and open valleys for culture through the rocks of their subterranean wilderness. From it they extract the light which supplies their lamps, finding it steadier, softer, and healthier than the other inflammable materials they had formerly used.

But the effects of the alleged discovery of the means to direct the more terrible force of vril were chiefly remarkable in their influence upon social polity. As these effects became familiarly known and skilfully administered, war between the Vril-discoverers ceased, for they brought the art of destruction to such perfection as to annul all superiority in numbers, discipline, or military skill. The fire lodged in the hollow of a rod directed by the hand of a child could shatter the strongest fortress, or cleave its burning way from the van to the rear of an embattled host. If army met army, and both had command of this agency, it could be but to the annihilation of each. The age of war was therefore gone, but with the cessation of war other effects bearing upon the social state soon became apparent. Man was so completely at the mercy of man, each whom he encountered being able, if so willing, to slay him on the instant, that all notions of government by force gradually vanished from political systems and forms of law. It is only by force that vast communities, dispersed through great distances of space, can be kept together; but now there was no longer either the necessity of self-preservation or the pride of aggrandisement to make one state desire to preponderate in population over another.

The Vril-discoverers thus, in the course of a few generations, peacefully split into communities of moderate size. The tribe amongst which I had fallen was limited to 12,000 families. Each tribe occupied a territory sufficient for all its wants, and at stated periods the surplus population departed to seek a realm of its own. There appeared no necessity for any arbitrary selection of these emigrants; there was always a sufficient number who volunteered to depart.

These subdivided states, petty if we regard either territory or population,—all appertained to one vast general family. They spoke the same language, though the dialects might slightly differ. They intermarried; they maintained the same general laws and customs; and so important a bond between these several communities was the knowledge of vril and the practice of its agencies, that the word A-Vril was synonymous with civilisation; and Vril-ya, signifying "The Civilised Nations," was the common name by which the communities employing the uses of vril distinguished themselves from such of the Ana as were yet in a state of barbarism.

The government of the tribe of Vril-ya I am treating of was apparently very complicated, really very simple. It was based upon a principle recognised in theory, though little carried out in practice, above ground—viz., that the object of all systems of philosophical thought tends to the attainment of unity, or the ascent through all intervening labyrinths to the simplicity of a single first cause or principle. Thus in politics, even republican writers have agreed that a benevolent autocracy would insure the best administration, if there were any guarantees for its continuance, or against its gradual abuse of the powers accorded to it. This singular community elected therefore a single supreme magistrate styled Tur; he held his office nominally for life, but he could seldom be induced to retain it after the first approach of old age. There was indeed in this society nothing to induce any of its members to covet the cares of office. No honours, no insignia of higher rank were assigned to it. The supreme magistrate was not distinguished from the rest by superior habitation or revenue. On the other hand, the duties awarded to him were marvellously light and easy, requiring no preponderant degree of energy or intelligence. There being no apprehensions of war, there were no armies to maintain; being no government of force, there was no police to appoint and direct. What we call crime was utterly unknown to the Vril-ya; and there were no courts of criminal justice. The rare instances of civil disputes were referred for arbitration to friends chosen by either party, or decided by the Council of Sages, which will be described later. There were no professional lawyers; and indeed their laws were but amicable conventions, for there was no power to enforce laws against an offender who carried in his staff the power to destroy his judges. There were customs and regulations to compliance with which, for several ages, the people had tacitly habituated themselves; or if in any instance an individual felt such compliance hard, he quitted the community and went elsewhere. There was, in fact, quietly established amid this state, much the same compact that is found in our private families, in which we virtually say to any independent grown-up member of the family whom we receive and entertain, "Stay or go, according as our habits and regulations suit or displease you." But though there were no laws such as we call laws, no race above ground is so law-observing. Obedience to the rule adopted by the community has become as much an instinct as if it were implanted by nature. Even in every household the head of it makes a regulation for its guidance, which is never resisted nor even cavilled at by those who belong to the family. They have a proverb, the pithiness of which is much lost in this paraphrase, "No happiness without order, no order without authority, no authority without unity." The mildness of all government among them, civil or domestic, may be signalised by their idiomatic expressions for such terms as illegal or forbidden— viz., "It is requested not to do so-and-so." Poverty among the Ana is as unknown as crime; not that property is held in common, or that all are equals in the extent of their possessions or the size and luxury of their habitations: but there being no difference of rank or position between the grades of wealth or the choice of occupations, each pursues his own inclinations without creating envy or vying; some like a modest, some a more splendid kind of life; each makes himself happy in his own way. Owing to this absence of competition, and the limit placed on the population, it is difficult for a family to fall into distress; there are no hazardous speculations, no emulators striving for superior wealth and rank. No doubt, in each settlement all originally had the same proportions of land dealt out to them; but some, more adventurous than others, had extended their possessions farther into the bordering wilds, or had improved into richer fertility the produce of their fields, or entered into commerce or trade. Thus, necessarily, some had grown richer than others, but none had become absolutely poor, or wanting anything which their tastes desired. If they did so, it was always in their power to migrate, or at the worst to apply, without shame and with certainty of aid, to the rich; for all the members of the community considered themselves as brothers of one affectionate and united family. More upon this head will be treated of incidentally as my narrative proceeds.

The chief care of the supreme magistrate was to communicate with certain active departments charged with the administration of special details. The most important and essential of such details was that connected with the due provision of light. Of this department my host, Aph-Lin, was the chief. Another department, which might be called the foreign, communicated with the neighbouring kindred states, principally for the purpose of ascertaining all new inventions; and to a third department, all such inventions and improvements in machinery were committed for trial. Connected with this department was the College of Sages—a college especially favoured by such of the Ana as were widowed and childless, and by the young unmarried females, amongst whom Zee was the most active, and, if what we call renown or distinction was a thing acknowledged by this people (which I shall later show it is not), among the most renowned or distinguished. It is by the female Professors of this College that those studies which are deemed of least use in practical life—as purely speculative philosophy, the history of remote periods, and such sciences as entomology,[4] conchology,[5] etc.—are the more diligently cultivated. Zee, whose mind, active as Aristotle's, equally embraced the largest domains and the minutest details of thought, had written two volumes on the parasite insect that dwells amid the hairs of a tiger's[6] paw, which work was considered the best authority on that interesting subject. But the researches of the sages are not confined to such subtle or elegant studies. They comprise various others more important, and especially the properties of vril, to the perception of which their finer nervous organisation renders the female Professors eminently keen. It is out of this college that the Tur, or chief magistrate, selects Councillors, limited to three, in the rare instances in which novelty of event or circumstance perplexes his own judgment.

There are a few other departments of minor consequence, but all are carried on so noiselessly and quietly that the evidence of a government seems to vanish altogether, and social order to be as regular and unobtrusive as if it were a law of nature. Machinery is employed to an inconceivable extent in all the operations of labour within and without doors, and it is the unceasing object of the department charged with its administration to extend its efficiency. There is no class of labourers or servants, but all who are required to assist or control the machinery are found in the children, from the time they leave the care of their mothers to the marriageable age, which they place at sixteen for the Gy-ei (the females), twenty for the Ana (the males). These children are formed into bands and sections under their own chiefs, each following the pursuits in which he is most pleased, or for which he feels himself most fitted. Some take to handicrafts, some to agriculture, some to household work, and some to the only services of danger to which the population is exposed; for the sole perils that threaten this tribe are, first, from those occasional convulsions within the earth, to foresee and guard against which tasks their utmost ingenuity—irruptions of fire and water, the storms of subterranean winds and escaping gases. At the borders of the domain, and at all places where such peril might be apprehended, vigilant inspectors are stationed with telegraphic[7] communication to the hall in which chosen sages take it by turns to hold perpetual sittings. These inspectors are always selected from the elder boys approaching the age of puberty, and on the principle that at that age observation is more acute and the physical forces more alert than at any other. The second service of danger, less grave, is in the destruction of all creatures hostile to the life, or the culture, or even the comfort, of the Ana. Of these the most formidable are the vast reptiles, of some of which ante-diluvian[8] relics are preserved in our museums, and certain gigantic winged creatures, half bird, half reptile.[9] These, together with lesser wild animals, corresponding to our tigers or venomous serpents, it is left to the younger children to hunt and destroy; because, according to the Ana, here ruthlessness is wanted, and the younger a child the more ruthlessly he will destroy. There is another class of animals in the destruction of which discrimination is to be used, and against which children of intermediate age are appointed—animals that do not threaten the life of man, but ravage the produce of his labour, varieties of the elk and deer species, and a smaller creature much akin to our rabbit, though infinitely more destructive to crops, and much more cunning in its mode of depredation. It is the first object of these appointed infants, to tame the more intelligent of such animals into respect for enclosures signalised by conspicuous landmarks, as dogs are taught to respect a larder, or even to guard the master's property. It is only where such creatures are found untamable to this extent that they are destroyed. Life is never taken away for food or for sport, and never spared where untamably inimical to the Ana. Concomitantly with these bodily services and tasks, the mental education of the children goes on till boyhood ceases. It is the general custom, then, to pass through a course of instruction at the College of Sages, in which, besides more general studies, the pupil receives special lessons in such vocation or direction of intellect as he himself selects. Some, however, prefer to pass this period of probation in travel, or to emigrate, or to settle down at once into rural or commercial pursuits. No force is put upon individual inclination.

CHAPTER 10

The word Ana (pronounced broadly Arna) corresponds with our plural men; An (pronounced Arn), the singular, with man. The word for woman is Gy (pronounced hard, as in Guy); it forms itself into Gy-ei for the plural, but the G becomes soft in the plural, like Jy-ei.[1] They have a proverb to the effect that this difference in pronunciation is symbolical, for that the female sex is soft, collectively, but hard to deal with in the individual. The Gy-ei are in the fullest enjoyment of all the rights of equality with males, for which certain philosophers above ground contend.

In childhood they perform the offices of work and labour impartially with boys; and, indeed, in the earlier age appropriated to the destruction of animals irreclaimably hostile, the girls are frequently preferred, as being by constitution more ruthless under the influence of fear or hate. In the interval between infancy and the marriageable age familiar intercourse between the sexes is suspended. At the marriageable age it is renewed, never with worse consequences than those which attend upon marriage. All arts and vocations allotted to the one sex are open to the other, and the Gy-ei arrogate to themselves a superiority in all those abstruse and mystical branches of reasoning, for which they say the Ana are unfitted by a duller sobriety of understanding, or the routine of their matter-of-fact occupations, just as young ladies in our own world constitute themselves authorities in the subtlest points of theological doctrine, for which few men, actively engaged in worldly business, have sufficient learning or refinement of intellect. Whether owing to early training in gymnastic exercises or to their constitutional organisation, the Gy-ei are usually superior to the Ana in physical strength (an important element in the consideration and maintenance of female rights). They attain to loftier stature, and amid their rounder proportions are embedded sinews and muscles as hardy as those of the other sex. Indeed they assert that, according to the original laws of nature, females were intended to be larger than males, and maintain this dogma by reference to the earliest formations of life in insects, and in the most ancient family of the vertebrate[2]—viz., fishes—in both of which the females are generally large enough to make a meal of their consorts if they so desire. Above all, the Gy-ei have a readier and more concentred power over that mysterious fluid or agency which contains the element of destruction, with a larger portion of that sagacity which comprehends dissimulation. Thus they can not only defend themselves against all aggressions from the males, but could, at any moment when he least suspected his danger, terminate the existence of an offending spouse. To the credit of the Gy-ei no instance of their abuse of this awful superiority in the art of destruction is on record for several ages. The last that occurred in the community I speak of appears (according to their chronology) to have been about two thousand years ago. A Gy, then in a fit of jealousy, slew her husband; and this abominable act inspired such terror among the males that they emigrated in a body and left all the Gy-ei to themselves. The history runs that the widowed Gy-ei, thus reduced to despair, fell upon the murderess when in her sleep (and therefore unarmed), and killed her, and then entered into a solemn obligation amongst themselves to abrogate for ever the exercise of their extreme conjugal powers, and to inculcate the same obligation for ever and ever on their female children. By this conciliatory process, a deputation despatched to the fugitive consorts succeeded in persuading many to return, but those who did return were mostly the elder ones. The younger, either from too craven a doubt of their consorts, or too high an estimate of their own merits, rejected all overtures, and, remaining in other communities, were caught up there by other mates, with whom perhaps they were no better off. But the loss of so large a portion of the male youth operated as a salutary warning on the Gy-ei, and confirmed them in the pious resolution to which they had pledged themselves. Indeed it is now popularly considered that, by long hereditary disuse, the Gy-ei have lost both the aggressive and the defensive superiority over the Ana which they once possessed, just as in the inferior animals above the earth many peculiarities in their original formation, intended by nature for their protection, gradually fade or become inoperative when not needed under altered circumstances. I should be sorry, however, for any An who induced a Gy to make the experiment whether he or she were the stronger.

From the incident I have narrated, the Ana date certain alterations in the marriage customs, tending, perhaps, somewhat to the advantage of the male. They now bind themselves in wedlock only for three years; at the end of each third year either male or female can divorce the other and is free to marry again. At the end of ten years the An has the privilege of taking a second wife, allowing the first to retire if she so please. These regulations are for the most part a dead letter; divorces and polygamy are extremely rare, and the marriage state now seems singularly happy and serene among this astonishing people;—the Gy-ei, notwithstanding their boastful superiority in physical strength and intellectual abilities, being much curbed into gentle manners by the dread of separation or of a second wife, and the Ana being very much the creatures of custom, and not, except under great aggravation, liking to exchange for hazardous novelties faces and manners to which they are reconciled by habit. But there is one privilege the Gy-ei carefully retain, and the desire for which perhaps forms the secret motive of most lady asserters of woman rights above ground. They claim the privilege, here usurped by men, of proclaiming their love and urging their suit; in other words, of being the wooing party rather than the wooed. Such a phenomenon as an old maid does not exist among the Gy-ei. Indeed it is very seldom that a Gy does not secure any An upon whom she sets her heart, if his affections be not strongly engaged elsewhere. However coy, reluctant, and prudish, the male she courts may prove at first, yet her perseverance, her ardour, her persuasive powers, her command over the mystic agencies of vril, are pretty sure to run down his neck into what we call "the fatal noose." Their argument for the reversal of that relationship of the sexes which the blind tyranny of man has established on the surface of the earth, appears cogent, and is advanced with a frankness which might well be commended to impartial consideration. They say, that of the two the female is by nature of a more loving disposition than the male—that love occupies a larger space in her thoughts, and is more essential to her happiness, and that therefore she ought to be the wooing party; that otherwise the male is a shy and dubitant[3] creature—that he has often a selfish predilection for the single state—that he often pretends to misunderstand tender glances and delicate hints—that, in short, he must be resolutely pursued and captured. They add, moreover, that unless the Gy can secure the An of her choice, and one whom she would not select out of the whole world becomes her mate, she is not only less happy than she otherwise would be, but she is not so good a being, that her qualities of heart are not sufficiently developed; whereas the An is a creature that less lastingly concentrates his affections on one object; that if he cannot get the Gy whom he prefers he easily reconciles himself to another Gy; and, finally, that at the worst, if he is loved and taken care of, it is less necessary to the welfare of his existence that he should love as well as be loved; he grows contented with his creature comforts, and the many occupations of thought which he creates for himself.

Whatever may be said as to this reasoning, the system works well for the male; for being thus sure that he is truly and ardently loved, and that the more coy and reluctant he shows himself, the more the determination to secure him increases, he generally contrives to make his consent dependent on such conditions as he thinks the best calculated to insure, if not a blissful, at least a peaceful life. Each individual An has his own hobbies, his own ways, his own predilections, and, whatever they may be, he demands a promise of full and unrestrained concession to them. This, in the pursuit of her object, the Gy readily promises; and as the characteristic of this extraordinary people is an implicit veneration for truth, and her word once given is never broken even by the giddiest Gy, the conditions stipulated for are religiously observed. In fact, notwithstanding all their abstract rights and powers, the Gy-ei are the most amiable, conciliatory, and submissive wives I have ever seen even in the happiest households above ground. It is an aphorism among them, that "where a Gy loves it is her pleasure to obey."[4] It will be observed that in the relationship of the sexes I have spoken only of marriage, for such is the moral perfection to which this community has attained, that any illicit connection is as little possible amongst them as it would be to a couple of linnets during the time they agreed to live in pairs.

CHAPTER **11**
Nothing had more perplexed me in seeking to reconcile my sense to the existence of regions extending below the surface of the earth, and habitable by beings, if dissimilar from, still, in all material points of organism, akin to those in the upper world, than the contradiction thus presented to the doctrine in which, I believe, most geologists and philosophers concur—viz., that though with us the sun is the great source of heat, yet the deeper we go beneath the crust of the earth, the greater is the increasing heat, being, it is said, found in the ratio of a degree for every foot, commencing from fifty feet below the surface. But though the domains of the tribe I speak of were, on the higher ground, so comparatively near to the surface, that I could account for a temperature, therein, suitable to organic life, yet even the ravines and valleys of that realm were much less hot than philosophers would deem possible at such a depth—certainly not warmer than the south of France, or at least of Italy. And according to all the accounts I received, vast tracts immeasurably deeper beneath the surface, and in which one might have thought only salamanders[1] could exist, were inhabited by innumerable races organized like ourselves. I cannot pretend in any way to account for a fact which is so at variance with the recognised laws of science, nor could Zee much help me towards a solution of it. She did but conjecture that sufficient allowance had not been made by our philosophers for the extreme porousness of the interior earth—the vastness of its cavities and irregularities, which served to create free currents of air and frequent winds—and for the various modes in which heat is evaporated and thrown off. She allowed, however, that there was a depth at which the heat was deemed to be intolerable to such organised life as was known to the experience of the Vril-ya, though their philosophers believed that even in

such places life of some kind, life sentient, life intellectual, would be found abundant and thriving, could the philosophers penetrate to it. "Wherever the All-Good builds," said she, "there, be sure, He places inhabitants. He loves not empty dwellings." She added, however, that many changes in temperature and climate had been effected by the skill of the Vril-ya, and that the agency of vril had been successfully employed in such changes. She described a sub-tle and life-giving medium called Lai, which I suspect to be identi-cal with the ethereal oxygen of Dr. Lewins,[2] wherein work all the correlative forces united under the name of vril; and contended that wherever this medium could be expanded, as it were, suf-ficiently for the various agencies of vril to have ample play, a tem-perature congenial to the highest forms of life could be secured. She said also, that it was the belief of their naturalists that flow-ers and vegetation had been produced originally (whether devel-oped from seeds borne from the surface of the earth in the earlier convulsions of nature, or imported by the tribes that first sought refuge in cavernous hollows) through the operations of the light constantly brought to bear on them, and the gradual improve-ment in culture. She said also, that since the vril light had super-seded all other light-giving bodies, the colours of flower and fo-liage had become more brilliant, and vegetation had acquired larger growth.

Leaving these matters to the consideration of those better com-petent to deal with them, I must now devote a few pages to the very interesting questions connected with the language of the Vril-ya.

CHAPTER 12

The language of the Vril-ya is peculiarly in-teresting, because it seems to me to exhibit with great clearness the traces of the three main transitions through which language passes in attaining to perfection of form.

One of the most illustrious of recent philologists, Max Müller, in arguing for the analogy between the strata of language and the strata of the earth, lays down this absolute dogma: "No language can, by any possibility, be inflectional without having passed through the agglutinative and isolating stratum. No language can be agglutinative without clinging with its roots to the underlying stratum of isolation."—'*On the Stratification of Language*,' *p.* 20.[1]

Taking then the Chinese language as the best existing type of the original isolating stratum, "as the faithful photograph of man in his leading-strings trying the muscles of his mind, groping his way, and so delighted with his first successful grasps that he repeats them again and again,"[2]—we have, in the language of the Vril-ya, still "clinging with its roots to the underlying stratum," the evidences of the original isolation. It abounds in monosyllables, which are the foundations of the language. The transition into the agglutinative form marks an epoch that must have gradually extended through ages, the written literature of which has only survived in a few fragments of symbolical mythology and certain pithy sentences which have passed into popular proverbs. With the extant literature of the Vril-ya the inflectional stratum commences. No doubt at that time there must have operated concurrent causes, in the fusion of races by some dominant people, and the rise of some great literary phenomena by which the form of language became arrested and fixed. As the inflectional stage prevailed over the agglutinative,[3] it is surprising to see how much more boldly the original roots of the language project from the surface that conceals them. In the old fragments and proverbs of the preceding stage the monosyllables which compose those roots vanish amidst words of enormous length, comprehending whole sentences from which no one part can be disentangled from the other and employed separately. But when the inflectional form of language became so far advanced as to have its scholars and grammarians, they seem to have united in extirpating all such polysynthetical[4] or polysyllabic monsters, as devouring invaders of the aboriginal forms. Words beyond three syllables became proscribed as barbarous, and in proportion as the language grew thus simplified it increased in strength, in dignity, and in sweetness. Though now very compressed in sound, it gains in clearness by that compression. By a single letter, according to its position, they contrive to express all that with civilised nations in our upper world it takes the waste, sometimes of syllables, sometimes of sentences, to express. Let me here cite one or two instances: An (which I will translate man), Ana (men); the letter *s* is with them a letter implying multitude, according to where it is placed; Sana means mankind; Ansa, a multitude of men.[5] The prefix of certain letters in their alphabet invariably denotes compound significations. For instance, Gl (which with them is a single letter, as *th* is a single letter with the Greeks) at the commencement of a word infers an assemblage or union of things, sometimes kindred, sometimes dissimilar—as Oon, a house; Gloon, a town (*i.e.*, an assemblage of houses). Ata is sorrow; Glata, a public calamity. Aur-an is the health or wellbeing of a man; Glauran, the well-being of the state, the good of the community; and a word constantly in their mouths is A-glauran, which denotes their political creed—viz., that "the first principle of a community is the good of all." Aub is invention; Sila, a tone in music.[6] Glaubsila, as uniting the ideas of invention and of musical intonation, is the classical word for poetry—abbreviated, in ordinary conversation, to Glaubs. Na, which with them is, like Gl, but a single letter, always, when an initial, implies something antagonistic to life or joy or comfort, resembling in this the Aryan root Nak, expressive of perishing or destruction.[7] Nax is darkness; Narl, death; Naria, sin or evil. Nas—an uttermost condition of sin and evil—corruption. In writing, they deem it irreverent to express the Supreme Being by any special name. He is symbolised by what may be termed the hieroglyphic of a pyramid, A. In prayer they address Him by a name which they deem too sacred to confide to a stranger, and I know it not. In conversation they generally use a periphrastic epithet, such as the All-Good. The letter V, symbolical of the inverted pyramid, where it is an initial, nearly always denotes excellence or power; as Vril, of which I have said so much; Veed, an immortal spirit; Veedya, immortality;[8] Koom, pronounced like the Welsh Cwm, denotes something of hollowness. Koom itself is a profound hollow, metaphorically a cavern; Koom-in; a hole; Zi-koom, a valley; Koom-zi, vacancy or void; Bodh-koom, ignorance (literally, knowledge-void). Koom-Posh is their name for the government of the many, or the ascendancy of the most ignorant or hollow. Posh is an almost untranslatable idiom, implying, as the reader will see later, contempt. The closest rendering I can give to it is our slang term, "bosh;" and thus Koom-Posh may be loosely rendered "Hollow-Bosh."[9] But when Democracy or Koom-Posh degenerates from popular ignorance into that popular passion or ferocity which precedes its decease, as (to cite illustrations from the upper world) during the French Reign of Terror,[10] or for the fifty years of the Roman Republic preceding the ascendancy of Augustus,[11] their name for that state of things is Glek-Nas. Ek is strife—Glek, the universal strife. Nas, as I before said, is corruption or rot; thus Glek-Nas may be construed, "the universal strife-rot." Their compounds are very expressive; thus, Bodh being knowledge,[12] and Too, a participle that implies the action of cautiously approaching,—Too-bodh is their word for Philosophy; Pah is a contemptuous exclamation analogous to our idiom, "stuff and nonsense;"[13] Pah-bodh (literally, stuff-and-nonsense-knowledge) is their term for futile or false philosophy, and is applied to a species of metaphysical or speculative ratiocination formerly in vogue, which consisted in making inquiries that could not be answered, and were not worth making; such, for instance, as, "Why does an An have five toes to his feet instead of four or six? Did the first An, created by the All-Good, have the same number of toes as his descendants? In the form by which an An will be recognised by his friends in the future state of being, will he retain any toes at all, and, if so, will they be material toes or spiritual toes?" I take these illustrations of Pah-bodh, not in irony or jest, but because the very inquiries I name formed the subject of controversy by the latest cultivators of that "science"—4000 years ago.

In the declension of nouns I was informed that anciently there were eight cases (one more than in the Sanskrit Grammar); but the effect of time has been to reduce these cases, and multiply, instead of these varying terminations, explanatory prepositions. At present, in the Grammar submitted to my study, there were four cases to nouns, three having varying terminations, and the fourth a differing prefix.

SINGULAR	PLURAL
Nom.: An, Man	Nom.: Ana, Men
Dat.: Ano, to Man	Dat.: Anoi, to Men
Ac.: Anam, Man	Ac.: Ananda, Men
Voc.: Hil-An, O Man	Voc.: Hil-Ananda, O Men

In the elder inflectional literature the dual form existed—it has long been obsolete.[14]

The genitive case with them is also obsolete; the dative supplies its place: they say the House *to* a Man, instead of the House *of* a Man. When used (sometimes in poetry), the genitive in the termination is the same as the nominative; so is the ablative, the preposition that marks it being a prefix or suffix at option, and generally decided by ear, according to the sound of the noun. It will be observed that the prefix Hil marks the vocative case. It is always retained in addressing another, except in the most intimate domestic relations; its omission would be considered rude: just as in our old forms of speech in addressing a king it would have been deemed disrespectful to say "King," and reverential to say "O King." In fact, as they have no titles of honour, the vocative adjuration supplies the place of a title, and is given impartially to all. The prefix Hil enters into the composition of words that imply distant communications, as Hil-ya, to travel.

In the conjugation of their verbs, which is much too lengthy a subject to enter on here, the auxiliary verb Ya, "to go," which plays so considerable a part in the Sanskrit, appears and performs a kindred office, as if it were a radical in some language from which both had descended. But another auxiliary of opposite signification also accompanies it and shares its labours—viz., Zi, to stay or

repose. Thus Ya enters into the future tense, and Zi in the preter-
ite of all verbs requiring auxiliaries. Yam, I go—Yiam, I may go—
Yani-ya, I shall go (literally, I go to go) Zam-poo-yan, I have gone
(literally, I rest from gone). Ya, as a termination, implies by analogy, progress, movement, efflorescence.[15] Zi, as a terminal, denotes fixity, sometimes in a good sense, sometimes in a bad, according to the word with which it is coupled. Iva-zi, eternal
goodness; Nan-zi, eternal evil. Poo (from) enters as a prefix to
words that denote repugnance, or things from which we ought to
be averse. Poo-pra, disgust; Poo-naria, falsehood, the vilest kind of
evil. Poosh or Posh I have already confessed to be untranslatable
literally. It is an expression of contempt not unmixed with pity.
This radical seems to have originated from inherent sympathy between the labial effort and the sentiment that impelled it, Poo being an utterance in which the breath is exploded from the lips with
more or less vehemence. On the other hand, Z, when an initial,
is with them a sound in which the breath is sucked inward, and
thus Zu, pronounced Zoo (which in their language is one letter), is
the ordinary prefix to words that signify something that attracts,
pleases, touches the heart—as Zummer, lover; Zutze, love; Zuzu-
lia, delight.[16] This indrawn sound of Z seems indeed naturally appropriate to fondness. Thus, even in our language, mothers say
to their babies, in defiance of grammar, "Zoo darling;" and I have
heard a learned professor at Boston call his wife (he had been only
married a month) "Zoo little pet."

I cannot quit this subject, however, without observing by what
slight changes in the dialects favoured by different tribes of the
same race, the original signification and beauty of sounds may
become confused and deformed. Zee told me with much indignation that Zummer (lover) which, in the way she uttered it, seemed
slowly taken down to the very depths of her heart, was, in some
not very distant communities of the Vril-ya, vitiated into the half-
hissing, half-nasal, wholly disagreeable, sound of Subber. I thought
to myself it only wanted the introduction of *n* before *u* to render it

into an English word significant of the last quality an amorous Gy would desire in her Zummer.

I will but mention another peculiarity in this language which gives equal force and brevity to its forms of expressions.

A is with them, as with us, the first letter of the alphabet, and is often used as a prefix word by itself to convey a complex idea of sovereignty or chiefdom, or presiding principle. For instance, Iva is goodness; Diva, goodness and happiness united; A-Diva is unerring and absolute truth. I have already noticed the value of A in A-glauran, so, in vril (to whose properties they trace their present state of civilisation), A-vril denotes, as I have said, civilisation itself.[17]

The philologist will have seen from the above how much the language of the Vril-ya is akin to the Aryan[18] or Indo-Germanic; but, like all languages, it contains words and forms in which transfers from very opposite sources of speech have been taken. The very title of Tur, which they give to their supreme magistrate, indicates theft from a tongue akin to the Turanian.[19] They say themselves that this is a foreign word borrowed from a title which their historical records show to have been borne by the chief of a nation with whom the ancestors of the Vril-ya were, in very remote periods, on friendly terms, but which has long become extinct, and they say that when, after the discovery of vril, they re-modelled their political institutions, they expressly adopted a title taken from an extinct race and a dead language for that of their chief magistrate, in order to avoid all titles for that office with which they had previous associations.

Should life be spared to me, I may collect into systematic form such knowledge as I acquired of this language during my sojourn amongst the Vril-ya. But what I have already said will perhaps suffice to show to genuine philological students that a language which, preserving so many of the roots in the aboriginal form, and clearing from the immediate, but transitory, polysynthetical stage so many rude incumbrances, has attained to such a union of simplicity and compass in its final inflectional forms, must have been the gradual work of countless ages and many varieties of mind; that it contains the evidence of fusion between congenial races, and necessitated, in arriving at the shape of which I have given examples, the continuous culture of a highly thoughtful people.

That, nevertheless, the literature which belongs to this language is a literature of the past; that the present felicitous state of society at which the Ana have attained forbids the progressive cultivation of literature, especially in the two main divisions of fiction and history,—I shall have occasion to show later.

CHAPTER 13 This people have a religion, and, whatever may be said against it, at least it has these strange peculiarities: firstly, that they all believe in the creed they profess; secondly, that they all practise the precepts which the creed inculcates. They unite in the worship of the one divine Creator and Sustainer of the universe. They believe that it is one of the properties of the all-permeating agency of vril, to transmit to the well-spring of life and intelligence every thought that a living creature can conceive; and though they do not contend that the idea of a Deity is innate, yet they say that the An (man) is the only creature, so far as their observation of nature extends, to whom the capacity of conceiving that idea, with all the trains of thought which open out from it, is vouchsafed. They hold that this capacity is a privilege that cannot have been given in vain, and hence that prayer and thanksgiving are acceptable to the divine Creator, and necessary to the complete development of the human creature. They offer their devotions both in private and public. Not being considered one of their species, I was not admitted into the building or temple in which the public worship is rendered; but I am informed that the service is exceedingly short, and unattended with any pomp of ceremony. It is a doctrine with the Vril-ya, that earnest devotion or complete abstraction from the actual world cannot, with benefit to itself, be maintained long at a stretch by the human mind, especially in public, and that all attempts to do so either lead to fanaticism or to hypocrisy. When they pray in private, it is when they are alone or with their young children.

They say that in ancient times there was a great number of books written upon speculations as to the nature of the Deity, and upon the forms of belief or worship supposed to be most agreeable to Him. But these were found to lead to such heated and angry disputations as not only to shake the peace of the community and divide families before the most united, but in the course of discussing the attributes of the Deity, the existence of the Deity Himself became argued away, or, what was worse, became invested with the passions and infirmities of the human disputants. "For," said my host, "since a finite being like an An cannot possibly define the Infinite, so, when he endeavours to realise an idea of the Divinity, he only reduces the Divinity into an An like himself." During the later ages, therefore, all theological speculations, though not forbidden, have been so discouraged as to have fallen utterly into disuse.

The Vril-ya unite in a conviction of a future state, more felicitous and more perfect than the present. If they have very vague notions of the doctrine of rewards and punishments, it is perhaps because they have no systems of rewards and punishments among themselves, for there are no crimes to punish, and their moral standard is so even that no An among them is, upon the whole, considered more virtuous than another. If one excels, perhaps, in one virtue, another equally excels in some other virtue; if one has his prevalent fault or infirmity, so also another has his. In fact, in their extraordinary mode of life, there are so few temptations to wrong, that they are good (according to their notions of goodness) merely because they live. They have some fanciful notions upon the continuance of life, when once bestowed, even in the vegetable world, as the reader will see in the next chapter.

CHAPTER 14

Though, as I have said, the Vril-ya discourage all speculations on the nature of the Supreme Being, they appear to concur in a belief by which they think to solve that great problem of the existence of evil which has so perplexed the philosophy of the upper world. They hold that wherever He has once given life, with the perceptions of that life, however faint it be, as in a plant, the life is never destroyed; it passes into new and improved forms, though not in this planet (differing therein from the ordinary doctrine of metempsychosis),[1] and that the living thing retains the sense of identity, so that it connects its past life with its future, and is *conscious* of its progressive improvement in the scale of joy. For they say that, without this assumption, they cannot, according to the lights of human reason vouchsafed to them, discover the perfect justice which must be a constituent quality of the All-Wise and the All-Good. Injustice, they say, can only emanate from three causes: want of wisdom to perceive what is just, want of benevolence to desire, want of power to fulfil it; and that each of these three wants is incompatible in the All-Wise, the All-Good, the All-Powerful. But that, while even in this life, the wisdom, the benevolence, and the power of the Supreme Being are sufficiently apparent to compel our recognition, the justice necessarily resulting from those attributes, absolutely requires another life, not for man only, but for every living thing of the inferior orders. That, alike in the animal and the vegetable world, we see one individual rendered, by circumstances beyond its control, exceedingly wretched compared to its neighbours—one only exists as the prey of another—even a plant suffers from disease till it perishes prematurely, while the plant next to it rejoices in its vitality and lives out its happy life free from a pang. That it is an erroneous analogy from human infirmities to reply by saying that the Supreme Being only acts by general laws, thereby making his own secondary causes so potent as to mar the essential kindness of the first Cause;[2] and a still meaner and more ignorant conception of the All-Good, to dismiss with a brief contempt all consideration of justice for the myriad forms into which He has infused life, and assume that justice is only due to the single product of the An. There is no small and no great in the eyes of the divine Life-Giver. But once grant that nothing, however humble, which feels that it lives and suffers, can perish through the series of ages, that all its suffering here, if continuous from the moment of its birth to that of its transfer to another form of being, would be more brief compared with eternity than the cry of the new-born is compared to the whole life of a man; and once suppose that this living thing retains its sense of identity when so transferred (for without that sense it could be aware of no future being), and though, indeed, the fulfilment of divine justice is removed from the scope of our ken, yet we have a right to assume it to be uniform and universal, and not varying and partial, as it would be if acting only upon general secondary laws; because such perfect justice flows of necessity from perfectness[3] of knowledge to conceive, perfectness of love to will, and perfectness of power to complete it.

However fantastic this belief of the Vril-ya may be, it tends perhaps to confirm politically the systems of government which, admitting differing degrees of wealth, yet establishes perfect equality in rank, exquisite mildness in all relations and intercourse, and tenderness to all created things which the good of the community does not require them to destroy. And though their notion of compensation to a tortured insect or a cankered flower may seem to some of us a very wild crotchet, yet, at least, it is not a mischievous one; and it may furnish matter for no unpleasing reflection to think that within the abysses of earth, never lit by a ray from the material heavens, there should have penetrated so luminous a conviction of the ineffable goodness of the Creator—so fixed an idea that the general laws by which He acts cannot admit of any partial injustice or evil, and therefore cannot be comprehended without reference to their action over all space and throughout all time. And since, as I shall have occasion to observe later, the intellectual conditions and social systems of this subterranean race comprise and harmonise great, and apparently antagonistic, varieties in philosophical doctrine and speculation which have from time to time been started, discussed, dismissed, and have re-appeared amongst thinkers or dreamers in the upper world, so I may perhaps appropriately conclude this reference to the belief of the Vril-ya, that self-conscious or sentient life once given is inde-structible among inferior creatures as well as in man, by an elo-quent passage from the work of that eminent zoologist, Louis Agassiz, which I have only just met with, many years after I had committed to paper those recollections of the life of the Vril-ya which I now reduce into something like arrangement and form: "The relations which individual animals bear to one another are of such a character that they ought long ago to have been considered as sufficient proof that no organised being could ever have been called into existence by other agency than by the direct interven-tion of a reflective mind. This argues strongly in favour of the exis-tence in every animal of an immaterial principle similar to that which by its excellence and superior endowments places man so much above animals; yet the principle unquestionably exists, and whether it be called sense, reason, or instinct, it presents in the whole range of organised beings a series of phenomena closely linked together, and upon it are based not only the higher manifes-tations of the mind, but the very permanence of the specific differ-ences which characterise every organism. Most of the arguments in favour of the immortality of man apply equally to the perma-nency of this principle in other living beings. May I not add that a future life in which man would be deprived of that great source of enjoyment and intellectual and moral improvement which results from the contemplation of the harmonies of an organic world would involve a lamentable loss? And may we not look to a spiri-tual concert of the combined worlds and all their inhabitants in the presence of their Creator as the highest conception of para-dise?"—'Essay on Classification,' sect. xvii, p. 97–99.[4]

CHAPTER 15

Kind to me as I found all in this household, the young daughter of my host was the most considerate and thoughtful in her kindness. At her suggestion I laid aside the habiliments in which I had descended from the upper earth, and adopted the dress of the Vril-ya, with the exception of the artful wings which served them, when on foot, as a graceful mantle. But as many of the Vril-ya, when occupied in urban pursuits, did not wear these wings, this exception created no marked difference between myself and the race among which I sojourned, and I was thus enabled to visit the town without exciting unpleasant curiosity. Out of the household no one suspected that I had come from the upper world, and I was but regarded as one of some inferior and barbarous tribe whom Aph-Lin entertained as a guest.

The city was large in proportion to the territory round it, which was of no greater extent than many an English or Hungarian nobleman's estate; but the whole of it, to the verge of the rocks which constituted its boundary, was cultivated to the nicest degree, except where certain allotments of mountain and pasture were humanely left free to the sustenance of the harmless animals they had tamed, though not for domestic use. So great is their kindness towards these humbler creatures, that a sum is devoted from the public treasury for the purpose of deporting them to other Vril-ya communities willing to receive them (chiefly new colonies), whenever they become too numerous for the pastures allotted to them in their native place. They do not, however, multiply to an extent comparable to the ratio at which, with us, animals bred for slaughter, increase. It seems a law of nature that animals not useful to man gradually recede from the domains he occupies, or even become extinct. It is an old custom of the various sovereign states amidst which the race of the Vril-ya are distributed, to leave between each state a neutral and uncultivated border-land. In the instance of the community I speak of, this tract, being a ridge of savage rocks, was impassable by foot, but was easily surmounted, whether by the wings of the inhabitants or the air-boats, of which I shall speak hereafter. Roads through it were also cut for the transit of vehicles impelled by vril. These intercommunicating tracts were always kept lighted, and the expense thereof defrayed by a special tax, to which all the communities comprehended in the denomination of Vril-ya contribute in settled proportions. By these means a considerable commercial traffic with other states, both near and distant, was carried on. The surplus wealth of this special community was chiefly agricultural. The community was also eminent for skill in constructing implements connected with the arts of husbandry. In exchange for such merchandise it obtained articles more of luxury than necessity. There were few things imported on which they set a higher price than birds taught to pipe artful tunes in concert. These were brought from a great distance, and were marvellous for beauty of song and plumage. I understood that extraordinary care was taken by their breeders and teachers in selection, and that the species had wonderfully improved during the last few years. I saw no other pet animals among this community except some very amusing and sportive creatures of the Batrachian[1] species, resembling frogs, but with very intelligent countenances, which the children were fond of, and kept in their private gardens. They appear to have no animals akin to our dogs or horses, though that learned naturalist, Zee, informed me that such creatures had once existed in those parts, and might now be found in regions inhabited by other races than the Vril-ya. She said that they had gradually disappeared from the more civilised world since the discovery of vril, and the results attending that discovery, had dispensed with their uses. Machinery and the invention of wings had superseded the horse as a beast of burden; and the dog was no longer wanted either for protection or the chase, as it had been when the ancestors of the Vril-ya feared the aggressions of their own kind, or hunted the lesser animals for food. Indeed, however, so far as the horse was concerned, this region was so rocky that a horse could have been, there, of little use either for pastime or burden. The only creature they use for the latter purpose is a kind of large goat which is much employed on farms. The nature of the surrounding soil in these districts may be said to have first suggested the invention of wings and air-boats. The largeness of space, in proportion to the rural territory occupied by the city, was occasioned by the custom of surrounding every house with a separate garden. The broad main street, in which Aph-Lin dwelt, expanded into a vast square, in which were placed the College of Sages and all the public offices; a magnificent fountain of the luminous fluid which I call naphtha (I am ignorant of its real nature) in the centre. All these public edifices have a uniform character of massiveness and solidity. They reminded me of the architectural pictures of Martin.[2] Along the upper stories of each ran a balcony, or rather a terraced garden, supported by columns, filled with flowering-plants, and tenanted by many kinds of tame birds. From the square branched several streets, all broad and brilliantly lighted, and ascending up the eminence on either side. In my excursions in the town I was never allowed to go alone; Aph-Lin or his daughter was my habitual companion. In this community the adult Gy is seen walking with any young An as familiarly as if there were no difference of sex.

The retail shops are not very numerous; the persons who attend on a customer are all children of various ages, and exceedingly intelligent and courteous, but without the least touch of importunity or cringing. The shopkeeper himself might or might not be visible; when visible, he seemed rarely employed on any matter connected with his professional business; and yet he had taken to that business from special liking to it, and quite independently of his general sources of fortune.

Some of the richest citizens in the community kept such shops. As I have before said, no difference of rank is recognisable, and therefore all occupations hold the same equal social status. An An, of whom I bought my sandals, was the brother of the Tur, or chief magistrate; and though his shop was not larger than that of any bootmaker in Bond Street or Broadway, he was said to be twice as rich as the Tur, who dwelt in a palace. No doubt, however, he had some country-seat.

The Ana of the community are, on the whole, an indolent set of beings after the active age of childhood. Whether by temperament or philosophy, they rank repose among the chief blessings of life. Indeed, when you take away from a human being the incentives to action which are found in cupidity or ambition, it seems to me no wonder that he rests quiet.

In their ordinary movements they prefer the use of their feet to that of their wings. But for their sports or (to indulge in a bold misuse of terms) their public *promenades,* they employ the latter, also for the aerial dances I have described, as well as for visiting their country places, which are mostly placed on lofty heights; and, when still young, they prefer their wings, for travel into the other regions of the Ana, to vehicular conveyances.

Those who accustom themselves to flight can fly, if less rapidly than some birds, yet from twenty-five to thirty miles an hour, and keep up that rate for five or six hours at a stretch. But the Ana generally, on reaching middle age, are not fond of rapid movements requiring violent exercise. Perhaps for this reason, as they hold a doctrine which our own physicians will doubtless approve—viz., that regular transpiration through the pores of the skin is essential to health, they habitually use the sweating-baths to which we give the name of Turkish or Roman, succeeded by douches of perfumed waters. They have great faith in the salubrious virtue of certain perfumes.

It is their custom also, at stated but rare periods, perhaps four times a-year when in health, to use a bath charged with vril.[3] They consider that this fluid, sparingly used, is a great sustainer of life; but used in excess, when in the normal state of health, rather tends to reaction and exhausted vitality. For nearly all their diseases, however, they resort to it as the chief assistant to nature in throwing off the complaint.

In their own way they are the most luxurious of people, but all their luxuries are innocent. They may be said to dwell in an atmosphere of music and fragrance. Every room has its mechanical contrivances for melodious sounds, usually tuned down to soft-murmured notes, which seem like sweet whispers from invisible spirits. They are too accustomed to these gentle sounds to find them a hindrance to conversation, nor, when alone, to reflection. But they have a notion that to breathe an air filled with continuous melody and perfume has necessarily an effect at once soothing and elevating upon the formation of character and the habits of thought. Though so temperate, and with total abstinence from other animal food than milk, and from all intoxicating drinks, they are delicate and dainty to an extreme in food and beverage; and in all their sports even the old exhibit a childlike gaiety. Happiness is the end at which they aim, not as the excitement of a moment, but as the prevailing condition of the entire existence; and regard for the happiness of each other is evinced by the exquisite amenity of their manners.

Their conformation of skull has marked differences from that of any known races in the upper world, though I cannot help thinking it a development, in the course of countless ages, of the Brachycephalic type of the Age of Stone in Lyell's "Elements of Geology," C. X., p. 113, as compared with the Dolichocephalic type of the beginning of the Age of Iron, correspondent with that now so prevalent amongst us, and called the Celtic type.[4] It has the same comparative massiveness of forehead, not receding like the Celtic—the same even roundness in the frontal organs; but it is far loftier in the apex, and far less pronounced in the hinder cranial hemisphere where phrenologists place the animal organs.[5] To speak as a phrenologist, the cranium common to the Vril-ya has the organs of weight, number, tune, form, order, causality, very largely developed; that of construction much more pronounced than that of ideality. Those which are called the moral organs, such as conscientiousness and benevolence, are amazingly full; amativeness and combativeness are both small; adhesiveness large; the organ of destructiveness (*i.e.,* of determined clearance of intervening obstacles) immense, but less than that of benevolence; and their philoprogenitiveness[6] takes rather the character of compassion and tenderness to things that need aid or protection than of the animal love of offspring. I never met with one person deformed or misshapen. The beauty of their countenances is not only in symmetry of feature, but in a smoothness of surface, which continues without line or wrinkle to the extreme of old age, and a serene sweetness of expression, combined with that majesty which seems to come from consciousness of power and the freedom of all terror, physical or moral. It is that very sweetness, combined with that majesty, which inspired in a beholder like myself, accustomed to strive with the passions of mankind, a sentiment of humiliation, of awe, of dread. It is such an expression as a painter might give to a demi-god, a genius, an angel. The males of the Vril-ya are entirely beardless; the Gy-ei sometimes, in old age, develop a small moustache.

I was surprised to find that the colour of their skin was not uniformly that which I had remarked in those individuals whom I had first encountered,—some being much fairer, and even with blue eyes, and hair of a deep golden auburn, though still of complexions warmer or richer in tone than persons in the north of Europe.

I was told that this admixture of colouring arose from intermarriage with other and more distant tribes of the Vril-ya, who, whether by the accident of climate or early distinction of race, were of fairer hues than the tribes of which this community formed one. It was considered that the dark-red skin showed the most ancient family of Ana; but they attached no sentiment of pride to that antiquity, and, on the contrary, believed their present excellence of breed came from frequent crossing with other families differing, yet akin; and they encourage such intermarriages, always provided that it be with the Vril-ya nations. Nations which, not conforming their manners and institutions to those of the Vril-ya, nor indeed held capable of acquiring the powers over the vril agencies which it had taken them generations to attain and transmit, were regarded with more disdain than citizens of New York regard the negroes.

I learned from Zee, who had more lore in all matters than any male with whom I was brought into familiar converse, that the superiority of the Vril-ya was supposed to have originated in the intensity of their earlier struggles against obstacles in nature amidst the localities in which they had first settled. "Wherever," said Zee, moralising, "wherever goes on that early process in the history of civilisation, by which life is made a struggle, in which the individual has to put forth all his powers to compete with his fellow, we invariably find this result,—viz., since in the competition a vast number must perish, nature selects for preservation only the strongest specimens. With our race, therefore, even before the discovery of vril, only the highest organisations were preserved; and there is among our ancient books a legend, once popularly believed, that we were driven from a region that seems to denote the world you come from, in order to perfect our condition and attain to the purest elimination of our species by the severity of the struggles our forefathers underwent; and that, when our education shall become finally completed, we are destined to return to the upper world, and supplant all the inferior races now existing therein."[7]

Aph-Lin and Zee often conversed with me in private upon the political and social conditions of that upper world, in which Zee so philosophically assumed that the inhabitants were to be exterminated one day or other by the advent of the Vril-ya. They found in my accounts,—in which I continued to do all I could (without launching into falsehoods so positive that they would have been easily detected by the shrewdness of my listeners) to present our powers and ourselves in the most flattering point of view, perpetual subjects of comparison between our most civilised populations and the meaner subterranean races which they considered hopelessly plunged in barbarism, and doomed to gradual if certain extinction. But they both agreed in desiring to conceal from their community all premature opening into the regions lighted by the sun; both were humane, and shrunk from the thought of annihilating so many millions of creatures; and the pictures I drew of our life, highly coloured as they were, saddened them. In vain I

boasted of our great men—poets, philosophers, orators, generals—
and defied the Vril-ya to produce their equals. "Alas!" said Zee, her
grand face softening into an angel-like compassion, "this predominance of the few over the many is the surest and most fatal
sign of a race incorrigibly savage. See you not that the primary
condition of mortal happiness consists in the extinction of that
strife and competition between individuals, which, no matter what
forms of government they adopt, render the many subordinate to
the few, destroy real liberty to the individual, whatever may be the
nominal liberty of the state, and annul that calm of existence, without which, felicity, mental, or bodily, cannot be attained? Our notion is, that the more we can assimilate life to the existence which
our noblest ideas can conceive to be that of spirits on the other
side of the grave, why, the more we approximate to a divine happiness here, and the more easily we glide into the conditions of
being hereafter. For, surely, all we can imagine of the life of gods,
or of blessed immortals, supposes the absence of self-made cares
and contentious passions, such as avarice and ambition. It seems
to us that it must be a life of serene tranquillity, not indeed without
active occupations to the intellectual or spiritual powers, but occupations, of whatsoever nature they be, congenial to the idio-
syncrasies of each, not forced and repugnant—a life gladdened by
the untrammelled interchange of gentle affections, in which the
moral atmosphere utterly kills hate and vengeance, and strife and
rivalry. Such is the political state to which all the tribes and families of the Vril-ya seek to attain, and towards that goal all our theories of government are shaped. You see how utterly opposed is
such a progress to that of the uncivilised nations from which you
come, and which aim at a systematic perpetuity of troubles, and
cares, and warring passions, aggravated more and more as their
progress storms its way onward. The most powerful of all the races
in our world, beyond the pale of the Vril-ya, esteems itself the best
governed of all political societies, and to have reached in that respect the extreme end at which political wisdom can arrive, so that
the other nations should tend more or less to copy it. It has estab-

lished, on its broadest base, the Koom-Posh—viz., the government of the ignorant upon the principle of being the most numerous. It has placed the supreme bliss in the vying with each other in all things, so that the evil passions are never in repose—vying for power, for wealth, for eminence of some kind; and in this rivalry it is horrible to hear the vituperation, the slanders, and calumnies which even the best and mildest among them heap on each other without remorse or shame."

"Some years ago," said Aph-Lin, "I visited this people, and their misery and degradation were the more appalling because they were always boasting of their felicity and grandeur as compared with the rest of their species. And there is no hope that this people, which evidently resembles your own, can improve, because all their notions tend to further deterioration. They desire to enlarge their dominion more and more, in direct antagonism to the truth that, beyond a very limited range, it is impossible to secure to a community the happiness which belongs to a well-ordered family; and the more they mature a system by which a few individuals are heated and swollen to a size above the standard slenderness of the millions, the more they chuckle and exact, and cry out, 'see by what great exceptions to the common littleness of our race we prove the magnificent results of our system!'"

"In fact," resumed Zee, "if the wisdom of human life be to approximate to the serene equality of immortals, there can be no more direct flying off into the opposite direction than a system which aims at carrying to the utmost the inequalities and turbulences of mortals. Nor do I see how, by any forms of religious belief, mortals, so acting, could fit themselves even to appreciate the joys of immortals to which they still expect to be transferred by the mere act of dying. On the contrary, minds accustomed to place happiness in things so much the reverse of godlike, would find the happiness of gods exceedingly dull, and would long to get back to a world in which they could quarrel with each other."

CHAPTER 16

I have spoken so much of the Vril Staff that my reader may expect me to describe it.[1] This I cannot do accurately, for I was never allowed to handle it for fear of some terrible accident occasioned by my ignorance of its use. It is hollow, and has in the handle several stops, keys, or springs by which its force can be altered, modified, or directed—so that by one process it destroys, by another it heals—by one it can rend the rock, by another disperse the vapour—by one it affects bodies, by another it can exercise a certain influence over minds. It is usually carried in the convenient size of a walking-staff, but it has slides by which it can be lengthened or shortened at will. When used for special purposes, the upper part rests in the hollow of the palm, with the fore and middle fingers protruded. I was assured, however, that its power was not equal in all, but proportioned to the amount of certain vril properties in the wearer, in affinity, or *rapport*, with the purposes to be effected. Some were more potent to destroy, others to heal, &c.; much also depended on the calm and steadiness of volition in the manipulator. They assert that the full exercise of vril power can only be acquired by constitutional temperament—*i.e.,* by hereditarily transmitted organisation—and that a female infant of four years old belonging to the Vril-ya races can accomplish feats with the wand placed for the first time in her hand, which a life spent in its practice would not enable the strongest and most skilled mechanician,[2] born out of the pale of the Vril-ya, to achieve. All these wands are not equally complicated; those entrusted to children are much simpler than those borne by sages of either sex, and constructed with a view to the special object in which the children are employed; which, as I have before said, is among the youngest children the most destructive. In the wands of wives and mothers the correlative destroying force is usually abstracted, the healing power fully charged. I wish I could say more in detail of this singular conductor of the vril fluid, but its machinery is as exquisite as its effects are marvellous.

I should say, however, that this people have invented certain tubes by which the vril fluid can be conducted towards the object it is meant to destroy, throughout a distance almost indefinite; at least I put it modestly when I say from 500 to 600 miles. And their mathematical science as applied to such purpose is so nicely accurate, that on the report of some observer in an air-boat, any member of the vril department can estimate unerringly the nature of intervening obstacles, the height to which the projectile instrument should be raised, and the extent to which it should be charged, so as to reduce to ashes within a space of time too short for me to venture to specify it, a capital twice as vast as London.

Certainly these Ana are wonderful mechanicians—wonderful for the adaptation of the inventive faculty to practical uses.

I went with my host and his daughter Zee over the great public museum, which occupies a wing in the College of Sages, and in which are hoarded, as curious specimens of the ignorant and blundering experiments of ancient times, many contrivances on which we pride ourselves as recent achievements. In one department, carelessly thrown aside as obsolete lumber are tubes for destroying life by metallic balls and an inflammable powder, on the principle of our cannons and catapults, and even still more murderous than our latest improvements.

My host spoke of these with a smile of contempt, such as an artillery officer might bestow on the bows and arrows of the Chinese. In another department there were models of vehicles and vessels worked by steam, and of a balloon which might have been constructed by Montgolfier.[3] "Such," said Zee, with an air of meditative wisdom—"such were the feeble triflings with nature of our savage forefathers, ere they had even a glimmering perception of the properties of vril!"

This young Gy was a magnificent specimen of the muscular force to which the females of her country attain. Her features were beautiful, like those of all her race: never in the upper world have

I seen a face so grand and so faultless, but her devotion to the severer studies had given to her countenance an expression of abstract thought which rendered it somewhat stern when in repose; and such sternness became formidable when observed in connection with her ample shoulders and lofty stature. She was tall even for a Gy, and I saw her lift up a cannon as easily as I could lift a pocket-pistol. Zee inspired me with a profound terror—a terror which increased when we came into a department of the museum appropriated to models of contrivances worked by the agency of vril; for here, merely by a certain play of her vril staff, she herself standing at a distance, she put into movement large and weighty substances. She seemed to endow them with intelligence, and to make them comprehend and obey her command. She set complicated pieces of machinery into movement, arrested the movement or continued it, until, within an incredibly short time, various kinds of raw material were reproduced as symmetrical works of art, complete and perfect. Whatever effect mesmerism or electrobiology produces over the nerves and muscles of animated objects, this young Gy produced by the motions of her slender rod over the springs and wheels of lifeless mechanism.

When I mentioned to my companions my astonishment at this influence over inanimate matter—while owning that in our world, I had witnessed phenomena which showed that over certain living organisations certain other living organisations could establish an influence genuine in itself, but often exaggerated by credulity or craft—Zee, who was more interested in such subjects than her father, bade me stretch forth my hand, and then, placing her own beside it, she called my attention to certain distinctions of type and character. In the first place, the thumb of the Gy (and, as I afterwards noticed, of all that race, male or female) was much larger, at once longer and more massive, than is found with our species above ground. There is almost, in this, as great a difference as there is between the thumb of a man and that of a gorilla. Secondly, the palm is proportionately thicker than ours—the texture of the skin infinitely finer and softer—its average warmth is greater. More remarkable than all this, is a visible nerve, perceptible under the skin, which starts from the wrist skirting the ball of the thumb, and branching, fork-like, at the roots of the fore and middle fingers. "With your slight formation of thumb," said the philosophical young Gy, "and with the absence of the nerve which you find more or less developed in the hands of our race, you can never achieve other than imperfect and feeble power over the agency of vril; but so far as the nerve is concerned, that is not found in the hands of our earliest progenitors, nor in those of the ruder tribes without the pale of the Vril-ya. It has been slowly developed in the course of generations, commencing in the early achievements, and increasing with the continuous exercise, of the vril power; therefore, in the course of one or two thousand years, such a nerve may possibly be engendered in those higher beings of your race, who devote themselves to that paramount science through which is attained command over all the subtler forces of nature permeated by vril. But when you talk of matter as something in itself inert and motionless, your parents or tutors surely cannot have left you so ignorant as not to know that no form of matter is motionless and inert: every particle is constantly in motion and constantly acted upon by agencies, of which heat is the most apparent and rapid, but vril the most subtle, and, when skilfully wielded, the most powerful. So that, in fact, the current launched by my hand and guided by my will does but render quicker and more potent the action which is eternally at work upon every particle of matter, however inert and stubborn it may seem. If a heap of metal be not capable of originating a thought of its own, yet, through its internal susceptibility to movement, it obtains the power to receive the thought of the intellectual agent at work on it; and which, when conveyed with a sufficient force of the vril power, it is as much compelled to obey as if it were displaced by a visible bodily force. It is animated for the time being by the soul thus infused into it, so that one may almost say that it lives and it reasons. Without this we could not make our automata supply the place of servants."

I was too much in awe of the thews[4] and the learning of the young Gy to hazard the risk of arguing with her. I had read somewhere in my schoolboy days that a wise man, disputing with a Roman emperor, suddenly drew in his horns; and when the emperor asked him whether he had nothing further to say on his side of the question, replied, "Nay, Cæsar, there is no arguing against a reasoner who commands twenty-five legions."

Though I had a secret persuasion that whatever the real effects of vril upon matter Mr. Faraday could have proved her a very shallow philosopher as to its extent or its causes, I had no doubt that Zee could have brained all the Fellows of the Royal Society,[5] one after the other, with a blow of her fist. Every sensible man knows that it is useless to argue with any ordinary female upon matters he comprehends; but to argue with a Gy seven feet high upon the mysteries of vril,—as well argue in a desert, and with a simoom![6]

Amid the various departments to which the vast building of the College of Sages was appropriated, that which interested me most was devoted to the archæology of the Vril-ya, and comprised a very ancient collection of portraits. In these the pigments and groundwork employed were of so durable a nature that even pictures said to be executed at dates as remote as those in the earliest annals of the Chinese, retained much freshness of colour. In examining this collection, two things especially struck me:—firstly, That the pictures said to be between 6000 and 7000 years old were of a much higher degree of art than any produced within the last 3000 or 4000 years; and, secondly, That the portraits within the former period much more resembled our own upper world and European types of countenance. Some of them, indeed, reminded me of the Italian heads which look out from the canvas of Titian[7]—speaking of ambition or craft, of care or of grief, with furrows in which the passions have passed with iron ploughshare. These were the countenances of men who had lived in struggle and conflict before the discovery of the latent forces of vril had changed the character of society—men who had fought with each other for power or fame as we in the upper world fight.

The type of face began to evince a marked change about a thousand years after the vril revolution, becoming then, with each generation, more serene, and in that serenity more terribly distinct from the faces of labouring and sinful men; while in proportion as the beauty and the grandeur of the countenance itself became more fully developed, the art of the painter became more tame and monotonous.

But the greatest curiosity in the collection was that of three portraits belonging to the pre-historical age, and, according to mythical tradition, taken by the orders of a philosopher, whose origin and attributes were as much mixed up with symbolical fable as those of an Indian Budh[8] or a Greek Prometheus.[9]

From this mysterious personage, at once a sage and a hero, all the principal sections of the Vril-ya race pretend to trace a common origin.

The portraits are of the philosopher himself, of his grandfather, and great-grandfather. They are all at full length. The philosopher is attired in a long tunic which seems to form a loose suit of scaly armour, borrowed, perhaps, from some fish or reptile, but the feet and hands are exposed: the digits in both are wonderfully long, and webbed. He has little or no perceptible throat, and a low receding forehead, not at all the ideal of a sage's. He has bright brown prominent eyes, a very wide mouth and high cheek-bones, and a muddy complexion. According to tradition, this philosopher had lived to a patriarchal age, extending over many centuries, and he remembered distinctly in middle life his grandfather as surviving, and in childhood his great-grandfather; the portrait of the first he had taken, or caused to be taken, while yet alive—that of the latter was taken from his effigies in mummy. The portrait of the grandfather had the features and aspect of the philosopher, only much more exaggerated: he was not dressed, and the colour of his body was singular; the breast and stomach yellow, the shoulders and legs of a dull bronze hue: the great-grandfather was a magnificent specimen of the Batrachian genus, a Giant Frog, *pur et simple*.[10]

Among the pithy sayings which, according to tradition, the philosopher bequeathed to posterity in rhythmical form and sententious brevity, this is notably recorded: "Humble yourselves, my descendants; the father of your race was a *twat*[11] (tadpole): exalt yourselves, my descendants, for it was the same Divine Thought which created your father that develops itself in exalting you."

Aph-Lin told me this fable while I gazed on the three Batrachian portraits. I said in reply: "You make a jest of my supposed ignorance and credulity as an uneducated Tish, but though these horrible daubs may be of great antiquity, and were intended, perhaps, for some rude caricature, I presume that none of your race, even in the less enlightened ages, ever believed that the great-grandson of a Frog became a sententious philosopher; or that any section, I will not say of the lofty Vril-ya, but of the meanest varieties of the human race, had its origin in a Tadpole."

"Pardon me," answered Aph-Lin: "in what we call the Wrangling[12] or Philosophical Period of History, which was at its height about seven thousand years ago, there was a very distinguished naturalist, who proved to the satisfaction of numerous disciples such analogical and anatomical agreements in structure between an An and a Frog, as to show that out of the one must have developed the other. They had some diseases in common; they were both subject to the same parasitical worms in the intestines; and, strange to say, the An has, in his structure, a swimming-bladder, no longer of any use to him, but which is a rudiment that clearly proves his descent from a Frog. Nor is there any argument against this theory to be found in the relative difference of size, for there are still existent in our world Frogs of a size and stature not inferior to our own, and many thousand years ago they appear to have been still larger."

"I understand that," said I, "because Frogs thus enormous are, according to our eminent geologists, who perhaps saw them in dreams, said to have been distinguished inhabitants of the upper world before the Deluge; and such Frogs are exactly the creatures likely to have flourished in the lakes and morasses of your subterranean regions. But pray, proceed."

"In the Wrangling Period of History, whatever one sage asserted another sage was sure to contradict.[13] In fact, it was a maxim in that age, that the human reason could only be sustained aloft by being tossed to and fro in the perpetual motion of contradiction; and therefore another sect of philosophers maintained the doctrine that the An was not the descendant of the Frog, but that the Frog was clearly the improved development of the An. The shape of the Frog, taken generally, was much more symmetrical than that of the An; beside the beautiful conformation of its lower limbs, its flanks and shoulders, the majority of the Ana in that day were almost deformed, and certainly ill-shaped. Again, the Frog had the power to live alike on land and in water—a mighty privilege, partaking of a spiritual essence denied to the An, since the disuse of his swimming-bladder clearly proves his degeneration from a higher development of species. Again, the earlier races of the Ana seem to have been covered with hair, and, even to a comparatively recent date, hirsute bushes deformed the very faces of our ancestors, spreading wild over their cheeks and chins, as similar bushes, my poor Tish, spread wild over yours. But the object of the higher races of the Ana through countless generations has been to erase all vestige of connection with hairy vertebrata, and they have gradually eliminated that debasing capillary excrement by the law of sexual selection; the Gy-ei naturally preferring youth or the beauty of smooth faces. But the degree of the Frog in the scale of the vertebrata is shown in this, that he has no hair at all, not even on his head. He was born to that hairless perfection which the most beautiful of the Ana, despite the culture of incalculable ages, have not yet attained. The wonderful complication and delicacy of a Frog's nervous system and arterial circulation were shown by this school to be more susceptible of enjoyment than our inferior, or at least simpler, physical frame allows us to be. The examination of a Frog's hand, if I may use that expression, accounted for its keener susceptibility to love, and to social life in general. In fact, gregarious and amatory as are the Ana, Frogs are still more so. In short, these two schools raged against each other; one asserting the An to be the perfected type of the Frog; the other that the Frog was the highest development of the An. The moralists were divided in opinion with the naturalists, but the bulk of them sided with the Frog-preference school. They said, with much plausibility, that in moral conduct (viz., in the adherence to rules best adapted to the health and welfare of the individual and the community) there could be no doubt of the vast superiority of the Frog. All history showed the wholesale immorality of the human race, the complete disregard, even by the most renowned among them, of the laws which they acknowledged to be essential to their own and the general happiness and well-being. But the severest critic of the Frog race could not detect in their manners a single aberration from the moral law tacitly recognised by themselves. And what, after all, can be the profit of civilisation if superiority in moral conduct be not the aim for which it strives, and the test by which its progress should be judged?

"In fine, the adherents to this theory presumed that in some remote period the Frog race had been the improved development of the Human; but that, from causes which defied rational conjecture, they had not maintained their original position in the scale of nature; while the Ana, though of inferior organisation, had, by dint less of their virtues than their vices, such as ferocity and cunning, gradually acquired ascendancy, much as among the human race itself tribes utterly barbarous have, by superiority in similar vices, utterly destroyed or reduced into insignificance tribes originally excelling them in mental gifts and culture. Unhappily these disputes became involved with the religious notions of that age; and as society was then administered under the government of the Koom-Posh, who, being the most ignorant, were of course the most inflammable class—the multitude took the whole question out of the hands of the philosophers; political chiefs saw that the Frog dispute, so taken up by the populace, could become a most valuable instrument of their ambition; and for not less than one thousand years war and massacre prevailed, during which period the philosophers on both sides were butchered, and the government of the Koom-Posh itself was happily brought to an end by the ascendancy of a family that clearly established its descent from the aboriginal tadpole, and furnished despotic rulers to the various nations of the Ana. These despots finally disappeared, at least from our communities, as the discovery of vril led to the tranquil institutions under which flourish all the races of the Vril-ya."

"And do no wranglers or philosophers now exist to revive the dispute; or do they all recognise the origin of your race in the tadpole?"

"Nay, such disputes," said Zee, with a lofty smile, "belong to the Pah-bodh of the dark ages, and now only serve for the amusement of infants. When we know the elements out of which our bodies are composed, elements common to the humblest vegetable plants, can it signify whether the All-Wise combined those elements out of one form more than another, in order to create that in which He has placed the capacity to receive the idea of Himself, and all the varied grandeurs of intellect to which that idea gives birth? The An in reality commenced to exist as An with the donation of that capacity, and with that capacity, the sense to acknowledge that, however through the countless ages his race may improve in wisdom, it can never combine the elements at its command into the form of a tadpole."

"You speak well, Zee," said Aph-Lin; "and it is enough for us short-lived mortals to feel a reasonable assurance that whether the origin of the An was a tadpole or not, he is no more likely to become a tadpole again than the institutions of the Vril-ya are likely to relapse into the heaving quagmire and certain strife-rot of a Koom-Posh."

CHAPTER 17

The Vril-ya, being excluded from all sight of the heavenly bodies, and having no other difference between night and day than that which they deem it convenient to make for themselves,—do not, of course, arrive at their divisions of time by the same process that we do; but I found it easy, by the aid of my watch, which I luckily had about me, to compute their time with great nicety. I reserve for a future work on the science and literature of the Vril-ya, should I live to complete it, all details as to the manner in which they arrive at their notation of time: and content myself here with saying, that in point of duration, their year differs very slightly from ours, but that the divisions of their year are by no means the same. Their day (including what we call night) consists of twenty hours of our time, instead of twenty-four, and of course their year comprises the correspondent increase in the number of days by which it is summed up. They subdivide the twenty hours of their day thus—eight hours,[1] called the "Silent Hours," for repose; eight hours, called the "Earnest Time," for the pursuits and occupations of life; and four hours, called the "Easy Time" (with which what I may term their day closes), allotted to festivities, sport, recreation, or family converse, according to their several tastes and inclinations. But, in truth, out of doors there is no night. They maintain, both in the streets and in the surrounding country, to the limits of their territory, the same degree of light at all hours. Only, within doors, they lower it to a soft twilight during the Silent Hours. They have a great horror of perfect darkness, and their lights are never wholly extinguished. On occasions of festivity they continue the duration of full light, but equally keep note of the distinction between night and day, by mechanical contrivances which answer the purpose of our clocks and watches. They are very fond of music; and it is by music that these chronometers strike the principal division of time. At every one of their hours, during their day, the sounds coming from all the timepieces in their public buildings, and caught up, as it were, by those of houses or hamlets scattered amidst the landscapes without the city, have an effect singularly sweet, and yet singularly solemn. But during the Silent Hours these sounds are so subdued as to be only faintly heard by a waking ear. They have no change of seasons, and, at least in the territory of this tribe, the atmosphere seemed to me very equable, warm as that of an Italian summer, and humid rather than dry; in the forenoon usually very still, but at times invaded by strong blasts from the rocks that made the borders of their domain. But time is the same to them for sowing or reaping as in the Golden Isles of the ancient poets.[2] At the same moment you see the younger plants in blade or bud, the older in ear or fruit. All fruit-bearing plants, however, after fruitage, either shed or change the colour of their leaves. But that which interested me most in reckoning up their divisions of time was the ascertainment of the average duration of life amongst them. I found on minute inquiry that this very considerably exceeded the term allotted to us on the upper earth. What seventy years are to us, one hundred years are to them. Nor is this the only advantage they have over us in longevity, for as few among us attain to the age of seventy, so, on the contrary, few among them die before the age of one hundred; and they enjoy a general degree of health and vigour which makes life itself a blessing even to the last. Various causes contribute to this result: the absence of all alcoholic stimulants; temperance in food; more especially, perhaps, a serenity of mind undisturbed by anxious occupations and eager passions. They are not tormented by our avarice or our ambition; they appear perfectly indifferent even to the desire of fame; they are capable of great affection, but their love shows itself in a tender and cheerful complaisance, and, while forming their happiness, seems rarely, if ever, to constitute their woe. As the Gy is sure only to marry where she herself fixes her choice, and as here, not less than above ground, it is the female on whom the happiness of home depends; so the Gy, having chosen the mate she prefers to all others, is lenient to his faults, consults his humours, and does her best to secure his attachment. The death of a beloved one is of course with them, as with us, a cause of sorrow; but not only is death with them so much more rare before that age in which it becomes a release, but when it does occur the survivor takes much more consolation than, I am afraid, the generality of us do, in the certainty of reunion in another and yet happier life.

All these causes, then, concur to their healthful and enjoyable

longevity, though, no doubt, much also must be owing to hereditary organisation. According to their records, however, in those
earlier stages of their society when they lived in communities resembling ours, agitated by fierce competition, their lives were considerably shorter, and their maladies more numerous and grave.
They themselves say that the duration of life, too, has increased,
and is still on the increase, since their discovery of the invigorating
and medicinal properties of vril, applied for remedial purposes.
They have few professional and regular practitioners of medicine,
and these are chiefly Gy-ei, who, especially if widowed and childless, find great delight in the healing art, and even undertake
surgical operations in those cases required by accident, or, more
rarely, by disease.

They have their diversions and entertainments, and, during the
Easy Time of their day, they are wont to assemble in great numbers
for those winged sports in the air which I have already described.
They have also public halls for music, and even theatres, at which
are performed pieces that appeared to me somewhat to resemble
the plays of the Chinese—dramas that are thrown back into distant
times for their events and personages, in which all classic unities are
outrageously violated, and the hero, in one scene a child, in the
next is an old man, and so forth. These plays are of very ancient
composition. They appeared to me extremely dull, on the whole,
but were relieved by startling mechanical contrivances, and a kind
of farcical broad humour, and detached passages of great vigour
and power expressed in language highly poetical, but somewhat
overcharged with metaphor and trope. In fine, they seemed to me
very much what the plays of Shakespeare seemed to a Parisian in
the time of Louis XV,[3] or perhaps to an Englishman in the reign of
Charles II.[4]

The audience, of which the Gy-ei constituted the chief portion,
appeared to enjoy greatly the representation of these dramas,
which, for so sedate and majestic a race of females, surprised me,
till I observed that all the performers were under the age of adoles-

cence, and conjectured truly that the mothers and sisters came to please their children and brothers.

I have said that these dramas are of great antiquity. No new plays, indeed no imaginative works sufficiently important to survive their immediate day, appear to have been composed for several generations. In fact, though there is no lack of new publications, and they have even what may be called newspapers, these are chiefly devoted to mechanical science, reports of new inventions, announcements respecting various details of business—in short, to practical matters. Sometimes a child writes a little tale of adventure, or a young Gy vents her amorous hopes or fears in a poem; but these effusions are of very little merit, and are seldom read except by children and maiden Gy-ei. The most interesting works of a purely literary character are those of explorations and travels into other regions of this nether world, which are generally written by young emigrants, and are read with great avidity by the relations and friends they have left behind.

I could not help expressing to Aph-Lin my surprise that a community in which mechanical science had made so marvellous a progress, and in which intellectual civilisation had exhibited itself in realising those objects for the happiness of the people, which the political philosophers above ground had, after ages of struggle, pretty generally agreed to consider unattainable visions, should, nevertheless, be so wholly without a contemporaneous literature, despite the excellence to which culture had brought a language at once rich and simple, vigorous and musical.

My host replied—"Do you not perceive that a literature such as you mean would be wholly incompatible with that perfection of social or political felicity at which you do us the honour to think we have arrived? We have at last, after centuries of struggle, settled into a form of government with which we are content, and in which, as we allow no differences of rank, and no honours are paid to administrators distinguishing them from others, there is no stimulus given to individual ambition. No one would read works advocating theories that involved any political or social change, and therefore no one writes them. If now and then an An feels himself dissatisfied with our tranquil mode of life, he does not attack it; he goes away. Thus all that part of literature (and to judge by the ancient books in our public libraries, it was once a very large part) which relates to speculative theories on society is become utterly extinct. Again, formerly there was a vast deal written respecting the attributes and essence of the All-Good, and the arguments for and against a future state; but now we all recognise two facts, that there *is* a Divine Being, and there *is* a future state, and we all equally agree that if we wrote our fingers to the bone, we could not throw any light upon the nature and conditions of that future state, or quicken our apprehensions of the attributes and essence of that Divine Being. Thus another part of literature has become also extinct, happily for our race; for in the times when so much was written on subjects which no one could determine, people seemed to live in a perpetual state of quarrel and contention. So, too, a vast part of our ancient literature consists of historical records of wars and revolutions during the times when the Ana lived in large and turbulent societies, each seeking aggrandisement at the expense of the other. You see our serene mode of life now; such it has been for ages. We have no events to chronicle. What more of us can be said than that 'they were born, they were happy, they died?' Coming next to that part of literature which is more under the control of the imagination, such as what we call Glaubsila, or colloquially 'Glaubs,' and you call poetry, the reasons for its decline amongst us are abundantly obvious.

"We find, by referring to the great masterpieces in that department of literature which we all still read with pleasure, but of which none would tolerate imitations, that they consist in the portraiture of passions which we no longer experience—ambition, vengeance, unhallowed love, the thirst for warlike renown, and such like. The old poets lived in an atmosphere impregnated with these passions, and felt vividly what they expressed glowingly. No one can express such passions now, for no one can feel them, or meet with any sympathy in his readers if he did. Again, the old poetry has a main element in its dissection of those complex mysteries of human character which conduce to abnormal vices and crimes, or lead to signal and extraordinary virtues. But our society, having got rid of temptations to any prominent vices and crimes, has necessarily rendered the moral average so equal, that there are no very salient virtues. Without its ancient food of strong passions, vast crimes, heroic excellences, poetry therefore is, if not actually starved to death, reduced to a very meagre diet. There is still the poetry of description—description of rocks, and trees, and waters, and common household life; and our young Gy-ei weave much of this insipid kind of composition into their love verses."

"Such poetry," said I, "might surely be made very charming; and we have critics amongst us who consider it a higher kind than that which depicts the crimes, or analyses the passions, of man. At all events, poetry of the insipid kind you mention is a poetry that nowadays commands more readers than any other among the people I have left above ground."

"Possibly; but then I suppose the writers take great pains with the language they employ, and devote themselves to the culture and polish of words and rhythms as an art?"

"Certainly they do: all great poets must do that. Though the gift of poetry may be inborn, the gift requires as much care to make it available as a block of metal does to be made into one of your engines."

"And doubtless your poets have some incentive to bestow all those pains upon such verbal prettinesses?"

"Well, I presume their instinct of song would make them sing as the bird does; but to cultivate the song into verbal or artificial prettiness, probably does need an inducement from without, and our poets find it in the love of fame—perhaps, now and then, in the want of money."

"Precisely so. But in our society we attach fame to nothing which man, in that moment of his duration which is called 'life,' can perform. We should soon lose that equality which constitutes the felicitous essence of our commonwealth if we selected any individual for pre-eminent praise: pre-eminent praise would confer pre-eminent power, and the moment it were given, evil passions, now dormant, would awake; other men would immediately covet praise, then would arise envy, and with envy hate, and with hate calumny and persecution. Our history tells us that most of the poets and most of the writers who, in the old time, were favoured with the greatest praise, were also assailed by the greatest vituperation, and even, on the whole, rendered very unhappy, partly by the attacks of jealous rivals, partly by the diseased mental constitution which an acquired sensitiveness to praise and to blame tends to engender. As for the stimulus of want; in the first place, no man in our community knows the goad of poverty; and, secondly, if he did, almost every occupation would be more lucrative than writing.

"Our public libraries contain all the books of the past which time has preserved; those books, for the reasons above stated, are infinitely better than any can write nowadays, and they are open to all to read without cost. We are not such fools as to pay for reading inferior books, when we can read superior books for nothing."

"With us, novelty has an attraction; and a new book, if bad, is read when an old book, though good, is neglected."

"Novelty, to barbarous states of society struggling in despair for something better, has no doubt an attraction, denied to us, who see nothing to gain in novelties; but, after all, it is observed by one of our great authors four thousand years ago, that 'he who studies old books will always find in them something new, and he who reads new books will always find in them something old.' But to return to the question you have raised, there being then among us no stimulus to painstaking labour, whether in desire of fame or in pressure of want, such as have the poetic temperament, no doubt, vent it in song, as you say the bird sings; but for lack of elaborate culture it fails of an audience, and, failing of an audience, dies out, of itself, amidst the ordinary avocations of life."

"But how is it that these discouragements to the cultivation of literature do not operate against that of science?"

"Your question amazes me. The motive to science is the love of truth apart from all consideration of fame, and science with us too is devoted almost solely to practical uses, essential to our social conservation and the comforts of our daily life. No fame is asked by the inventor, and none is given to him; he enjoys an occupation congenial to his tastes, and needing no wear and tear of the passions. Man must have exercise for his mind as well as body; and continuous exercise, rather than violent, is best for both. Our most ingenious cultivators of science are, as a general rule, the longest lived and the most free from disease. Painting is an amusement to many, but the art is not what it was in former times, when the great painters in our various communities vied with each other for the prize of a golden crown, which gave them a social rank equal to that of the kings under whom they lived. You will thus doubtless have observed in our archæological department how superior in point of art the pictures were several thousand years ago. Perhaps it is because music is, in reality, more allied to science than it is to poetry, that, of all the pleasurable arts, music is that which flourishes the most amongst us. Still, even in music the absence of stimulus in praise or fame has served to prevent any great superiority of one individual over another; and we rather excel in choral music, with the aid of our vast mechanical instruments, in which we make great use of the agency of water,[5] than in single performers. We have had scarcely any original composer for some ages. Our favourite airs are very ancient in substance, but have admitted many complicated variations by inferior, though ingenious, musicians."

"Are there no political societies among the Ana which are animated by those passions, subjected to those crimes, and admitting those disparities in condition, in intellect, and in morality, which the state of your tribe, or indeed of the Vril-ya generally, has left behind in its progress to perfection? If so, among such societies perhaps Poetry and her sister arts still continue to be honoured and to improve?"

"There are such societies in remote regions, but we do not

admit them within the pale of civilised communities; we scarcely even give them the name of Ana, and certainly not that of Vril-ya. They are barbarians, living chiefly in that low stage of being, Koom-Posh, tending necessarily to its own hideous dissolution in Glek-Nas. Their wretched existence is passed in perpetual contest and perpetual change. When they do not fight with their neighbours, they fight among themselves. They are divided into sections, which abuse, plunder, and sometimes murder each other, and on the most frivolous points of difference that would be unintelligible to us if we had not read history, and seen that we too have passed through the same early state of ignorance and barbarism. Any trifle is sufficient to set them together by the ears. They pretend to be all equals, and the more they have struggled to be so, by removing old distinctions and starting afresh, the more glaring and intolerable the disparity becomes, because nothing in hereditary affections and associations is left to soften the one naked distinction between the many who have nothing and the few who have much. Of course the many hate the few, but without the few they could not live. The many are always assailing the few; sometimes they exterminate the few; but as soon as they have done so, a new few starts out of the many, and is harder to deal with than the old few. For where societies are large, and competition to have something is the predominant fever, there must be always many losers and few gainers. In short, the people I speak of are savages groping their way in the dark towards some gleam of light, and would demand our commiseration for their infirmities, if, like all savages, they did not provoke their own destruction by their arrogance and cruelty. Can you imagine that creatures of this kind, armed only with such miserable weapons as you may see in our museum of antiquities, clumsy iron tubes charged with saltpetre, have more than once threatened with destruction a tribe of the Vril-ya, which dwells nearest to them, because they say they have thirty millions of population—and that tribe may have fifty thousand—if the latter do not accept their notions of Soc-Sec (money-getting) on some trading principles which they have the impudence to call a 'law of civilisation?'"

"But thirty millions of population are formidable odds against fifty thousand!"

My host stared at me astonished. "Stranger," said he, "you could not have heard me say that this threatened tribe belongs to the Vril-ya; and it only waits for these savages to declare war, in order to commission some half-a-dozen small children to sweep away their whole population."

At these words I felt a thrill of horror, recognising much more affinity with "the savages," than I did with the Vril-ya, and remembering all I had said in praise of the glorious American institutions, which Aph-Lin stigmatised as Koom-Posh. Recovering my self-possession, I asked if there were modes of transit by which I could safely visit this temerarious and remote people.

"You can travel with safety, by vril agency, either along the ground or amid the air, throughout all the range of the communities with which we are allied and akin; but I cannot vouch for your safety in barbarous nations governed by different laws from ours; nations, indeed, so benighted, that there are among them large numbers who actually live by stealing from each other, and one could not with safety in the Silent Hours even leave the doors of one's own house open."

Here our conversation was interrupted by the entrance of Taë, who came to inform us that he, having been deputed to discover and destroy the enormous reptile which I had seen on my first arrival, had been on the watch for it ever since his visit to me, and had begun to suspect that my eyes had deceived me, or that the creature had made its way through the cavities within the rocks to the wild regions in which dwelt its kindred race,—when it gave evidences of its whereabouts by a great devastation of the herbage bordering one of the lakes. "And," said Taë, "I feel sure that within that lake it is now hiding. So" (turning to me) "I thought it might amuse you to accompany me to see the way we destroy such unpleasant visitors." As I looked at the face of the young child, and called to mind the enormous size of the creature he proposed to exterminate, I felt myself shudder with fear for him, and perhaps fear for myself, if I accompanied him in such a chase. But my curiosity to witness the destructive effects of the boasted vril, and my unwillingness to lower myself in the eyes of an infant by betraying apprehensions of personal safety, prevailed over my first impulse. Accordingly, I thanked Taë for his courteous consideration for my amusement, and professed my willingness to set out with him on so diverting an enterprise.

CHAPTER 18

As Taë and myself, on quitting the town, and leaving to the left the main road which led to it, struck into the fields, the strange and solemn beauty of the landscape, lighted up, by numberless lamps, to the verge of the horizon, fascinated my eyes, and rendered me for some time an inattentive listener to the talk of my companion.

Along our way various operations of agriculture were being carried on by machinery, the forms of which were new to me, and for the most part very graceful; for among these people art being so cultivated for the sake of mere utility, exhibits itself in adorning or refining the shapes of useful objects. Precious metals and gems are so profuse among them, that they are lavished on things devoted to purposes the most commonplace; and their love of utility leads them to beautify its tools, and quickens their imagination in a way unknown to themselves.

In all service, whether in or out of doors, they make great use of automaton figures, which are so ingenious, and so pliant to the operations of vril, that they actually seem gifted with reason. It was scarcely possible to distinguish the figures I beheld, apparently guiding or superintending the rapid movements of vast engines, from human forms endowed with thought.

By degrees, as we continued to walk on, my attention became

roused by the lively and acute remarks of my companion. The intelligence of the children among this race is marvellously precocious, perhaps from the habit of having entrusted to them, at so early an age, the toils and responsibilities of middle age. Indeed, in conversing with Taë, I felt as if talking with some superior and observant man of my own years. I asked him if he could form any estimate of the number of communities into which the race of the Vril-ya is subdivided.

"Not exactly," he said, "because they multiply, of course, every year as the surplus of each community is drafted off. But I heard my father say that, according to the last report, there were a million and a half of communities speaking our language, and adopting our institutions and forms of life and government; but, I believe, with some differences, about which you had better ask Zee. She knows more than most of the Ana do. An An cares less for things that do not concern him than a Gy does; the Gy-ei are inquisitive creatures."

"Does each community restrict itself to the same number of families or amount of population that you do?"

"No; some have much smaller populations, some have larger—varying according to the extent of the country they appropriate, or to the degree of excellence to which they have brought their machinery. Each community sets its own limit according to circumstances, taking care always that there shall never arise any class of poor by the pressure of population upon the productive powers of the domain; and that no state shall be too large for a government resembling that of a single well-ordered family. I imagine that no Vril community exceeds thirty thousand households. But, as a general rule, the smaller the community, provided there be hands enough to do justice to the capacities of the territory it occupies, the richer each individual is, and the larger the sum contributed to the general treasury,—above all, the happier and the more tranquil is the whole political body, and the more perfect the products of its industry. The state which all tribes of the Vril-ya acknowledge to be the highest in civilisation, and which has brought the vril force to its fullest development, is perhaps the smallest. It limits itself to four thousand families; but every inch of its territory is cultivated to the utmost perfection of garden ground; its machinery excels that of every other tribe, and there is no product of its industry in any department which is not sought for, at extraordinary prices, by each community of our race. All our tribes make this state their model, considering that we should reach the highest state of civilisation allowed to mortals if we could unite the greatest degree of happiness with the highest degree of intellectual achievement; and it is clear that the smaller the society the less difficult that will be. Ours is too large for it."

This reply set me thinking. I reminded myself of that little state of Athens, with only twenty thousand free citizens, and which to this day our mightiest nations regard as the supreme guide and model in all departments of intellect. But then Athens permitted fierce rivalry and perpetual change, and was certainly not happy. Rousing myself from the reverie into which these reflections had plunged me, I brought back our talk to the subjects connected with emigration.

"But," said I, "when, I suppose yearly, a certain number among you agree to quit home and found a new community elsewhere, they must necessarily be very few, and scarcely sufficient, even with the help of the machines they take with them, to clear the ground, and build towns, and form a civilised state with the comforts and luxuries in which they had been reared."

"You mistake. All the tribes of the Vril-ya are in constant communication with each other, and settle amongst themselves each year what proportion of one community will unite with the emigrants of another, so as to form a state of sufficient size; and the place for emigration is agreed upon at least a year before, and pioneers sent from each state to level rocks, and embank waters, and construct houses; so that when the emigrants at last go, they find a city already made, and a country around it at least partially cleared. Our hardy life as children makes us take cheerfully to travel and adventure. I mean to emigrate myself when of age."

"Do the emigrants always select places hitherto uninhabited and barren?"

"As yet generally, because it is our rule never to destroy except where necessary to our wellbeing. Of course, we cannot settle in lands already occupied by the Vril-ya; and if we take the cultivated lands of the other races of Ana, we must utterly destroy the previous inhabitants. Sometimes, as it is, we take waste spots, and find that a troublesome, quarrelsome race of Ana, especially if under the administration of Koom-Posh or Glek-Nas, resents our vicinity, and picks a quarrel with us; then, of course, as menacing our welfare, we destroy it: there is no coming to terms of peace with a race so idiotic that it is always changing the form of government which represents it. Koom-Posh," said the child, emphatically, "is bad enough, still it has brains, though at the back of its head, and is not without a heart; but in Glek-Nas the brain and heart of the creatures disappear, and they become all jaws, claws, and belly."[1]

"You express yourself strongly. Allow me to inform you that I myself, and I am proud to say it, am the citizen of a Koom-Posh!"

"I no longer," answered Taë, "wonder to see you here so far from your home. What was the condition of your native community before it became a Koom-Posh?"

"A settlement of emigrants—like those settlements which your tribe sends forth—but so far unlike your settlements, that it was dependent on the state from which it came. It shook off that yoke, and, crowned with eternal glory, became a Koom-Posh."

"Eternal glory! how long has the Koom-Posh lasted?"

"About 100 years."

"The length of an An's life—a very young community. In much less than another 100 years your Koom-Posh will be a Glek-Nas."

"Nay, the oldest states in the world I come from, have such faith in its duration, that they are all gradually shaping their institutions so as to melt into ours, and their most thoughtful politicians say that, whether they like it or not, the inevitable tendency of these old states is towards Koom-Posh-erie."

"The old states?"

"Yes, the old states."

"With populations very small in proportion to the area of productive land?"

"On the contrary, with populations very large in proportion to that area."

"I see! old states indeed!—so old as to become drivelling if they don't pack off that surplus population as we do ours—very old states!—very, very old! Pray, Tish, do you think it wise for very old men to try to turn head-over-heels as very young children do?[2] And if you asked them why they attempted such antics, should you not laugh if they answered that by imitating very young children they could become very young children themselves? Ancient history abounds with instances of this sort a great many thousand years ago—and in every instance a very old state that played at Koom-Posh soon tumbled into Glek-Nas. Then, in horror of its own self, it cried out for a master, as an old man in his dotage cries out for a nurse; and after a succession of masters or nurses, more or less long, that very old state died out of history. A very old state attempting Koom-Posh-erie is like a very old man who pulls down the house to which he has been accustomed, but he has so exhausted his vigour in pulling it down, that all he can do in the way of rebuilding is to run up a crazy hut, in which himself and his successors whine out 'How the wind blows! How the walls shake!'"

"My dear Taë, I make all excuse for your unenlightened prejudices, which every schoolboy educated in a Koom-Posh could easily controvert, though he might not be so precociously learned in ancient history as you appear to be."

"I learned! not a bit of it. But would a schoolboy, educated in your Koom-Posh, ask his great-great-grandfather or great-great-grandmother to stand on his or her head with the feet uppermost? and if the poor old folks hesitated—say, 'What do you fear?—see how I do it!'"[3]

"Taë, I disdain to argue with a child of your age. I repeat, I make allowances for your want of that culture which a Koom-Posh alone can bestow."

"I, in my turn," answered Taë, with an air of the suave but lofty good breeding which characterises his race, "not only make allowances for you as not educated among the Vril-ya, but I entreat you to vouchsafe me your pardon for insufficient respect to the habits and opinions of so amiable a—Tish!"

I ought before to have observed that I was commonly called Tish by my host and his family, as being a polite and indeed a pet name, metaphorically signifying a small barbarian, literally a Froglet; the children apply it endearingly to the tame species of Frog which they keep in their gardens.

We had now reached the banks of a lake, and Taë here paused to point out to me the ravages made in fields skirting it. "The enemy certainly lies within these waters," said Taë. "Observe what shoals of fish are crowded together at the margin. Even the great fishes with the small ones, who are their habitual prey and who generally shun them, all forget their instincts in the presence of a common destroyer. This reptile certainly must belong to the class of the Krek-a,[4] a class more devouring than any other, and said to be among the few surviving species of the world's dreadest inhabitants before the Ana were created. The appetite of a Krek is insatiable—it feeds alike upon vegetable and animal life; but for the swift-footed creatures of the elk species it is too slow in its movements. Its favourite dainty is an An when it can catch him unawares; and hence the Ana destroy it relentlessly whenever it enters their dominion. I have heard that when our forefathers first cleared this country, these monsters, and others like them, abounded, and, vril being then undiscovered, many of our race were devoured. It was impossible to exterminate them wholly till that discovery which constitutes the power and sustains the civilisation of our race. But after the uses of vril became familiar to us, all creatures inimical to us were soon annihilated. Still, once a-year or so, one of these enormous reptiles wanders from the unreclaimed and savage districts beyond, and within my memory one seized upon a young Gy who was bathing in this very lake. Had she been on land and armed with her staff, it would not have dared even to show itself; for, like all savage creatures, the reptile has a marvellous instinct, which warns it against the bearer of the vril wand. How they teach their young to avoid him, though seen for the first time, is one of those mysteries which you may ask Zee to explain, for I cannot.[5] So long as I stand here, the monster will not stir from its lurking-place; but we must now decoy it forth."

"Will not that be difficult?"

"Not at all. Seat yourself yonder on that crag (about one hundred yards from the bank), while I retire to a distance. In a short time the reptile will catch sight or scent of you, and, perceiving that you are no vril-bearer, will come forth to devour you. As soon as it is fairly out of the water, it becomes my prey."

"Do you mean to tell me that I am to be the decoy to that horrible monster which could engulf me within its jaws in a second! I beg to decline."

The child laughed. "Fear nothing," said he; "only sit still."

Instead of obeying this command, I made a bound, and was about to take fairly to my heels, when Taë touched me lightly on the shoulder, and, fixing his eyes steadily on mine, I was rooted to the spot. All power of volition left me. Submissive to the infant's gesture, I followed him to the crag he had indicated, and seated myself there in silence. Most readers have seen something of the effects of electro-biology, whether genuine or spurious. No professor of that doubtful craft had ever been able to influence a thought or a movement of mine, but I was a mere machine at the will of this terrible child. Meanwhile he expanded his wings, soared aloft, and alighted amidst a copse at the brow of a hill at some distance.

I was alone; and turning my eyes with an indescribable sensation of horror towards the lake, I kept them fixed on its water, spell-bound. It might be ten or fifteen minutes, to me it seemed ages, before the still surface, gleaming under the lamplight, began to be agitated towards the centre. At the same time the shoals of fish near the margin evinced their sense of the enemy's approach by splash and leap and bubbling circle. I could detect their hurried flight hither and thither, some even casting themselves ashore.

A long, dark, undulous furrow came moving along the waters, nearer and nearer, till the vast head of the reptile emerged—its jaws bristling with fangs, and its dull eyes fixing themselves hungrily on the spot where I sat motionless. And now its fore feet were on the strand—now its enormous breast, scaled on either side as in armour, in the centre showing corrugated skin of a dull venomous yellow; and now its whole length was on the land, a hundred feet or more from the jaw to the tail.[6] Another stride of those ghastly feet would have brought it to the spot where I sat. There was but a moment between me and this grim form of death, when what seemed a flash of lightning shot through the air, smote, and, for a space in time briefer than that in which a man can draw his breath, enveloped the monster; and then, as the flash vanished, there lay before me a blackened, charred, smouldering mass, a something gigantic, but of which even the outlines of form were burned away, and rapidly crumbling into dust and ashes. I remained still seated, still speechless, ice-cold with a new sensation of dread: what had been horror was now awe.

I felt the child's hand on my head—fear left me—the spell was broken—I rose up. "You see with what ease the Vril-ya destroy their enemies," said Taë; and then, moving towards the bank, he contemplated the smouldering relics of the monster, and said quietly, "I have destroyed larger creatures, but none with so much pleasure. Yes, it is a Krek; what suffering it must have inflicted while it lived!" Then he took up the poor fishes that had flung themselves ashore, and restored them mercifully to their native element.

CHAPTER 19
As we walked back to the town, Taë took a new and circuitous way, in order to show me what, to use a familiar term, I will call the "station," from which emigrants or travellers to other communities commence their journeys. I had, on a former occasion, expressed a wish to see their vehicles. These I

found to be of two kinds, one for land-journeys, one for aerial voyages: the former were of all sizes and forms, some not larger than an ordinary carriage, some movable houses of one story and containing several rooms, furnished according to the ideas of comfort or luxury which are entertained by the Vril-ya. The aerial vehicles were of light substances, not the least resembling our balloons, but rather our boats and pleasure-vessels, with helm and rudder, with large wings as paddles, and a central machine worked by vril. All the vehicles both for land or air were indeed worked by that potent and mysterious agency.

I saw a convoy set out on its journey, but it had few passengers, containing chiefly articles of merchandise, and was bound to a neighbouring community; for among all the tribes of the Vril-ya there is considerable commercial interchange. I may here observe, that their money currency does not consist of the precious metals, which are too common among them for that purpose. The smaller coins in ordinary use are manufactured from a peculiar fossil shell, the comparatively scarce remnant of some very early deluge, or other convulsion of nature, by which a species has become extinct. It is minute, and flat as an oyster, and takes a jewel-like polish. This coinage circulates among all the tribes of the Vril-ya. Their larger transactions are carried on much like ours, by bills of exchange, and thin metallic plates which answer the purpose of our bank-notes.

Let me take this occasion of adding that the taxation among the tribe I became acquainted with was very considerable, compared with the amount of population. But I never heard that any one grumbled at it, for it was devoted to purposes of universal utility, and indeed necessary to the civilisation of the tribe. The cost of lighting so large a range of country, of providing for emigration, of maintaining the public buildings at which the various operations of national intellect were carried on, from the first education of an infant to the departments in which the College of Sages were perpetually trying new experiments in mechanical science: all these involved the necessity for considerable state funds. To these I must add an item that struck me as very singular. I have said that all the human labour required by the state is carried on by children up to the marriageable age. For this labour the state pays, and at a rate immeasurably higher than our remuneration to labour even in the United States. According to their theory, every child, male or female, on attaining the marriageable age, and there terminating the period of labour, should have acquired enough for an independent competence during life. As, no matter what the disparity of fortune in the parents, all the children must equally serve, so all are equally paid according to their several ages or the nature of their work. When the parents or friends choose to retain a child in their own service, they must pay into the public fund in the same ratio as the state pays to the children it employs; and this sum is handed over to the child when the period of service expires. This practice serves, no doubt, to render the notion of social equality familiar and agreeable; and if it may be said that all the children form a democracy, no less truly it may be said that all the adults form an aristocracy. The exquisite politeness and refinement of manners among the Vril-ya, the generosity of their sentiments, the absolute leisure they enjoy for following out their own private pursuits, the amenities of their domestic intercourse, in which they seem as members of one noble order that can have no distrust of each other's word or deed, all combine to make the Vril-ya the most perfect nobility which a political disciple of Plato or Sidney could conceive for the ideal of an aristocratic republic.[1]

CHAPTER 20

From the date of the expedition with Taë which I have just narrated, the child paid me frequent visits. He had taken a liking to me, which I cordially returned. Indeed, as he was not yet twelve years old, and had not commenced the course of scientific studies with which childhood closes in that country, my intellect was less inferior to his than to that of the elder members of his race, especially of the Gy-ei, and most especially of the accomplished Zee. The children of the Vril-ya, having upon their minds the weight of so many active duties and grave responsibilities, are not generally mirthful; but Taë, with all his wisdom, had much of the playful good-humour one often finds the characteristic of elderly men of genius. He felt that sort of pleasure in my society which a boy of a similar age in the upper world has in the company of a pet dog or monkey. It amused him to try and teach me the ways of his people, as it amuses a nephew of mine to make his poodle walk on his hind legs or jump through a hoop. I willingly lent myself to such experiments, but I never achieved the success of the poodle. I was very much interested at first in the attempt to ply the wings which the youngest of the Vril-ya use as nimbly and easily as ours do their legs and arms; but my efforts were attended with contusions serious enough to make me abandon them in despair.

The wings, as I before said, are very large, reaching to the knee, and in repose thrown back so as to form a very graceful mantle. They are composed from the feathers of a gigantic bird that abounds in the rocky heights of the country—the colour mostly white, but sometimes with reddish streaks. They are fastened round the shoulders with light but strong springs of steel; and, when expanded, the arms slide through loops for that purpose, forming, as it were, a stout central membrane. As the arms are raised, a tubular lining beneath the vest or tunic becomes, by mechanical contrivance, inflated with air, increased or diminished at will by the movement of the arms, and serving to buoy the whole form as on bladders. The wings and the balloon-like apparatus are highly charged with vril; and when the body is thus wafted upward, it seems to become singularly lightened of its weight. I found it easy enough to soar from the ground; indeed, when the wings were spread it was scarcely possible not to soar, but then came the difficulty and the danger. I utterly failed in the power to use and direct the pinions, though I am considered among my own race unusually alert and ready in bodily exercises, and am a very practised swimmer. I could only make the most confused and blundering efforts at flight. I was the servant of the wings; the wings were not my servants—they were beyond my control; and when by a violent strain of muscle, and, I must fairly own, in that abnormal strength which is given by excessive fright, I curbed their gyrations and brought them near to the body, it seemed as if I lost the sustaining power stored in them and the connecting bladders, as when air is let out of a balloon, and found myself precipitated again to earth; saved, indeed, by some spasmodic flutterings, from being dashed to pieces, but not saved from the bruises and the stun of a heavy fall. I would, however, have persevered in my attempts, but for the advice or the commands of the scientific Zee, who had benevolently accompanied my flutterings, and indeed on the last occasion, flying just under me, received my form as it fell on her own expanded wings, and preserved me from breaking my head on the roof of the pyramid from which we had ascended.

"I see," she said, "that your trials are in vain, not from the fault of the wings and their appurtenances, nor from any imperfectness and malformation of your own corpuscular system, but from irremediable, because organic, defect in your power of volition. Learn that the connection between the will and the agencies of that fluid which has been subjected to the control of the Vril-ya was never established by the first discoverers, never achieved by a single generation; it has gone on increasing, like other properties of race, in proportion as it has been uniformly transmitted from parent to child, so that, at last, it has become an instinct; and an infant An of our race, wills to fly as intuitively and unconsciously as he wills to walk. He thus plies his invented or artificial wings with as much safety as a bird plies those with which it is born. I did not think sufficiently of this when I allowed you to try an experiment which allured me, for I longed to have in you a companion. I shall abandon the experiment now. Your life is becoming dear to me." Herewith the Gy's voice and face softened, and I felt more seriously alarmed than I had been in my previous flights.

Now that I am on the subject of wings, I ought not to omit mention of a custom among the Gy-ei which seems to me very pretty and tender in the sentiment it implies. A Gy wears wings habitually while yet a virgin—she joins the Ana in their aerial sports—she adventures alone and afar into the wilder regions of the sunless world: in the boldness and height of her soarings, not less than in the grace of her movements, she excels the opposite sex. But from the day of marriage, she wears wings no more, she suspends them with her own willing hand over the nuptial couch, never to be resumed unless the marriage tie be severed by divorce or death.

Now when Zee's voice and eyes thus softened—and at that softening I prophetically recoiled and shuddered—Taë, who had accompanied us in our flights, but who, child-like, had been much more amused with my awkwardness than sympathising in my fears or aware of my danger, hovered over us, poised amidst the still radiant air, serene and motionless on his outspread wings, and hearing the endearing words of the young Gy, laughed aloud. Said he, "If the Tish cannot learn the use of wings, you may still be his companion, Zee, for you can suspend your own."

CHAPTER 21

I had for some time observed in my host's highly informed and powerfully proportioned daughter that kindly and protective sentiment which, whether above the earth or below it, an all-wise Providence has bestowed upon the feminine division of the human race. But until very lately I had ascribed it to that affection for "pets" which a human female at every age shares with a human child. I now became painfully aware that the feeling with which Zee deigned to regard me was different from that which I had inspired in Taë. But this conviction gave me none of that complacent gratification which the vanity of man ordinarily conceives from a flattering appreciation of his personal merits on the part of the fair sex; on the contrary, it inspired me with fear. Yet of all the Gy-ei in the community, if Zee were perhaps the wisest and the strongest, she was, by common repute, the gentlest, and she was certainly the most popularly beloved. The desire to aid, to succour, to protect, to comfort, to bless, seemed to pervade her whole being. Though the complicated miseries that originate in penury and guilt are unknown to the social system of the Vril-ya, still, no sage had yet discovered in vril an agency which could banish sorrow from life; and wherever amongst her people sorrow found its way, there Zee followed in the mission of comforter. Did some sister Gy fail to secure the love she sighed for? Zee sought her out, and brought all the resources of her lore, and all the consolations of her sympathy, to bear upon a grief that so needs the solace of a confidant. In the rare cases, when grave illness seized upon childhood or youth, and the cases, less rare, when, in the hardy and adventurous probation of infants, some accident, attended with pain and injury, occurred, Zee forsook her studies and her sports, and became the healer and the nurse. Her favourite flights were towards the extreme boundaries of the domain where children were stationed on guard against outbreaks of warring forces in nature, or the invasions of devouring animals, so that she might warn them of any peril which her knowledge detected or foresaw, or be at hand if any harm should befall. Nay, even in the exercise of her scientific acquirements there was a concurrent benevolence of purpose and will. Did she learn any novelty in invention that would be useful to the practitioner of some special art or craft? she hastened to communicate and explain it. Was some veteran sage of the College perplexed and wearied with the toil of an abstruse study? she would patiently devote herself to his aid, work out details for him, sustain his spirits with her hopeful smile, quicken his wit with her luminous suggestion, be to him, as it were, his own good genius made visible as the strengthener and inspirer. The same tenderness she exhibited to the inferior creatures. I have often known her bring home some sick and wounded animal, and tend and cherish it as a mother would tend and cherish her stricken child. Many a time when I sat in the balcony, or hanging garden, on which my window opened, I have watched her rising in the air on her radiant wings, and in a few moments groups of infants below, catching sight of her, would soar upward with joyous sounds of greeting; clustering and sporting around her, so that she seemed a very centre of innocent delight. When I have walked with her amidst the rocks and valleys without the city, the elk-deer would scent or see her from afar, come bounding up, eager for the caress of her hand, or follow her footsteps, till dismissed by some musical whisper that the creature had learned to comprehend. It is the fashion among the virgin Gy-ei to wear on their foreheads a circlet, or coronet, with gems resembling opals, arranged in four points or rays like stars. These are lustreless in ordinary use, but if touched by the vril wand they take a clear lambent flame, which illuminates, yet not burns. This serves as an ornament in their festivities, and as a lamp, if, in their wanderings beyond their artificial lights, they have to traverse the dark. There are times, when I have seen Zee's thoughtful majesty of face lighted up by this crowning halo, that I could scarcely believe her to be a creature of mortal birth, and bent my head before her as the vision of a being among the celestial orders. But never once did my heart feel for this lofty type of the noblest womanhood a sentiment of human love. Is it that, among the race I belong to, man's pride so far influences his passions that woman loses to him her special charm of woman if he feels her to be in all things eminently superior to himself? But by what strange infatuation could this peerless daughter of a race which, in the supremacy of its powers and the felicity of its conditions, ranked all other races in the category of barbarians, have deigned to honour me with her preference? In personal qualifications, though I passed for good-looking among the people I came from, the handsomest of my countrymen might have seemed insignificant and homely beside the grand and serene type of beauty which characterised the aspect of the Vril-ya.

That novelty, the very difference between myself and those to whom Zee was accustomed, might serve to bias her fancy was probable enough, and as the reader will see later, such a cause might suffice to account for the predilection with which I was distinguished by a young Gy scarcely out of her childhood, and very inferior in all respects to Zee. But whoever will consider those tender characteristics which I have just ascribed to the daughter of Aph-Lin, may readily conceive that the main cause of my attraction to her was in her instinctive desire to cherish, to comfort, to protect, and, in protecting, to sustain and to exalt. Thus, when I look back, I account for the only weakness unworthy of her lofty nature, which bowed the daughter of the Vril-ya to a woman's affection for one so inferior to herself as was her father's guest. But be the cause what it may, the consciousness that I had inspired such affection thrilled me with awe—a moral awe of her very perfections, of her mysterious powers, of the inseparable distinctions between her race and my own; and with that awe, I must confess to my shame, there combined the more material and ignoble dread of the perils to which her preference would expose me.

Could it be supposed for a moment that the parents and friends of this exalted being could view without indignation and disgust the possibility of an alliance between herself and a Tish? Her they could not punish, her they could not confine nor restrain. Neither in domestic nor in political life do they acknowledge any law of force amongst themselves; but they could effectually put an end to her infatuation by a flash of vril inflicted upon me.

Under these anxious circumstances, fortunately, my conscience and sense of honour were free from reproach. It became clearly my duty, if Zee's preference continued manifest, to intimate it to my host, with, of course, all the delicacy which is ever to be preserved by a well-bred man in confiding to another any degree of favour by which one of the fair sex may condescend to distinguish him. Thus, at all events, I should be freed from responsibility or suspicion of voluntary participation in the sentiments of Zee; and the superior wisdom of my host might probably suggest some sage extrication from my perilous dilemma. In this resolve I obeyed the ordinary instinct of civilised and moral man, who, erring though he be, still generally prefers the right course in those cases where it is obviously against his inclinations, his interests, and his safety to elect the wrong one.

CHAPTER 22

As the reader has seen, Aph-Lin had not favoured my general and unrestricted intercourse with his countrymen. Though relying on my promise to abstain from giving any information as to the world I had left, and still more on the promise of those to whom had been put the same request, not to question me, which Zee had exacted from Taë, yet he did not feel sure that, if I were allowed to mix with the strangers whose curiosity the sight of me had aroused, I could sufficiently guard myself against their inquiries. When I went out, therefore, it was never alone; I was always accompanied either by one of my host's family, or my child-friend Taë. Bra, Aph-Lin's wife, seldom stirred beyond the gardens which surrounded the house, and was fond of reading the ancient literature, which contained something of romance and adventure not to be found in the writing of recent ages, and presented pictures of a life unfamiliar to her experience and interesting to her imagination; pictures, indeed, of a life more resembling that which we lead every day above-ground, coloured by our sorrows, sins, and passions, and much to her what the Tales of the Genii or the Arabian Nights are to us. But her love of reading did not prevent Bra from the discharge of her duties as mistress of the largest household in the city. She went daily the round of the chambers, and saw that the automata and other mechanical contrivances were in order, that the numerous children employed by Aph-Lin, whether in his private or public capacity, were carefully tended. Bra also inspected the accounts of the whole estate, and it was her great delight to assist her husband in the business connected with his office as chief administrator of the Lighting Department, so that her avocations necessarily kept her much within doors. The two sons were both completing their education at the College of Sages; and the elder, who had a strong passion for mechanics, and especially for works connected with the machinery of timepieces and automata, had decided in devoting himself to these pursuits, and was now occupied in constructing a shop, or warehouse, at which his inventions could be exhibited and sold. The younger son preferred farming and rural occupations; and when not attending the College, at which he chiefly studied the theories of agriculture, was much absorbed by his practical application of that science to his father's lands. It will be seen by this how completely equality of ranks is established among this people—a shopkeeper being of exactly the same grade in estimation as the large landed proprietor. Aph-Lin was the wealthiest member of the community, and his oldest son preferred keeping a shop to any other avocation; nor was this choice thought to show any want of elevated notions on his part.

This young man had been much interested in examining my watch, the works of which were new to him, and was greatly pleased when I made him a present of it.[1] Shortly after, he returned the gift with interest, by a watch of his own construction, marking both the time as in my watch and the time as kept among the Vril-ya. I have that watch still, and it has been much admired by many among the most eminent watchmakers of London and Paris. It is of gold, with diamond hands and figures, and it plays a favourite tune among the Vril-ya in striking the hours: it only requires to be wound up once in ten months, and has never gone wrong since I had it.

These young brothers being thus occupied, my usual companions in that family, when I went abroad, were my host or his daughter. Now, agreeably with the honourable conclusions I had come to, I began to excuse myself from Zee's invitations to go out alone with her, and seized an occasion when that learned Gy was delivering a lecture at the College of Sages to ask Aph-Lin to show me his country-seat. As this was at some little distance, and as Aph-Lin was not fond of walking, while I had discreetly relinquished all attempts at flying, we proceeded to our destination in one of the aerial boats belonging to my host. A child of eight years old, in his employ, was our conductor. My host and myself reclined on cushions, and I found the movement very easy and luxurious.

"Aph-Lin," said I, "you will not, I trust, be displeased with me, if I ask your permission to travel for a short time, and visit other tribes or communities of your illustrious race. I have also a strong desire to see those nations which do not adopt your institutions, and which you consider as savages. It would interest me greatly to notice what are the distinctions between them and the races whom we consider civilised in the world I have left."

"It is utterly impossible that you should go hence alone," said Aph-Lin. "Even among the Vril-ya you would be exposed to great dangers. Certain peculiarities of formation and colour, and the extraordinary phenomenon of hirsute bushes upon your cheeks and chin, denoting in you a species of An distinct alike from our race and any known race of barbarians yet extant, would attract, of course, the special attention of the College of Sages in whatever community of Vril-ya you visited, and it would depend upon the individual temper of some individual sage whether you would be received, as you have been here, hospitably, or whether you would not be at once dissected for scientific purposes. Know that when the Tur first took you to his house, and while you were there put to sleep by Taë in order to recover from your previous pain or fatigue, the sages summoned by the Tur were divided in opinion whether you were a harmless or an obnoxious animal. During your unconscious state your teeth were examined, and they clearly showed that you were not only graminivorous,[2] but carnivorous. Carnivorous animals of your size are always destroyed, as being of dangerous and savage nature. Our teeth, as you have doubtless observed,[3] are not those of the creatures who devour flesh. It is, indeed, maintained by Zee and other philosophers, that as, in remote ages, the Ana did prey upon living beings of the brute species, their teeth must have been fitted for that purpose. But, even if so, they have been modified by hereditary transmission, and suited to the food on which we now exist; nor are even the barbarians, who adopt the turbulent and ferocious institutions of Glek-Nas, devourers of flesh like beasts of prey.

"In the course of this dispute it was proposed to dissect you; but Taë begged you off, and the Tur being, by office, averse to all novel experiments at variance with our custom of sparing life, except where it is clearly proved to be for the good of the community to take it, sent to me, whose business it is, as the richest man of the state, to afford hospitality to strangers from a distance. It was at my option to decide whether or not you were a stranger whom I could safely admit. Had I declined to receive you, you would have been handed over to the College of Sages, and what might there have befallen you I do not like to conjecture. Apart from this danger, you might chance to encounter some child of four years old, just put in possession of his vril staff; and who, in alarm at your strange appearance, and in the impulse of the moment, might reduce you to a cinder. Taë himself was about to do so when he first saw you, had his father not checked his hand. Therefore I say you cannot travel alone, but with Zee you would be safe; and I have no doubt that she would accompany you on a tour round the neighbouring communities of Vril-ya (to the savage states, No!): I will ask her."

Now, as my main object in proposing to travel was to escape from Zee, I hastily exclaimed, "Nay, pray do not! I relinquish my design. You have said enough as to its dangers to deter me from it; and I can scarcely think it right that a young Gy of the personal attractions of your lovely daughter should travel into other regions without a better protector than a Tish of my insignificant strength and stature."

Aph-Lin emitted the soft sibilant sound which is the nearest approach to laughter that a full-grown An permits to himself ere he replied: "Pardon my discourteous but momentary indulgence of mirth at any observation seriously made by my guest. I could not but be amused at the idea of Zee, who is so fond of protecting others that children call her 'THE GUARDIAN,' needing a protector herself against any dangers arising from the audacious admiration of males. Know that our Gy-ei, while unmarried, are accustomed to travel alone among other tribes, to see if they find there some An who may please them more than the Ana they find at home. Zee has already made three such journeys, but hitherto her heart has been untouched."

Here the opportunity which I sought was afforded to me, and I said, looking down, and with faltering voice, "Will you, my kind host, promise to pardon me, if what I am about to say gives you offence?"

"Say only the truth, and I cannot be offended; or, could I be so, it would be not for me, but for you to pardon."

"Well, then, assist me to quit you, and, much as I should have liked to witness more of the wonders, and enjoy more of the felicity, which belong to your people, let me return to my own."

"I fear there are reasons why I cannot do that; at all events, not without permission of the Tur, and he, probably, would not grant it. You are not destitute of intelligence; you may (though I do not think so) have concealed the degree of destructive powers possessed by your people; you might, in short, bring upon us some danger; and if the Tur entertains that idea, it would clearly be his duty either to put an end to you, or enclose you in a cage for the rest of your existence. But why should you wish to leave a state of society which you so politely allow to be more felicitous than your own?"

"Oh, Aph-Lin! my answer is plain. Lest in aught, and unwittingly, I should betray your hospitality; lest, in that caprice of will which in our world is proverbial among the other sex, and from which even a Gy is not free, your adorable daughter should deign to regard me, though a Tish, as if I were a civilised An, and—and—and——"

"Court you as her spouse," put in Aph-Lin, gravely, and without any visible sign of surprise or displeasure.

"You have said it."

"That would be a misfortune," resumed my host, after a pause, "and I feel that you have acted as you ought in warning me. It is, as you imply, not uncommon for an unwedded Gy to conceive tastes as to the object she covets which appear whimsical to others; but there is no power to compel a young Gy to any course opposed to that which she chooses to pursue. All we can do is to reason with her, and experience tells us that the whole College of Sages would find it vain to reason with a Gy in a matter that concerns her choice in love. I grieve for you, because such a marriage would be against the Aglauran, or good of the community, for the children of such a marriage would adulterate the race: they might even come into the world with the teeth of carnivorous animals; this could not be allowed: Zee, as a Gy, cannot be controlled; but you, as a Tish, can be destroyed. I advise you, then, to resist her addresses; to tell her plainly that you can never return her love. This happens constantly. Many an An, however ardently wooed by one Gy, rejects her, and puts an end to her persecution by wedding another. The same course is open to you."

"No; for I cannot wed another Gy without equally injuring the community, and exposing it to the chance of rearing carnivorous children."

"That is true. All I can say, and I say it with the tenderness due to a Tish, and the respect due to a guest, is frankly this—if you yield, you will become a cinder. I must leave it to you to take the best way you can to defend yourself. Perhaps you had better tell Zee that she is ugly. That assurance on the lips of him she woos generally suffices to chill the most ardent Gy. Here we are at my country-house."

CHAPTER 23 I confess that my conversation with Aph-Lin and the extreme coolness with which he stated his inability to control the dangerous caprice of his daughter, and treated the idea of the reduction into a cinder to which her amorous flame might expose my too seductive person, took away the pleasure I should otherwise have had in the contemplation of my host's country-seat, and the astonishing perfection of the machinery by which his farming-operations were conducted. The house differed in appearance from the massive and sombre building which Aph-Lin inhabited in the city, and which seemed akin to the rocks out of which the city itself had been hewn into shape. The walls of the country-seat were composed by trees placed a few feet apart from each other, the interstices being filled in with the transparent metallic substance which serves the purpose of glass among the Ana. These trees were all in flower, and the effect was very pleasing, if not in the best taste. We were received at the porch by lifelike automata, who conducted us into a chamber, the like to which I never saw before, but have often on summer days dreamily imagined. It was a bower—half room, half garden. The walls were one mass of climbing flowers. The open spaces, which we call windows, and in which, here, the metallic surfaces were slided back, commanded various views; some, of the wide landscape with its lakes and rocks; some, of small limited expanse answering to our conservatories, filled with tiers of flowers. Along the sides of the room were flower-beds, interspersed with cushions for repose. In the centre of the floor were a cistern and a fountain of that liquid light which I have presumed to be naphtha. It was luminous and of a roseate hue; it sufficed without lamps to light up the room with a subdued radiance. All around the fountain was carpeted with a soft deep lichen, not green (I have never seen that colour in the vegetation of this country), but a quiet brown, on which the eye reposes with the same sense of relief as that with which in the upper world it reposes on green. In the outlets upon flowers (which I have compared to our conservatories) there were singing-birds innumerable, which, while we remained in the room, sang in those harmonies of tune to which they are, in these parts, so wonderfully trained. The roof was open. The whole scene had charms for every sense—music from the birds, fragrance from the flowers, and varied beauty to the eye at every aspect. About all was a voluptuous repose. What a place, methought, for a honeymoon, if a Gy bride were a little less formidably armed not only with the rights of woman, but with the powers of man! but when one thinks of a Gy, so learned, so tall, so stately, so much above the standard of the creature we call woman as was Zee, no! even if I had felt no fear of being reduced to a cinder, it is not of her I should have dreamed in that bower so constructed for dreams of poetic love.

The automata reappeared, serving one of those delicious liquids which form the innocent wines of the Vril-ya.

"Truly," said I, "this is a charming residence, and I can scarcely conceive why you do not settle yourself here instead of amid the gloomier abodes of the city."

"As responsible to the community for the administration of light, I am compelled to reside chiefly in the city, and can only come hither for short intervals."

"But since I understand from you that no honours are attached to your office, and it involves some trouble, why do you accept it?"

"Each of us obeys without question the command of the Tur. He said, 'Be it requested that Aph-Lin shall be Commissioner of Light,' so I had no choice; but having held the office now for a long time, the cares, which were at first unwelcome, have become, if not pleasing, at least endurable. We are all formed by custom— even the difference of our race from the savage is but the transmitted continuance of custom, which becomes, through hereditary descent, part and parcel of our nature. You see there are Ana who even reconcile themselves to the responsibilities of chief magistrate, but no one would do so if his duties had not been rendered so light, or if there were any questions as to compliance with his requests."

"Not even if you thought the requests unwise or unjust?"

"We do not allow ourselves to think so, and indeed, everything goes on as if each and all governed themselves according to immemorial custom."

"When the chief magistrate dies or retires, how do you provide for his successor?"

"The An who has discharged the duties of chief magistrate for many years is the best person to choose one by whom those duties may be understood, and he generally names his successor."

"His son, perhaps?"

"Seldom that; for it is not an office any one desires or seeks, and a father naturally hesitates to constrain his son. But if the Tur himself decline to make a choice, for fear it might be supposed that he owed some grudge to the person on whom his choice would settle, then there are three of the College of Sages who draw lots among themselves which shall have the power to elect the chief. We consider that the judgment of one An of ordinary capacity is better than the judgment of three or more, however wise they may be; for among three there would probably be disputes; and where there are disputes, passion clouds judgment. The worst choice made by one who has no motive in choosing wrong, is better than the best choice made by many who have many motives for not choosing right."

"You reverse in your policy the maxims adopted in my country."

"Are you all, in your country, satisfied with your governors?"

"All! certainly not; the governors that most please some are sure to be those most displeasing to others."

"Then our system is better than yours."

"For you it may be; but according to our system a Tish could not be reduced to a cinder if a female compelled him to marry her; and as a Tish I sigh to return to my native world."

"Take courage, my dear little guest; Zee can't compel you to marry her. She can only entice you to do so. Don't be enticed. Come and look round my domain."

We went forth into a close, bordered with sheds; for though the Ana keep no stock for food there are some animals which they rear for milking and others for shearing. The former have no resemblance to our cows, nor the latter to our sheep, nor do I believe such species exist amongst them. They use the milk of three varieties of animal: one resembles the antelope, but is much larger, being as tall as a camel; the other two are smaller, and, though differing somewhat from each other, resemble no creature I ever saw on earth. They are very sleek and of rounded proportions; their colour that of the dappled deer, with very mild countenances and beautiful dark eyes. The milk of these three creatures differs in richness and in taste. It is usually diluted with water, and flavoured with the juice of a peculiar and perfumed fruit, and in itself is very nutritious and palatable. The animal whose fleece serves them for clothing and many other purposes, is more like the Italian she-goat than any other creature, but is considerably larger, has no horns, and is free from the displeasing odour of our goats. Its fleece is not thick, but very long and fine; it varies in colour, but is never white, more generally of a slate-like or lavender hue. For clothing it is usually worn dyed to suit the taste of the wearer. These animals were exceedingly tame, and were treated with extraordinary care and affection by the children (chiefly female) who tended them.

We then went through vast storehouses filled with grains and fruits. I may here observe that the main staple of food among these people consists—firstly, of a kind of corn much larger in ear than our wheat, and which by culture is perpetually being brought into new varieties of flavour; and, secondly, of a fruit of about the size of a small orange, which, when gathered, is hard and bitter. It is stowed away for many months in their warehouses, and then becomes succulent and tender. Its juice, which is of dark-red colour, enters into most of their sauces. They have many kinds of fruit of the nature of the olive, from which delicious oils are extracted. They have a plant somewhat resembling the sugar-cane, but its juices are less sweet and of a delicate perfume. They have no bees nor honey-kneading insects, but they make much use of a sweet gum that oozes from a coniferous plant, not unlike the araucaria. Their soil teems also with esculent roots and vegetables, which it is the aim of their culture to improve and vary to the utmost. And I never remember any meal among this people, however it might be confined to the family household, in which some delicate novelty in such articles of food was not introduced. In fine, as I before observed, their cookery is exquisite, so diversified and nutritious that one does not miss animal food; and their own physical forms suffice to show that with them, at least, meat is not required for superior production of muscular fibre. They have no grapes—the drinks extracted from their fruits are innocent and refreshing. Their staple beverage, however, is water, in the choice of which they are very fastidious, distinguishing at once the slightest impurity.

"My younger son takes great pleasure in augmenting our produce," said Aph-Lin is we passed through the storehouses, "and therefore will inherit these lands, which constitute the chief part of my wealth. To my elder son such inheritance would be a great trouble and affliction."

"Are there many sons among you who think the inheritance of vast wealth would be a great trouble and affliction?"

"Certainly; there are indeed very few of the Vril-ya who do not consider that a fortune much above the average is a heavy burden. We are rather a lazy people after the age of childhood, and do not like undergoing more cares than we can help, and great wealth does give its owner many cares. For instance, it marks us out for public offices, which none of us like and none of us can refuse. It necessitates our taking a continued interest in the affairs of any of our poorer countrymen, so that we may anticipate their wants and see that none fall into poverty. There is an old proverb amongst us which says, 'The poor man's need is the rich man's shame——'"

"Pardon me, if I interrupt you for a moment. You then allow that some, even of the Vril-ya, know want, and need relief?"

"If by want you mean the destitution that prevails in a Koom-Posh, *that* is impossible with us, unless an An has, by some extraordinary process, got rid of all his means, cannot or will not emigrate, and has either tired out the affectionate aid of his relations or personal friends, or refuses to accept it."

"Well, then, does he not supply the place of an infant or automaton, and become a labourer—a servant?"

"No; then we regard him as an unfortunate person of unsound reason, and place him, at the expense of the State, in a public building, where every comfort and every luxury that can mitigate his affliction are lavished upon him. But an An does not like to be considered out of his mind, and therefore such cases occur so seldom that the public building I speak of is now a deserted ruin, and the last inmate of it was an An whom I recollect to have seen in my childhood. He did not seem conscious of loss of reason, and wrote glaubs (poetry). When I spoke of wants, I meant such wants as an An with desires larger than his means sometimes entertains— for expensive singing-birds, or bigger houses, or country-gardens; and the obvious way to satisfy such wants is to buy of him something that he sells. Hence Ana like myself, who are very rich, are obliged to buy a great many things they do not require, and live on a very large scale where they might prefer to live on a small one. For instance, the great size of my house in the town is a source of much trouble to my wife, and even to myself; but I am compelled to have it thus incommodiously large, because, as the richest An of the community, I am appointed to entertain the strangers from the other communities when they visit us, which they do in great crowds twice a-year, when certain periodical entertainments are held, and when relations scattered throughout all the realms of the Vril-ya joyfully reunite for a time. This hospitality, on a scale so extensive, is not to my taste, and therefore I should have been happier had I been less rich. But we must all bear the lot assigned to us in this short passage through time that we call life. After all, what are a hundred years, more or less, to the ages through which we must pass hereafter? Luckily, I have one son who likes great wealth. It is a rare exception to the general rule, and I own I cannot myself understand it."

After this conversation I sought to return to the subject which continued to weigh on my heart—viz., the chances of escape from Zee. But my host politely declined to renew that topic, and summoned our air-boat. On our way back we were met by Zee, who, having found us gone, on her return from the College of Sages, had unfurled her wings and flown in search of us.

Her grand, but to me unalluring, countenance brightened as she beheld me, and, poising herself beside the boat on her large outspread plumes, she said reproachfully to Aph-Lin—"Oh father, was it right in you to hazard the life of your guest in a vehicle to which he is so unaccustomed? He might, by an incautious movement, fall over the side; and, alas! he is not like us, he has no wings. It were death to him to fall. Dear one!" (she added, accosting my shrinking self in a softer voice), "have you no thought of me, that you should thus hazard a life which has become almost a part of mine? Never again be thus rash, unless I am thy companion. What terror thou hast stricken into me!"

I glanced furtively at Aph-Lin, expecting, at least, that he would indignantly reprove his daughter for expressions of anxiety and affection, which, under all the circumstances, would, in the world above ground, be considered immodest in the lips of a young female, addressed to a male not affianced to her, even if of the same rank as herself.

But so confirmed are the rights of females in that region, and so absolutely foremost among those rights do females claim the privilege of courtship, that Aph-Lin would no more have thought of reproving his virgin daughter, than he would have thought of disobeying the Tur. In that country, custom, as he implied, is all and all.

He answered mildly, "Zee, the Tish was in no danger, and it is my belief that he can take very good care of himself."

"I would rather that he let me charge myself with his care. Oh, heart of my heart, it was in the thought of thy danger that I first felt how much I loved thee!"

Never did man feel in so false a position as I did. These words were spoken loud in the hearing of Zee's father—in the hearing of the child who steered. I blushed with shame for them, and for her, and could not help replying, angrily: "Zee, either you mock me, which, as your father's guest, misbecomes you, or the words you utter are improper for a maiden Gy to address even to an An of her own race, if he has not wooed her with the consent of her parents. How much more improper to address them to a Tish, who has never presumed to solicit your affections, and who can never regard you with other sentiments than those of reverence and awe!"

Aph-Lin made me a covert sign of approbation, but said nothing.

"Be not so cruel!" exclaimed Zee, still in sonorous accents. "Can love command itself where it is truly felt? Do you suppose that a maiden Gy will conceal a sentiment that it elevates her to feel? What a country you must have come from!"

Here Aph-Lin gently interposed, saying, "Among the Tish-a the rights of your sex do not appear to be established, and at all events my guest may converse with you more freely if unchecked by the presence of others."

To this remark Zee made no reply, but, darting on me a tender reproachful glance, agitated her wings and fled homeward.

"I had counted, at least, on some aid from my host," said I, bitterly, "in the perils to which his own daughter exposes me."

"I gave you the best aid I could. To contradict a Gy in her love affairs is to confirm her purpose. She allows no counsel to come between her and her affections."

CHAPTER 24

On alighting from the air-boat, a child accosted Aph-Lin in the hall with a request that he would be present at the funeral obsequies of a relation who had recently departed from that nether world.

Now, I had never seen a burial-place or cemetery amongst this people, and, glad to seize even so melancholy an occasion to defer an encounter with Zee, I asked Aph-Lin if I might be permitted to witness with him the interment of his relation; unless, indeed, it were regarded as one of those sacred ceremonies to which a stranger to their race might not be admitted.

"The departure of an An to a happier world," answered my host, "when, as in the case of my kinsman, he has lived so long in this as to have lost pleasure in it, is rather a cheerful though quiet festival than a sacred ceremony, and you may accompany me if you will."

Preceded by the child-messenger, we walked up the main street to a house at some little distance, and, entering the hall, were conducted to a room on the ground-floor, where we found several persons assembled round a couch on which was laid the deceased. It was an old man, who had, as I was told, lived beyond his 130th year. To judge by the calm smile on his countenance, he had passed away without suffering. One of the sons, who was now the head of the family, and who seemed in vigorous middle life, though he was considerably more than seventy, stepped forward with a cheerful face and told Aph-Lin "that the day before he died his father had seen in a dream his departed Gy, and was eager to be reunited to her, and restored to youth beneath the nearer smile of the All-Good."

While these two were talking, my attention was drawn to a dark metallic substance at the farther end of the room. It was about twenty feet in length, narrow in proportion, and all closed round, save, near the roof, there were small round holes through which might be seen a red light. From the interior emanated a rich and sweet perfume; and while I was conjecturing what purpose this machine was to serve, all the time-pieces in the town struck the hour with their solemn musical chime; and as that sound ceased, music of a more joyous character, but still of a joy subdued and tranquil, rang throughout the chamber, and from the walls beyond, in a choral peal. Symphonious with the melody, those present lifted their voice in chant. The words of this hymn were simple. They expressed no regret, no farewell, but rather a greeting to the new world whither the deceased had preceded the living. Indeed, in their language, the funeral hymn is called the "Birth Song." Then the corpse, covered by a long cerement, was tenderly lifted up by six of the nearest kinsfolk and borne towards the dark thing I have described. I pressed forward to see what happened. A sliding door or panel at one end was lifted up—the body deposited within, on a shelf—the door reclosed—a spring at the side touched—a sudden *whishing*, sighing sound heard from within; and lo! at, the other end of the machine the lid fell down, and a small handful of smouldering dust dropped into a *patera* placed to receive it. The son took up the *patera* and said (in what I understood afterwards was the usual form of words), "Behold how great is the Maker! To this little dust He gave form and life and soul. It needs not this little dust for Him to renew form and life and soul to the beloved one we shall soon see again."[1]

Each present bowed his head and pressed his hand to his heart. Then a young female child opened a small door within the wall, and I perceived, in the recess, shelves on which were placed many *pateræ* like that which the son held, save that they all had covers. With such a cover a Gy now approached the son, and placed it over the cup, on which it closed with a spring. On the lid were engraven the name of the deceased, and these words:—"Lent to us" (here the date of birth). "Recalled from us" (here the date of death).

The closed door shut with a musical sound, and all was over.

CHAPTER 25

"And this," said I, with my mind full of what I had witnessed—"this, I presume, is your usual form of burial?"

"Our invariable form," answered Aph-Lin. "What is it amongst your people?"

"We inter the body whole within the earth."

"What! to degrade the form you have loved and honoured, the wife on whose breast you have slept, to the loathsomeness of corruption?"

"But if the soul lives again, can it matter whether the body waste within the earth or is reduced by that awful mechanism, worked, no doubt by the agency of vril, into a pinch of dust?"

"You answer well," said my host, "and there is no arguing on a matter of feeling; but to me your custom is horrible and repulsive, and would serve to invest death with gloomy and hideous associations. It is something, too, to my mind, to be able to preserve the token of what has been our kinsman or friend within the abode in which we live. We thus feel more sensibly that he still lives, though not visibly so to us. But our sentiments in this, as in all things, are created by custom. Custom is not to be changed by a wise An, any more than it is changed by a wise Community, without the gravest deliberation, followed by the most earnest conviction. It is only thus that change ceases to be changeability, and once made is made for good."

When we regained the house, Aph-Lin summoned some of the children in his service and sent them round to several of his friends, requesting their attendance that day, during the Easy Hours, to a festival in honour of his kinsman's recall to the All-Good. This was the largest and gayest assembly I ever witnessed during my stay among the Ana, and was prolonged far into the Silent Hours.

The banquet was spread in a vast chamber reserved especially for grand occasions. This differed from our entertainments, and was not without a certain resemblance to those we read of in the luxurious age of the Roman empire. There was not one great table set out, but numerous small tables, each appropriated to eight guests. It is considered that beyond that number conversation languishes and friendship cools. The Ana never laugh loud, as I have before observed, but the cheerful ring of their voices at the various tables betokened gaiety of intercourse. As they have no stimulant drinks, and are temperate in food, though so choice and dainty, the banquet itself did not last long. The tables sank through the floor, and then came musical entertainments for those who liked them. Many, however, wandered away:—some of the younger ascended on their wings, for the hall was roofless, forming aerial dances; others strolled through the various apartments, examining the curiosities with which they were stored, or formed themselves into groups for various games, the favourite of which is a complicated kind of chess played by eight persons. I mixed with the crowd, but was prevented joining in their conversation by the constant companionship of one or the other of my host's sons, appointed to keep me from obtrusive questionings. The guests, however, noticed me but slightly; they had grown accustomed to my appearance, seeing me so often in the streets, and I had ceased to excite much curiosity.

To my great delight Zee avoided me, and evidently sought to excite my jealousy by marked attentions to a very handsome young An, who (though, as is the modest custom of the males when addressed by females, he answered with downcast eyes and blushing cheeks, and was demure and shy as young ladies new to the world are in most civilised countries, except England and America) was evidently much charmed by the tall Gy, and ready to falter a bashful "Yes" if she had actually proposed. Fervently hoping that she would, and more and more averse to the idea of reduction to a cinder after I had seen the rapidity with which a human body can be hurried into a pinch of dust, I amused myself by watching the manners of the other young people. I had the satisfaction of observing that Zee was no singular assertor of a female's most valued rights. Wherever I turned my eyes, or lent my ears, it seemed to me that the Gy was the wooing party, and the An the coy and reluctant one. The pretty innocent airs which an An gave himself on being thus courted, the dexterity with which he evaded direct answer to professions of attachment, or turned into jest the flattering compliments addressed to him, would have done honour to the most accomplished coquette. Both my male chaperons were subjected greatly to these seductive influences, and both acquitted themselves with wonderful honour to their tact and self-control.

I said to the elder son, who preferred mechanical employments to the management of a great property, and who was of an eminently philosophical temperament,—"I find it difficult to conceive how at your age, and with all the intoxicating effects on the senses, of music and lights and perfumes, you can be so cold to that impassioned Gy who has just left you with tears in her eyes at your cruelty."

The young An replied with a sigh, "Gentle Tish, the greatest misfortune in life is to marry one Gy if you are in love with another."

"Oh! you are in love with another?"

"Alas! yes."

"And she does not return your love?"

"I don't know. Sometimes a look, a tone, makes me hope so; but she has never plainly told me that she loves me."

"Have you not whispered in her own ear that you love her?"

"Fie! what are you thinking of? What world do you come from? Could I so betray the dignity of my sex? Could I be so un-Anly[1]—so lost to shame, as to own love to a Gy who has not first owned hers to me?"

"Pardon: I was not quite aware that you pushed the modesty of your sex so far. But does no An ever say to a Gy, 'I love you,' till she says it first to him?"

"I can't say that no An has ever done so, but if he ever does, he is disgraced in the eyes of the Ana, and secretly despised by the Gy-ei. No Gy, well brought up, would listen to him; she would consider that he audaciously infringed on the rights of her sex, while outraging the modesty which dignifies his own. It is very provoking," continued the An, "for she whom I love has certainly courted no one else, and I cannot but think she likes me. Sometimes I suspect that she does not court me because she fears I would ask some unreasonable settlement as to the surrender of her rights. But if so, she cannot really love me, for where a Gy really loves she foregoes all rights."

"Is this young Gy present?"

"Oh yes. She sits yonder talking to my mother."

I looked in the direction to which my eyes were thus guided, and saw a Gy dressed in robes of bright red, which among this people is a sign that a Gy as yet prefers a single state. She wears grey, a neutral tint, to indicate that she is looking about for a spouse; dark purple if she wishes to intimate that she has made a choice; purple and orange when she is betrothed or married; light blue when she is divorced or a widow and would marry again. Light blue is of course seldom seen.

Among a people where all are of so high a type of beauty, it is difficult to single out one as peculiarly handsome. My young friend's choice seemed to me to possess the average of good looks; but there was an expression in her face that pleased me more than did the faces of the young Gy-ei generally, because it looked less bold—less conscious of female rights. I observed that, while she talked to Bra, she glanced, from time to time, sidelong at my young friend.

"Courage," said I; "that young Gy loves you."

"Ay, but if she will not say so, how am I the better for her love?"

"Your mother is aware of your attachment?"

"Perhaps so. I never owned it to her. It would be un-Anly to confide such weakness to a mother. I have told my father; he may have told it again to his wife."

"Will you permit me to quit you for a moment and glide behind your mother and your beloved? I am sure they are talking about you. Do not hesitate. I promise that I will not allow myself to be questioned till I rejoin you."

The young An pressed his hand on his heart, touched me lightly on the head, and allowed me to quit his side. I stole unobserved behind his mother and his beloved. I overheard their talk.

Bra was speaking; said she, "There can be no doubt of this: either my son, who is of marriageable age, will be decoyed into marriage with one of his many suitors, or he will join those who emigrate to a distance and we shall see him no more. If you really care for him, my dear Lo, you should propose."

"I do care for him, Bra; but I doubt if I could really ever win his affections. He is fond of his inventions and timepieces; and I am not like Zee, but so dull that I fear I could not enter into his favourite pursuits, and then he would get tired of me, and at the end of three years divorce me, and I could never marry another—never."

"It is not necessary to know about timepieces to know how to be so necessary to the happiness of an An who cares for timepieces, that he would rather give up the timepieces than divorce his Gy. You see, my dear Lo," continued Bra, "that precisely because we are the stronger sex, we rule the other, provided we never show our strength. If you were superior to my son in making timepieces and automata, you should, as his wife, always let him suppose you thought him superior in that art to yourself. The An tacitly allows the pre-eminence of the Gy in all except his own special pursuit. But if she either excels him in that, or affects not to admire him for his proficiency in it, he will not love her very long; perhaps he may even divorce her. But where a Gy really loves, she soon learns to love all that the An does."

The young Gy made no answer to this address. She looked down musingly, then a smile crept over her lips, and she rose, still silent, and went through the crowd till she paused by the young An who loved her. I followed her steps, but discreetly stood at a little distance while I watched them. Somewhat to my surprise, till I recollected the coy tactics among the Ana, the lover seemed to receive her advances with an air of indifference. He even moved away, but she pursued his steps, and, a little time after, both spread their wings and vanished amid the luminous space above.

Just then I was accosted by the chief magistrate, who mingled with the crowd distinguished by no signs of deference or homage. It so happened that I had not seen this great dignitary since the day I had entered his dominions, and recalling Aph-Lin's words as to his terrible doubt whether or not I should be dissected, a shudder crept over me at the sight of his tranquil countenance.

"I hear much of you, stranger, from my son Taë," said the Tur, laying his hand politely on my bended head. "He is very fond of your society, and I trust you are not displeased with the customs of our people."

I muttered some unintelligible answer, which I intended to be an assurance of my gratitude for the kindness I had received from the Tur, and my admiration of his countrymen, but the dissecting-knife gleamed before my mind's eye and choked my utterance. A softer voice said, "My brother's friend must be dear to me." And looking up I saw a young Gy, who might be sixteen years old, standing beside the magistrate and gazing at me with a very benignant countenance. She had not come to her full growth, and was scarcely taller than myself (viz., about 5 feet 10 inches), and, thanks to that comparatively diminutive stature, I thought her the loveliest Gy I had hitherto seen. I suppose something in my eyes revealed that impression, for her countenance grew yet more benignant.

"Taë tells me," she said, "that you have not yet learned to accustom yourself to wings. That grieves me, for I should have liked to fly with you."

"Alas!" I replied, "I can never hope to enjoy that happiness. I am assured by Zee that the safe use of wings is a hereditary gift, and it would take generations before one of my race could poise himself in the air like a bird."

"Let not that thought vex you too much," replied this amiable Princess, "for, after all, there must come a day when Zee and myself must resign our wings for ever. Perhaps when that day comes we might be glad if the An we chose was also without wings."

The Tur had left us, and was lost amongst the crowd. I began to feel at ease with Taë's charming sister, and rather startled her by the boldness of my compliment in replying "that no An she could choose would ever use his wings to fly away from her." It is so against custom for an An to say such civil things to a Gy till she has declared her passion for him, and been accepted as his betrothed, that the young maiden stood quite dumbfounded for a few moments. Nevertheless she did not seem displeased. At last recovering herself, she invited me to accompany her into one of the less crowded rooms and listen to the songs of the birds. I followed her steps as she glided before me, and she led me into a chamber almost deserted. A fountain of naphtha was playing in the centre of the room; round it were ranged soft divans, and the walls of the room were open on one side to an aviary in which the birds were chanting their artful chorus. The Gy seated herself on one of the divans, and I placed myself at her side. "Taë tells me," she said, "that Aph-Lin has made it the law[2] of his house that you are not to be questioned as to the country you come from or the reason why you visit us. Is it so?"

"It is."

"May I, at least, without sinning against that law, ask at least if the Gy-ei in your country are of the same pale colour as yourself, and no taller?"

"I do not think, O beautiful Gy, that I infringe the law of Aph-Lin, which is more binding on myself than any one, if I answer questions so innocent. The Gy-ei in my country are much fairer of hue than I am, and their average height is at least a head shorter than mine."

"They cannot then be so strong as the Ana amongst you? But I suppose their superior vril force makes up for such extraordinary disadvantage of size?"

"They do not profess the vril force as you know it. But still they are very powerful in my country, and an An has small chance of a happy life if he be not more or less governed by his Gy."

"You speak feelingly," said Taë's sister, in a tone of voice half sad, half petulant. "You are married, of course?"

"No—certainly not."

"Nor betrothed?"

"Nor betrothed."

"Is it possible that no Gy has proposed to you?"

"In my country the Gy does not propose; the An speaks first."

"What a strange reversal of the laws of nature!" said the maiden, "and what want of modesty in your sex! But have you never proposed, never loved one Gy more than another?"

I felt embarrassed by these ingenuous questionings, and said, "Pardon me, but I think we are beginning to infringe upon Aph-Lin's injunction. Thus much only will I say in answer, and then, I implore you, ask no more. I did once feel the preference you speak of; I did propose, and the Gy would willingly have accepted me, but her parents refused their consent."

"Parents! Do you mean seriously to tell me that parents can interfere with the choice of their daughters?"

"Indeed they can, and do very often."

"I should not like to live in that country," said the Gy, simply; "but I hope you will never go back to it."

I bowed my head in silence. The Gy gently raised my face with her right hand, and looked into it tenderly. "Stay with us," she said; "stay with us, and be loved."

What I might have answered, what dangers of becoming a cinder I might have encountered, I still tremble to think, when the light of the naphtha fountain was obscured by the shadow of wings; and Zee, flying through the open roof, alighted beside us. She said not a word, but, taking my arm with her mighty hand, she drew me away, as a mother draws a naughty child, and led me through the apartments to one of the corridors, on which, by the mechanism they generally prefer to stairs, we ascended to my own room. This gained, Zee breathed on my forehead, touched my breast with her staff, and I was instantly plunged into a profound sleep.

When I awoke some hours later, and heard the song of the birds in the adjoining aviary, the remembrance of Taë's sister, her gentle looks and caressing words, vividly returned to me; and so impossible is it for one born and reared in our upper world's state of society to divest himself of ideas dictated by vanity and ambition, that I found myself instinctively building proud castles in the air.

"Tish though I be," thus ran my meditations—"Tish though I be, it is then clear that Zee is not the only Gy whom my appearance can captivate. Evidently I am loved by A PRINCESS,[3] the first maiden of this land, the daughter of the absolute Monarch whose autocracy they so idly seek to disguise by the republican title of chief magistrate. But for the sudden swoop of that horrible Zee, this Royal Lady would have formally proposed to me; and though it may be very well for Aph-Lin, who is only a subordinate minister, a mere Commissioner of Light, to threaten me with destruction if I accept his daughter's hand, yet a Sovereign, whose word is law, could compel the community to abrogate any custom that forbids intermarriage with one of a strange race and which in itself is a contradiction to their boasted equality of ranks.

"It is not to be supposed that his daughter, who spoke with such incredulous scorn of the interference of parents, would not have sufficient influence with her Royal Father to save me from the combustion to which Aph-Lin would condemn my form. And if I were exalted by such an alliance, who knows but what the Monarch might elect me as his successor. Why not? Few among this indolent race of philosophers like the burden of such greatness. All might be pleased to see the supreme power lodged in the hands of an accomplished stranger who has experience of other and livelier forms of existence; and, once chosen, what reforms I would institute! What additions to the really pleasant but too monotonous life of this realm my familiarity with the civilised nations above ground would effect! I am fond of the sports of the field. Next to war, is not the chase a king's pastime? In what varieties of strange game does this nether world abound! How interesting to strike down creatures that were known above ground before the Deluge! But how? By that terrible vril, in which, from want of hereditary transmission, I could never be a proficient. No, but by a civilised handy breech-loader,[4] which these ingenious mechanicians could not only make, but no doubt improve; nay, surely I saw one in the Museum. Indeed, as absolute king, I should discountenance vril altogether, except in cases of war. *Apropos* of war, it is perfectly absurd to stint a people so intelligent, so rich, so well armed, to a petty limit of territory sufficing for 10,000 or 12,000 families. Is not this restriction a mere philosophical crotchet, at variance with the aspiring element in human nature, such as has been partially, and with complete failure, tried in the upper world by the late Mr. Robert Owen.[5] Of course one would not go to war with neighbouring nations as well armed as one's own subjects; but then, what of those regions inhabited by races unacquainted with vril, and apparently resembling, in their democratic institutions, my American countrymen? One might invade them without offence to the vril nations, our allies, appropriate their territories, extending, perhaps, to the most distant regions of the nether earth, and thus rule over an empire in which the sun never sets.[6] (I forgot, in my enthusiasm, that over those regions there was no sun to set.) As for the fantastical notion against conceding fame or renown to an eminent individual, because, forsooth, bestowal of honours insures contest in the pursuit of them, stimulates angry passions, and mars the felicity of peace—it is opposed to the very elements, not only of the human but the brute creation, which are all, if tamable, participators in the sentiment of praise and emulation. What renown would be given to a king who thus extended his empire! I should be deemed a demigod."[7]

Thinking of that, the other fanatical notion of regulating this life by reference to one which, no doubt, we Christians firmly believe in, but never take into consideration, I resolved that enlightened philosophy compelled me to abolish a heathen religion so superstitiously at variance with modern thought and practical action. Musing over these various projects, I felt how much I should have liked at that moment to brighten my wits by a good glass of whisky-and-water. Not that I am habitually a spirit-drinker, but certainly there are times when a little stimulant of alcoholic nature, taken with a cigar, enlivens the imagination. Yes; certainly among these herbs and fruits there would be a liquid from which one could extract a pleasant vinous alcohol; and with a steak cut off one of those elks (ah! what offence to science to reject the animal food which our first medical men agree in recommending to the gastric juices of mankind!) one would certainly pass a more exhilarating hour of repast. Then, too, instead of those antiquated dramas performed by childish amateurs, certainly, when I am king, I will introduce our modern opera and a *corps de ballet,* for which one might find, among the nations I shall conquer, young females of less formidable height and thews than the Gy-ei—not armed with vril, and not insisting upon one's marrying them.

I was so completely rapt in these and similar reforms, political, social, and moral, calculated to bestow on the people of the nether world[8] the blessings of a civilisation known to the races of the upper, that I did not perceive that Zee had entered the chamber till I heard a deep sigh, and raising my eyes, beheld her standing by my couch.

I need not say that, according to the manners of this people, a

Gy can, without indecorum, visit an An in his chamber, though an An would be considered forward and immodest to the last degree if he entered the chamber of a Gy without previously obtaining her permission to do so. Fortunately I was in the full habiliments I had worn when Zee had deposited me on the couch. Nevertheless I felt much irritated, as well as shocked, by her visit, and asked in a rude tone what she wanted.

"Speak gently, beloved one, I entreat you," said she, "for I am very unhappy. I have not slept since we parted."

"A due sense of your shameful conduct to me as your father's guest might well suffice to banish sleep from your eyelids. Where was the affection you pretend to have for me, where was even that politeness on which the Vril-ya pride themselves, when, taking advantage alike of that physical strength in which your sex, in this extraordinary region, excels our own, and of those detestable and unhallowed powers[9] which the agencies of vril invest in your eyes and finger-ends, you exposed me to humiliation before your assembled visitors, before Her Royal Highness—I mean, the daughter of your own chief magistrate,—carrying me off to bed like a naughty infant, and plunging me into sleep, without asking my consent? "

"Ungrateful! Do you reproach me for the evidences of my love? Can you think that, even if unstung by the jealousy which attends upon love till it fades away in blissful trust when we know that the heart we have wooed is won, I could be indifferent to the perils to which the audacious overtures of that silly little child might expose you?"

"Hold! Since you introduce the subject of perils, it perhaps does not misbecome me to say that my most imminent perils come from yourself, or at least would come if I believed in your love and accepted your addresses. Your father has told me plainly that in that case I should be consumed into a cinder with as little compunction as if I were the reptile whom Taë blasted into ashes with the flash of his wand."

"Do not let that fear chill your heart to me," exclaimed Zee, dropping on her knees and absorbing my right hand in the space of her ample palm. "It is true, indeed, that we two cannot wed as those of the same race wed; true that the love between us must be pure as that which, in our belief, exists between lovers who reunite in the new life beyond that boundary at which the old life ends. But is it not happiness enough to be together, wedded in mind and in heart? Listen: I have just left my father. He consents to our union on those terms. I have sufficient influence with the College of Sages to insure their request to the Tur not to interfere with the free choice of a Gy, provided that her wedding with one of another race be but the wedding of souls. Oh, think you that true love needs ignoble union? It is not that I yearn only to be by your side in this life, to be part and parcel of your joys and sorrows here: I ask here for a tie which will bind us for ever and for ever in the world of immortals. Do you reject me?"

As she spoke, she knelt, and the whole character of her face was changed; nothing of sternness left to its grandeur; a divine light, as that of an immortal, shining out from its human beauty. But she rather awed me as angel than moved me as woman, and after an embarrassed pause, I faltered forth evasive expressions of gratitude, and sought, as delicately as I could, to point out how humiliating would be my position amongst her race in the light of a husband who might never be permitted the name of father.

"But," said Zee, "this community does not constitute the whole world. No; nor do all the populations comprised in the league of the Vril-ya. For thy sake I will renounce my country and my people. We will fly together to some region where thou shalt be safe. I am strong enough to bear thee on my wings across the deserts that intervene. I am skilled enough to cleave open, amid the rocks, valleys in which to build our home. Solitude and a hut with thee would be to me society and the universe. Or wouldst thou return to thine own world, above the surface of this, exposed to the uncertain seasons, and lit but by the changeful orbs which constitute by thy description the fickle character of those savage regions? If so, speak the word, and I will force the way for thy return, so that I am thy companion there, though, there as here, but partner of thy soul, and fellow-traveller with thee to the world in which there is no parting and no death.[10]

I could not but be deeply affected by the tenderness, at once so pure and so impassioned, with which these words were uttered, and in a voice that would have rendered musical the roughest sounds in the rudest tongue. And for a moment it did occur to me that I might avail myself of Zee's agency to effect a safe and speedy return to the upper world. But a very brief space for reflection sufficed to show me how dishonourable and base a return for such devotion it would be to allure thus away, from her own people and a home in which I had been so hospitably treated, a creature to whom our world would be so abhorrent, and for whose barren, if spiritual love, I could not reconcile myself to renounce the more human affection of mates less exalted above my erring self. With this sentiment of duty towards the Gy combined another of duty towards the whole race I belonged to. Could I venture to introduce into the upper world a being so formidably gifted—a being that with a movement of her staff could in less than an hour reduce New York and its glorious Koom-Posh into a pinch of snuff? Rob her of one staff, with her science she could easily construct another; and with the deadly lightnings that armed the slender engine her whole frame was charged. If thus dangerous to the cities and populations of the whole upper earth, could she be a safe companion to myself in case her affection should be subjected to change or embittered by jealousy? These thoughts which it takes so many words to express, passed rapidly through my brain and decided my answer.

"Zee," I said, in the softest tones I could command, and pressing respectful lips on the hand into whose clasp mine had vanished—"Zee, I can find no words to say how deeply I am touched, and how highly I am honoured, by a love so disinterested and self-immolating. My best return to it is perfect frankness. Each nation has its customs. The customs of yours do not allow you to wed me; the customs of mine are equally opposed to such a union between those of races so widely differing. On the other hand, though not deficient in courage among my own people, or amid dangers with which I am familiar, I cannot, without a shudder of horror, think of constructing a bridal home in the heart of some dismal chaos, with all the elements of nature, fire and water and mephitic [11] gases, at war with each other, and with the probability that at some moment, while you were busied in cleaving rocks or conveying vril into lamps, I should be devoured by a krek which your operations disturbed from its hiding-place. I, a mere Tish, do not deserve the love of a Gy, so brilliant, so learned, so potent as yourself. Yes, I do not deserve that love, for I cannot return it."

Zee released my hand, rose to her feet, and turned her face away to hide her emotions; then she glided noiselessly along the room, and paused at the threshold. Suddenly, impelled as by a new thought, she returned to my side and said, in a whispered tone,—

"You told me you would speak with perfect frankness. With perfect frankness, then, answer me this question, If you cannot love me, do you love another?"

"Certainly, I do not."

"You do not love Taë's sister?"

"I never saw her before last night."

"That is no answer. Love is swifter than vril. You hesitate to tell me. Do not think it is only jealousy that prompts me to caution you. If the Tur's daughter should declare love to you—if in her ignorance she confides to her father any preference that may justify his belief that she will woo you—he will have no option but to request your immediate destruction, as he is specially charged with the duty of consulting the good of the community, which could not allow a daughter of the Vril-ya to wed a son of the Tish-a, in that sense of marriage which does not confine itself to union of the souls. Alas! there would then be for you no escape. She has no strength of wing to uphold you through the air; she has no science wherewith to make a home in the wilderness. Believe that here my friendship speaks, and that my jealousy is silent."

With those words Zee left me. And recalling those words, I

thought no more of succeeding to the throne of the Vril-ya, or of the political, social, and moral reforms I should institute in the capacity of Absolute Sovereign.

CHAPTER 26

After the conversation with Zee just recorded, I fell into a profound melancholy. The curious interest with which I had hitherto examined the life and habits of this marvellous community was at an end. I could not banish from my mind the consciousness that I was among a people who, however kind and courteous, could destroy me at any moment without scruple or compunction. The virtuous and peaceful life of the people which, while new to me, had seemed so holy a contrast to the contentions, the passions, the vices of the upper world, now began to oppress me with a sense of dulness and monotony. Even the serene tranquillity of the lustrous air preyed on my spirits. I longed for a change, even to winter, or storm, or darkness. I began to feel that, whatever our dreams of perfectibility, our restless aspirations towards a better, and higher, and calmer sphere of being, we, the mortals of the upper world, are not trained or fitted to enjoy for long the very happiness of which we dream or to which we aspire.

Now, in this social state of the Vril-ya, it was singular to mark how it contrived to unite and to harmonise into one system nearly all the objects which the various philosophers of the upper world have placed before human hopes as the ideals of a Utopian future. It was a state in which war, with all its calamities, was deemed impossible,—a state in which the freedom of all and each was secured to the uttermost degree, without one of those animosities which make freedom in the upper world depend on the perpetual strife of hostile parties. Here the corruption which debases democracies was as unknown as the discontents which undermine the thrones of monarchies. Equality here was not a name; it was a reality. Riches were not persecuted, because they were not envied. Here those problems connected with the labours of a working class, hitherto insoluble above ground, and above ground conducing to such bitterness between classes, were solved by a process the simplest,—a distinct and separate working class was dispensed with altogether. Mechanical inventions, constructed on principles that baffled my research to ascertain, worked by an agency infinitely more powerful and infinitely more easy of management than aught we have yet extracted from electricity or steam, with the aid of children whose strength was never overtasked, but who loved their employment as sport and pastime, sufficed to create a Public-wealth so devoted to the general use that not a grumbler was ever heard of. The vices that rot our cities, here had no footing. Amusements abounded, but they were all innocent. No merry-makings conduced to intoxication, to riot, to disease. Love existed, and was ardent in pursuit, but its object, once secured, was faithful. The adulterer, the profligate, the harlot, were phenomena so unknown in this commonwealth, that even to find the words by which they were designated one would have had to search throughout an obsolete literature composed thousands of years before. They who have been students of theoretical philosophies above ground, know that all these strange departures from civilised life do but realise ideas which have been broached, canvassed, ridiculed, contested for, sometimes partially tried, and still put forth in fantastic books, but have never come to practical result. Nor were these all the steps towards theoretical perfectibility which this community had made. It had been the sober belief of Descartes that the life of man could be prolonged, not, indeed, on this earth, to eternal duration, but to what he called the age of the patriarchs, and modestly defined to be from 100 to 150 years average length. Well, even this dream of sages was here fulfilled—nay, more than fulfilled; for the vigour of middle life was preserved even after the term of a century was passed. With this longevity was combined a greater blessing than itself—that of continuous health. Such diseases as befell the race were removed with ease by scientific applications of that agency—life-giving as life-destroying—which is inherent in vril. Even this idea is not unknown above ground, though it has generally been confined to enthusiasts or charlatans, and emanates from confused notions about mesmerism, odic force, &c. Passing by such trivial contrivances as wings, which every schoolboy knows has been tried and found wanting, from the mythical or pre-historical period, I proceed to that very delicate question, urged of late as essential to the perfect happiness of our human species by the two most disturbing and potential influences on upper-ground society,—Womankind and Philosophy. I mean, the Rights of Women.[1]

Now, it is allowed by jurisprudists[2] that it is idle to talk of rights where there are not corresponding powers to enforce them; and above ground, for some reason or other, man, in his physical force, in the use of weapons offensive and defensive, when it comes to positive personal contest, can, as a rule of general application, master women. But among this people there can be no doubt about the rights of women, because, as I have before said, the Gy, physically speaking, is bigger and stronger than the An; and her will being also more resolute than his, and will being essential to the direction of the vril force, she can bring to bear upon him, more potently than he on herself, the mystical agency which art can extract from the occult properties of nature. Therefore all that our female philosophers above ground contend for as to rights of women, is conceded as a matter of course in this happy commonwealth. Besides such physical powers, the Gy-ei have (at least in youth) a keen desire for accomplishments and learning which exceeds that of the male; and thus they are the scholars, the professors—the learned portion, in short, of the community.

Of course, in this state of society the female establishes, as I have shown, her most valued privilege, that of choosing and courting her wedding partner. Without that privilege she would despise all the others. Now, above ground, we should not unreasonably apprehend that a female, thus potent and thus privileged, when she had fairly hunted us down and married us, would be very imperious and tyrannical. Not so with the Gy-ei: once married, the wings once suspended, and more amiable, complacent, docile mates, more sympathetic, more sinking their loftier capacities into the study of their husbands' comparatively frivolous tastes and whims, no poet could conceive in his visions of conjugal bliss. Lastly, among the more important characteristics of the Vril-ya, as distinguished from our mankind—lastly, and most important on the bearings of their life and the peace of their commonwealths, is their universal agreement in the existence of a merciful beneficent Deity, and of a future world to the duration of which a century or two are moments too brief to waste upon thoughts of fame and power and avarice; while with that agreement is combined another—viz., since they can know nothing as to the nature of that Deity beyond the fact of His supreme goodness, nor of that future world beyond the fact of its felicitous existence, so their reason forbids all angry disputes on insoluble questions. Thus they secure for that state in the bowels of the earth what no community ever secured under the light of the stars—all the blessings and consolations of a religion without any of the evils and calamities which are engendered by strife between one religion and another.

It would be, then, utterly impossible to deny that the state of existence among the Vril-ya is thus, as a whole, immeasurably more felicitous than that of super-terrestrial races, and, realising the dreams of our most sanguine philanthropists, almost approaches to a poet's conception of some angelical order. And yet, if you would take a thousand of the best and most philosophical of human beings you could find in London, Paris, Berlin, New York, or even Boston, and place them as citizens in this beatified community, my belief is, that in less than a year they would either die of *ennui*, or attempt some revolution by which they would militate against the good of the community, and be burnt into cinders at the request of the Tur.

Certainly I have no desire to insinuate, through the medium of this narrative, any ignorant disparagement of the race to which I belong. I have, on the contrary, endeavoured to make it clear that the principles which regulate the social system of the Vril-ya forbid them to produce those individual examples of human greatness which adorn the annals of the upper world. Where there are no wars there can be no Hannibal,[3] no Washington,[4] no Jackson,[5] no Sheridan;[6]—where states are so happy that they fear no danger and desire no change, they cannot give birth to a Demosthenes,[7] a Webster,[8] a Sumner,[9] a Wendel [sic] Holmes,[10] or a Butler;[11] and where a society attains to a moral standard, in which there are no crimes and no sorrows from which tragedy can extract its aliment of pity and sorrow, no salient vices or follies on which comedy can lavish its mirthful satire, it has lost the chance of producing a Shakespeare, or a Molière,[12] or a Mrs. Beecher Stowe.[13] But if I have no desire to disparage my fellow-men above ground in showing how much the motives that impel the energies and ambition of individuals in a society of contest and struggle—become dormant or annulled in a society which aims at securing for the aggregate the calm and innocent felicity which we presume to be the lot of beatified immortals; neither, on the other hand, have I the wish to represent the commonwealths of the Vril-ya as an ideal form of political society, to the attainment of which our own efforts of reform should be directed. On the contrary, it is because we have so combined, throughout the series of ages, the elements which compose human character, that it would be utterly impossible for us to adopt the modes of life, or to reconcile our passions to the modes of thought, among the Vril-ya,—that I arrived at the conviction that this people—though originally not only of our human race, but, as seems to me clear by the roots of their language, descended from the same ancestors as the great Aryan family, from which in varied streams has flowed the dominant civilisation of the world; and having, according to their myths and their history, passed through phases of society familiar to ourselves,—had yet now developed into a distinct species with which it was impossible that any community in the upper world could amalgamate: And that if they ever emerged from these nether recesses into the light of day, they would, according to their own traditional persuasions of their ultimate destiny, destroy and replace our existent varieties of man.

It may, indeed, be said, since more than one Gy could be found to conceive a partiality for so ordinary a type of our superterrestrial[14] race as myself, that even if the Vril-ya did appear above ground, we might be saved from extermination by intermixture of race. But this is too sanguine a belief. Instances of such *mésalliance* would be as rare as those of intermarriage between the Anglo-Saxon emigrants and the Red Indians. Nor would time be allowed for the operation of familiar intercourse. The Vril-ya, on emerging, induced by the charm of a sunlit heaven to form their settlements above ground, would commence at once the work of destruction, seize upon the territories already cultivated, and clear off, without scruple, all the inhabitants who resisted that invasion. And considering their contempt for the institutions of Koom-Posh or Popular Government, and the pugnacious valour of my beloved countrymen, I believe that if the Vril-ya first appeared in free America—as, being the choicest portion of the habitable earth, they would doubtless be induced to do—and said, "This quarter of the globe we take; Citizens of a Koom-Posh, make way for the development of species in the Vril-ya," my brave compatriots would show fight, and not a soul of them would be left in this life, to rally round the Stars and Stripes, at the end of a week.

I now saw but little of Zee, save at meals, when the family assembled, and she was then reserved and silent. My apprehensions of danger from an affection I had so little encouraged or deserved, therefore, now faded away, but my dejection continued to increase. I pined for escape to the upper world, but I racked my brains in vain for any means to effect it. I was never permitted to wander forth alone, so that I could not even visit the spot on which I had alighted, and see if it were possible to re-ascend to the mine. Nor even in the Silent Hours, when the household was locked in sleep, could I have let myself down from the lofty floor in which my apartment was placed. I knew not how to command the automata who stood mockingly at my beck beside the wall, nor could I ascertain the springs by which were set in movement the platforms that supplied the place of stairs. The knowledge how to avail myself of these contrivances had been purposely withheld from me. Oh, that I could but have learned the use of wings, so freely here at the service of every infant, then I might have escaped from the casement, regained the rocks, and buoyed myself aloft through the chasm of which the perpendicular sides forbade place for human footing!

CHAPTER 27

One day, as I sat alone and brooding in my chamber, Taë flew in at the open window and alighted on the couch beside me. I was always pleased with the visits of a child, in whose society, if humbled, I was less eclipsed than in that of Ana who had completed their education and matured their understanding. And as I was permitted to wander forth with him for my companion, and as I longed to revisit the spot in which I had descended into the nether world, I hastened to ask him if he were at leisure for a stroll beyond the streets of the city. His countenance seemed to me graver than usual as he replied, "I came hither on purpose to invite you forth."

We soon found ourselves in the street, and had not got far from the house when we encountered five or six young Gy-ei, who were returning from the fields with baskets full of flowers, and chanting a song in chorus as they walked. A young Gy sings more often than she talks. They stopped on seeing us, accosting Taë with familiar kindness, and me with the courteous gallantry which distinguishes the Gy-ei in their manner towards our weaker sex.

And here I may observe that, though a virgin Gy is so frank in her courtship to the individual she favours, there is nothing that approaches to that general breadth and loudness of manner which those young ladies of the Anglo-Saxon race, to whom the distinguished epithet of "fast" is accorded, exhibit towards young gentlemen whom they do not profess to love. No: the bearing of the Gy-ei towards males in ordinary is very much that of high-bred men in the gallant societies of the upper world towards ladies whom they respect but do not woo; deferential, complimentary, exquisitely polished—what we should call "chivalrous."

Certainly I was a little put out by the number of civil things addressed to my *amour propre*,[1] which were said to me by these courteous young Gy-ei. In the world I came from, a man would have thought himself aggrieved, treated with irony, "chaffed" (if so vulgar a slang word may be allowed on the authority of the popular novelists who use it so freely), when one fair Gy complimented me on the freshness of my complexion, another on the choice of colours in my dress, a third, with a sly smile, on the conquests I had made at Aph-Lin's entertainment. But I knew already that all such language was what the French call *banal*, and did but express in the female mouth, below earth, that sort of desire to pass for amiable with the opposite sex which, above earth, arbitrary custom and hereditary transmission demonstrate by the mouth of the male. And just as a high-bred young lady, above earth, habituated to such compliments, feels that she cannot, without impropriety, return them, nor evince any great satisfaction at receiving them; so I, who had learned polite manners at the house of so wealthy and dignified a Minister of that nation, could but smile and try to look pretty in bashfully disclaiming the compliments showered upon me. While we were thus talking, Taë's sister, it seems, had seen us from the upper rooms of the Royal Palace at the entrance of the town, and, precipitating herself on her wings, alighted in the midst of the group.

Singling me out, she said, though still with the inimitable deference of manner which I have called "chivalrous," yet not without a certain abruptness of tone which, as addressed to the weaker sex, Sir Philip Sidney might have termed "rustic," "Why do you never come to see us?"

While I was deliberating on the right answer to give to this unlooked-for question, Taë said quickly and sternly, "Sister, you forget—the stranger is of my sex. It is not for persons of my sex, having due regard for reputation and modesty, to lower themselves by running after the society of yours."

This speech was received with evident approval by the young Gy-ei in general; but Taë's sister looked greatly abashed. Poor thing!—and a PRINCESS too!

Just at this moment a shadow fell on the space between me and the group; and, turning round, I beheld the chief magistrate coming close upon us, with the silent and stately pace peculiar to the Vril-ya. At the sight of his countenance, the same terror which had seized me when I first beheld it returned. On that brow, in those eyes, there was that same indefinable something which marked the being of a race fatal to our own—that strange expression of serene exemption from our common cares and passions, of conscious superior power, compassionate and inflexible as that of a judge who pronounces doom. I shivered, and, inclining low, pressed the arm of my child-friend, and drew him onward silently. The Tur placed himself before our path, regarded me for a moment without speaking, then turned his eye quietly on his daughter's face, and, with a grave salutation to her and the other Gy-ei, went through the midst of the group,—still without a word.

CHAPTER 28

When Taë and I found ourselves alone on the broad road that lay between the city and the chasm through which I had descended into this region beneath the light of the stars and sun, I said under my breath, "Child and friend, there is a look in your father's face which appals me. I feel as if, in its awful tranquillity, I gazed upon death."

Taë did not immediately reply. He seemed agitated, and as if debating with himself by what words to soften some unwelcome intelligence. At last he said, "None of the Vril-ya fear death: do you?"

"The dread of death is implanted in the breasts of the race to which I belong. We can conquer it at the call of duty, of honour, of love. We can die for a truth, for a native land, for those who are dearer to us than ourselves. But if death do really threaten me now and here, where are such counteractions to the natural instinct

138

which invests with awe and terror the contemplation of severance between soul and body?"

Taë looked surprised, but there was great tenderness in his voice as he replied, "I will tell my father what you say. I will entreat him to spare your life."

"He has, then, already decreed to destroy it?"

"'Tis my sister's fault or folly," said Taë, with some petulance. "But she spoke this morning to my father; and, after she had spoken, he summoned me, as a chief among the children who are commissioned to destroy such lives as threaten the community, and he said to me, 'Take thy vril staff, and seek the stranger who has made himself dear to thee. Be his end painless and prompt.'"

"And," I faltered, recoiling from the child—"and it is, then, for my murder that thus treacherously thou hast invited me forth? No, I cannot believe it. I cannot think thee guilty of such a crime."

"It is no crime to slay those who threaten the good of the community; it would be a crime to slay the smallest insect that cannot harm us."

"If you mean that I threaten the good of the community because your sister honours me with the sort of preference which a child may feel for a strange plaything, it is not necessary to kill me. Let me return to the people I have left, and by the chasm through which I descended. With a slight help from you, I might do so now. You, by the aid of your wings, could fasten to the rocky ledge within the chasm the cord that you found, and have no doubt preserved. Do but that; assist me but to the spot from which I alighted, and I vanish from your world for ever, and as surely as if I were among the dead."

"The chasm through which you descended! Look round; we stand now on the very place where it yawned. What see you? Only solid rock. The chasm was closed, by the orders of Aph-Lin, as soon as communication between him and yourself was established in your trance, and he learned from your own lips the nature of the world from which you came. Do you not remember when Zee bade me not question you as to yourself or your race? On quitting you that day, Aph-Lin accosted me, and said, 'No path between the stranger's home and ours should be left unclosed, or the sorrow and evil of his home may descend to ours. Take with thee the children of thy band, smite the sides of the cavern with your vril staves till the fall of their fragments fills up every chink through which a gleam of our lamps could force its way.'"

As the child spoke, I stared aghast at the blind rocks before me. Huge and irregular, the granite masses, showing by charred discoloration where they had been shattered, rose from footing to roof-top; not a cranny!

"All hope, then, is gone,"[1] I murmured, sinking down on the craggy wayside, "and I shall nevermore see the sun." I covered my face with my hands, and prayed to Him whose presence I had so often forgotten when the heavens had declared His handiwork. I felt His presence in the depths of the nether earth, and amid the world of the grave. I looked up, taking comfort and courage from my prayers, and gazing with a quiet smile into the face of the child, said, "Now, if thou must slay me, strike."

Taë shook his head gently. "Nay," he said, "my father's request is not so formally made as to leave me no choice. I will speak with him, and I may prevail to save thee. Strange that thou shouldst have that fear of death which we thought was only the instinct of the inferior creatures, to whom the conviction of another life has not been vouchsafed. With us, not an infant knows such a fear. Tell me, my dear Tish," he continued, after a little pause, "would it reconcile thee more to departure from this form of life to that form which lies on the other side of the moment called 'death,' did I share thy journey? If so, I will ask my father whether it be allowable for me to go with thee. I am one of our generation destined to emigrate, when of age for it, to some regions unknown within this world. I would just as soon emigrate now to regions unknown, in another world. The All-Good is no less there than here. Where is He not?"

"Child," said I, seeing by Taë's countenance that he spoke in serious earnest, "it is a crime in thee to slay me; it were a crime not less in me to say, 'slay thyself.' The All-Good chooses His own time to give us life, and His own time to take it away. Let us go back. If, on speaking with thy father, he decides on my death, give me the longest warning in thy power, so that I may pass the interval in self-preparation."

We walked back to the city, conversing but by fits and starts. We could not understand each other's reasonings, and I felt for the fair child, with his soft voice and beautiful face, much as a convict feels for the executioner who walks beside him to the place of doom.

CHAPTER 29 In the midst of those hours set apart for sleep and constituting the night of the Vril-ya, I was awakened from the disturbed slumber into which I had not long fallen, by a hand on my shoulder. I started, and beheld Zee standing beside me.

"Hush," she said, in a whisper; "let no one hear us. Dost thou think that I have ceased to watch over thy safety because I could not win thy love? I have seen Taë. He has not prevailed with his father, who had meanwhile conferred with the three sages whom, in doubtful matters, he takes into council, and by their advice he has ordained thee to perish when the world re-awakens to life. I will save thee.[1] Rise and dress."

Zee pointed to a table by the couch on which I saw the clothes I had worn on quitting the upper world, and which I had exchanged subsequently for the more picturesque garments of the Vril-ya. The young Gy then moved towards the casement and stepped into the balcony, while hastily and wonderingly I donned my own habiliments.[2] When I joined her on the balcony, her face was pale and rigid. Taking me by the hand, she said softly, "See how brightly the art of the Vril-ya has lighted up the world in which they dwell. Tomorrow that world will be dark to me." She drew me back into the room without waiting for my answer, thence into the corridor, from which we descended into the hall. We passed into the deserted streets and along the broad upward road which wound beneath the rocks. Here, where there is neither day nor night, the Silent Hours are unutterably solemn,—the vast space illumined by mortal skill is so wholly without the sight and stir of mortal life. Soft as were our footsteps, their sounds vexed the ear, as out of harmony with the universal repose. I was aware in my own mind, though Zee said it not, that she had decided to assist my return to the upper world, and that we were bound towards the place from which I had descended. Her silence infected me, and commanded mine. And now we approached the chasm. It had been reopened; not presenting, indeed, the same aspect as when I had emerged from it, but, through that closed wall of rock before which I had last stood with Taë, a new cleft had been riven, and along its blackened sides still glimmered sparks and smouldered embers. My upward gaze could not, however, penetrate more than a few feet into the darkness of the hollow void, and I stood dismayed, and wondering how that grim ascent was to be made.

Zee divined my doubt. "Fear not," said she, with a faint smile; "your return is assured. I began this work when the Silent Hours commenced, and all else were asleep: believe that I did not pause till the path back into thy world was clear. I shall be with thee a little while yet. We do not part until thou sayest, 'Go, for I need thee no more.'"

My heart smote me with remorse at these words. "Ah!" I exclaimed, "would that thou wert of my race or I of thine, then I should never say, 'I need thee no more.'"

"I bless thee for those words, and I shall remember them when thou art gone," answered the Gy, tenderly.

During this brief interchange of words, Zee had turned away from me, her form bent and her head bowed over her breast. Now, she rose to the full height of her grand stature, and stood fronting me. While she had been thus averted from my gaze, she had lighted up the circlet that she wore round her brow, so that it blazed as if it were a crown of stars. Not only her face and her form, but the atmosphere around, were illumined by the effulgence of the diadem.

"Now," said she, "put thine arms around me for the first and last time. Nay, thus; courage, and cling firm."

As she spoke her form dilated, the vast wings expanded. Clinging to her, I was borne aloft through the terrible chasm. The starry light from her forehead shot around and before us through the darkness. Brightly, and steadfastly, and swiftly as an angel may soar heavenward with the soul it rescues from the grave, went the flight of the Gy, till I heard in the distance the hum of human voices, the sounds of human toil. We halted on the flooring of one of the galleries of the mine, and beyond, in the vista, burned the dim, rare, feeble lamps of the miners. Then I released my hold. The Gy kissed me on my forehead passionately, but as with a mother's passion, and said, as the tears gushed from her eyes, "Farewell for ever. Thou wilt not let me go into thy world— thou canst never return to mine. Ere our household shake off slumber, the rocks will have again closed over the chasm, not to be re-opened by me, nor perhaps by others, for ages yet unguessed. Think of me sometimes, and with kindness. When I reach the life that lies beyond this speck in time, I shall look round for thee. Even there, the world consigned to thyself and thy people may have rocks and gulfs which divide it from that in which I rejoin those of my race that have gone before, and I may be powerless to cleave way to regain thee as I have cloven way to lose."

Her voice ceased. I heard the swan-like sough of her wings, and saw the rays of her starry diadem receding far and farther through the gloom.[3]

I sate myself down for some time, musing sorrowfully; then I rose and took my way with slow footsteps towards the place in which I heard the sounds of men. The miners I encountered were strange to me, of another nation than my own. They turned to look at me with some surprise, but finding that I could not answer their brief questions in their own language, they returned to their work and suffered me to pass on unmolested. In fine, I regained the mouth of the mine, little troubled by other interrogatories;—save those of a friendly official to whom I was known, and luckily he was too busy to talk much with me. I took care not to return to my former lodging, but hastened that very day to quit a neighbourhood where I could not long have escaped inquiries to which I could have given no satisfactory answers. I regained in safety my own country, in which I have been long peacefully settled, and engaged in practical business, till I retired, on a competent fortune, three years ago. I have been little invited and little tempted to talk of the rovings and adventures of my youth. Somewhat disappointed, as most men are, in matters connected with household love and domestic life, I often think of the young Gy as I sit alone at night, and wonder how I could have rejected such a love, no matter what dangers attended it, or by what conditions it was restricted. Only, the more I think of a people calmly developing, in regions excluded from our sight and deemed uninhabitable by our sages, powers surpassing our most disciplined modes of force, and virtues to which our life, social and political, becomes antagonistic in proportion as our civilisation advances,—the more devoutly I pray that ages may yet elapse before there emerge into sunlight our inevitable destroyers. Being, however, frankly told by my physician that I am afflicted by a complaint which, though it gives little pain and no perceptible notice of its encroachments, may at any moment be fatal, I have thought it my duty to my fellow-men to place on record these forewarnings of The Coming Race.[4]

THE END

During his editorship of the *New Monthly Magazine* from 1832 to 1833 Bulwer-Lytton published "Asmodeus at Large," a serial combining social satire with metaphysical speculation. Asmodeus, named after the devil in Tobias 3:8, is the persona of a cynical, worldly-wise observer. Bulwer-Lytton's choice of title probably derives from Charles Sedley's 1808 novel *Asmodeus; or, The Devil in London* (described by Michael Sadleir in his *Bulwer and His Wife* as a "pastiche on contemporary manners"). Kosem Kesamim, the narrator's second guide, is an Eastern seer. In Number 4 of the serial the narrator falls into an induced sleep and awakes to find himself in an underground labyrinth.

When I woke, I found myself alone in a sort of cell formed of the most brilliant spars. A vast but continuous and steady noise, as of the march of a mighty sea, sounded in my ears—a voice of inexpressible power, depth, and intenseness. I was awed, but not startled. I rose gradually from the rude couch on which I was lying, and gazed round. Through an aperture in my cell, I caught the perspective of gigantic arches and mighty columns of some rough and gloomy substance which I did not recognize as familiar. A vague, silent alarm seized me. I rose, and cautiously quitting my cave, looked forth on the scene without. Wonderful! Far as I could see, stupendous halls, arches whose height soared aloft into dim and impenetrable show—courts opening one into the other, thousands and tens of thousands, with areas in which cities might have stood—stretched in solemn and deep solitude around me. Every where gloomed the majesty of immeasurable space: it seemed the sepulchre of some giant world. And now, as my steps involuntarily glided on, millions of rills and waterfalls broke down the dark sides of the mighty walls around me: this seemed to account for the sound that had so appalled me. There was no heaven above this vast domain. My eye penetrated far, far as the eagle might soar, but still rose the rocks and walls around me, shadow their only roof and canopy. This new world, for such it seemed to me, was lighted by strange, unsteady fires, that flashed, danced, and crept around the pillars and crags at close intervals; and these playing against the waters that rolled or glided down the steeps, gave forth a changeful, but ruby-like and universal glow.

"Is this enchantment?" said I, inly, "or is it the Dread World of Death?"

The ground beneath me was rough and uneven, and looking down I beheld large fragments of gold and silver ore. Was it possible that I was in some mighty mine as yet undiscovered by human avarice? While I asked myself this question, from a dim, sulphurous cave, at a little distance beyond, over which a dull smoke simmered, as it were, there suddenly burst forth a column of dazzling fire, and soared rapidly aloft, like some wonderful fountain of flame, higher and higher, till it illumined the whole gigantic space around; and looking up, I beheld it disappear through another dark aperture in an opposite wall. But still the cavern continued to pour forth, pile after pile of this deep, and it almost seemed, solid flame, and still pile after pile wound regularly through the aperture above, emerging and vanishing like the defiles of a demon army.

"Thus Ætna is supplied," said a voice at my side. I turned hastily, and beheld the dark figure of Kosem Kesamim, all unrelieved by the lurid glow that played on all else—dull, shadowy, and indistinct, as if seen at a distance by the uncertain twilight; yet was he within touch of my head, and the red light of unnumbered fires burnt fiercely round him.

"Fear not," said that mournful and solemn voice, "knowest thou on what spot we stand?"

"Great Enchanter, no!"

"It is a spot where fear should be unknown, though awe may wake; for here crime and war, and man's guilty deeds, have come not since eternity. This is the Centre of the Earth. Behold the womb of the round world! Is it not a goodly palace? Shrink not the petty rocks and towers that crown its surface, into mole-hills and bull-rushes, beside its stately walls and immeasurable arches? In this gigantic laboratory all the operations of Nature perform their ever-lasting course. Here, around the arch secret of our orb; here, around the magnet which makes our affinity with the stars, and holds the solid earth on its airy axis; here are the seeds and germs of all things—the elements of elements. This is the Hades of Earth —the dark Reign of Shadow—the Mystery of Mysteries—the Wheel of the Vast Machine—the Mother that bears—the Grave that con-cealeth all! Welcome, stranger! I—human, like thyself, alone with thee in these awful depths—I bid thee welcome." Thereat a cold-ness and chill penetrated into my marrow, although my heart beat with a wild exulting joy to find myself thus privileged above my race. I bowed down my head, and after a pause, in which I endeav-oured to nerve and to collect myself, I replied:—

"Dark and mysterious Shade! I know not well in what words to answer thee; for I cannot persuade myself that I do not dream. From that gay, light, wild revel of last night, how drear and solemn a transition! Something in my adventures hitherto has been hu-man and familiar. I might imagine Asmodeus of my own race, and the witches of my own flesh. These occasioned me the surprise of amusement, not the marvel of awe. I am past the growth of mind when curiosity or fear is powerful; and I have known enough of mortal friendships not to be very much alarmed at having a devil for a companion; but now my heart is at once roused and appalled. Tell me, O magician! Where are those whom I saw yesternight? Do they, too, inhabit these realms, or were they but creatures raised by thy wand—gay yet grotesque delusions, the incongruous but not terrible beings of a dream,—but thou of that dream the mystic and mighty God, moved not, relaxing not, at the fantastic mirth of the phantoms thou createdst?"

"They thou speakest of," replied Kosem Kesamim, "*are* yet pal-pable and living, as they seemed to thee; but their homes penetrate not into these stern recesses. They hold the purlieus of the temple, but their steps cross not the veil."

"And why, Enchanter, am I distinguished above them?"

"Because thou darest more. Thou wouldst cross an ocean of fire for a novelty on the other shore; and in this temper I recognize what once was my own. The key to all mysteries is the thirst to discover: the search for novelty is the invention of truth."

"But how comes it, O Kosem Kesamim, that these ladies ever arrived at the dignity of witchcraft? Some of them, I grant, silent and weird, looked fitting receptacles for such solemn gifts of the spirit; but my buxom coquette, my lively Jesthah, appears somewhat too earthly a lamp for so preternatural a light.

"Ask not these questions now," replied the sad voice, that dampened, as it spoke, my returning vivacity; "but while yet in these hoar recesses, summon thy graver powers to seize advantage of the occasions offered them."

"I am prepared," said I, in a subdued tone, "for all thou canst show me."

We moved on silently; but I found by the current of air that rushed against my face, and by the swiftness with which arch and column glided by, that some unseen power unconsciously winged my steps, and that our progress was suited to the mighty space that we traversed. And now we paused below a circular chasm in the rocks, that seemed to rise spirally and lessening upward; and from this chasm I heard a wild and loud hubbub, but no distinct sound.

"Is this the Cavern of the Winds?" said I, stunned by the mingled uproar.

"This is as the Ear of the Earth," replied the Enchanter, "and through this channel come down all the tidings of the million tribes of mankind. From the first breath in Paradise, from the first whisper of Eve's virgin love—from the first murmur of Adam's repenting soul, to the universal clamour of contending interests, crimes, and passions that now agitate the crowded world—all come mellowed and separate down, confused, indeed, to thy ear, but distinct and intelligible to that Being which the sounds are destined to reach and guide."

"And who is that Being?" said I, wonderingly.

"Look yonder!" answered Kesamim, raising his shadowy arm.

I looked in the quarter to which he pointed, and beheld, on a Throne of grey stone, gigantic, motionless—an aged Man, or rather a manlike Shape. His vast countenance was unutterably and dreadly calm. His brows, like the Olympian Jove's, overhung his majestic features; but the orbs beneath were dull and lifeless— there was no ray in them.

"Is that death?" said I, shrinking back; "if so, it is the death of a god."

"Look again," said the deep voice of the magician, and I obeyed. Then I saw that around him—so that he sat, as it were, in the midst—was a web of numberless fine and subtle threads, the ends of which disappeared among the million apertures round, pores, as it were, of the rock; and then as my eye, waxing bold, gazed more intently, I found, that with every hollow blast that descended momentarily from the upper world—his hands scarce moving, so quiet *was* the motion, touched some one or other of these meshes, and straight threads here and there snapped asunder, and the shape of the web changed, but slightly, and only in parts. Then saw I that the dullness of the eyes was not of Death, but Blindness.

"And who," said I, within my breath, "is that dread old man?"

"He," answered Kesamim, "who moves in blindness, but with method, the strings of the external world. He moves the puppets, men and kings: he snaps or weaves the meshes of life; he sends forth through those webs the electric orders to the lower delegates of the universe—the Monster King, whom you call Ocean, and the Spirit of the leaping Fires. He, so mute and worn with years, is yet the life and principle of the restless machine of earth. How far wise or gifted none know;—himself a mystery, he unravels none. And it is the dark, relentless, inscrutable office he wields, from which men, shuddering at the unseen power, have taken the dream of Destiny; and others, noting blindness amidst the power, have conceived the term of Chance. But he himself is *Nameless*."

While I was yet gazing, I felt myself hurried on. The grey old man vanished gradually from my eyes, and the descent of the sounds of earth faded on my ear as the voice of a distant waterfall. We now travelled upward; and darting through one of the intricate chasms that yawned on the side of a lofty rock, we glided on till a more cheerful light than that which had hitherto guided us, streamed down; and, making towards it, I suddenly found myself in a most beautiful city, not, indeed, vast and gloomy, like the nature-formed palaces I had just left, but a city built by human hands for human habitation. Theatres, circuses, squares, met me on every side. Yet still I noted that there was no heaven above, and that the light which illumined the place was from artificial sources; but they were rosy and cheerful lights, such as should look on the meetings of lovers, or the revelry of voluptuous gardens. And all around, the inscriptions on the walls, the shapes of the buildings, the fashion of the streets,—was unfamiliar, though evidently human. "And what, O Enchanter! What new wonder is this?"

But the Enchanter was gone, and by my side stood Asmodeus, helping his nose to a pinch of snuff.

"Your obedient servant, sir," said the Devil coolly; "having looked at the figures of the dial so long, what think you now of the clockwork?"

"Asmodeus, is that really you? What a vision have I seen! But where is the Great Enchanter?"

"Gone! He loves not these lightsome abodes. Humanity in thine inferior shape will not bear, too long at a time, the solemn marvels to which thou hast been admitted. He has, therefore, kindly conducted thee hither, for a short respite, and will reveal to thee more of the stern secrets of his wisdom anon. Meanwhile, thou art in a city which an antiquary would give his ears to visit.

Know, that above thee glows an eastern sun, and these stately buildings are not far beneath the surface of the Earth."

"And is this the work of Kesasim?"

"The work of fiddlestick!" replied Asmodeus, tartly,—"of mere vulgar mechanics, some four thousand years ago. At some short distance from the spot on which this city formerly stood, is a lofty mountain, once a volcano; but the flames have been dried these thirty centuries, and this city, in an hour of revelry and feasting, became its prey. The camels of the traveller pass over it; none (not even tradition) know what hath been. This is no vulgar Pompeii, no hacknied Herculaneum. It is a treasure known but to us and our agreeable friends the witches."

There then follows a discussion of Frances Trollope's *Domestic Manners of Americans* (1832) and English politics. Number 5 opens as follows:

I find, dear reader, that narrating my adventures to you only once a month, and sometimes not so often—I am forced to leave frequent gaps in my recital. It requires a long stride to keep up with the March of Events, and to talk to you only on those matters which are either interesting at all times, or interesting from their connection with the moment. How much then must I omit!—What scenes with my dear Witches!—What delightful hours with my beloved Jesthah!—Yes, reader, I still remain in that old buried City, with its gigantic arches, and porphyry temples, and silent fountains, and unechoing areas. Every evening is spent with the Witches, in the most agreeable rattling conversation, over the romance, the anecdote, the scandal of the past. Such stories are ripped up, that Time had stowed away in his budget, never dreaming they could again be routed forth into day—the amours of all Courts, from the Egyptian Ptolemies to the English Anne, (for no Witch had been enrolled in the free list at Cyprolis since the latter period) are detailed to me with the most refreshing earnestness! I listen, shrug my shoulders, swear the world was very bad in those days, and ask leave to teach Jesthah the last fashion in kissing. Happy hours! One man among so many ladies, though they be Witches, need be no Wizard to be a little in request. Happy hours! —I shall look back to you as a dream.—Yet you are realities, and I shall remember as much of you, as men ever remember of that past in which they once lived. I remember as much of you as a Rector does of Greek—as a Politician of the Public—as the World does of Virtue—as Virtue of the World;—yet how many silly people will say that I am deceiving them—that I never saw Jesthah—that I never talked with Kosem Kesamim—that Asmodeus exists not— and that my life, my very life, my thoughtful, bustling, various life, is but a drop of ink, created by a goose-quill, and passed on no broader superficies than a sheet of paper! Alas, what is real if the mind be not? Is that which in the dim chambers of our decaying memory lies all mouldering and unheeded, more real, more palpable, more living than the bright creatures of our fancy? No! Fancy is a life itself, and the world we create has as much of truth as the world that was created for us. The all-merciful Father blessed us with imagination as a counterpoise to the sufferings of experience.

And every day I walk forth among those ruins, and by the help of Witch-lore, decipher the language of four thousand years back, which is engraved on many a marble wall, and many an archived scroll. I here see how Wisdom has travelled from age to age—as a river that flows through our mortality—visible in its course—but in its sources undiscovered. For in these scrolls I behold the doc-trines claimed by the Greeks—their beautiful thoughts—their high and endearing dreams, all bodied forth in the more luxuriant im-agery of the East, and, indeed, they were rather simplified than en-larged by those bright purloiners, who stole from the Heaven of Fame the fire that belonged not to their race, but which so stolen never can expire.

And every morning to breakfast, previous to my adventurous rovings, comes my attentive Demon, full of the news of the upper world, laden with books and journals, reports and truths—and making me as much conversant with the little squabbles on the world's surface, as if I were, as heretofore, a partner of them!

The underground city anticipates the setting of *The Coming Race*. Here underground location is figured as a source of energy and life as well as Hades; and it also functions as a conveniently distanced point from which to comment satirically on contemporary England. The blind deity controlling destiny through a network of threads partially anticipates the impassive, sphinx-like expressions of the Vril-ya. At the beginning of Number 6, Kosem Kesamim takes the narrator back to the month of the access cavern and he rejoins life on the surface of the earth. There then follows the inset "Tale of Kosem Kesamim," which describes the latter's encounter with an emotionless priest-like figure surrounded by flames rising from the earth. He identifies himself as "The Living Principle of the World," and the seer expresses his awe with the same movements that will be repeated by the narrator of *The Coming Race*: "I bowed my face, and covered it with my hands, and my voice left me." The encounter takes place in an enormous cavern lit by naphtha lamps. The High Priest as he is called sits impassively at an altar within a rich hall whose pillars are decorated with inlaid jewels. In Number 7, as Kosem Kesamim continues with his tale, he is interrupted by a spiritual form whose appearance anticipates that of Zee in her height, starry diadem, and sphinx-like expression:

It was a female form, or rather likeness of a form, of exceeding height. The face was beautiful—but severe and fearful—and set, as it were, in a profound and death-like calm. It wore a pale, yet luminous diadem on its head, from which the locks, which were dark, parted in a regular and majestic flow. The diadem seemed wrought of light itself, impalpable and tremulous; and as the face—still and motionless in a stony repose—looked upon us, it recalled to me the images of those gigantic Sphinxes whose like-ness has outlived their worship; but yet the more did it recall to me some vague and inexpressible dreams, as of a countenance I had seen long years before, though not in my present state of existence,—a memory faint and confused, retained by the soul from the wrecks of a former being.

NOTES

INTRODUCTION, pp. xiii–liii

1   "Satiric Utopias," *The Spectator* (3 June 1871): 666.

2   Richard Stang, *The Theory of the Novel in England, 1850–1870* (New York: Columbia University Press, 1966), 153–55.

3   Quoted in Robert Lee Wolff, *Strange Stories and Other Explorations in Victorian Fiction* (Boston: Gambit Press, 1971), 216.

4   Edward Bulwer-Lytton, *Caxtoniana: A Series of Essays on Life, Literature, and Manners* (Edinburgh and London: William Blackwood, 1863), 2:148–49. In this same essay Bulwer-Lytton argues that the following is a characteristic of nineteenth-century narratives: "Instead of appending to the fable a formal moral, a moral signification runs throughout the whole fable, but so little obtrusively, that, even at the close, it is to be divined by the reader, not explained by the author" (151).

5   Malcolm Orthell Usrey, "The Letters of Sir Edward Bulwer-Lytton to the Editors of *Blackwood's Magazine*, 1840–1873, in the National Library of Scotland" (Ph.D. diss., Texas Technological College, 1963; Ann Arbor, Mich.: University Microfilms International 64–4856), 414, 413, 411.

6   Victor Alexander, second earl of Lytton, *The Life of Edward Bulwer, First Lord Lytton, by His Grandson* (London: Macmillan, 1913), 2:309.

7   T. H. S. Escott, "Bulwer's Last Three Books," *Fraser's Magazine* (June 1874): 767.

8   Darko Suvin, *Victorian Science Fiction in the UK: The Discourses of Knowledge and Power* (Boston: G. K. Hall, 1983), 344, 345, 346. Robert Lee Wolff states more baldly that the main target of the novel is the "concept of equality"; Wolff, *Strange Stories*, 324.

9   H. Bruce Franklin, ed. *Future Perfect: American Science Fiction of the Nineteenth Century* (New York: Oxford University Press, 1966), 141–50. The utopian story is "Recollections of Six Days' Journey in the Moon," published by "An Aerio-Nautical Man."

10 I. F. Clarke, introduction to *The Battle of Dorking and When William Came* (Oxford: Oxford University Press, 1997), x; C. A. Simmons, "Anglo-Saxonism, the Future, and the Franco-Prussian War," *Studies in Medievalism* 7 (1995): 139.

11 James L. Campbell Sr. "Edward Bulwer-Lytton's *The Coming Race* as a Condemnation of Advanced Ideas," *Essays in Arts and Sciences* 16 (May 1987): 55.

12 "The Coming Race," *Athenaeum* 2274 (27 May 1871): 649.

13 Fiona J. Stafford, *The Last of the Race: The Growth of a Myth from Milton to Darwin* (Oxford: Clarendon Press, 1994), 278, 281.

14 Lytton, *Life of Edward Bulwer* (London: Macmillan, 1913), 1:440; Edward Bulwer-Lytton, *England and the English* (London: George Routledge, 1874), 304.

15 Quoted in William Feaver, *The Art of John Martin* (Oxford: Clarendon Press, 1975), 232.

16 Ibid., 208.

17 William Henry Smith, "The Coming Race," *Blackwood's Magazine* 110 (1871): 49.

18 Walter E. Houghton, *The Victorian Frame of Mind, 1830–1870* (New Haven: Yale University Press, 1957), 1.

19 *England and the English*, 280, 281.

20 Charles Darwin, *On the Origin of Species*, ed. Joseph Carroll (Peterborough, Ont.: Broadview Press, 2003), 145.

21 Lytton, *Life of Edward Bulwer*, 1:465.

22 Ibid. 2:465, 466.

23 Gillian Beer, *Darwin's Plots: Evolutionary Narrative in Darwin, George Eliot, and Nineteenth-Century Fiction* (London: Routledge Kegan Paul, 1983), 143.

24 Ibid., 44.

25 F. Max Müller, "Comparative Philology" (1851), quoted in Linda Dowling, *Language and Decadence in the Victorian Fin de Siècle* (Princeton: Princeton University Press, 1986), 68. Dowling discusses the impact of Max Müller and philology generally in chapter 2 of her book.

26 In chapter 6 of *Zanoni* we are told that the sage's name derives from the Chaldean for "sun," which signals that character's promethean hunger for knowledge. Lytton here discusses etymology as a series of "mutilations" or "corruptions" of pristine ancient terms.

27 F. Max Müller, *Chips from a German Workshop*, vol. 4: *Essays Chiefly on the Science of Language* (London: Longmans, Green, 1875), 78.

28 Usrey, "The Letters of Sir Edward Bulwer-Lytton," 415.

29 Max Müller, *Chips*, 79.

30 Simmons, "Anglo-Saxonism," 137.

31 John Stuart Mill, *On Liberty, Representative Government, The Subjection of Women: Three Essays*, ed. M. G. Fawcett (London and New York: Oxford University Press, 1912), 451.

32 Darwin, *Descent of Man*, chap. 8.

33 Campbell, "Edward Bulwer-Lytton's *The Coming Race*," 59.

34 Herbert Van Thal, *Eliza Lynn Linton: The Girl of the Period* (London and Boston: Allen and Unwin, 1979), 85.

35 Suvin, *Victorian Science Fiction in the UK*, 347. Geoffrey Wagner also notes these linkages when he describes Lytton's "vision of American society as a tyranny of the majority, subsumed by feminine values in league with the machine"; Wagner, "A Forgotten Satire: Bulwer-Lytton's *The Coming Race*," *Nineteenth-Century Fiction* 19 (1964): 384–85.

36 Smith, "The Coming Race," 52.

37 Newspaper article of 1871 quoted in "Fictions of the Future," *Dublin Review* 70 (1872): 82–83. This review included discussion of John Francis Maguire's *The Next Generation*, another novel dealing with women's rights.

38 Mary E. Bradley Lane, *Mizora: A Prophecy*, ed. Jean Pfaelzer (Syracuse, N.Y.: Syracuse University Press, 2000), 45.

39 Simmons, "Anglo-Saxonism," 132. This essay is invaluable for situating *The Coming Race* historically and extends an earlier discussion in Simmons's "'Iron-Worded Proof': Victorian Identity and the Old English Language," *Studies in Medievalism* 4 (1992): 202–14. In a letter to his editor Lytton described *The Battle of Dorking* as a "marvellous piece of good writing"; Usrey, "The Letters of Sir Edward Bulwer-Lytton," 419.

40 Léon Poliakoff, *The Aryan Myth: A History of Racist and Nationalist Ideas in Europe*, trans. Edmund Howard (New York: New American Library, 1977), 50–51.

41 H. G. Wells, *A Modern Utopia* (1905), chap. 10, sect. ii.

42 Beer, *Darwin's Plots*, 115.

43 Edward Bulwer-Lytton, *The Haunted and the Haunters* (London: Simpkin, Marshall, Hamilton, Kent, 1925), 40, 41. The allusion in the second quotation is to the universal force that Baron von Reichenbach posited as running throughout nature, which he named the *Od*. This notion gained currency in Britain in the 1850s.

44 Edward Bulwer-Lytton, *Pamphlets and Sketches* (London: Routledge, 1875), 331.

45 Edward Bulwer-Lytton, *Miscellaneous Prose Works* (London: Richard Bentley, 1868), 2:212–13.

46 Marie Mulvey Roberts, *Gothic Immortals: The Fiction of the Brotherhood of the Rosy Cross* (London and New York: Routledge, 1990), 170.

47 Usrey, "The Letters of Sir Edward Bulwer-Lytton," 212.

48 Bulwer-Lytton wrote but dropped from the final version of the novel a chapter mostly in dialogue that comments at length on spiritualism, "supernatural agency" in literature, and related issues. This chapter was published for the first time by Andrew Brown: "The 'Supplementary Chapter' to Bulwer Lytton's *A Strange Story,*" *Victorian Literature and Culture* 26.i (1998): 157–82. I am grateful to Andrew Brown for his generous help in preparing the present edition.

49 Wolff, *Strange Stories,* 253.

50 Lytton, *Life of Edward Bulwer,* 2:44.

51 The 1973 reprint from the Philosophical Publishing Company contains glosses on the symbolic importance of vril and other matters important to the "Great Work," and also carries an appendix outlining the "Aeth Arcanum." The editor claims that Bulwer-Lytton was a member of the Rosicrucian Council of Three; Emerson M. Clymer, "The Vril," foreword to *The Coming Race* (Quakertown, Pa.: Philosophical Publishing Company), v.

52 Leslie Mitchell, *Bulwer Lytton: The Rise and Fall of a Victorian Man of Letters* (London and New York: Hambledon and London, 2003), 138–39.

53 Lytton, *Life of Edward Bulwer,* 2:466–67.

54 A. C. Christensen, *Edward Bulwer Lytton: The Fiction of New Regions* (Athens: University of Georgia Press, 1976), 179.

55 William C. Rubinstein, "*The Coming Race,*" in *Survey of Science Fiction Literature,* ed. Frank N. Magill (Englewood Cliffs, N.J.: Salem Press, 1979), 1:421.

56 Susan Stone-Blackburn, "Consciousness, Evolution, and Early Telepathic Tales," *Science-Fiction Studies* 20.ii (1993): 247.

57 In that respect Bulwer-Lytton's treatment of vril resembles Verne's refusal to explain electricity. The latter's enigma, Arthur Evans has argued, serves as a "kind of evocative magic wand used to solve certain narrative problems in addition to purely fictional ones"; Evans, *Jules Verne Rediscovered: Didacticism and the Scientific Novel* (Westport, Conn.: Greenwood Press, 1988), p. 71.

58 Bruce Clarke, *Energy Forms: Allegory and Science in the Era of Classic Thermodynamics* (Ann Arbor: University of Michigan Press, 2001), 50.

59 For example, "X.Y.Z.," *The Vril Staff* (London: D. Stott, 1891); and William Walker Atkinson, *Vril* (Chicago: A. C. McClurg, 1911).

60 *Vril; or, Vital Magnetism* (Escondido, Calif.: The Book Tree, 1999), 8, 15, 18. As published originally by A. C. McClurg of Chicago in 1911, the full title of this pamphlet read *Vril; or, Vital Magnetism; Being Volume Six of the Arcane Teaching or Secret Doctrine of Ancient Atlantis, Egypt, Chaldea, and Greece*. A further pamphlet, titled *Vril! Or What?*, was published in the 1930s for the Rosicrucian Fellowship Auditorium by Max Heindel.

61 Peter Hadley, *The History of Bovril Advertising* (London: Bovril Ltd., 1972), p.13; supplemented with information from the Archive Collection of Unilever Bestfoods UK. Bovril was promoted by the British War Office in a campaign that reached its ultimate ingenuity when it was claimed in the *Manchester Evening Chronicle* for 7 April 1900 that Lord Roberts's march on Kimberley and Bloemfontein inscribed the word "Bovril" on the African landscape.

62 George Griffith, *Olga Romanoff; or, The Syren of the Skies* (Westport, Conn.: Hyperion Press, 1974), 45.

63 Cf. William Q. Judge's "Kali Yuga and the Coming Race" (published in the *Path* for January 1895), available at http://www.blavatsky.net/theosophy/judge/articles/kali-yuga-coming-race.htm. Blavatsky's allusions to vril occur in *The Secret Doctrine*, vol. 1, bk. 3, chap. 10. An interviewer in the 1880s described how meeting Madame Blavatsky was like seeing an incarnation of *Zanoni* and *The Coming Race*; "More about the Theosophists: An Interview with Madame Blavatsky," *Pall Mall Gazette* (26 April 1884): 3–4.

64 Annie Besant, *Evolution and Man's Destiny* (London: Theosophical Society, 1924), 94. Besant believed that each root-race had a guiding deity or Manu whose role was to accelerate evolution: "The work of the Manu is . . . to choose out those who show in consciousness the germs of the new stage which is to evolve in the coming Race" (83).

65 Nicholas Goodrick-Clarke, *The Occult Roots of Nazism: Secret Aryan Cults and Their Influence on Nazi Ideology* (London and New York: I. B. Tauris, 1992), 19, 27. Lytton's ideas were promoted by the German astrologer Friedrich Schwickert, and in 1930 a Theosophical publication by Johannes Täufer appeared with the title *Vril: Die Kosmische Urkraft*

(*Vril: The Primal Cosmic Force*) (Berlin: Astrologischer Verlag Wilhelm Becker). Täufer's call "Deutschland, wach' auf!" closely resembles the Nazi slogan "Deutschland, erwache!" (i.e., "Germany awake!").

66 Louis Pauwels and Jacques Bergier, *The Dawn of Magic*, trans. Rollo Myers (London: Anthony Gibbs and Phillips, 1963), 147.

67 Willy Ley, "Pseudoscience in Naziland," *Astounding Science Fiction* 39.iii (May 1947): 92.

68 Goodrick-Clark, *The Occult Roots of Nazism*, 218–20. Further commentary on this subject can be found in "Rudolf Steiner and the Vril Society Myth" (from the Institute for Sociology and the History of Ideas) at http://sociologyesoscience.com/steinerschauberger.html.

69 Peter Raby, *Samuel Butler: A Biography* (London: Hogarth Press, 1991), 119.

70 George Eliot, *Impressions of Theophrastus Such* (Edinburgh and London: William Blackwood, 1879), 253–54.

71 Isaac Asimov, "The Machine and the Robot," in Asimov, *Robot Visions* (London and New York: Guild Publishing, 1990), 346–50.

72 Stephen Derry, "The Time Traveller's Utopian Books and His Reading of the Future," *Foundation* 65 (Autumn 1995): 21.

73 B. G. Knepper, "Shaw's Debt to *The Coming Race*," *Journal of Modern Literature* 1 (1971): 340, 342.

74 George Bernard Shaw, *Back to Methuselah: A Metabiological Pentateuch* (London: Constable, 1949), 142.

75 Ludvig Holberg, *Journey of Neils Klim to the World Underground*, ed. James I. McNelis Jr. (Lincoln: University of Nebraska Press, 1960), 90. Among the different editions of this novel, Bulwer-Lytton could have known the one published by Thomas North in London in 1828.

76 The claim for authorship is made by J. O. Bailey in his introduction to *Symzonia: A Voyage of Discovery* (Gainesville, Fla.: Scholars' Facsimiles and Reprints, 1965). Brian Stableford discusses this work's ambiguity of tone in "Symzonia," in *Survey of Science Fiction Literature*, ed. Frank N. Magill (Englewood Cliffs, N.J.: Salem Press, 1979), 5:2207–10.

77 Olivier Dumas, Piero Gondola della Riva, and Volker Dehs, eds. *Correspondance inédite de Jules Verne*, vol. 2: *1875–1878* (Geneva: Slatkine, 2001), 82–83. I am grateful to Arthur Evans for this reference. *Les Indes noires* has appeared in English translations with the titles *The Black Indies*, *The Child of the Cavern*, *The Underground City*, and *Black Diamonds*.

78 In a note to the second edition of the novel, Hyne states that he had been accused of plagiarizing *The Coming Race*, among other works.

79 The allusions to Rome suggest Mussolini's new Roman empire. Although O'Neill's setting resembles Lytton's, Robert Crossley has described a letter from O'Neill to Wells where he admits the latter was his true model; "Dystopian Nights," *Science-Fiction Studies* 14.i (1987): 95. Stanley A. Coblentz's *Hidden World* describes two travelers' discovering a world similar to O'Neill's at the bottom of a mineshaft. Here citizens are classified by number, the lower ranks being required to swear regular oaths of fidelity. Social conformity is ensured by the application of an "anti-thought serum."

80 William R. Bradshaw, *The Goddess of Atvatabar: Being the History of the Discovery of the Interior World and the Conquest of Atvatabar* (1891; Kila, Mont.: Kessinger, 1996),139.

81 William Alexander Taylor, *Intermere* (1901; Makelumne Hill, Calif.: Health Research, 1969), 128.

82 Wyndham's novel was published in 1936 in Odham's *Passing Show,* a weekly periodical, but was not printed in book form until 1972. Verne's *L'Invasion de la mer* (1905) was reissued in a new translation as *Invasion of the Sea* in 2001 by Wesleyan University Press.

83 Suvin, *Victorian Science Fiction in the UK,* 14, 315–25.

THE COMING RACE

DEDICATION, p. 3

Bulwer-Lytton was at one point considering dedicating the novel to Max Müller in Vril-ya as: *"No [or Vo] & Too Bodho,"* but decided that "the humour of it might be too farcical"; Malcolm Orthell Usrey, "The Letters of Sir Edward Bulwer-Lytton to the Editors of *Blackwood's Magazine,* 1840–1873, in the National Library of Scotland," Ph.D. diss., Texas Technological College, 1963. Ann Arbor, Mich.: University Microfilms International 64–4856, p. 418.

CHAPTER I, pp. 5–7

I The self-definition in the opening line partly echoes that of Mary Shelley's *The Last Man* (1826): "I am the native of a sea-surrounded nook." Bulwer-Lytton was an enthusiastic admirer of Mary Shelley's works. The narrator's evident pride in lineage demonstrates an American national contradiction identified by James L. Campbell Sr. as a desire for rank that tugs against a democratic leveling of society; "Edward Bulwer-Lytton's *The Coming Race* as a Condemnation of Advanced Ideas," *Essays in Arts and Sciences* 16 (May 1987): 57. The narrator also echoes Cain's description of himself as an outcast in Genesis 4:14. In his essays from 1862–63 Bulwer-Lytton distinguishes the American from the English national character as follows: "Our American kinsfolk[,] . . . to use their own phrase, are 'a go-ahead' population. They look at distant objects with a more sanguine and eager ken than we of the Old World are disposed to do; they do not weigh the pros and cons which ought first to be placed in the balance"; *Caxtoniana* (London: George Routledge, 1875), 164. Bulwer-Lytton commented further on America in his essay "The Disputes with America," *Quarterly Review* 99 (June 1856): 235–86.

2 Term used from the 1850s onward to denote a frame or carriage used as a vertical hoist in a mineshaft.

3 Gas lighting was introduced in London in 1807, and the provision of plentiful lighting formed part of John Martin's schemes for urban improvement (see n. 2 to chap. 15).

4 H. U. Seeber notes the accuracy of Bulwer-Lytton's allusion to miners' superstitions as described in Agricola among other writers; "Bulwer-Lytton's Underworld: *The Coming Race* (1871)," *Moreana: Bulletin Thomas More* 30 (1971): 40.

CHAPTER 3, pp. 9–11

1 "World without a sun" is a quotation from Thomas Campbell's poem "Pleasures of Hope," pt. 2, line 21. The section reads:
   "And say, without our hopes, without our fears,
   Without the home that plighted love endears,
   Without the smile from partial beauty won,
   Oh! What were man?—a world without a sun."
   In addition to the Campbell quotation, Bulwer-Lytton also glances at the paradoxical composition of place in Milton's *Samson Agonistes* where Samson is caught in darkness "amid the blaze of noon" (l. 80). Bulwer-Lytton's narrator finds himself in a double paradox where the expected darkness is reversed by artificial lighting. Campbell's poem builds up to a climactic final topic: "the predominance of a belief in a future state over the terrors attendant on dissolution" ("Analysis of Part II").

1   Lytton's debt here is to Robert Paltock's novel *The Life and Adventures of Peter Wilkins* (1751), which combines the robinsonnade genre (a castaway narrative modeled on *Robinson Crusoe*) with a hollow earth, lost race theme. The title page of the novel summarizes the narrative as describing "his shipwreck near the South Pole; his wonderful passage thro' a subterranean cavern into a kind of new world; his there meeting with a Gawry or flying woman, whose life he preserv'd, and afterwards married her; his extraordinary conveyance to the country of Glums and Gawrys, or men and women that fly. Likewise a description of this strange country, with the laws, customs, and manners of its inhabitants, and the author's remarkable transactions among them." The wings of these creatures are compared to a kind of second skin, closely folded over the body and supported by devices resembling whalebone.

2   In *The Last Days of Pompeii* (1834) the Egyptian sorcerer Arbaces dreams of being transported to an enormous cavern "in the bowels of the earth" where he confronts a giantess whose features anticipate those of the Vril-ya: "The countenance of the giantess was solemn and hushed, and beautifully serene. It was as the face of some colossal sculpture of his own ancestral sphinx. No passion—no human emotion, disturbed its brooding and unwrinkled brow: there was neither sadness, nor joy, nor memory, nor hope: it was free from all with which the human heart can sympathise" (*The Last Days of Pompeii*, bk. 5, chap. 1). This figure resembles a human form but lacks those features that would induce identification. She is the "Incarnation of the Sublime," a personification of Nature who demonstrates how the underground galleries embody different aspects of humanity's fate. Specifically she can foresee the future and the imminent destruction of Pompeii. This figure of enigma recurs in H. G. Wells's *The Time Machine* (1895), where the Time Traveller encounters a colossal carved figure apparently of white stone with the following features: "It chanced that the face was towards me; the sightless eyes seemed to watch me; there was the faint shadow of a smile on the lips" (chap. 3). In 1897 Jules Verne published *Le Sphinx des glaces* (translated into English as *An Antarctic Mystery* and *The Sphinx of the Ice*) as a continuation of Edgar Allen Poe's *Narrative of Arthur Gordon Pym* (1838), where the mystery of the Antarctic is reified in an enormous block of magnetized iron. As the sailors approach it, the sphinx induces

the reactions typical of the sublime: "The monster grew larger as we neared it, but lost none of its mythological shape. Alone on that vast plain it produced a sense of awe"; Edgar Allen Poe, *The Narrative of Arthur Gordon Pym of Nantucket*, ed. Harold Beaver (Harmondsworth, Eng.: Penguin, 1975), 309.

3 The final sentence is a set phrase used by writers such as William Godwin denoting a reaction of great distress or grief. The narrator of Mary Shelley's "Transformation" (1831) witnesses a shipwreck followed by the cries of drowning victims. He describes his reactions thus: "I had been fascinated to gaze till the end: at last I sank on my knees—I covered my face with my hands"; Betty T. Bennett and Charles E. Robinson, eds., *The Mary Shelley Reader* (New York and Oxford: Oxford University Press, 1990), 292. In *A Strange Story* the character Louis Grayle falls on his knees and covers his eyes with awe before the sage Haroun of Aleppo, who has discovered the "Principle of Animal Life" (chap. 39).

CHAPTER 5, pp. 12–20

1 Paved with small square blocks such as those used in mosaics. This is a verbal link with the huge building that H. G. Wells's Time Traveller enters. There too the floor is paved with metal blocks, the latter term being stressed in Wells's text.

2 This term signifies either a machine that imitates the actions of a living creature or a living creature viewed materially or as a machine. Apart from mechanical birds or other creatures described as far back as classical antiquity, human automata are depicted in nineteenth-century writings like E. T. A. Hoffmann's "The Sandman" (1817), which contains a mechanical dancing figure. In 1769 Baron von Kempellen invented an automaton that apparently played chess. Exhibited in the United States in the 1830s, it provoked Edgar Allen Poe's spoof "Maelzel's Chess-Player" (1836). The tradition of androids or artificial simulations of humans is often taken to include *Frankenstein*, which Bulwer-Lytton knew well, but in *The Coming Race* the automata resemble servants performing their domestic functions in silence and with idealized ease. In his reading of the novel, Darko Suvin takes them as a class metaphor, an image of domestic servants dehumanized into abstract mechanical functions. In Disraeli's *Coningsby* (1844) a princess turns the description of a genteel social gathering as having "bon-ton" against the mem-

bers by inquiring, "Have these automata indeed souls?" (bk. 4, chap. 11).

3   The modern meaning of this term as a contrivance for raising people or goods in hotels and mansions dates from the Great Exhibition of 1851. The term became current during the 1860s, sometimes occurring within scare quotes as here.

4   Sharp and piercing, like a lance.

5   Lucas Cranach (1472–1553) was a German painter of religious subjects, remembered for his famous portrait of Martin Luther. His early works were particularly brightly colored and posed his foregrounded figures against backgrounds made to seem close by discontinuities in the perspective.

6   *Peri*: "In Persian mythology a beautiful malevolent sprite of a class which caused comets, eclipses, crop failure, etc. In later myths a fairy descendant of disobedient angels doing earthly penance until readmitted into paradise. The Peri directed with a wand the way to heaven to the pure in mind"; Gertrude Jobes, *Dictionary of Mythology, Folklore and Symbols* (New York: Scarecrow Press, 1962), 1255. They occur in William Beckford's *Vathek* (1786) and in poems by the Romantics on oriental subjects. For instance, Thomas Moore's poem "Lalla Rookh" has an inset fable called "Paradise and the Peri," in which the latter nymph is described as a "child of air." This poem contains a description of a dance by two other nymphs, whom Bulwer-Lytton may have conflated with the mythical creature. In *Leila; or, The Siege of Granada* (1838) the performance of the Arab maids of Granada is compared to the Dance of the Peri "summoned to beguile the sated leisure of a youthful Solomon" (bk. 1, chap. 1). Bulwer-Lytton's composition of this and other luxurious dwellings in *The Coming Race* draws on Romantic descriptions of oriental scenes.

7   A special form of "sabbath" used in application to witches. The *OED* cites the instance of Bulwer-Lytton's *A Strange Story* (1861) where the physician narrator witnesses a grotesquely energetic dance performed by elderly characters that causes him to reflect: "I could have fancied myself at a witches' sabbat" (chap. 26). The term occurs several times in *A Strange Story*, which partly investigates the connections between ancient magic and the contemporary world.

1   An allusion to the species created in Genesis 1 over which man is given dominion.

2   Bulwer-Lytton elsewhere writes: "The American citizens, fondly colonising Futurity, proclaimed, in every crisis of popular excitement, the Monroe doctrine, that the whole continent of America—the whole fourth quarter of the globe—was the destined appendage of their Republic One and Indivisible"; *Caxtoniana* (London: George Routledge, 1875), 164–65. In 1823, when it appeared that the European powers might try to reestablish colonies in America, President James Monroe in his annual Message to Congress formulated the position that came to be known as the Monroe Doctrine, according to which the American continents should not be seen as "subjects for future colonization." This declaration of political interest in the hemisphere underlay a growing conviction about the expansionist future of America, summed up in the term "manifest destiny." "America's claim to the continent derives not from ambition but merely from the recognition of a destiny rooted in the earth, a law of nature assigning fragments of adjacent territory to the proximate power rather than the distant"; Albert K. Weinberg, *Manifest Destiny: A Study of National Expansionism in American History* (Chicago: Quadrangle Books, 1963), 61. Bulwer-Lytton's ironic allusion recognizes the importance of the U.S. arms business that was flourishing in the wake of the Civil War. This doctrine of expansionism was expressed through figures of growth without limits and through the metaphor of a national body that never aged, implying a "unique biology devoid of death" (ibid., 217). The ending of the Civil War triggered a wave of commercial speculation centered on the railways, among other concerns. In 1870 Speaker of the House James G. Blaine's support for Jay Cooke's Northern Pacific railroad was "purchased" by a generous loan, an instance virtually as blatant as the one that Lytton describes; Matthew Josephson, *The Robber Barons: The Great American Capitalists, 1861–1901* (London: Eyre and Spottiswoode, 1962), 95. American exceptionalism is turned on its head in chapter 26 when the narrator imagines the Vril-ya taking over American territory and in the act echoing a phrase ("this corner of the globe") used by Jefferson to Madison in a letter of 1789 where he contrasts American fund-raising with Old World inherited privilege.

3   Probably a contraction of "virile," though New Age commentators have also suggested "vitriol" as its origin. On 20 March 1870 Lytton explained vril to John Forster as follows: "I did not mean Vril for mesmerism, but for electricity, developed into uses as yet only dimly guessed, and including whatever there may be genuine in mesmerism, which I hold to be a mere branch current of the one great fluid pervading all nature. . . . Now, as some bodies are charged with electricity like the torpedo or electric eel, and can never communicate that power to other bodies, so I suppose the existence of a race charged with that electricity and having acquired the art to concentre and direct it—in a word, to be conductors of its lightnings. If you can suggest any other idea of carrying out that idea of a destroying race, I should be glad. Probably even the notion of Vril might be more cleared from mysticism or mesmerism by being simply defined to be electricity and conducted by those staves or rods, omitting all about mesmeric passes, etc. Perhaps too, it would be safe to omit all reference to the power of communicating with the dead"; Victor Alexander, second earl of Lytton, *The Life of Edward Bulwer, First Lord Lytton, by His Grandson* (London: Macmillan, 1913), 2:466–67. Without citing a specific work, Louis Pauwels and Jacques Bergier state: "The notion of the 'vril' is mentioned for the first time in the works of the French writer [Louis] Jacolliot." They also quote Willy Ley on the German secret society the Luminous Lodge as stating that "the disciples believed they had secret knowledge that would enable them to change their race and become equals of the men hidden in the bowels of the Earth"; *The Dawn of Magic*, trans. Rollo Myers (London: Anthony Gibbs and Phillips, 1963), p. 147. Vril is introduced into the novel as a benign therapeutic force before being identified as a weapon. Clearly it served as a synthesizing concept for Bulwer-Lytton, linking different areas of experience. This notion emerged in his writings as early as the 1840s: in *Zanoni* (1842) the Eastern sage Mejnour "professed to find a link between all intellectual beings in the existence of a certain all-pervading and invisible fluid resembling electricity, yet distinct from the known operations of that mysterious agency" (bk. 4, chap. 5). Just as vril is repeatedly related to the will in *The Coming Race*, so the physician narrator of *A Strange Story* (1862), Allen Fenwick, conducts experiments on inducing an electric current by the exercise of will. Critics have seen vril as an anticipation of nuclear power and laser weapons.

4 "Electricity developed by chemical means" (*OED*), sometimes used for its therapeutic applications; named after the experimenter Luigi Galvani. Galvanism is also named by Mary Shelley in her 1831 introduction to *Frankenstein* as the force that might reanimate a corpse or realize the possibility that the "component parts of a creature might be manufactured, brought together, and endued with vital warmth"; Betty T. Bennett and Charles E. Robinson, eds., *The Mary Shelley Reader* (New York and Oxford: Oxford University Press, 1990), 170.

5 The opening lines of Michael Faraday's 1845 paper "Action of Magnets on Light" in Faraday, *Experimental Researches in Electricity* (London: Richard Taylor and William Francis, 1855), 3:1–2. Faraday held force to be a constant in nature. In *Zanoni* the Middle Eastern scientist Mejnour locates a "link between all intellectual beings in the existence of a certain all-pervading and invisible fluid resembling electricity, yet distinct from the known operations of that mysterious agency." This extends into a principle of connectedness between mind and matter: "If the doctrine were true, all human knowledge became attainable through a medium established between the brain of the individual enquirer and all the farthest and obscurest regions in the universe of ideas" (bk. 4, chap. 5).

6 In the 1840s Faraday formulated this concept to explain the circulation of thermomagnetic currents in the earth's atmosphere. These could be measured partly as lines of force.

7 I.e., hypnotism, named after its founder, Anton Mesmer. Another term denoting hypnotism in the nineteenth century was "animal magnetism." Bulwer-Lytton had been interested in mesmerism since the 1840s and defended Dr. John Elliotson, one of its leading proponents, against hostile criticism following the latter's public lecture of 1846. Bulwer-Lytton's letter of support appeared in the *Zoist* for that year and is reproduced in Robert Lee Wolff's *Strange Stories and Other Explorations in Victorian Fiction* (Boston: Gambit Press, 1971), 237.

8 Electro-biology: "the branch of electricity which deals with the electrical phenomena of living beings" (*OED*). Dating from circa 1845, it is the name given to a form of hypnotism induced by the subject's contemplation of a bright object.

9 Baron von Reichenbach in his *Dynamics* (English translation, 1850) posited a force in all nature designated the *Od*, which manifested itself

in sensitive individuals through their fingertips and in crystals, magnets, heat, light, etc. "It has been held to explain the phenomena of mesmerism and animal magnetism" (*OED*).

10 In his essay "On the Normal Clairvoyance of the Imagination," Bulwer-Lytton gives a rather ironic account of the "wonders recorded of mesmeric clairvoyance," which involve the belief that "a person in this abnormal state can penetrate into the most secret thoughts of another —traverse, in spirit, the region of time and space"; *Miscellaneous Prose Works* (London: Richard Bentley, 1868), 3:27. Bulwer-Lytton argues that mesmeric clairvoyance constantly falls short of the claims made by its advocates and points instead to the "immeasurably more wonderful" quasi-clairvoyant faculty of a writer's imagination: "The imagination is but the faculty of glassing [*sic*] images; and it is with exceeding difficulty, and by the imperative will of the reasoning faculty resolved to mislead it, that it glasses images which have no prototype in truth and nature" (ibid., 36).

CHAPTER 9, pp. 29–37

1 The lamp-lit underground dome of Eblis is one of the most spectacular scenes in William Beckford's *Vathek* (1786).

2 In his *England and the English* (1833) Bulwer-Lytton praises John Martin's (see n. 2 to chap. 15) painting of the Deluge as the simplest and "most awful" of his works. "With an imagination that pierces from effects to the ghastly and sublime agency," Bulwer-Lytton continues, "Martin gives, in the same picture, a possible solution to the phenomenon he records, and in the gloomy and perturbed heaven you see the conjunction of the sun, the moon, and a comet!"; *England and the English* (London: George Routledge, 1874), 304, 305.

3 This college echoes, though less ludicrously, the Grand Academy of Lagado in book 3 of *Gulliver's Travels*. Bulwer-Lytton thought *Gulliver's Travels* the finest work of its age and describes it in terms directly relevant to the method of *The Coming Race*: "The satirical design of *Gulliver's Travels* is certainly not that which philanthropists would commend to the approval of youth. It seeks to mock away all by which man's original nature is refined, softened, exalted, and adorned; it directs the edge of its ridicule at the very roots of those interests and motives by which society has called cities from the quarry, and gardens from the

wild; and closes all its assaults upon the framework of civilised communities with the most ruthless libel upon man himself that ever gave the venom of Hate to the stingings of wit." Nevertheless, *Gulliver's Travels* is second only to Shakespeare "in its power of 'imagining new worlds,' [such] that, age after age, it will contribute to the adornment and improvement of the human race, by perpetual suggestions to the inventive genius by which, from age to age, the human race is adorned or improved"; *Caxtoniana* (London: George Routledge, 1875), pp. 114–15.

4 The study of insects.

5 The study of shells and shellfish.

6 The narrator's note to the text: "The animal here referred to has many points of difference from the tiger of the upper world. It is larger, and with a broader paw, and still more receding frontal. It haunts the sides of lakes and pools, and feeds principally on fishes, though it does not object to any terrestrial animal of inferior strength that comes its way. It is becoming very scarce even in the wild districts, where it is devoured by gigantic reptiles. I apprehend that it clearly belongs to the tiger species, since the parasite animalcule found its paw, like that found in the Asiatic tiger's, is a miniature image of itself." This is one of the many instances where the narrator casts himself as a well-informed naturalist.

7 The electric telegraph was devised in the 1790s and pioneered in Great Britain in the 1840s by the Great Western Railway. In 1869 the Telegraph Act nationalized the different companies and brought them under the remit of the postmaster general.

8 Belonging to the period before the Flood.

9 The combination of bird and reptile suggests a pterodactyl.

CHAPTER 10, pp. 37–42

1 *An:* contraction of Classical Greek *aner* (man). *Gy-ei:* taken from Classical Greek *gyne* (woman); plural *gynai*. Bulwer-Lytton's singular is a homophone of the American word "guy," used in the nineteenth century to designate males. The English sense of the verb "guy," meaning "to mimic," further complicates the associations of Bulwer-Lytton's term, which suggests gender crossing and imitation.

2 Having a spinal column or backbone.

3 Doubting or hesitant.

4 The phrase "pleasure to obey" usually occurs in a Christian theological context to describe the believer's willingness to obey God.

CHAPTER 11, pp. 42–43

1 "Lizard-like creature supposed to live in fire" (*OED*).

2 Robert Lewins formulated the doctrine of "hylo-idealism," which held that "reality belongs to the immediate object of belief as such: material or somatic idealism, sensuous subjectivism" (*OED*). One possible source could have been *Biology versus Theology; or, Identity of the Cosmical and Vital Forces, according to Dr. Lewins*, published in 1870 under the pseudonym "Julian."

CHAPTER 12, pp. 43–50

1 Friedrich Max Müller (1823–1900), the German-born philologist and orientalist, held the Taylorian chair in modern languages at Oxford University and in 1868 delivered the Rede Lecture at Cambridge, titled "On the Stratification of Language." This lecture attempted to consolidate what Max Müller called a "science of language" analogous to geology; hence his title. Just as fluctuations of the temperature of the earth's crust has produced variations in the variations in geological strata, so the vagaries of history have frozen languages at different phases in their development. Bulwer-Lytton's first quotation displays Max Müller's guiding principle that all languages go through evolutionary phases from juxtaposition to combination and inflection. This approach, as recent commentators have shown, privileges the status of the Aryan family of languages, producing the Teutonic group that included English and German. Indeed, Max Müller had a clear political agenda at the time of the Franco-Prussian War (i.e., at the time of the publication of *The Coming Race*) to cement a cultural alliance between Britain, Germany, and the United States. Max Müller's classifications situated Chinese as a "primitive" language frozen in the childhood of the human era, which is suggested in Bulwer-Lytton's second quotation; F. Max Müller, *Chips from a German Workshop* (London: Longmans, Green, 1875), 4:86, 79. This entire chapter draws heavily on Max Müller's writings, although Bulwer-Lytton had been interested in etymology for some considerable time. The summary of the Vril-ya language presents it as a summary of Indo-European linguistic change.

2 The narrator's note to the text: "Max Müller, 'Stratification of Language,' p. 13."

3 Type of language in which simple words are joined to form increasingly complex compounds.

4 Term applied to the American Indian languages by Max Müller in the sense of agglutinative, that is, blending different words and particles into a single word. In Max Müller's evolutionary schema this would be an early and therefore "primitive" form of language out of which the simplicity of the Vril-ya's language has emerged.

5 The term *an* is the first in a series of instances where Lytton follows the methods of philology to demonstrate word formation, which in English of course suggests the indefinite article and dialect variations of "one." Lytton's plural *ana* is a Greek prefix suggesting recurrence. *Sana* resembles some of Max Müller's Sanskrit examples, which he repeatedly used in his demonstrations, and also signifies "healthy" (fem.) in Latin. Bulwer-Lytton again and again uses a strategy of juxtaposing actual with invented instances in order to authenticate the Vril-ya language. His cross-linguistic echoes also play thematically on aspects of the Vril-ya culture relating to gender roles, spiritual as against material values, and so on.

6 Cf. French *aube* (dawn) and English "alb." *Sila* is formed from So/Si + La, the two adjacent notes in a musical scale.

7 This example of root-formation is taken almost verbatim from Max Müller. The relevant passage reads: "There is, for instance, a root nak, expressive of perishing or destruction. We have it in nak, night; Latin *nox*, Greek *nyx*, meaning originally the waning, the disappearing, the death of day. We have the same root in composition, as, for instance, giva-nak, life-destroying; and by means of suffixes Greek has formed from it *nek-ros*, a dead body, *nek-ys*, dead, and *nek-y-es*, in the plural, the departed. In Sanskrit this root is turned into a simple verb, *nas-ya-ti*, he perishes. But in order to give to it a more distinctly neuter meaning, a new verbal base is formed by composition with ya, nas-ya-ti, he goes to destruction" (*Chips*, p. 94).

8 Cf. Sanskrit *veda* (sacred knowledge). This is further documentation of the spirituality of the Vril-ya.

9 Bulwer-Lytton familiarizes the term *koom* through a comparison with the Welsh homophone *cwm* (valley), but the English term "comb" car-

ries the same meaning and sound value. *Bodh* is taken from the Sanskrit *bodhi* ("enlightenment"). *Koom-posh* makes an implicit ironic comment on the rule of the many, *posh* being glossed on an analogy with the English "bosh" ("rubbish"). However, the social connotations of the English slang "posh" give Bulwer-Lytton's term the connotation of "pseudo-elegant." B. G. Knepper argues that *koom-posh* and *glek-nas* "corre-spond to two of Plato's imperfect societies": an ironic version of mid-nineteenth-century democracy and a condition of universal strife; "Shaw's Debt to Bulwer Lytton," *Journal of Modern Literature* 1 (1971): 350–51. Knepper notes Bulwer-Lytton's allusion to Plato's famous cave image, glossed in the novel as a place of ignorance and emptiness. Socrates demonstrates the limits to human enlightenment in the following figure: "Human beings living in an underground den, which has a mouth open towards the light and reaching all along the den; here they have been from their childhood, and have their legs and necks chained so that they cannot move, and can only see before them. . . . Above and behind them a fire is blazing at a distance, and between the fire and the prisoners there is a raised way; and you will see, if you look, a low wall built along the way, like the screen which marionette players have in front of them, over which they show the puppets"; *The Republic of Plato*, trans. Benjamin Jowett (Oxford: Clarendon Press, 1888), 214. The prisoners' position means that they only see the shadows of things, which are constantly mistaken for realities.

10 The wave of executions in France directed by the Committee of Public Safety in 1793–94.

11 The first emperor of Rome, who ruled from 63 B.C. to A.D. 14.

12 Enlightenment or awakening(Sanskrit).

13 *Too* and *pah* are examples taken directly from English, the first being used in the sense of "to" or "toward," the second as an exclamation.

14 The declension of nouns follows Indo-European languages like Latin, which similarly lost a case (the locative) and, as can be seen in the history of English inflections, changes over time. The reduction of cases supports one of the main characteristics of the Vril-ya language that Bulwer-Lytton stresses, namely its economy of expression. The obsolete dual number is taken from Homeric Greek.

15 *Ya* is a Sanskrit radical, meaning "to go," which Bulwer-Lytton takes from Max Müller (*Chips*, p. 94) and weaves into his history of the Vril-

ya language so as to locate it within the Aryan languages. *Yam* is a Sanskrit termination. Bulwer-Lytton's *yami* is an altered form of *iyam* taken from Max Müller (*Chips*, p. 95).

16 Bulwer-Lytton draws here on the German prefix *zu-*, meaning "addition" or "convergence." *Zummer* is a homophone of German *Summer* (buzzer). *Zutze* partly echoes German *Suesse* ("sweet/heart"). *Zoo* of course is an English noun here masked as a transliteration and one cognate with Greek *zoon* ("creature"). The incorporation of prefixes and nouns that resemble German has a cultural symbolism in creating a pedigree for the Vril-ya language that combines aspects of English, German, Latin, Classical Greek, and Sanskrit.

17 Used by analogy with the "alpha privative" in Classical Greek where the prefix means "without." *Diva* in Latin means "divine" (fem.).

18 Key term used by Max Müller to name one of the main linguistic families, deriving ultimately from northern India. This and Semitic, Max Müller notes, "include, no doubt, the most important languages of the world." "Aryan" derives from Sanskrit *arya* ("noble") but has also been interpreted as a racial name. From Gobineau's *Essay on the Inequality of the Human Races* (1855) through to the ideologues of Nazism, the term was exploited to promote the cause of racial purity in contrast with the members of the Semitic group. For a history of the concepts clustering around this term, see Léon Poliakov, *The Aryan Myth: A History of Racist and Nationalist Ideas in Europe*, trans. Edmund Howard (London: Chatto and Windus Heinemann, 1974). "Indo-Germanic" was used as an alternative to "Aryan" and "Indo-European" in nineteenth-century discussions of philology and race, but it became increasingly criticized for being too narrow in meaning.

19 An example of a loanword that Bulwer-Lytton dramatizes as a "theft." A "tur" is a kind of wild goat found in parts of Russia, possibly connected with the adjective "Turanian," which Max Müller promoted vigorously. This denoted the Ural-Altaic group of languages, then became used to describe a language that was neither Indo-European nor Semitic, extended further in the 1860s (particularly by Max Müller) to mean the speakers of these languages, that is, as an ethnic indicator. By the end of the nineteenth century, "Turanian" had become a synonym for "barbaric" or "wild."

1 Term signifying the passage of the soul of a person or animal into a new body after death; promoted through the Pythagorean cult. In 1874 Mortimer Collins published a novel called *Metempsychosis,* which concerns a series of incarnations of the narrator after his death.

2 Belief in God as the designer or first mover of the universe.

3 A less common term than "perfection," but it was used particularly in relation to religion.

4 In 1859 the American naturalist Louis Agassiz (1807–73) published *An Essay on Classification,* in which he discussed the interrelation, metamorphosis, and succession of species. A central part of his discussion argues that any evidence of thought in nature is "direct proof of the existence of a thinking God." The quoted passage does indeed come from the opening of section 17 ("The Relation of Individuals to One Another") but omits a substantial passage after "reflective mind," where Agassiz considers the notion that "physical agents" might produce species. It is an untenable proposition, he argues, because it cannot explain how new species come into existence or begin to decompose. "The relations upon which the maintenance of species is based," he insists, "have really nothing to do with external conditions of existence; they indicate only relations of individuals to individuals, beyond their connexions with the material world in which they live." While these relations undoubtedly have an organic dimension, Agassiz adds that there are signs of a "psychological character" that closes up the gap between animals and humanity. Of animals he states: "The range of their passions is even as extensive as that of the human mind. . . . The gradations of the moral faculties among the higher animals and man are moreover so imperceptible, that, to deny to the first a certain sense of responsibility and consciousness, would certainly be an exaggeration of the differences which distinguish animals and men. There exists, besides, as much individuality, within their respective capabilities, among animals, as among men"; Louis Agassiz, *An Essay on Classification* (London: Longmans and Co., 1859), 96–97. In the rest of the passage, there then follows Agassiz's conclusion about an "immaterial principle."

CHAPTER 15, pp. 55–63

1 Of or relating to frogs.

2 John Martin (1789–1854) was a printmaker and painter famous for his series of illustrations to the Bible and to *Paradise Lost*. Bulwer-Lytton was a fervent admirer of his works, and the two men became friends. In 1849 Martin wrote to Bulwer-Lytton to express his appreciation of the latter's responses to his work: "There are few capable of justly appreciating the *sentiment* in imaginative pictures, the judgement of the less refined critics being limited to the material detail, whilst the higher spiritual aim is entirely overlooked"; quoted in William Feaver, *The Art of John Martin* (Oxford: Clarendon Press, 1975), 232. Bulwer-Lytton's allusion to "massiveness and solidity" could refer to such works by Martin as the *Fall of Nineveh*, *Fall of Babylon*, or *Pandemonium*. In *England and the English* (1833) Bulwer-Lytton describes Martin as the "greatest, the most lofty, the most permanent, the most original genius of his age." He praises him for the scale of his works: "Vastness is his sphere. . . . Alone and guideless, he has penetrated the remotest caverns of the past, and gazed on the primeval shapes of the gone world"; *England and the English* (London: George Routledge, 1874), 304.

3 The narrator's note to the text: "I once tried the effect of the vril bath. It was very similar in its invigorating powers to that of the baths at Gastein, the virtues of which are ascribed by many physicians to electricity; but though similar, the effect of the vril bath was more lasting." Gastein or Bad-Gastein was a fashionable spa town near Salzburg. Toward the end of the nineteenth century, it was discovered that the hot springs contained radium, to which their healing properties were attributed. After following a water treatment at Malvern, Bulwer-Lytton visited Gastein in 1847 and wrote to the actor William Macready, "I have had something like the real feeling of health here"; Victor Alexander, second earl of Lytton, *The Life of Edward Bulwer, First Lord Lytton, by His Grandson* (London: Macmillan, 1913), 2:96.

4 Sir Charles Lyell (1797–1875) established the notion of the evolutionary sequence of species in his *Principles of Geology* (1830–33), where he argues that the extension of species threatened and eventually wiped out other species. His *Elements of Geology* (1838) further elaborates on the layered history of land areas over many thousands of years. In *The Geological Evidence of the Antiquity of Man* (1863), he summarizes the succession of

ages from stone through bronze to iron, the names taken from the materials that were used for implements. In chapter 5 he summarizes Thomas Huxley's comments on the ancient skulls discovered at Engis and the Neanderthal, which the latter described as dolichocephalic (see below), situating them between the skull dimensions of chimpanzees and humans. He pronounced them the "most brutal of all known human skulls." Lyell's *Elements of Geology* (1838) was a classic nineteenth-century study of the stratification of minerals and fossils. This work offered Max Müller a metaphor for his Rede Lecture (see n. 1 to chap. 12) where he refers to Lyell's study. "Brachycephalic" literally means "short-headed"; it is a term from craniology, the study of the shape of the skull as revealing faculties. Skulls were measured against a "cranial index" and classified as either brachycephalic ("short-headed"), if their breadth was at least four-fifths of their length, or dolichocephalic ("long-headed"), if their breadth was less than four-fifths of their length. Briefly Bulwer-Lytton dons the persona of a Victorian naturalist like T. H. Huxley, who pioneered the study of skulls to reveal racial characteristics.

5   Phrenology was a system that attempted to relate the shape of the cranium to character and has been described as one of the "classificatory" sciences of the Victorian age. See David de Giustino, *Conquest of Mind: Phrenology and Victorian Social Thought* (London: Croom Helm, 1975), 35. The science was pioneered on the Continent by Johann Spurzheim and Franz Josef Gall and was promoted in Britain particularly from the 1830s onward. Phrenology involved a kind of cranial mapping where different areas ("organs" in the jargon) were related to behavior traits. Thus "amativeness" (i.e., sexual energy) was located at the rear base of the skull and "adhesiveness" (the "propensity" to form friendships) to the left of center at the rear of the skull. Phrenology became routinely adapted to character descriptions in much nineteenth-century fiction, being used by Edgar Allen Poe, for example, who earlier had reviewed Bulwer-Lytton's *Rienzi* (1835). It was used by Bulwer-Lytton himself in his description of the Egyptian priest in *The Last Days of Pompeii* (1834), whose "shaven skull was so low and narrow in the front as nearly to approach to the conformation of that of an African savage, save only towards the temples, where, in that organ styled acquisitiveness by the pupils of a science modern in name, but best practically known (as their sculpture teaches us) amongst the ancients, two huge and almost pre-

ternatural protuberances yet more distorted the unshapely head" (*Last Days*, Knebworth Edition, p. 47). Phrenology is briefly discussed in *A Strange Story*, where its premises are said to have been exploded in Sir W. Hamilton's *Lecture on Metaphysics* (1859). Bulwer-Lytton had witnessed the taking of a phrenological cast. In the account of the Vril-ya he borrows the categories of phrenology, among which the organs of weight, number, tune, and so on, are located in arches immediately over the eyes. These are the organs of perception, while the moral faculties are exceptionally developed. In his *System of Phrenology* the Scottish pioneer George Combe explains the latter as follows: "It is the faculty of Conscientiousness . . . which produces the feeling of natural right on the part of one to demand, and of natural obligation on another to perform." And of benevolence he writes: "The faculty produces desire of the happiness of others, and delight in the diffusion of enjoyment. It disposes to active goodness and, in cases of distress, to compassion"; George Combe, *A System of Craniology*, 5th ed. (Edinburgh: Maclachlan Stewart, 1843), 1:419, 384. Bulwer-Lytton carefully modifies the point about destructiveness by a parenthesis similar to Combe's explanation that the faculty involves the "removal of objects that annoy us." In fact Combe had difficulties with putting a positive gloss on this faculty, which was well developed "in the heads of cool and deliberate murderers" (1:261), eventually arguing that it was really a sign of activity: "The real effect of Destructiveness appears to me to be to communicate ability to act with energy in certain situations," adding that it can prompt the "conception of images of terror, which become sublime or horrible," citing Byron's poem "Darkness" as a clear example (1:266). If one decodes the phrenological jargon, the Vril-ya emerge as perceptive, high minded, practically intelligent, and irresistible. The features of individuals in their smooth skin, domed foreheads, and lack of expression closely resemble those of the phrenological busts that were popular throughout the nineteenth century.

6   Producing many offspring. In the context of phrenology it also meant "loving offspring."

7   Zee's explanation of the history of civilization is pure social Darwinism. In chapter 3 of *The Origin of Species* (1859), "Struggle for Existence," Darwin presents his famous account of a natural state of war existing between different members of the same species. In the following chap-

ter he explains the process of "survival of the fittest" by drawing an analogy with different human groups within the same country competing for living space. Zee adopts the twin premises of life as a struggle and the survival of the fittest to justify the Vril-ya's subjection or conquest of other groups as a racial and evolutionary inevitability. Her conviction that the Vril-ya are "destined to return to the upper world, and supplant all the inferior races now existing therein" not only predicts the demise of the narrator's society; it was also adopted with enthusiasm by the German mystical organizations incorporated into the Nazi movement. In chapter 16 Aph-Lin's explanation of how the Ana (Bulwer-Lytton's equivalent at once to civilized beings and the Aryan race) gradually lost their body hair presents a Darwinian form of species variation, but one brought about by the exercise of the collective will.

CHAPTER 16, pp. 64–73

1 The vril staff is a version of the magician's wand. In *A Strange Story* the narrator Fenwick takes possession of a similar object of Middle Eastern origin, which is used to induce a trance by either pointing at or touching another. The "wand" (Bulwer-Lytton's term) is, like the vril staff, hollow, but with a fine wire running through it. In both novels the wand is carried within a conventional walking stick. In *A Strange Story* the wand carries hieroglyphics that cannot be deciphered and is described as an ancient implement similar to those described in the Bible or used for rhabdomancy (divination by staff). Fenwick speculates on the "vital power" contained in the wand, comparing it to the "odic" force. With it in his grasp he feels he is losing his uncertainties and becoming the very personification of "Intellectual Man." The repeated comparisons with electricity anticipate Bulwer-Lytton's descriptions of vril, as does Fenwick's speculation about the force contained in the wand: "What if this rod be charged with some occult fluid, that runs through all creation, and can be so disciplined as to establish communication wherever life and thought can reach to beings that live and think?" (*A Strange Story*, chap. 61). The wand in the earlier novel induces trances similar to those described in *The Coming Race* when the narrator is learning about the culture of the Vril-ya. The self-evident phallic symbolism of the staff suggests that the narrator's helplessness before its effects amounts to a form of emasculation.

2 "One skilled in the construction of machinery" (*OED*).

3 Joseph and Etienne Montgolfier were pioneer balloonists who demonstrated the first flight of a hot-air balloon in 1783. R. M. Ballantyne's novel of balloon voyages, *Up in the Clouds,* was published in 1869.

4 Sinews or muscles.

5 The Royal Society of London for the Improvement of Natural Knowledge was founded in 1660. Its presidents included Isaac Newton, and it was satirized in *Gulliver's Travels.*

6 A hot, dry, dusty wind encountered in the Arabian desert.

7 Tiziano Vecelli, a Renaissance Italian painter famous for religious and mythological subjects as well as for his portraits.

8 A holy wise man like the Buddha. The term is from the Sanskrit *budh* ("to know").

9 In mythology the Greek hero who stole fire from the gods.

10 Bulwer-Lytton clearly uses the frog as a substitute for the ape that figured prominently in Victorian discussions of evolution. Writing to his editor at Blackwood's, probably in 1872, to comment on the activities of the French "Communalists," Bulwer-Lytton expressed his fear of the chaos that might result from the breakup of established government and commented sardonically: "The sooner the Coming race derived from frogs demolishes the present race derived from monkeys the better"; Malcolm Orthell Usrey, "The Letters of Sir Edward Bulwer-Lytton to the Editors of *Blackwood's Magazine,* 1840–1873, in the National Library of Scotland" (Ph.D. diss., Texas Technological College, 1963; Ann Arbor, Mich.: University Microfilms International 64–4856) 514.

11 By the nineteenth century this word (of unknown origin) had been established as a slang term for the female genitals. Bulwer-Lytton is either producing a howler or making a tortuous cross-gender pun about human birth and evolution. The first seems more likely.

12 Wrangling literally means "disputatious," but Bulwer-Lytton may also have had in mind the honorary intellectual title. A "wrangler" was one awarded a first class in the Cambridge Mathematical Tripos.

13 One reviewer compared the following account of social conflict with the stages of political decay described in book 8 of Plato's *Republic*; T. H. S. Escott, "Bulwer's Last Three Books" *Fraser's Magazine* (June 1874): 769.

CHAPTER 17, pp. 73–84

1   The narrator's note to the text: "For the sake of convenience, I adopt the words hours, days, years, &c., in any general reference to the subdivisions of time among the Vril-ya—those terms but loosely corresponding, however, with such subdivisions."

2   A conflation of early pastoral and the ancient belief in the Fortunate Isles or Isles of the Blest, where the souls of the favored lived in a state of paradise.

3   Louis XV reigned as king of France from 1723 to 1774.

4   Charles II ruled as king of England from 1660 to 1685.

5   The narrator's note to the text: "This may remind the student of Nero's invention of a musical machine, by which water was made to perform the part of an orchestra, and on which he was employed when the conspiracy against him broke out." The device referred to is the hydraulis or water-organ, invented by Ktesibius of Alexandria in the third century B.C. Water was used to control the pressure of the different pipes. The Roman emperor Nero was reported to have performed on this instrument; he survived a conspiracy in A.D. 65.

CHAPTER 18, pp. 84–91

1   The Koom-Posh are a parody of democracy, their name suggesting cwm, that is, "valley" and therefore "hollow"; the "hollow/would-be posh." The Glek-Nas represent Bulwer-Lytton's equivalent to Swift's Yahoos, brutalized beings existing in a state of violent predation, in "Nature, red in tooth and claw" (Tennyson, *In Memoriam* [1850] lyric 56, line 15).

2   An allusion to Lewis Carroll's comic question-and-answer poem "You are old, Father William" in *Alice in Wonderland*, where the old man perversely refuses to behave according to his age:

> "You are old, Father William," the young man said,
> "And your hair has become very white;
> And yet you incessantly stand on your head—
> Do you think, at your age, it is right?"

Carroll's poem was itself a parody of Robert Southey's "The Old Man's Comforts."

3   A further allusion to *Alice in Wonderland;* see the preceding note.

4   Bulwer-Lytton's enormous reptile resembles in name the Kraken, a

mythical Norwegian sea monster described in Tennyson's poem "The Kraken" (1830), which in turn inspired John Wyndham's novel *The Kraken Wakes* (1953).

5 The narrator's note to the text: "The reptile in this instinct does but resemble our wild birds and animals, which will not come in reach of a man armed with a gun. When the electric wires were first put up, partridges struck against them in their flight, and fell down wounded. No younger generations of partridges meet with a similar accident."

6 Bulwer-Lytton composes this embodiment of ultimate predation from different sources; the gradual emergence of the monster from the deeps, for instance, recalls *Revelation* 13:1. The scaled skin of the creature suggests a form of dinosaur, implying that the narrator has penetrated geological time, while the details of its yellow skin and dull eyes echo the features of Frankenstein's creation.

CHAPTER 19, pp. 91–93

1 Plato's republic is governed by an elite group of Guardians chosen for their "natural gifts"; specially educated, they are trained to serve as magistrates and soldiers. In his *Arcadia* (1590; augmented, 1593), Sir Philip Sidney (1554–86) describes the country retreat of the prince Basileus, where courtly behavior is played out. Sidney's pastoralism probably informs the lush and idealized description of Aph-Lin's country seat in chapter 23.

CHAPTER 22, pp. 100–105

1 The young man's interest in the narrator's watch echoes that of the emperor of Lilliput in Gulliver's chronometer.

2 Grass-eating, as distinct from "carnivorous," flesh-eating.

3 The narrator's note to the text: "I never had observed it; and, if I had, am not physiologist enough to have distinguished the difference."

CHAPTER 24, pp. 113–15

1 The casket device described is a form of crematorium; a *patera* in Roman antiquity was a shallow dish used for libations at sacrifices. The introduction of this detail enables Bulwer-Lytton to describe what is in effect a religious ceremony. Cremation was illegal in England at the time that Bulwer-Lytton was writing. It was an issue extensively debated

during the 1870s, and the first working crematorium was built at Woking in Surrey in 1879.

CHAPTER 25, pp. 115–30

1 A transparent version of "un-manly."

2 The narrator's note to the text: "Literally 'has said, in this house be it requested.' Words synonymous with law, as implying forcible obligation, are avoided by this singular people. Even had it been decreed by the Tur that his College of Sages should dissect me, the decree would have run blandly thus,—'Be it requested that, for the good of the community, the carnivorous Tish be requested to submit himself to dissection.'" In this respect the Tur resembles the emperor of Lilliput, who decrees savage punishment but declares that his decrees are evidence of his "lenity and tenderness."

3 A possible allusion to Tennyson's poem *The Princess* (1847), which describes an imperious and, by implication for Tennyson, unfeminine princess who ultimately gives up all power to serve her lover as his wife. Bulwer-Lytton's Gy characters simultaneously and paradoxically combine a similar strength of will with a submissiveness to their male partners. In chapter 26 Bulwer-Lytton's narrator reflects ironically on the "rights of women," repeating the catchphrase taken from Mary Wollstonecraft's *A Vindication of the Rights of Women* (1792). One reviewer of *The Coming Race* commented that its depiction of the relations between the sexes was its most topical element, but he remarked on the fact that Lytton's female characters were stronger yet more obedient: "We presume all this is burlesque"; William Henry Smith, "The Coming Race," *Blackwood's Magazine* 110 (1871): 52. The debate over women's rights was addressed in William Francis Maguire's *The Next Generation* (1871), which was covered with *The Coming Race* by a number of reviewers, one of whom noted the alarming speed with which American women were "invading" all those areas of social activity that were previously the domain of men, including sports (newspaper article of 1871 quoted in the anonymous "Fictions of the Future," *Dublin Review* 70 [1872]: 82–83).

4 A gun loaded through the back part of the weapon, not its muzzle.

5 Between 1800 and 1824 Robert Owen (1771–1858) managed a model factory devoted mainly to cotton weaving in New Lanark, Scotland.

Owen was a fervent social reformer and used New Lanark as the prototype of "Villages of Unity and Mutual Co-operation," which were to
be self-managed communities of a limited size. Although the commercial imperative lay behind this scheme, in his book of essays, *A New
View of Society* (1813), Owen made it clear that he saw such communities as experiments in social planning, particularly in redirecting the
influence of circumstances on individuals, which would reshape the
character of a community's inmates and ultimately usher in a millenarian change in society. Cooperative Owenite communities were founded
in the United States as well as in Britain. Bulwer-Lytton visited Owen's
model schools in 1824. Although the reference here is negative, suggesting that such communities are petty dictatorships ruled over by despotic managers, Bulwer-Lytton had earlier found a positive side to Owen's
experiments: "There is this germ of truth in the Owenite principle of
co-operation: Co-operation is power; in proportion as people combine,
they know their strength; civilization itself is but the effect of combining"; *England and the English* (London: George Routledge, 1874), 100.

6   A popular phrase originating in Christopher North [John Wilson],
     Noctes Ambrosianae no. 20 (April 1829): "His Majesty's dominions, on
     which the sun never sets," transposed from the British to a future
     American Empire.

7   In imperialistic terms the narrator indulges the same fantasy of power
     as Victor Frankenstein, who dreams of a similarly godlike role: "a new
     species would bless me as its creator" (*Frankenstein*, chap. 4). The term
     is also used in *Paradise Lost* to denote the highest ranks of the fallen an-
     gels. Bulwer-Lytton described the portrait of Byron given in Lady Caro-
     line Lamb's novel *Glenarvon* as "half demon, and yet demigod"; Victor
     Alexander, second earl of Lytton, *The Life of Edward Bulwer, First Lord
     Lytton, by His Grandson* (London: Macmillan, 1913), 1:120.

8   A phrase applied to the earth in relation to the heavens, and more fre-
     quently to the regions perceived as lying beneath the surface of the
     earth, and thus Hell. In the nineteenth century the phrase was applied
     by Lyell to lower geological layers of the earth's surface, and in 1889 it
     was adopted by George Gissing as the title for his novel about the Lon-
     don poor.

9   In her 1831 introduction to *Frankenstein* Mary Shelley describes her pro-
     tagonist as the "pale student of unhallowed arts." Frankenstein himself

records himself dabbling "among the unhallowed damps of the grave" (chap. 4), where once again the term suggests areas of knowledge beyond divine sanction and therefore, in a sense, unnatural.

10 The phrase partly echoes George Eliot's *Scenes from Clerical Life* (1857): "In every parting there is an image of death" ("Amos Barton," chap. 10).

11 Mephitic, that is, noxious, gases were associated with mines and volcanoes, and were also a standard feature in descriptions of Hell.

CHAPTER 26, pp. 130–36

1 The short title of Mary Wollstonecraft's *A Vindication of the Rights of Women* (1792). This cause was taken up by John Stuart Mill in his pamphlet *The Subjection of Women* (1869). The 1860s saw vigorous campaigns for married women's property rights and full female suffrage.

2 Specialists versed in human law. The more common term would be "jurists."

3 Carthaginian general who invaded Italy from Spain in the Second Punic War.

4 George Washington (1732–99), commander-in-chief of the American army in the revolution and the first president of the United States.

5 Andrew Jackson (1767–1845), the seventh president of the United, who defeated the British in the War of 1812.

6 Philip Henry Sheridan (1831–88), leading officer in the Union army during the American Civil War

7 Famous Athenian orator of the fourth century B.C.

8 Daniel Webster (1782–1852), American statesman who pursued the cause of national unity and who attempted to find a compromise between the northern and southern states in the 1850s.

9 Charles Sumner (1811–74), American statesman promoting the cause of the abolition of slavery.

10 Oliver Wendell Holmes Sr. (1809–94), American physician and man of letters, famous for his "Breakfast-Table" essay collections from the 1850s to the 1870s.

11 Probably Samuel Butler (1612–80), British poet famous for his satire of Puritanism in *Hudibras*.

12 French comic dramatist of the seventeenth century famous for *The Miser, The Hypochondriac,* and other works.

13 Author of the antislavery novel *Uncle Tom's Cabin* (1852), an ardent cam-

paigner for abolition. In the 1860s Stowe wrote on domestic subjects and was coauthor of *The American Woman's Home* (1869).

14 Living on the surface of the earth.

CHAPTER 27, pp. 136–38

1 Self-respect (French).

CHAPTER 28, pp. 138–41

1 The narrator's despair relates to the presentation of the underground world as a kind of hell. Over the portal of Dante's Inferno is inscribed "Abandon hope all ye who enter."

CHAPTER 29, pp. 141–44

1 Zee acts as the narrator's savior and here echoes promises of salvation made in the Bible, as in Ezekiel 36:29.

2 Clothes.

3 H. U. Seeber notes that the narrator's rescue is heavily loaded with symbolism: "The flight is a resurrection from Utopia to the world as we know it"; "Bulwer-Lytton's Underworld: *The Coming Race* (1871)," *Moreana: Bulletin Thomas More* 30 (1971): 40. The starry diadem worn by Zee echoes an image of royalty used by Lovelace, Marlowe, and other writers; it also resembles a halo and has even broader connotations since in other works Bulwer-Lytton uses the epithet "starry" to denote the influence of the stars. The spiritual suggestions of this image contrast with the ironic reference to the national emblem of the Stars and Stripes in chapter 26. The figure of ascent occurs in Bulwer-Lytton's dialogue poem "The Mind and the Body," published in *Blackwood's Edinburgh Magazine* 95 (Jan.–June 1864): 43–48. On the death of the Body, Mind, "like a young bird," hovers over the corpse's obsequies and then soars upward to the "gates which Mind enters as Soul" (47–48).

4 The sense of Bulwer-Lytton's title is anticipated in an essay of the 1860s called "Motive Power," where he describes a young man who is a prodigy of learning in the "Positive Sciences," an athlete, and the possessor of a critical intellect. Observers declared: "See the Coming Man!"; *Caxtoniana: A Series of Essays on Life, Literature, and Manners* (Edinburgh and London: William Blackwood, 1863), 9.

BIBLIOGRAPHY

The bibliography is divided into the following sections:
Works of Edward Bulwer-Lytton
    Novels and Stories
    Poetry
    Plays
    Prose Works and Translations
    Collected Editions
    Letters
    Editions of *The Coming Race*
Secondary Sources on Edward Bulwer-Lytton and His Works
Hollow Earth and Underground Worlds Writing

Works of Edward Bulwer-Lytton

For full details of works published in Bulwer-Lytton's lifetime, see Andrew Brown's entry in *The Cambridge Bibliography of English Literature*, 3rd ed., vol. 4.

NOVELS AND STORIES

Falkland. London: Henry Colburn, 1827 (anon.).

Pelham; or, The Adventures of a Gentleman. London: Henry Colburn, 1828 (anon.).

The Disowned. London: Henry Colburn, 1828.

Devereux: A Tale. London: Henry Colburn, 1829.

Paul Clifford. London: Henry Colburn and Richard Bentley, 1830.

Eugene Aram: A Tale. London: Henry Colburn, 1832.

Godolphin: A Novel. London: Richard Bentley, 1833 (anon.).

The Pilgrims of the Rhine. London: Saunders and Otley, 1834.

The Last Days of Pompeii. . London: Richard Bentley, 1834.

Rienzi, the Last of the Tribunes. London: Saunders and Otley, 1835.

Ernest Maltravers. London: Saunders and Otley, 1837.

Alice; or, The Mysteries. London: Saunders and Otley, 1838.

Leila; or, The Siege of Granada and Calderon the Courtier. London: Longman, Orme, Brown, Green, and Longmans for Charles Heath, 1838.

Night and Morning. London: Saunders and Otley, 1841.

Zanoni. London: Saunders and Otley, 1842.

Eva: A True Story of Light and Darkness; The Ill-Omened Marriage, and Other Tales and Poems. London: Saunders and Otley, 1842.

The Last of the Barons. London: Saunders and Otley, 1843.

Lucretia; or, The Children of Night. London: Saunders and Otley, 1846.

Harold, the Last of the Saxon Kings. London: Richard Bentley, 1848.

The Caxtons: A Family Picture. Edinburgh and London: William Blackwood, 1849. Serialized in *Blackwood's Magazine,* April 1848 to October 1849.

"My Novel" by Pisistratus Caxton; or, Varieties in English Life. Edinburgh and London: William Blackwood, 1853. Serialized in *Blackwood's Magazine,* September 1850 to January 1853.

The Haunted and the Haunters; or, The House and the Brain. Glasgow and London: Gowan's International Library, 1905. Printed in *Blackwood's Magazine,* August 1859.

What Will He Do with It? by Pisistratus Caxton. Edinburgh and London: William Blackwood, 1858. Serialized in *Blackwood's Magazine,* June 1857 to January 1859.

A Strange Story. London: Sampson and Low, 1862. Serialized in *All the Year Round,* 10 August 1861 to 8 March 1862.

The Coming Race. Edinburgh and London: William Blackwood, 1871 (anon.).

The Parisians. Edinburgh and London: William Blackwood, 1873. Serialized in *Blackwood's Magazine,* October 1872 to January 1874.

Kenelm Chillingly: His Adventures and Opinions. Edinburgh and London: William Blackwood, 1873.

Pausanias the Spartan: An Unfinished Historical Romance. Ed. E. R. B. Lytton, Earl of Lytton. London: George Routledge, 1876.

POETRY

Ismael: An Oriental Tale, with Other Poems. London: J. Hatchard, 1820.

Delmour; or, The Tale of a Sylphid, and Other Poems. London: Carpenter and Son, 1823 (anon.).

Weeds and Wildflowers. Privately printed in Paris, 1826.

O'Neill; or, The Rebel. London: Henry Colburn, 1827 (anon.).

The Siamese Twins: A Satirical Tale of the Times, with Other Poems. London: Henry Colburn, 1831.

Eva: A True Story of Light and Darkness; The Ill-Omened Marriage, and Other Tales and Poems. London: Saunders and Otley, 1842.

The Crisis: A Satire of the Day. London: John Ollivier, 1845.

The New Timon: A Romance of London. London: Henry Colburn, 1846 (anon.).

King Arthur. London: Henry Colburn, 1848.

St. Stephens: A Poem. Edinburgh and London: William Blackwood, 1860 (anon.).

The Boatman, by Pisistratus Caxton. Edinburgh and London: William Blackwood, 1864.

Poems, Collected and Revised. London: John Murray, 1865.

The Lost Tales of Miletus. Edinburgh and London: William Blackwood, 1866.

PLAYS

The Duchess de la Valiere. London: Saunders and Otley, 1836.

The Lady of Lyons; or, Love and Pride. London: Saunders and Otley, 1838.

Richelieu; or, The Conspiracy. London: Saunders and Otley, 1839.

The Sea Captain; or, The Birthright. London: Saunders and Otley, 1839.

Money. London: Saunders and Otley, 1840.

Not So Bad as We Seem; or, Many Sides to a Character. London: Chapman and Hall, 1851.

Collected Dramatic Works. London: George Routledge, 1860.

The Rightful Heir. London: John Murray, 1868.

Walpole; or, Every Man Has His Price. Edinburgh and London: William Blackwood, 1869.

Darnley. London: George Routledge, 1882.

PROSE WORKS AND TRANSLATIONS

England and the English. London: Richard Bentley, 1833.

Asmodeus at Large. London: Henry Colburn, 1833 (anon.).

A Letter to a Late Cabinet Minister on the Present Crisis. London: Richard Bentley, 1834.

The Student: A Series of Papers. London: Saunders and Otley, 1835.

Athens, Its Rise and Fall, with Views of the Literature, Philosophy, and Social Life of the Athenian People. London: Saunders and Otley, 1837.

The Poems and Ballads of Schiller, Translated, with a Brief Sketch of Schiller's Life. Edinburgh and London: William Blackwood, 1844.

Confessions and Observations of a Water-Patient. Leipzig: Tauchnitz, 1845.

A Word to the Public. London: Saunders and Otley, 1847.

Letters to John Bull, Esq., on Affairs Connected with His Landed Property and the Persons Who Live Thereon. London: Chapman and Hall, 1851.

Caxtoniana: A Series of Essays on Life, Literature, and Manners. Edinburgh and London: William Blackwood, 1863.

Miscellaneous Prose Works. London: Richard Bentley, 1868.

The Odes and Epodes of Horace. Edinburgh and London: William Blackwood, 1869.

COLLECTED EDITIONS

Library Edition. 40 vols. Edinburgh and London: William Blackwood, 1859–74.

Knebworth Edition. 37 vols. London: George Routledge, 1873–77.

New Library Edition. 40 vols. Boston: Estes and Lauriat, 1892–93.

New Knebworth Edition. 29 vols. London: George Routledge, 1895–98.

LETTERS

Devey, Louisa, ed. *The Letters of the Late Edward Bulwer, Lord Lytton, to His Wife*. London: W. Swan Sonnenschein, 1884.

Matthews, James Brander, ed. *Letters of Bulwer-Lytton to Macready, 1836–1866*. Newark, N.J.: Carteret Brook Club, 1911.

Shattuck, Charles H., ed. *Bulwer and Macready: A Chronicle of Early Victorian Theatre*. Urbana: University of Illinois Press, 1958.

Usrey, Malcolm Orthell, ed. "The Letters of Sir Edward Bulwer-Lytton to the Editors of *Blackwood's Magazine*, 1840–1873, in the National Library of Scotland." Ph.D. Diss., Texas Technological College, 1963. Ann Arbor, Mich.: University Microfilms International 64-4856.

Wolff, Robert Lee. "Devoted Disciple: The Letters of Mary Elizabeth Braddon to Sir Edward Bulwer-Lytton, 1862-1873." *Harvard Library Bulletin* 22 (1974): 5–35; 129–61.

EDITIONS OF *The Coming Race*

1871: Anon., *The Coming Race*. Edinburgh and London: William Blackwood; 8 eds. by 1873.

1871: As *The Coming Race; or, The New Utopia*. New York: Francis B. Felt; Toronto: Adam, Stevenson and Co.

1873: Leipzig: Bernhard Tauchnitz.

1873: New York: Henry L. Hinton.

1874: New York: Harper's.

N.d.: As *The Coming Race; or, The New Utopia*. New York: Hurst.

1882: As *The Coming Race; or, The New Utopia*. New York: J.W. Lovell.

1890s?: New York: Mershon Co.

1893: As *Collection of British Writers: The Coming Race*. Leipzig and Paris: Tauchnitz.

1928: With *The Haunted and the Haunters*. Introduction by F. J. Harvey Darton. Oxford: Oxford University Press.

1967: Pomeroy, Wash.: Health Research.

c. 1970: Mokelumne Hill, Calif.: Occult Facsimiles.

1972: As *Vril: The Power of the Coming Race*. Introduction by Paul M. Allen. Blauvelt, N.Y.: Rudolf Steiner Publications.

1973: Introduction by Manuela Auerbach. Quakertown, Pa.: Philosophical Publishing.

1975: As *Vril; or, The Power of the Coming Race*. N.p.: Multimedia/Biograf.

1986: Hastings, Eng.: Society of Metaphysicians.

1986: As *Vril: The Power of the Coming Race*. New York: Spiritual Fiction Publications.

1989: As *The Coming Race: A First in Science Fiction*. Introduction by John Weeks. Santa Barbara, Calif.: Woodbridge Press.

1995: Introduction by Julian Wolfreys. Stroud, Eng., and Dover, N.H.: Alan Sutton.

2001: Murrieta, Calif.: Classic Books.

2001: As *The Coming Race: With Commentaries*. Palm Springs, Calif.: Scientist of New Atlantis.

2001: Introduction by I. F. Clarke. In *British Future Fiction*, ed. I. F. Clarke, 1:145–436. London: Pickering and Chatto. 7 vols.

2002: As *Vril, the Power of the Coming Race*. Holicong, Pa.: Wildside Press.

2002: Introduction by Brian Aldiss. Peterborough, Ont.: Broadview Press.

[Translations: Italian and German, 1874; Hungarian, 1880; French, 1888; Spanish, 1893?]

SECONDARY SOURCES ON
EDWARD BULWER-LYTTON AND HIS WORKS

For a full listing of nineteenth-century and early-twentieth-century
commentary on Bulwer-Lytton, see Andrew Brown's entry in *The
Cambridge Bibliography of English Literature,* 3rd ed., vol. 4.

"A.J.O." "Readings and Re-Readings: *Zanoni.*" *Theosophical Review* 31
(December 1902): 338–46.
Aldiss, Brian. Introduction to *The Coming Race.* Peterborough, Ont.:
Broadview Press, 2002.
Allen, Paul M. Introduction to *Vril: The Power of the Coming Race.* Blauvelt,
N.Y.: Rudolph Steiner Publications, 1972.
Armitage, Harold. "Lytton the Mystic." Introduction to *The Haunted and
the Haunters.* London: Simpkin, Marshall, Hamilton, Kent, 1925.
Ashley, Mike. "Bulwer-Lytton, (Sir) Edward (George Earle Lytton), First
Baron Lytton (1803–1873)." In *The Encyclopedia of Fantasy,* ed. John Clute
and John Grant, 149. London: Little, Brown, 1997.
"The *Athenaeum* and Bulwer Lytton." *Notes and Queries* 168 (February
1935): 128-29.
Atkinson, William Walker. *Vril.* Chicago: A. C. McClurg, 1911.
Auerbach, Manuela. "Commentary." In *The Coming Race,* iii–iv.
Quakertown, Pa.: Philosophical Publishing, 1973.
Barnes, James J. "Edward Bulwer Lytton and the Publishing Firm of
Harper & Bros." *American Literature* 38 (1966): 35-48.
Bayer-Berenbaum, L. B. *The Expansion of Consciousness in Gothic Literature
and Art.* London: Associated University Presses, 1982.
Belcher, Margaret E. "Bulwer's Mr. Bluff: A Suggestion for *Hard Times.*"
The Dickensian 78.ii (Summer 1982): 105–9.
Bell, E. G. *Introductions to the Prose Romances, Plays and Comedies of Edward
Bulwer, Lord Lytton.* Chicago: W. M. Hill, 1914.
Besant, Annie. "Lord Lytton a Great Occultist." *The Theosophist* 44
(February 1923): 448.
Bevis, Richard. "'Mightier than the Sword': The Anatomy of Power
in Bulwer-Lytton's *Richelieu.*" *Essays in Theatre* 8.ii (May 1990):
95–106.
Blain, Virginia. "Rosina Bulwer Lytton and the Rage of the Unheard."
Huntington Library Quarterly 53.iii (1990): 210–36.

Bleiler, E. F. "Edward George Bulwer-Lytton." In *Supernatural Fiction Writers*, ed. E. F. Bleiler, 195–204. New York: Scribner's, 1985.

Blake, Robert. "Bulwer-Lytton." *Cornhill Magazine* 1077 (1973): 67–76.

———. *Disraeli*. New York: St. Martin's Press, 1967.

Boos, Florence S. "William Morris, Robert Bulwer-Lytton, and the Arthurian Poetry of the 1850s." *Arthuriana* 6.iii (1996): 31–53.

Bradford, Sarah. *Disraeli*. New York: Stein and Day, 1983.

Brown, Andrew. "Bulwer Lytton, Sir Edward George Earle Lytton, 1st Lord Lytton, 1803–1873." In *The Cambridge Bibliography of English Literature*, 3rd ed., ed. Joanne Shattock, 4:1144–60. Cambridge: Cambridge University Press, 1999.

———. "Metaphysics and Melodrama: Bulwer's *Rienzi*." *Nineteenth-Century Fiction* 36.iii (December 1981): 261–76.

———. "The 'Supplementary Chapter' to Bulwer Lytton's *A Strange Story*." *Victorian Literature and Culture* 26.i (1998): 157–82.

Campbell, James L., Sr. *Edward Bulwer-Lytton*. Boston: Twayne, 1986.

Caracciolo, Peter. "George Eliot, Goethe, and the 'Passionless Mejnour.'" *Notes and Queries* 37.i (March 1990): 38.

Christensen, Allan C. "Bulwer, Bloch, Bussotti, and the Filial Muse: Recalled and Foreseen Sources of Inspiration." *Mosaic* 26.iii (Summer 1993): 37–52.

———. *Edward Bulwer-Lytton: The Fiction of New Regions*. Athens: University of Georgia Press, 1976.

———. "Edward Bulwer-Lytton of Knebworth, 25 May 1803–18 January 1873." *Nineteenth-Century Fiction* 28.i (June 1973): 85–86.

———, ed. *The Subverting Vision of Bulwer Lytton: Bicentennial Reflections*. Newark: University of Delaware Press, 2004.

Clarke, Bruce. *Energy Forms: Allegory and Science in the Era of Classical Thermodynamics*. Ann Arbor: University of Michigan Press, 2001.

Clarke, I. F. "The Coming Race." In *British Future Fiction*, ed. I. F. Clarke, 1:139–41. London: Pickering and Chatto, 2001.

Cloy, John. "Two Altered Endings: Dickens and Bulwer-Lytton." *University of Mississippi Studies in English* 10 (1992): 170–72.

Clute, John. "Lytton (Edward George Earle Lytton Bulwer), First Baron (1803–1873)." In *The Encyclopedia of Science Fiction*, ed. John Clute and Peter Nicholls, 743–44. London: Orbit, 1993.

Clymer, Emerson M. "The Vril," foreword to *The Coming Race.* Quakertown, Pa.: Philosophical Publishing, 1973

Coates, John. "*Zanoni* by Bulwer-Lytton: A Discussion of Its 'Philosophy' and Its Possible Influences." *Durham University Journal* 76.ii (1984): 223–33.

"The Coming Race." *Athenaeum* 2274 (27 May 1871): 649.

"The Coming Race." *Saturday Review* (27 May 1871): 674–75.

Cooper, Thompson. *Lord Lytton: A Biography.* London and New York: George Routledge, 1873.

Cragg, William E. "Bulwer's *Godolphin:* The Metamorphosis of the Fashionable Novel. *Studies in English Literature* 26.iv (1986): 675–90.

Cronin, Richard. "Mary Shelley and Edward Bulwer: *Lodore* as Hybrid Fiction." *Mary Shelley's Fictions: From Frankenstein to Falkner,* ed. Michael Eberle-Sinatra, 39–54. Basingstoke, Eng.: Macmillan; New York: St. Martin's Press, 2000.

Dahl, Curtis. "Benjamin Disraeli and Edward Bulwer-Lytton." In *Victorian Fiction: A Guide to Research,* ed. Lionel Stevenson, 35–43. Cambridge, Mass.: Harvard University Press, 1966.

———. "Bulwer-Lytton and the School of Catastrophe." *Philosophical Quarterly* 32 (1953): 428–42.

———. "Edward Bulwer-Lytton." In *Victorian Fiction: A Second Guide to Research,* ed. George H. Ford, 28–33. New York: Modern Language Association of America, 1978.

———. "History on the Hustings: Bulwer-Lytton's Historical Novels of Politics." In *From Jane Austen to Joseph Conrad: Essays Collected in Memory of James T. Hill ,* ed. Robert C. Rathburn and Martin Steinmann Jr., 60–71. Minneapolis: University of Minnesota Press, 1958.

———. "Recreations of Pompeii." *Archaeology* 9 (1956): 182–91.

Davis, Philip. "Debatable Lands: Variety of Form and Genre in the Early Victorian Novel." In *The Oxford English Literary History,* vol. 8: *1830–1880: The Victorians,* 272–90. Oxford and New York: Oxford University Press, 2002.

Dolvers, Horst. "'Quite a Serious Division of Creative Literature': Lord Lytton's Fables in Song and R. L. Stevenson's Prose Fables." *Archiv für das Studium der Neueren Sprachen und Literaturen* 230.i (1993): 62–77.

Eigner, Edwin M. "Bulwer-Lytton and the Changed Ending of *Great Expectations.*" *Nineteenth-Century Fiction* 25.i (June 1970): 104–8.

————. *The Metaphysical Novel in England and America: Dickens, Bulwer, Melville, and Hawthorne.* Berkeley: University of California Press, 1978.

————. *"The Pilgrims of the Rhine:* The Failure of the German Bildungsroman in England." *Victorian Newsletter* 68 (Fall 1985): 19–21.

————. "Raphael in Oxford Street: Bulwer's Accommodation to the Realists." In *The Nineteenth-Century Writer and His Audience,* ed. Harold Orel and George J. Worth, 61–74. Lawrence: University of Kansas Humanistic Studies, no. 40, 1969.

Eigner, Edwin M., and Joseph I. Fradin. "Bulwer-Lytton and Dickens' Jo." *Nineteenth-Century Fiction* 24.i (June1969): 98–102.

Eigner, Edwin M., and David Thomas. "The Authorship of *Mephistopheles in England." Nineteenth-Century Fiction* 39.i (June 1984): 91–94.

Engel, Elliot, and Margaret F. King. *The Victorian Novel before Victoria: British Fiction during the Reign of William IV, 1830–1837.* New York: St. Martin's Press, 1984.

Escott, T. H. S., "Bulwer's Last Three Books," *Fraser's Magazine* (June 1874): 765–77.

————. *Edward Bulwer, First Baron Lytton of Knebworth: A Social, Personal, and Political Monograph.* London: Routledge, 1910.

"Fictions of the Future." *Dublin Review* 70 (1872): 76–103.

Findlay, Ian. "Edward Bulwer-Lytton and the Rosicrucians." *Literature and the Occult: Essays in Comparative Literature,* ed. Luann Frank, 137–46. Arlington: University of Texas Press, 1977.

Fisher, James. "'The Arithmetic and Logic of Life': The Forces of Commerce and Capital in a Revival of Edward Bulwer-Lytton's *Money." Journal of Dramatic Theory and Criticism* 15.ii (2001): 115–32.

Fleishman, Avrom. *The English Historical Novel: Walter Scott to Virginia Woolf.* Baltimore: Johns Hopkins University Press, 1971.

Flower, Sybilla Jane. *Bulwer-Lytton: An Illustrated Life of the First Baron Lytton, 1803–1873.* Aylesbury, Eng.: Shire Publishing, 1973.

————. "Charles Dickens and Edward Bulwer-Lytton." *The Dickensian* 69 (1973): 79–89.

Ford, Eric J. *Bernard Shaw and Bulwer-Lytton: The Influence of "The Coming Race."* [London?]: The Lytton Circle, 1974.

Fradin, Joseph I. "'The Absorbing Tyranny of Every-Day Life': Bulwer Lytton's *A Strange Story." Nineteenth Century Fiction* 16 (1961): 1–16.

Friedman, Stanley. "*Bleak House* and Bulwer-Lytton's *Not So Bad as We Seem*." *Dickens Quarterly* 9.i (1992): 25–29.

Frost, William A. *Bulwer Lytton: An Exposure of the Errors of His Biographers.* N.p., 1911.

Gosse, Edmund. "The Life of Lord Lytton." *Fortnightly Review* 100 (December 1913): 1033–46.

Graham, Peter W. "Bulwer the Moraliste." *Dickens Studies Annual: Essays on Victorian Fiction* 9 (1981): 143–61.

———. "Pelham as Paragon: Bulwer's Ideal Aristocrat." *Victorians Institute Journal* 9 (1980–81): 71–81.

Greig, James C. J. "Buchan, Donisarius, and Bulwer Lytton." *John Buchan Journal* 19 (Autumn 1998): 16–18.

Hammond, Alexander. "Poe's 'Lionizing' and the Design of Tales of the Folio Club." *ESQ* 18 (1972): 154–65.

Harlan, Aurelia Brooks. *Owen Meredith: A Critical Biography of Robert, First Earl of Lytton.* New York: Columbia University Press, 1946.

Harvey, Geoffrey M. "Bulwer-Lytton and the Rhetorical Design of Trollope's *Orley Farm*." *Ariel* 6.i (1975): 68–79.

Hawes, Donald. "Thackeray, Tennyson, and Bulwer Lytton." *Notes and Queries* 36.ii (1989): 182–83.

Heilman, Robert B. "Lampedusa and Bulwer: Sic Transit in Different Keys." *Northwest Review* 7.ii (1965–66): 21–28.

Henkin, Leo J. *Darwinism in the English Novel, 1860–1910.* New York: Corporate Press, 1940.

Hollingsworth, Keith. *The Newgate Novel, 1830–1847: Bulwer, Ainsworth, Dickens, and Thackeray.* Detroit: Wayne State University Press, 1963.

Honan, Park. Introduction to *Falkland,* ed. Herbert Van Thal. London: Cassel, 1967.

Hook, Van. "The Master Who Was Lord Lytton." *The Theosophist* 44 (January 1923): 399, 402.

Howe, Susanne. *Wilhelm Meister and His English Kinsmen: Apprentices to Life.* New York: Columbia University Press, 1930.

Jerrold, William B. *The Best of All Good Company.* N.p., 1871.

Jowett, Benjamin. *Lord Lytton, the Man and the Author.* London: N.p., 1873.

Kelly, Richard. "The Haunted House of Bulwer-Lytton." *Studies in Short Fiction* 8 (1971): 581–87.

King, Margaret F., and Elliot Engel. "The Emerging Carlylean Hero in

Bulwer's Novels of the 1830s." *Nineteenth-Century Fiction* 36.iii (December 1981): 277–95.

Knepper, B.G. "Shaw's Debt to *The Coming Race*." *Journal of Modern Literature* 1 (1971): 339–53.

———. "*The Coming Race:* Hell? Or Paradise Foretasted?" In *No Place Else: Explorations in Utopian and Dystopian Fiction,* ed. Eric S. Rabkin, Martin H. Greenberg, and Joseph Olander, 11–32. Carbondale: Southern Illinois University Press, 1983.

Kurata, Marilyn J. "Wrongful Confinement: The Betrayal of Women by Men, Medicine, and Law." In *Victorian Scandals: Representations of Gender and Class* ed. K. O. Garrigan, 43–68. Athens: University of Ohio Press, 1992.

Liljegren, S. B. *Bulwer-Lytton's Novels and Isis Unveiled.* Upsala University Essays and Studies in English Language and Literature, 18. Lund, Sweden: Carl Blom; Cambridge, Mass.: Harvard University Press, 1957.

———. "Quelques romans anglais, source partielle d'une religion moderne." In *Mélanges d'histoire générale et comparée offerts à Fernand Baldensperger,* 2:60–67. Paris: n.p., 1930.

Lindsay, Jack. "Clairvoyance of the Normal: The Aesthetic Theory of Bulwer-Lytton." *Nineteenth Century and After* 145 (January 1949): 29–38.

Lloyd, Michael. "Bulwer-Lytton and the Idealising Principle." *English Miscellany* 7 (1956): 25–39.

Lord, Walter Frewin. "Lord Lytton's Novels." *Nineteenth Century* 50 (September 1901): 172–89. Collected in W. F. Lord, *The Mirror of the Century.* London and New York: John Lane, 1906.

"Lord Lytton." In *Chambers's Cyclopaedia of English Literature,* ed. David Patrick, 3:332–36. London and Edinburgh: Chambers, 1903.

Lytton, Robert, first earl of. *The Life, Letters, and Literary Remains of Edward Bulwer, Lord Lytton, by His Son.* 2 vols. London: Kegan Paul Trench, 1883.

Lytton, Rosina Bulwer. *A Blighted Life.* Bristol, Eng.: Thoemmes Press, 1994.

Lytton, Victor Alexander, second earl of. *Bulwer-Lytton.* Denver: Allan Swallow, 1948.

———. *The Life of Edward Bulwer, First Lord Lytton, by His Grandson.* 2 vols. London: Macmillan, 1913.

Macainsh, Noel. "Queensland, Rosicrucians, and *A Strange Story:* Aspects of Literary Occultism." *LiNQ* 11.iii (1983): 1–18.

Masson, David. *British Novelists and Their Styles*. London: Macmillan, 1859.

Mazlish, Bruce. "A Triptych: Freud's *The Interpretation of Dreams*, Rider Haggard's *She*, and Bulwer-Lytton's *The Coming Race*." *Comparative Studies in Society and History* 35.iv (1993): 726–45.

McClary, B. H. "Earl Lytton to Alexander Ireland on Emerson." *ESQ: A Journal of the American Renaissance* 43 (1966): 70–73.

McGann, Jerome J. Introduction to *Pelham; or, The Adventures of a Gentleman*, ed. Jerome J. McGann. Lincoln: University of Nebraska Press, 1972.

Merriman, James D. "The Last Days of the Eighteenth-Century Epic: Bulwer-Lytton's Arthuriad." *Studies in Medievalism* 2.iv (Fall 1983): 15–37.

Mitchell, Leslie. *Bulwer Lytton: The Rise and Fall of a Victorian Man of Letters*. London and New York: Hambledon and London, 2003.

Moore, John S. "Bulwer-Lytton" at http://www.mith.demon.co.uk/Bulwer.htm.

Mulvey-Roberts, Marie. "Edward Bulwer-Lytton." In *Gothic Writers: A Critical and Bibliographical Guide*, ed. Douglas H. Thomson, Jack G. Voller, and Frederick S. Frank, 83–89. Westport, Conn.: Greenwood Press.

———. "Fame, Notoriety, and Madness: Edward Bulwer-Lytton Paying the Price of Greatness." *Critical Survey* 13.ii (2001): 115–34.

———. *Gothic Immortals: The Fiction of the Brotherhood of the Rosy Cross*. London and New York: Routledge, 1990.

———. Introduction to *A Blighted Life: A True Story*, by Rosina Bulwer Lytton. Bristol: Thoemmes Press, 1994.

Murray, Christopher. "Richelieu at the Theatre Royal, Dublin, 1839." *Theatre Notebook* 37.iii (1983): 128–31.

Myer, Valerie Grosvenor. "Bulwer-Lytton, Edward George Earle Lytton, First Lord Lytton (1803–1873)." In *Victorian Britain: An Encyclopedia*, ed. Sally Mitchell, 103. New York: Garland Press, 1988.

Nickerson, Charles C. "Disraeli's *The Young Duke*." *Disraeli Newsletter* 3.ii (1978): 18–38.

Oakley, John. "The Boundaries of Hegemony: Lytton." In *1848: The Sociology of Literature: Proceedings of the Essex Conference on the Sociology of Literature, July 1977*, ed. Francis Barker et al., 166–84. Wivenhoe: University of Essex Press, 1978.

Oakley, J. W. "The Reform of Honor in Bulwer's *Pelham*." *Nineteenth-Century Literature* 47.i (June 1992): 49–71.

Paroissien, Davi. "Dickens' Ralph Nickleby and Bulwer Lytton's William Brandon: A Note on the Antagonists." *Dickens Studies Newsletter* 9 (1978): 10–15.

Piacentino, Edward J. "An Error in Poe's Review of *Rienzi*." *ANQ* 1.iv (1988): 136–37.

Poe, Edgar Allan. "Edward Lytton Bulwer" [reviews of *Rienzi* (1836), *Night and Morning* (1841), and *Critical and Miscellaneous Writings* (1841)]. In E. A. Poe, *Essays and Reviews*, ed. G. R. Thompson, 142–63. New York and Cambridge: Library of America, 1984.

Pollin, Burton R. "Bulwer Lytton and 'The Tell-Tale Heart.'" *American Notes and Queries* 4 (September 1965): 7–8.

———. "Bulwer-Lytton's Influence on Poe's Works and Ideas, Especially for an Author's 'Preconceived Design.'" *Edgar Allen Poe Review* 1.i (2000): 5–12.

———. "Poe's Invention of the 'Psychological Autobiographists.'" *Poe Studies* 11 (June 1978): 15–16.

Posten, Laurence. "Beyond the Occult: The Godwinian Nexus of Bulwer's *Zanoni*." *Studies in Romanticism* 37.ii (1998): 131–61.

Price, Lawrence M. "Karl Gutzkow and Bulwer Lytton." *Journal of English and German Philology* 16 (1917): 397–415.

Purton, Valeri. "Dickens and Bulwer Lytton: The Dandy Reclaimed." *The Dickensian* 74 (1978): 25–29.

Richards, Bernard. "Stopping the Press in Marius." *English Literature in Transition (1880–1920)* 27.ii (1984): 90–99.

Roberts, Adam. "Dickens's Jarndyce and Lytton's Gawtrey." *Notes and Queries* 43.i (March 1996): 45–46.

Robillard, Douglas. "A Possible Source for Melville's Goetic and Theurgic Magic." *Melville Society Extracts* 49 (February 1982): 5–6.

Rosa, M. W. *The Silver-Fork School: Novels of Fashion Preceding "Vanity Fair."* New York: Columbia University Press, 1936.

Rubinstein, William C. "*The Coming Race*." In *Survey of Science Fiction Literature*, ed. Frank N. Magill, 1:421. Englewood Cliffs, N.J.: Salem Press, 1979.

Sadleir, Michael T. H. *Bulwer: A Panorama. Edward and Rosina, 1803–1836.*

London: Constable, 1931. Retitled *Bulwer and His Wife: A Panorama, 1803–1836*. London: Constable, 1933.

Sanders, Andrew. *The Victorian Historical Novel, 1840–1880*. London: Macmillan, 1978.

"Satiric Utopias." *The Spectator* (3 June 1871): 665–67.

Seeber, Hans. "Bulwer-Lytton's Underworld: *The Coming Race* (1871)." *Moreana: Bulletin Thomas More* 30 (1971): 39–40.

Simmons, James C. "Bulwer and Vesuvius: The Topicality of *The Last Days of Pompeii*." *Nineteenth-Century Fiction* 24.i (June 1969): 103–5.

———. "The Novelist as Historian: An Unexplored Tract of Historiography." *Victorian Studies* 14 (1971): 293–305.

Simpson, Roger. "The Nannau Oak: Bulwer Lytton and His Midsummer Knight at the Westminster Round Table." *Arthuriana* 7.iii (1997): 124–36.

Sinnema, Peter W. "Domesticating Bulwer-Lytton's 'Colonial' Fiction: Mentorship and Masculinity in the Caxtons Trilogy." *English Studies in Canada* 26.ii (2000): 155–84.

Small, Helen. "Bulwer-Lytton, Edward George Earle (1803–1873)." In *The Handbook to Gothic Literature*, ed. Marie Mulvey-Roberts, 33–35. New York: New York University Press; Basingstoke, Eng.: Macmillan, 1998.

Smith, William Henry. "The Coming Race." *Blackwood's Magazine* 110 (1871): 46–61.

Snyder, Charles Willis. *Liberty and Morality: A Political Biography of Edward Bulwer-Lytton*. New York: Peter Lang, 1995.

Sparks, Julie. "The Evolution of Human Virtue: Precedents for Shaw's 'World Betterer' in the Utopias of Bellamy, Morris, and Bulwer-Lytton." In *Shaw and Other Matters: A Festschrift for Stanley Weintraub on the Occasion of His Forty-second Anniversary at the Pennsylvania State University*, ed. Susan Rusinko, 63–82. Selinsgrove, Pa.: Associated University Presses, 1998.

Spies, George H. "Edgar Allan Poe's Changing Critical Evaluation of the Novels of Edward Bulwer-Lytton." *Kyushu American Literature* 17 (1976): 1–6.

Stableford, Brian. "Bulwer-Lytton, Edward (George Earle; 1st Baron Lytton of Knebworth)." In *St. James Guide to Horror, Ghost, and Gothic Writers*, ed. David Pringle, 105–7. Detroit, Mich.: St. James Press/Gale, 1998.

Stafford, Fiona J. *The Last of the Race: The Growth of a Myth from Milton to Darwin*. Oxford: Clarendon Press, 1994.

Stephen, Leslie. "Lytton, Edward George Earle Lytton Bulwer, first Lord Lytton (1803–1873)." In *Dictionary of National Biography*, ed. Sidney Lee, 34: 380–87. London: Smith, Elder, 1893.

Stephens, J. R. "E. Bulwer Lytton: A Misattributed Article Identified." *Notes and Queries* 33.ii (1986): 161.

Stewart, C. Nelson. *Bulwer Lytton as Occultist*. London: Theosophical Publishing House, 1927.

Stone-Blackburn, Susan. "Consciousness, Evolution, and Early Telepathic Tales." *Science-Fiction Studies* 20.ii (1993): 241–50.

Sutherland, J. A. "Lytton, John Blackwood, and the Serialisation of *Middlemarch*." *The Bibliotheck* 7 (1975): 98–104.

Suvin, Darko. "The Extraordinary Voyage, the Future War, and Bulwer's *The Coming Race:* Three Sub-Genres in British Science Fiction, 1871–1885." *Literature and History* 10.ii (Autumn 1984): 231–48. Collected in D. Suvin, *Victorian Science Fiction in the UK: The Discourses of Knowledge and of Power*, 344–49. Boston: G. K. Hall, 1983.

Swift, S. F. "Toward the Vampire as Savior: Chelsea Quinn Yarbro's Saint-Germain Series Compared with Edward Bulwer-Lytton's *Zanoni*." In *The Blood Is the Life: Vampires in Literature*, ed. Leonard G. Heldreth and Mary Pharr, 155–64. Bowling Green, Ohio: Popular Press, 1999.

Täufer, Johannes. *Vril: Die Kosmische Urkraft*. Berlin: Astrologischer Verlag Wilhelm Becker.

Thompson, G. R. "Poe's Reading of *Pelham:* Another Source for 'Tintinnabulation' and Other Piquant Expressions." *American Literature* 41 (1969): 251–55.

Trela, D. J. "Carlyle, Bulwer and *The New Monthly Magazine*." *Victorian Periodicals Review* 22.iv (1989): 157–62.

Trodd, Anthea. "Michael Angelo Titmarsh and the Knebworth Apollo." *Costerus* 2 (1974): 59–81.

Tyson, N. J. *Eugene Aram: Literary History and Typology of the Scholar Criminal*. Hamden, Conn.: Archon, 1983.

———. "Thackeray and Bulwer: Between the Lines in *Barry Lyndon*." *English Language Notes* 27.ii (1989): 53–56.

Underwood, Ted. "Historical Difference as Immortality in the Mid-

Nineteenth-Century Novel." *Modern Language Quarterly* 63.iv (2002): 441–69.

Waddell, Gabrielle de R. "Reminiscences and Letters of Bulwer Lytton." *Century Magazine* 88 (July 1914): 469–72.

Waddington, Patrick. "Two Authors of Strange Stories: Bulwer-Lytton and Turgenev." *New Zealand Slavonic Journal* (1992): 31–54.

Wagner, Geoffrey. "A Forgotten Satire: Bulwer-Lytton's *The Coming Race*." *Nineteenth-Century Fiction* 19.iv (March 1965): 379–85.

Walker, C. S. "A Lost Prologue by Bulwer Lytton." *Century Magazine* 79 (December 1909): 313–14.

Watts, Harold C. "Lytton's Theories of Prose Fiction." *PMLA* 50 (1935): 274–89.

Weeks, Donald. "One Hundred Years (+) On: Edward Bulwer-Lytton." *Slightly Soiled* 3–4 (December 1986): 29–30.

Weeks, John. Introduction to *The Coming Race*. Santa Barbara, Calif.: Woodbridge Press, 1989.

"What We Are Come To." *The Month* (July 1871): 162–66.

Wildman, John H. "Unsuccessful Return from Avalon." *Victorian Poetry* 12 (1974): 291–96.

Wilkinson, Mrs. "*King Arthur* by Lord Lytton: Three Mystic Toils." *Theosophical Review* 30 (July 1902): 457; 31 (Sept.–Oct. 1902): 62, 137.

Williams, Raymond. "Utopia and Science Fiction." In *Science Fiction: A Critical Guide*, ed. Patrick Parrinder, 52–66. London: Longman, 1979.

Witemeyer, Hugh. "George Eliot's Romola and Bulwer Lytton's Rienzi." *Studies in the Novel* 15.i (1983): 62–73.

Wolff, Robert Lee. "'Devoted Disciple': The Letters of Mary Elizabeth Braddon to Sir Edward Bulwer-Lytton, 1862–1873." *Harvard Library Bulletin* 22 (1974): 5–35, 129–61.

———. *Sensational Victorian: The Life and Fiction of Mary Elizabeth Bradden*. New York: Garland, 1979.

———. *Strange Stories and Other Explorations in Victorian Fiction*. Boston: Gambit Press, 1971.

Wolfreys, Julian. Introduction to *The Coming Race*. Stroud, Eng., and Dover, N.H.: Allen Sutton, 1995.

"X.Y.Z." *The Vril Staff*. London: D. Stott, 1891.

Zipser, Richard A. *Edward Bulwer Lytton and Germany*. Berne and Frankfurt am Main: Herbert Lang, 1974.

Asterisked titles have been reprinted by Health Research Books, Pomeroy, Washington.

"Adams, Jack" [Alcanoan O. Grigsby and Mary P. Lowe]. *Nequa; or, The Problem of the Ages* [1890]. Topeka, Kan.: Equity Publishing Co., 1900.

Aston, B. G. *The Eye of the God.* London and Glasgow: Blackie, 1927.

Beale, Charles Willing. *The Secret of the Earth.* New York and London: F. Tennyson Neely, 1899.

Bell, George W. *Mr Oseba's Last Discovery.* Wellington, N.Z.: New Zealand Times, 1904.

*Bernard, Raymond W. *The Hollow Earth: The Greatest Geographical Discovery in History Made by Admiral Richard E. Byrd in the Mysterious Land beyond the Poles, The True Origin of Flying Saucers.* New York: University Books, 1964.

*Bradshaw, William R. *The Goddess of Atvatabar: Being the History of the Discovery of the Interior World and the Conquest of Atvatabar.* New York: J. F. Douthitt, 1892.

Burroughs, Edgar Rice. *Back to the Stone Age.* Tarzana, Calif.: Burroughs, 1937.

———. *Land of Terror.* Tarzana, Calif.: Burroughs, 1944.

———. *Pellucidar.* Chicago: McClurg, 1923.

———. *Tanar of Pellucidar.* New York: Metropolitan, 1930.

———. *Tarzan at the Earth's Core.* New York: Metropolitan, 1930.

Carter, Bruce [Richard Hough]. *The Perilous Descent into a Strange World.* London: Bodley Head, 1952. As *Into a Strange World:* New York: Crowell, 1953.

Carter, Lin. *Journey to the Underground World.* New York: DAW, 1979.

Casanova, Giacomo. *Icosameron, ou Histoire d'Edouard et d'Elizabeth Qui Passerent Quatre-Vingt Un Ans chez les Megamicres Habitans Aborigenes du Protocosme dans l'Interieur de Notre Globe* [1788]. Paris: François Bourin, 1988. Translated and abridged as *Casanova's "Icosameron"; or, The Story of Edward and Elizabeth: Who Spent Eighty-One Years in the Land of the Megamicres, Original Inhabitants of Protocosmos in the Interior of Our Globe.* New York: Jenna Press, 1986.

Channing, Mark. *White Python.* London: Hutchinson, 1934.

Clark, P. "The Symmes Theory of the Earth." *Atlantic Monthly* 31 (1878): 471–80.

Clock, Herbert, and Eric Boetzel. *The Light in the Sky*. New York: Coward-McCann, 1929.

Coblentz, Stanley A. *Hidden World*. New York: Avalon, 1957. As *In Caverns Below*. New York: Garland, 1975.

Emerson, Willis George. *The Smoky God; or, A Voyage to the Inner World*. Chicago: Forbes, 1908.

Fitting, Peter, ed. *Subterranean Worlds: A Critical Anthology*. Middletown CT: Wesleyan University Press, 2004.

Galouye, Daniel F. *Dark Universe*. New York: Bantam, 1961.

*Gardner, Marshall B. *A Journey to the Earth's Interior; or, Have the Poles Really Been Discovered?* Aurora, Ill.: [the author], 1913; revised and enlarged 1920.

Haggard, H. Rider. *When the World Shook: Being an Account of the Great Adventure of Bastin, Bickley, and Arbuthnot*. London: Cassell; New York: Longman, 1919.

Harben, William Nathaniel. *The Land of the Changing Sun*. New York: Merriam, 1894.

*Hartman, Franz. *Among the Gnomes* [1896]. New York: Arno Press, 1978.

Hay, William Delisle. *Three Hundred Years Hence; or, A Voice from Posterity*. London: Newman, 1881.

Heydon, J. K. [Hal P. Trevarthen]. *World D: Being a Brief Account of the Founding of Helioxenon*. New York: Sheed and Ward, 1935.

Holberg, Ludvig. *A Journey to the World Under-Ground, by Nicolas Klimius*. London: T. Astley, 1742. As *Journey of Neils Klim to the World Underground*: Ed. James I. McNelis Jr., Lincoln: University of Nebraska Press, 1960.

Hyne, C.J. Cutcliffe. *Beneath Your Very Boots: Being a Few Striking Episodes from the Life of Anthony Merlwood Haltoun, Esq*. London: Digby Long, 1889.

Kearns, William H., and B. L. Britton. *The Silent Continent*. New York: Harper, 1955.

Lane, Mary E. Bradley [Vera Zarovitch]. *Mizora: A Prophecy*. New York: G. W. Dillingham, 1890. As *Mizora: A World of Women*: Lincoln: University of Nebraska Press, 1999; ed. Jean Pfaelzer, Syracuse, N.Y.: Syracuse University Press, 2000.

*Lloyd, John Uri. *Etidorpha; or, The End of Earth: The Strange History of a*

Mysterious Being and the Account of a Remarkable Journey. Cincinnati: Robert Clarke, 1895.

*Lockwood, Ingersoll. *Baron Trump's Marvellous Underground Journey*. Boston: Lee and Shepard, 1893.

Lupoff, Richard A. *Circumpolar!* New York: Timescape, 1984.

MacLellan, Alec. *The Lost World of Agharti: The Mystery of Vril Power*. London: Souvenir Press, 1982.

Madden, E. F. "Symmes and His Theory." *Harper's New Monthly Magazine* 65 (1882): 740–44.

Merritt, Abraham. *Dwellers in the Mirage*. New York: Liveright, 1932.

———. *The Moon Pool*. New York: G. P. Putnam's, 1919.

Mitchell, Alexander. *A Treatise on Natural Philosophy, in Vindication of Symmes's Theory of the Earth Being a Hollow Sphere*. Eaton, Ohio: S. Tizzard, 1826.

Moore, M. Louise. *Al Modad; or, Life Scenes beyond the Polar Circumflex*. Shell Bank, Cameron Parish, La.: M. L. Moore and M. Beauchamp, 1892.

Obruchev, Vladimir Afanasevich. *Plutonia* [1924]. Trans. Fainne Solarko. Moscow: Raduga; Chicago: Imported Publications, 1957.

O'Neill, Joseph. *Land under England*. London: Victor Gollancz; New York: Simon and Schuster, 1935.

Paltock, Robert. *The Life and Adventures of Peter Wilkins, a Cornish Man* [1751]. London: Dent; New York: Dutton, 1915. New York: Garland, 1974.

Powell, Frank. *The Wolf-Men: A Tale of Amazing Adventure in the Under-World* [1905]. London: Cassell, 1906.

*Reed, William. *The Phantom of the Poles*. New York: Walter S. Rockey, 1906.

Rockwood, Roy. *Five Thousand Miles Underground; or, The Mystery of the Centre of the Earth*. New York: Cupples and Leon, 1908.

Rucker, Rudy. *The Hollow Earth: The Narrative of Mason Algiers Reynolds of Virginia*. Ed. Rudy Rucker. New York: Morrow, 1990.

*Savile, Frank. *Beyond the Great South Wall: The Secret of the Antarctic*. New York: Grosset and Dunlap, 1901.

Scott-Elliot, W. *The Story of Atlantis: A Geographical, Historical, and Ethnological Sketch*. N.p., 1896. With *The Lost Lemuria*: London: Theosophical Publishing House; Wheaton Ill.: Theosophical Press, 1972.

Scrymsour, Ella M. *The Perfect World: A Romance of Strange People and Strange Places.* New York: Frederick A. Stokes, 1922.

"Seaborn, Adam." *Symzonia: A Voyage of Discovery.* New York: J. Seymour, 1820. Gainesville, Fla.: Scholars' Facsimiles and Reprints, 1965. New York: Arno Press, 1975.

Shaw, William J. *Under the Auroras: A Marvellous Tale of the Interior World.* New York: Excelsior, 1888.

Sherman, M.L. *The Hollow Globe; or, The World's Agitator and Reconciler, a Treatise on the Physical Conformation of the Earth.* Chicago: Religio-Philosophical Publishing House, 1871.

Smyth, Clifford. *The Gilded Man.* New York: Boni and Liveright, 1918.

[Symmes, A.?] as "Citizen of the United States." *The Symmes's Theory of Concentric Spheres, Demonstrating That the Earth Is Hollow, Habitable Within, and Widely Open about the Poles.* Cincinnati: N.p., 1826. As by A. Symmes, title extended: *Compiled by Americus Symmes from the Writing of His Father, Capt. John Cleves Symmes.* Louisville, Ky.: N.p., 1878.

*Taylor, William Alexander. *Intermere.* Columbus, Ohio: XX Century Publishing, 1901.

Thomas, Eugene E. *Brotherhood of Mt. Shasta.* Los Angeles: De Vorss, 1946.

Thorpe, Fred [i.e., Albert Stearns] *Through the Earth; or, Jack Nelson's Invention.* New York: Street and Smith, n.d..

Tooker, Richard. *Inland Deep.* Philadelphia: Penn Publishing Co., 1936.

Verne, Jules. *Les Indes noires* [1877]. As *The Black Indies,* translator unknown. Munro, 1877. Other titles: *The Child of the Cavern, The Underground City, Black Diamonds.*

———. *Voyage au centre de la terre* [1864]. As *Journey to the Centre of the Earth,* trans. William Butcher. Oxford: Oxford University Press, 1992.

Waldrop, Howard, and Steven Utley. "Black as the Pit, from Pole to Pole." In Robert Silverberg, ed. *New Dimensions 7.* New York: Harper and Row, 1977, 39-81..

*Warren, William F. *Paradise Found; or, The Cradle of the Human Race at the North Pole: A Study of the Prehistoric World.* Boston: Houghton Mifflin, 1885.

Wedde, Ian. *Symmes Hole.* London: Faber, 1986.

Welcome, S. Byron. *From Earth's Centre: A Polar Gateway Message.* Chicago: C. H. Kerr, 1894.

Wells, H. G. *The Time Machine*. London: Heinemann; New York: Holt,
1895. Original serial title in *Science Schools Journal* (1888): *The Chronic
Argonauts*.

Wheatley, Dennis. *The Man Who Missed the War*. London: Hutchinson, 1947.

Winthrop, Park. "The Land of the Central Sun." *Argosy* 221-227 (July
1902–January 1903).

[Wood, Mrs. J.]. *Pantaletta: A Romance of Sheheland*. New York: American
News Co., 1882.

Wright, Sydney Fowler. *The Hidden Tribe*. London: Hale, 1938.

———. *The World Below*. London: Collins, 1929. As *The Dwellers:* London:
Panther, 1954.

Wyndham, John [John Beynon]. *The Secret People*. London: Newnes, 1935.

Edward George Earle Lytton Bulwer (from 1843 onward known as Bulwer-Lytton) was born on 25 May 1803 in London to the heiress of Knebworth, afterward Bulwer-Lytton's family seat, and a general in the Norfolk Rangers. Educated at first by private tutors, he was to claim in his unfinished autobiography that he had started writing poetry by the age of seven. He showed an early appetite for reading (entering the "City of the Dead" as he called it), and in 1820 he had his first book of poems published. Poetry remained an important part of Bulwer-Lytton's output, building up to a peak with his long and poorly received *King Arthur* of 1848, which he described as the "grand literary effort of my literary life." Bulwer-Lytton graduated from Cambridge University in 1826. An early influence on him came from Byron, and Bulwer-Lytton became briefly involved with Lady Caroline Lamb. In 1824, during a tour of the North, he visited Robert Owen at New Lanark and was captivated by the latter's utopian energy, later recording: "I listened with wonder to his projects for upsetting society and remodelling the world" (Robert, first earl of Lytton, *The Life, Letters, and Literary Remains of Edward Bulwer, Lord Lytton, by His Son* [London: Kegan Paul Trench, 1883], 1:88). After serving as a second in a duel in northern France, Bulwer-Lytton returned to London where he met and married Rosina Wheeler despite opposition from his mother. His biographer Michael Sadleir has described the youthful Bulwer-Lytton as a morbid, introspective, but talented fool who fell prey to a series of women, the last of whom was his young bride.

This marriage very quickly showed signs of strain, and matters came to a head when Rosina publicly confronted Bulwer-Lytton during an electoral campaign accusing him of cruelty and infidelity. The couple had officially separated in 1836, and Rosina began her own career as a writer, publishing her first novel, *Cheveley,* in 1839. She campaigned for the rights of wives, who at that time were severely restricted by law. Coincidentally, Bulwer-Lytton too became involved in these issues and exchanged correspondence with the reformer Caroline Norton over the 1838 Custody of Infants Bill, which proposed giving separated wives access to their children. In 1858 Rosina was certified insane and confined to an asylum in Brentford. She published her own account of this process in an autobiographical memoir published in 1880 with the title *A Blighted Life*, a "true Woman's Record of sad suffering." Here she accused Bulwer-Lytton again of different forms of cruelty and conspiracy, but also used her own case to speak out against the law that allowed husbands to commit their wives to asylums if they could get the endorsement of two doctors.

Bulwer-Lytton's literary career really took off when the newly married couple moved to London in 1829. Over ten years he produced a series of novels, more volumes of poetry, a history of Athens, and numerous essays and tales. In 1831–32 he edited the *New Monthly Magazine*, taking the journal over from Thomas Campbell and running it on reformist lines. From this period dates one of Bulwer-Lytton's most long-standing literary friendships, that with Disraeli. In 1833 Bulwer-Lytton published a study of his nation's culture, *England and the English*, which remains one of his most consulted works. Here he argued that England's aristocracy, unlike their German counterparts, had not held themselves aloof from national life, and as a result "the English aristocracy extended their moral influence throughout the whole of society" (*England and the English* [London: Routledge, 1874], 30). In presenting his report on the spirit of the age, Bulwer-Lytton expressed deep misgivings about the rampant commercialism of English life and focused his comments on two contrasting reformers: Robert Owen and Jeremy Bentham. Owen he applauded for fostering a spirit of cooperation, adding that "civilization itself is but the spirit of combining" (100). In contrast he saw Bentham as promoting a creed of the practical through utilitarianism, at the expense of the spiritual. For Bulwer-Lytton, Bentham was also encouraging a spirit of skeptical and destructive inquiry, which was responding to change by guiding that change in certain directions. *England and the English* attempts a delicate balancing act between evoking the stability of permanent features of the national character on the one hand and recognizing the irresistible forces of historical change on the other. The latter produces some of the gloomiest statements from Bulwer-Lytton about his age, such as the following:

> I have said that we live in an age of visible transition—an age of disquietude and doubt—of the removal of time-worn landmarks, and the breaking up of the hereditary elements of society—old opinions, feelings—ancestral customs and institutions are crumbling away, and both the spiritual and temporal worlds are darkened by the shadow of

change. The commencement of one of these epochs—periodical in the history of mankind—is hailed by the sanguine as the coming of a new Millennium—a great iconoclastic reformation, by which all false gods shall be overthrown. To me such epochs are but as the dark passages in the appointed progress of mankind—the times of greatest unhappiness to our species—passages into which we have no reason to rejoice at our entrance, save from the hope of being sooner landed on the opposite side. Uncertainty is the greatest of all our evils (281).

Bulwer-Lytton's sense of unease is reflected in the breaking up of his prose, and this passage goes a long way to explaining recurring themes in his fiction: his preoccupation with eras coming to an end, his interest in the occult as an ancient and timeless body of wisdom, and his perception of lost values. His projection of himself here as the helpless witness to change anticipates the predicament of the narrator of *The Coming Race,* who quite literally falls into the future and is helpless to escape without the help of a young woman from that future. Again and again he strains to see into the distance of the underground world, but the perspective will only carry his eyes a certain distance. In that sense the perspective acts as a visual representation of evolutionary time, teasing him toward a future he cannot quite make out. Bulwer-Lytton's preoccupation with lineage is reflected not only in his choice of literary themes but also in the changes to his name. Born as Bulwer, he was knighted in 1838 and changed his surname to Bulwer-Lytton in 1843 when he came into his mother's inheritance. Finally in 1866 he became Baron Lytton of Knebworth. Critics discussing his works have continued to use all three names.

The 1830s were a period of exceptional productivity for Bulwer-Lytton, who soon established a tendency to make forays into a wide range of literary genres. His fiction included Byronic romance (*Falkland,* 1827), a Newgate novel (*Paul Clifford,* 1830), a psychological study of criminality in *Eugene Aram* (published in 1832 and praised enthusiastically by Pierce Egan, the author of *Tom and Jerry*), and historical romance in *The Last Days of Pompeii* (1834) with its famous description of the eruption of Vesuvius. *Godolphin* (1833) describes the trials and tribulations in romance of its young protagonist Percy Godolphin, set against a motif of astrology that cannot be woven easily into the novel's social themes. However, the very presence of an astrologer reflects a concern with the paranormal that was to extend right through Bulwer-Lytton's career. When this seer speculates on the relation between the animate and inanimate, he is addressing a linkage that emerges in later novels like *Zanoni*, *A Strange Story*, and *The Coming Race*. Positing sympathy as a faculty located in the nerves, he asks: "Well, mark me: do not these nerves have attraction and sympathy—not only with human suffering, but with the powers of what is falsely termed inanimate nature?" (*Godolphin*, chap. 30). Such a link was to emerge again and again in Bulwer-Lytton's writing on the supernatural and occult.

During the 1830s Bulwer-Lytton was working out an aesthetic for his novels, and in 1838 he made his contribution to the public debate over the nature of the novel in his essay "On Art in Fiction," which was at first published anonymously. Here he stresses throughout the prime importance of a grand conception and draws a distinction between mechanical and intellectual art. Without ever quite dismissing execution and structure, Bulwer-Lytton nevertheless insists that "intellectual art is exercised in the highest degree . . . in proportion as it realises the Ideal" (*Pamphlets and Sketches* [London: Routledge, 1875], 319). The essay pays considerable attention to structure and distinguishes between the novel and play in terms of the one tending toward the diffuse and the other toward compression, an important point since Bulwer-Lytton was pursuing a tandem career in the theater. He particularly privileges what he calls the role of "sentiment" in fiction, meaning by this term a combination of moral impact and a sense of the whole work. Bulwer-Lytton is careful not to pin this elusive term down too specifically since it does not show itself in words: "it evinces itself insensibly and invisibly" (*Pamphlets*, 332). Throughout his career Bulwer-Lytton was opposed to the method of documentary realism in fiction, and in this essay he made out a case for valuing the grandeur of conception he found in a small number of writers, such as Victor Hugo, Walter Scott, and Goethe.

As Richard A. Zipser has shown, from his youth Bulwer-Lytton had been strongly drawn to the speculative energy of German literature, especially to the writings of Schiller (which he translated) and Goethe. Indeed, Bulwer-Lytton's novel *Ernest Maltravers* (1837) was directly modeled on *Wilhelm Meister*. His historical novel *Rienzi* was used by Wagner for his third opera. The energy that Bulwer-Lytton found in German writing matched his eagerness to address issues in his own writings. In his biography of Schiller he identified this quality in the following words: "Books which dispose the mind to abstract reverie or speculation, exercise a greater influence over the Germans than they do over us; a theory appears to them the more seductive in proportion as it is detached from the experience of practical life" (*Pamphlets*, 208). The practical was one of the key factors of contemporary English culture that Bulwer-Lytton resisted, and in recoil he was drawn to such techniques as creating characters that were "personifications of certain trains of mind," as A. C. Christensen puts it in one of the best studies of Bulwer-Lytton's work (*Edward Bulwer Lytton: The Fiction of New Regions* [Athens: University of Georgia Press, 1976], 18). Christensen takes his cues from Bulwer-Lytton's stated admiration for works like *Wilhelm Meister* and from the essay on fiction discussed above, and suggests that Bulwer-Lytton's works should be read around symbolic motifs such as recurrent Edens and cave images. Bulwer-Lytton emerges from this account as a speculator who constantly investigates the relation of surfaces to depths and externals to internals. For instance, *Pelham* (1828) describes the adventures in London and abroad of a young gentleman who then receives a brief but effective education from his uncle to be a "wholly impartial inquirer." As a result Pelham gradually turns away from the superficial gaiety of high society and enters politics.

There is an autobiographical dimension to Pelham's change since, after corresponding with William Godwin on the implications of the move, Bulwer-Lytton himself entered Parliament in 1831 as MP for St. Ives and actively campaigned for the new Reform Bill, which became law the following year. The bill removed his constituency, and Bulwer-Lytton was returned for Lincoln in 1832. He pursued a number of reforms including the abolition of Negro apprenticeship in the West Indies and the emendation of the laws relating to the licensing of theaters and stage censorship. In 1834 when the king dismissed Lord Melbourne's government, Bulwer-Lytton had a notable success with a pamphlet titled *A Letter to a Late Cabinet Minister on the Current Crisis*, which ran through 30,000 copies. The year 1835 appears to have been a moment of decision for Bulwer-Lytton in choosing between politics and literature, and he retired from Parliament in 1841. While pursuing his political activities he began a correspondence with John Stuart Mill, whose essays he admired greatly. For instance, *The Last of the Barons* (1843) deals with a particular phase in the history of the English nobility and, typically of Bulwer-Lytton's historical novels, situates his characters in moments of transition.

In *Liberty and Morality: A Political Biography of Edward Bulwer-Lytton*

(New York: Peter Lang, 1995), Charles W. Snyder has surveyed Bulwer-Lytton's parliamentary speeches to show how he started his political career as an independent Radical and then gradually drifted over to the Conservative cause. In fact political activity took its toll on Bulwer-Lytton, who wrote in a journal from the mid-1840s: "Parliament fatigues and exhausts me." In 1843 his mother died, and his grief, combined no doubt with his ongoing marital troubles, brought about a collapse. Typically, Bulwer-Lytton turned even this episode to good use by producing a pamphlet on his cure called "Confessions of a Water-Patient." Here he asserts "I have always had a great belief in the power of WILL" (his emphasis) and discusses the water-cure methods practiced at Malvern, where he took a course of treatment over some ten weeks. This system had been recently introduced into England on the model of a Silesian spa, and Bulwer-Lytton's therapy may explain why the use of water by the Vril-ya is given such prominence in *The Coming Race*.

Like many Victorian novelists, Bulwer-Lytton tried his hand at writing for the stage. His first play to be produced was *The Lady of Lyons* (1838), followed by *Richelieu* the next year. His most popular play was the comedy *Money*, which ran from 1840 to 1841 at the Haymarket Theatre. The Theatre Regulation Act (known as "Bulwer's Bill") that was passed in 1843 conferred status on smaller theaters and at the same time extended the licensing power of the Lord Chamberlain. Amateur theatricals at Knebworth in 1850 cemented the friendship between Dickens and Bulwer-Lytton, and the two writers raised funds to establish a Guild of Literature and Art to give financial support to writers. Bulwer-Lytton wrote a comedy specifically for this project, *Many Sides to a Character*, which was performed to a royal audience in 1851. Although an act of Parliament was passed in 1854 to establish this guild, the organization proved to be a failure.

Throughout his career Bulwer-Lytton remained drawn to the occult, and there is evidence that he had begun reading up on ancient lore as early as the 1830s. One result of these researches was the publication of his novel *Zanoni* in 1842. This unusual work has enjoyed a continuing popularity in occult circles and was an expansion on a sketch titled "Zicci," published the previous year in the *Monthly Chronicle*. *Zanoni* drew on a number of sources including the writings of William Godwin, but moved decisively away from the stereotypical Gothic figures of power like Zampieri in Godwin's *St. Leon* or Shelley's *Zastrozzi*. Bulwer-Lytton still draws on the evocative suggestions of the final initial letter of the alphabet and links his character with the ancient wisdom of Chaldea. Although Zanoni has a limited role in the novel, it is nevertheless a crucial one since he embodies a resistance to the fashionable materialism growing at the time of the novel's action, the late eighteenth century. In fact the novel makes a critical comment on the current developments in France, which Bulwer-Lytton sums up sardonically: "It was then the period, when a feverish spirit of change was working its way to that hideous mockery of human aspiration, the Revolution of France" (*Zanoni*, bk. 2, chap. 2). Bulwer-Lytton had digested Carlyle's *French Revolution*, which had presented a spectacle of anarchy and cruelty, and the same year in which his novel was published he wrote to John Forster that "Mob Rule will always be vile and bloody, and as such it seems to me should be exposed" (Lytton, *Life*, 2:52).

One of the most appreciative readers of *Zanoni* was the novelist Harriet Martineau, who sent Bulwer-Lytton an interpretive key. Martineau had already championed mesmerism, which she felt had cured her ailments, and Bulwer-Lytton, no doubt flattered by her intelligent attention, attached her key to editions of the novel after 1853, but without acknowledging its authorship. This addition to *Zanoni* is important for revealing Bulwer-Lytton's concern for a meaningful subtext. In his "Note" he declares: "We have no right to expect the most ingenious reader to search for the inner meaning, if the obvious course of the narrative be tedious and displeasing." So, the immediate narrative must function as a kind of inducement to a transcendental meaning, and for this reason Bulwer-Lytton stresses as a general principle that "Art in itself, if not necessarily typical, is essentially a suggester of something subtler than that which it embodies to the sense." Martineau's key, "Zanoni Explained," rather belies Bulwer-Lytton's insistence that the novel was not allegory because she glosses each character as the personification of an impulse or faculty. Thus Zanoni represents "Contemplation of the Ideal" and the young Englishman Glyndon "Unsustained Aspiration." Without necessarily accepting Martineau's key to a schematic meaning in the novel, we can nevertheless appreciate Bulwer-Lytton's insistence on his writing possessing implications deeper than the obvious as a comment on his general purpose in writing.

Bulwer-Lytton's interest in the paranormal has to date been best documented in Robert Lee Wolff's *Strange Stories and Other Explorations in Victorian Fiction* (1971), which questions the reading of *Zanoni* as a Rosicrucian novel, although there seems no doubt that Bulwer-Lytton was a member of that organization. He investigated a number of cases of spirit rapping and attended séances where he believed he was visited by the spirit of his dead daughter Emily, but Bulwer-Lytton retained a healthy skepticism about spiritualism, which he felt failed to live up to its promises. Similarly he knew of Dr. John Elliotson's 1846 defense of mesmerism and publicly supported him in the journal the *Zoist*. Bulwer-Lytton was also interested in phrenology, which is woven into *The Coming Race*, and, according to Wolff (237, 241), witnessed the taking of a cast on at least one occasion. Bulwer-Lytton's comment on communication with spirits in 1854 anticipates Arthur C. Clarke's point that the technology of one culture can seem magical to another. Faced with the question of whether spirit manifestations are real, Bulwer-Lytton remarks: "We can only answer as yet, as a sensible savage would answer of communication by the electric telegraph—'We don't know yet'" (Lytton, *Life*, 2:45). His approach to such phenomena was thus a combination of skepticism and fascination, skepticism toward the obvious frauds and fascination with phenomena he felt should be investigated in a scientific spirit. In 1861 he met the French occultist Eliphas Levi, and the two formed a group to study clairvoyance, magic, and other paranormal phenomena. Bulwer-Lytton was particularly drawn in the 1860s and early 1870s to scientists who opened the door to links between mind and matter. In the first of his *Caxtoniana* essays (1862-63) he notes Sir Humphry Davy's writing on aspects of instinct that could be related to the spirit; and in *The Coming Race* he accumulates instances of scientists linking the animate with the inanimate.

In 1860 Dickens asked Bulwer-Lytton to contribute a story to his journal *All the Year Round,* and the result was one of his most engaging metaphysical narratives, *A Strange Story*, published as a novel the following year. In his correspondence with Dickens Bulwer-Lytton explained that he had written much of it in dialogue form in order to anticipate and answer the reader's objections to the supernatural. A chapter consisting of an extended dialogue on the supernatural was dropped from the text as being too explanatory but was edited and published in 1998 by Andrew Brown. In his earlier story "Zicci," Bulwer-Lytton had described the search for the elixir of life, but now the language used to deal with this subject has become carefully scientific. Characters constantly discuss the "vital principle" as a force running through nature rather than as a substance to be used. *A Strange*

Story virtually assembles an encyclopedia of the supernatural and includes instances of clairvoyance ("the images of things to come"), ectoplasm, mesmerism, and somnambulism. But above all it concentrates on a mysterious wand—a clear anticipation of the *vril* staff in *The Coming Race*—possessed by an adept that seems to possess a mysterious force. The narrator Fenwick speculates: "What if this rod be charged with some occult fluid, that runs through all creation, and can be so disciplined as to establish communication wherever life and thought can reach to beings that live and think?" (*A Strange Story*, chap. 61). The novel traces the intellectual search of the narrator to come to an understanding of this force. Once again, as in *Zanoni*, Bulwer-Lytton uses characters who are emblematic of faculties. Fenwick, he told Dickens, represented the "type of the intellect that divorces itself from the spiritual"(Lytton, *Life*, 2:346). The continuity between *A Strange Story* and *The Coming Race* is clear. The later novel develops Bulwer-Lytton's speculations on the relation between mind and matter.

Bulwer-Lytton returned to politics in 1852 when he was returned as MP for Hertfordshire, and he spoke out several times on the Conservative side during the Crimean War, which he supported without reservation. In 1858 he was offered the post of secretary of state for the colonies in Lord Derby's administration and presided over the incorporation of British Columbia as a colony. However, declining health led to his resignation the following year. According to Bulwer-Lytton's grandson, the novel was essentially more suited to an aristocratic age; just as the 1860s saw a reduction of aristocratic rule in England, Bulwer-Lytton retired more and more from politics to pursue writing and the duties of running his Knebworth estate. In 1863, following the abdication of King Otho, Bulwer-Lytton was offered the throne of Greece (perhaps because of his diplomatic service in Corfu) but declined it in preference for the "calm Academe of Knebworth." In 1870 he accepted the Order of St. Michael and St. George. He died on 18 January 1873. His tradition of activity was in some ways followed by Bulwer-Lytton's son Robert, who combined the career of a diplomat (like that of Bulwer-Lytton's brother Sir Henry Bulwer), which reached its peak when he became viceroy of India, with the pursuit of writing. Under the pen name of Owen Meredith he published a series of well-received volumes of poetry and shared with his father a deep interest in spiritualism, the two attending at least one séance together.

Throughout his writing career Bulwer-Lytton courted controversy. His first novel *Falkland* and later works such as *Eugene Aram* were attacked for supposedly endorsing immorality and *Lucretia* (1846) for basing a character on the forger and poisoner Thomas Wainewright. By the end of the 1840s there were signs of Bulwer-Lytton moving toward subjects that were perceived to be more acceptable. Carlyle ridiculed the fashionable society novels that Bulwer-Lytton was producing in the 1820s and Thackeray burlesqued his early style in "Novels by Eminent Hands"; the latter was almost called out for a duel by Bulwer-Lytton, who had mistaken the authorship of a particularly hostile notice. Although he greatly admired his skill in plot construction, Edgar Allen Poe took Bulwer-Lytton to task for his overly elaborate and ponderous style, a criticism that persisted with commentators on Bulwer-Lytton right up to the present. Possibly as a defensive strategy against adverse criticism, Bulwer-Lytton published a number of his novels anonymously (*Falkland, Godolphin,* and others), and some under the pen name Pisistratus Stratus (*My Novel,* 1853; *What Will He Do with It?* 1858). The decision to issue *The Coming Race* anonymously was thus in line with his earlier practice, though the reasons Bulwer-Lytton gave were rather contradictory. On the one hand, he thought it would "cause a sensation"; on the other, he admitted that the book had a "certain dryness" that might be counteracted by the resulting curiosity over the subject (Second Earl of Lytton, *Life of Edward Bulwer* [London: Macmillan, 1913], 2:466; and G. de R. Waddell, "Reminiscences and Letters of Bulwer Lytton," *Century Magazine,* July 1914).

In his biography, *Bulwer Lytton: The Rise and Fall of a Victorian Man of Letters* (2003), Leslie Mitchell presents Bulwer-Lytton as an extraordinarily varied figure, active in politics, theater reform, and psychical research, to name only three fields. But, although he was one of the most widely read writers of his age, he was never comfortable within the Victorian literary establishment. He criticized Britain and British culture constantly, and he used his family home Knebworth as a refuge from the disputes of the time, content to act out the role of a landed baron. He was in many ways a man at odds with his age, driven by opposition to industrialization and the rise of the commercial spirit. It was this opposition that gave him his intellectual restlessness and that led him to experiment in many different kinds of writing.

ABOUT THE EDITOR

David Seed is a well-known British scholar of early science fiction. He holds a personal chair in American Literature in the English Department at the University of Liverpool, where he developed a graduate program in Science Fiction Studies, the first such course in Britain. He is series editor of *Science Fiction Texts and Studies* published by Liverpool University Press. His most recent major publication (for which he was editor) appeared in *Anticipations: Essays on Early Science Fiction and its Precursors* (Liverpool/Syracuse, 1995). He is a member of the editorial board of the *Journal of American Studies* and of the board of consulting editors of *Science-Fiction Studies*.